Eighth Winter

JILLIAN KAE REIMANN

ISBN: 978-1-953735-68-3

Published by Satin Romance
An Imprint of Melange Books, LLC
White Bear Lake, MN 55110
www.satinromance.com

Cover Design by Caroline Andrus

For those who have loved and lost,
and those who have recovered lost love.

Dear Trayten,

I cannot travel far enough from where your memory lingers,
to feel the ache subside, to let my love diminish.

I see your face in crowds, shifting among strangers.

And hopeful that my vision is true, I follow, reaching out to you.

But the mirage dissolves away and I have fooled myself again.

Didn't you always think that I was clever?

What good is cleverness, without you to admire it?

What value lies in living, if I should never find you?

The truth remains in hiding.

What has become of you?

This question rules my mind, and the echo of your words,
when anguish darkened your eyes; 'Be free' you said to me.

Forever I'll remember. But am I the only one?

You are lost for the choices that I made.

If it were only possible, my fate with yours I'd trade.

For I am left to wonder in the blackness left behind,

And trapped in a world without you, to wander I avow,

For if I had followed you then, I wouldn't be seeking you now.

Forever Yours,
    Katherine

Winter 1909

Battling westward from the coast of Cherbourg, *Courier II* braved Le Raz Blanchard, the Race of Alderney, where wind and wave rioted in concert. The tremendous display of tidal fury caused the ship to dive and leap, riding the rolling sea. Set upon her course, and well acquainted with the tempestuous attitude of the strait, she endured every knock and slam with resolve.

Pallid hues overwhelmed the view, hanging from low lying clouds and rising from foam frosted waters. They enclosed the vessel in whiteness and shortened the foreseeable distance, until a splatter of gold made known the before imperceptible horizon. The promise of land fueled hope for a lady with anxious eyes. She withstood the turbulent sea and clung to the life rail of the bow.

Stark against the paleness surrounding her, she was clothed in only black. A silhouette, a shadow. Her soft wool coat was trimmed with mink, from the Medici collar that framed her neck, to the hem that dusted the deck. Beneath the shade of her colossal chapeaux, her chestnut colored hair conformed with the ensemble, and appeared black as the feathers of a crow.

The biting wind painted a blush on her porcelain complexion, and her eyes were blue and deep as ocean water. With the steamer she rode the waves, bearing the billows and facing the assault of polar gusts. A sigh escaped her. A shudder expelled in a thin cloud of warmth. Though unmoved, her poise could not cover the agitation running rampant beneath her skin. Fixated on the little shore ahead, her feet rooted restlessly on the slick wooden planks of the bow.

Farther along the deck, a young couple meandered with their arms encircling one another. Their laughter skipped carelessly across the air. The girl beamed, innocent ambition alighting her features. The gentleman upon whose arm she dangled kissed her cheek and kept her close.

As she perceived them from the corner of her eye, the lady in black was afflicted with a menacing mixture of envy and annoyance, for their innocent delight was to her, like laughter at a funeral. She looked away, forcing their joy from her perspective. Still, their voices reached her ears, carrying the same tone of bliss that shone in their faces.

Turning back to the sea, she attempted to concentrate on the sprays of water splashing against the hull of the ship.

"Mrs. Koryn?" A voice startled her.

She pivoted and the young crewman appeared apologetic to have disturbed her diligent study of the water.

"Pardon ma'am." He bowed. "We'll be weighing anchor at Braye Harbour in a moment."

"Yes." She faintly smiled. "Thank you."

"Would you like me to have the steward ready your things?"

"I would."

He offered his arm to escort her across the deck. Her hand drifted from the rail to follow her footsteps forward. With troubled shadows darkening her eyes, Mrs. Koryn glanced over her shoulder, first to the young couple in their rapture, then beyond them to the island of Alderney.

۞

The *Courier II* was received into the stillness of Braye Harbour, embraced by the arc of the bay on the east side and the break-water extending from the northwest. Mrs. Koryn stepped onto the causeway and considered its length, a granite path rising high and stretching toward Alderney across the bay.

Treeless, the land sloped gradually from the northern coast, the blonde beach of Braye giving way to a meadow of tall grasses, busy bending with the breeze. The sky reigned and domi-nated the scene, limiting the land. Fort Albert imperiously guarded the eastern headland of the bay. It was one of eighteen similar forts and batteries spotting the coasts of Alderney. An angular, sprawling mass, the fort looked like an ice castle sculpted to crown the mound of the snow-strewn eastern point.

The muttering of the crewmen hovered cloud-like; a deep, slug-gish murmur as they pulled back from the shore to leave her. She shifted her weight, swaying to balance a bag in one hand with a suitcase in the other, watching the steamer slide into the fog and take with it all human sound. The silence left behind was deafening.

"Yer that lady come from Portsmouth, yea? The one's wrote to Miss Boley saying she's arriving today and expecting an escort to the Inn?"

Mrs. Koryn might have tripped on the short, portly maid who appeared in her path.

"Miss Boley, yes. I wrote to her requesting accommodations, indeed. I am Katherine Koryn."

"I figured. Follow me." The girl swept the suitcase from Katherine's hand and started shuffling toward a road at the end of the breakwater.

Between breaths she said, "It's exciting to have a person from

Portsmouth come stay with us. It's been a while, to be sure. What did ye come all this way for anyhow?"

"Ah." Katherine nodded, swallowing hard. "Well, special interests I should say. A local physician, Doctor Danby informed me that there's a man living at the Inn—"

"Ye mean our cripple?"

Katherine stumbled on the smooth brick pavement and stammered, "Crip…cripple? Is he?"

"Don't *ye* know? Didn't the doctor inform ye?"

Katherine inhaled to collect her composure. "I received very few details about him. You see, Doctor Danby merely indicated his existence here."

Slinging the suitcase onto her back with a swift thrust, the maid said, "Round here he's quite well-known. Marian, ah, that's Miss Boley, she and me, we take care of him and we're *delighted* to do it!" Raising her voice with the declaration, she stopped momentarily. "I never thought anyone beyond Alderney would know of him."

"I had sent letters to hospitals and asylums across England and throughout the Channel Islands inquiring after persons who were lost, those who had gone missing." Katherine broadened the scope of the search as she described it to the maid, withholding the fact that she had inquired after one person in particular. Instinct begged her to protect the desperation of that search and shield her emotional investment in its prize.

Quickening her pace to catch up, Katherine continued, "Doctor Danby responded to one of my letters and said that a man, a stranger, was found at sea and brought here. He gave me the post address of Miss Boley and she confirmed such a man lived at the Inn with her."

They reached the end of the breakwater and continued west along a sandy road. To the north was the sea and inland, a cluster of buildings formed the town, St. Anne. They ascended a hill as the road narrowed. Smoke coiled into the sky from the chimneys of houses beyond the road. Golden grass covered the ground, rooted in sand and a light dusting of snow. The raw quiet was a foreign phenomenon to a lady from the congested boroughs of Portsmouth.

They ventured north into a smaller road toward Fort Doyle, then followed Platte Saline Road west. At last they drew upon a large house on a small rise over Platte Saline Beach. The cracked yellow siding and broad, tall windows glowed in the pale winter light. Shutters, once the color of the sun, hung worn and bleached on bent hinges. Three stories high against the empty sky, it turned its back to the water. There, a rounded tower was set in the crux of two short wings and capped with a round cupola. A boardwalk extended from the back portico to the beach.

With a thundering heartbeat, Katherine followed the maid up the shallow, snow-packed steps and directly into the house. The warmth of the hallway burned her face after so long in the frigid air.

"I'll have ye wait in the parlor." The maid directed Katherine past a narrow staircase and through the polished mahogany arch of the front room. Then she disappeared, racing up the stairs in a clamor of creaking.

Katherine held her bag and remained concealed in her coat. The room was small and paved with plush burgundy carpet. The walls were lined with glass-faced curio cabinets. Every square foot was occupied, with a settee at one end, and a small, upholstered armchair and pianoforte at the other. In the center of the parlor, a low tea-table served to fill the last possible reach of open space.

She made a careful lap around the room, gazing through the glass at shells, statuettes, pictures, and figurines of crystal. Decorative plates and pottery of varied designs filled the shelves. An impressive number of collectable objects crowded into the cramped enclosures. Katherine traced a gloved finger along the textured wallpaper, where burgundy cherries dotted creeping vines in endless repetition.

Voices sounded from upstairs. A thump startled her, followed by muted yelling. She froze, her gaze darting to the low ceiling. She could discern nothing more distinct than a murmur. Her heart beat fiercely, vibrating through her bones. In order to subdue the excitement that threatened her tenuous self-possession, she focused on breathing slowly.

Setting her bag near her suitcase in the archway, she removed her trembling hands from black leather gloves. The ring on her left hand glittered, a flash of diamonds covering the top of the band. Examining it, she stiffened, troubled by the sight of them. Her jaw tightened.

Hurried, heavy footsteps alerted her, and a new voice snapped, "Get that mess cleared and fix another plate!"

"Heavens! Well, I see she let you in," exclaimed the boisterous creature as she swung around the corner from the staircase, catching Katherine by surprise.

Katherine opened her mouth to speak, however she was outdone.

"I'm Marian Boley. This is *my* house. Rather grand for Alderney, I'm sure you noticed, but of course I let rooms out upstairs. Sorry, I misplace minor details, your name is?"

"Mrs. Katherine Koryn of Portsmouth." She held out her hand. "I wrote to you—"

"Mrs., yea?" Marian withheld her hand. "And you travel alone? Not the behavior one expects from a lady of Portsmouth, or of *good* society, at least."

"My husband has been dead for eight years."

"Oh, I see. Well, pardon *that*. Have a seat. I'll take your coat." She peeled the garment from Katherine's shoulders before an objection might be made. Her velvet town dress was black like the woolen paletot.

Katherine sat down, crossed her ankles under the settee, and studied Miss Boley carefully. She had billowy, bright red hair that waved, frizzed, and refused to lie flat despite being cinched tightly into a severe knot on the top of her head. Her features were sharp and wild, with hazel eyes and white, freckled skin.

Marian's dress called to mind the bygone fashion of the nineties, with its enormous puff sleeves and tight, banded collar in gray ratine fabric. She chewed at her lips and moved without the grace found in other women. Her mannerisms, as she scooted around the tea-table and plopped into the armchair, were careless, masculine, and unrefined.

"Well, here you are, as you forewarned in your last letter. You said you were coming and here you are. But what business do you presume to have here, Mrs. Koryn?" Marian raised her chin.

Imagining that if she spoke, her voice would break and falter, Katherine stared back in silence. She took as much time as possible to blink while that instinct to protect her true plight returned. First, she needed to be sure that it was him.

"I would like to meet this man the doctor told me about," the words finally manifested. "And talk with him, evaluate him."

"Well, you might have saved yourself the trip if you had the forethought to ask that in your letter. I would've told you not to waste your time here. He's not friendly and despises meeting people."

"Consider it more of a clinical evaluation than a social call," Katherine offered.

"I should tell you straight away that I'm very much opposed to psychoists." Marian waved her hand as though declining an invitation.

"I'm not a *psychiatrist*." Katherine assumed she meant psychiatrist even though she said it wrong.

"Well *any* sort of psycho-ist. I'm strictly opposed. All are alike in my estimation; scheming, manipulative snoops with pompous ideas, thinking they know people, when one can never *really* know." A feral light flashed from Marian's eyes.

"I'd really only wish to talk with him. Manipulation has nothing whatsoever to do with it. Why don't you tell me more about him?"

"I can't say much, and neither can he! He has no memory. I

suppose the doctor called it…retrograde *ambrosia,* something or other."

"Retrograde *amnesia*?" Katherine gasped. Suddenly, the room seemed to spin.

"That's what I said. Fishermen pulled him from the water somewhere up north and brought him to me, yes to *me*. They fish in my bay and stay here often. They love my cooking so much they go out of their way to stay here." Marian beamed with pride.

"And what condition was he in when he arrived?" Katherine closed her eyes tightly and folded her trembling hands to restrain them.

"He wasn't doing well! He was wounded, apart from his feeble mind. He was unconscious when they brought him in. When he woke, he didn't know his name, which is how I discovered he couldn't remember what had happened to him. I tried to help him with his memory. Nothing. Not even his own name."

"Are you quite sure he remembers nothing? Not any person from his life? Not anything that he did?" There was the crack in her voice that she had hoped to avoid.

"*Quite* sure, of course! I'm not a *liar*," Marian snapped.

"I would not have presumed such a thing," Katherine replied twice as sharply. She fell back into silence and after studying the carpet asked, "Did you give him one?"

"One what?"

"A name. A person is no one without a name. A name is…it's —" Katherine straightened. "Did you give him one?"

"There were initials, etched inside a tin we found on him: T.B.."

Katherine caught and held onto her breath. The room around her burned fiery red, and Marian's sharp appearance stoked the flames. Those piercing hazel eyes pinned Katherine with a heated stare.

"Are you *sweating*, Mrs. Koryn? It's not too warm in here."

"Go on." Katherine shook her head. "Please, go on."

"We call him T.B.. And he's an ill-tempered man. Not one to be poked at and prodded. I can't permit you to *disturb* him."

"Permit? You're right in that you cannot *permit*. Neither can you *prevent*. You're not his master because you own his room, with all due respect, Miss Boley." Blood rushed to Katherine's face.

"They brought him to me." Marian squared her shoulders. "And here he has stayed under my absolute care. He's completely pathetic. He can't get on by himself. He has no one. I'm the *only* one."

"You may not be the *only* one. Have you considered that?"

Marian offered no response.

Katherine sighed, reeling her emotion back in. "If you would please allow me to stay here, I will pay of course, so that I may work with him."

"As long as you pay you may stay. But I'll warn you now, he'll not be agreeable and *that* I can't help with. If he refuses to allow you to see him, I will ensure he's not disturbed. And if you *do* see him, you'll understand if I supervise from time to time. I will be watching you."

"I'm not afraid of being watched. It's your home. May I go up now?" Katherine stood.

"No, not yet. After supper. We had a mess up there, he has these fits, the room needs cleaning, and he needs rest." Marian rushed to stand between Katherine and the hallway.

"Very well, I understand." With a deep sigh, Katherine put her hands back into her gloves and her excitement back under restraint. "May I leave my things here while I go into town?"

"Of course. I'll have Suzan put your bags in a room. I'm sure if you don't stay longer you'll at least stay for the night."

"Thank you. That is kind of you, Miss Boley."

Katherine made her way along the spacious, snow laced lanes of Victoria Street. Although the buildings clung to one another, arrayed in bright and various hues, the village was not the least bit crowded. St. Anne was void of bustle and filled with unobstructed breezes.

As she walked, she traced with her gaze the spaces between the cobblestones, reviewing the meandering and painful path that brought her to Alderney. A cautious mind fought against the excitement in her heart, for she knew that her journey might not be at an end. She braced herself to accept that her search would have to continue, and yet she hoped that her mourning might be turned into rejoicing after all.

The sound of footsteps other than her own caused her to raise her eyes. Two ladies tarried in the street ahead, the shorter one waving a handkerchief in friendly surrender. Both wore bright mantels, one pink and the other striped with dark and light greens. Both wore their sandy blonde hair in plaits, and both had upturned noses and brown, wide-set eyes.

"You're a stranger here, though we've seen you pass at least twice already now," the plumper of the pair said. She grinned with a thin mouth, which was crowded between her large doughy cheeks. Through the spectacles perched at the end of her nose, she eyed Katherine.

"I'm staying at Marian Boley's house."

"Whatever *for*? A lady such as you?" the smaller of the pair gasped. "Captain Scott's is at least suitable accommodation." Her mouth turned upward in an easy grin.

Katherine smiled warmly, delighted by her lack of censorship. "I might be looking in on the man that lives there."

"That delirious cripple?" The smaller one's companion slapped a plump hand over her mouth.

"Forgive my sister Louisa. *Half*-sister, really. We are familiar with them. I'm Mary Saunders."

"I am charmed to meet you both. Katherine Koryn."

Mary let loose of Louisa, who pronounced, "We are dressmakers, and this is our shop." She swept her arm back to present the front of their establishment. "You're well dressed enough. Still we'd be happy to tailor something new for you."

"I would be honored. Perhaps, another day. I'm rather anxious to return to Miss Boley's," Katherine said.

"Strange, indeed very strange." Louisa shook her head.

"Never mind her," Mary told Katherine. "You have important work to do, no doubt. Let's not stand in her way, Louisa."

"But Mary, doesn't she look familiar?" Louisa asked. "Look at her face!"

Katherine crinkled her forehead.

Louisa laughed loudly. "I'm sure I've seen you before!"

"I've never been to Alderney," Katherine admitted.

"Strange," Mary said.

Together they stared at her until she began to squirm. When Katherine stepped back, Mary shrugged. "Course, we get a bit imaginative from time to time."

Louisa giggled as a child would.

"I'd better get on," Katherine said. "It was wonderful to meet you both."

"Do come to call whenever you like," Mary offered. "We are always here."

"I should be delighted." Katherine smiled.

"Yes and tell Marian *hello* from the Saunders sisters!" Louisa grinned mischievously and stabbed her sister with an elbow.

Katherine waved and continued on. The laughter of the sisters bounced on the air and faded as they retreated into their shop.

☙❧

"You must understand and abide by these necessary rules," Marian warned, guarding a bedroom door in the lamp-lit hallway upstairs.

Katherine's heart beat powerfully, while her knees weakened. Her stomach protested loudly, for she had denied it any food, unable to trust its resolve. In a housedress and robe she wavered like a waif, the gauzy fabric hanging freely from her shoulders without form. As liberated, her hair reached to the small of her back and waved incongruously. Its irregular style was the result of having been twisted and pinned beneath her hat all day. She pressed a hand to her stomach and nodded to Marian, willing to comply with anything in order to pass through the door.

Sucking in her cheeks, Marian appeared skeletal, for shadows filled the cavities of her face. "He's sensitive to his injuries and you must be calm about him, easy with him."

"I shall be."

"I'll wait out here." Marian moved aside, waving a hand to the door.

Katherine entered, closing the door inside with her back to the rest of the room. She held her breath, closed her eyes, and opened them to the door. Shyly she turned and her heart stopped beating.

A bed below the window faced the sea. Moonlight through the glass painted squares of blue on the blanket covering his body. On a table beside the bed a candle flickered, and its erratic light splashed his cheeks with burnt orange, the brightness broken only by a thicket of black stubble. His black hair was long and unkempt, yet it was swept back from his forehead as he lay sleeping to reveal dark eyebrows and a straight nose. His lips rest, full and well-formed. His jawline was square and strong.

His arm hung over the edge of the bed, fingers dusting the floor. Drawn to his hand, Katherine there fixed her gaze. A pale, silvery scar followed the line of his knuckles. She inhaled and held onto her neck.

A chair sat in the corner, one with large wheels in front, smaller wheels in the back, and footplates hanging from the seat. The hardwood floor creaked when she moved, drawn to the edge of the bed. Katherine sank to her knees and her eyes filled with tears.

As the atmosphere thickened, she struggled to breathe in it. "Are you *really* here?"

Unable to resist, she took his fallen hand. Sensation raced through her at the feel of his skin. He stirred, yet she formed his hand against her own, then touched his face. Tears washed her cheeks when she blinked.

He jolted, breaking the stillness.

With an unconscious reflex his hand closed around her wrist and her response was an involuntary scream. His eyes snapped open, hazy, vacant, a glassy brown somehow bright in the dark, and he let out a terrible yell. He pulled her arm in his writhing until she twisted away and fell backward onto the floor.

As one tortured and without sense he thrashed and hollered. He flailed in the bed, his upper body fighting the air and his legs remaining still beneath the covers.

Marian burst into the room. "It's a fit, a fit! Mrs. Koryn, go!"

Katherine was shoved aside.

Restraining him, Marian screeched, "Suzan! Get my bag!" As she was rocked and quaked by the force of his resistance, gripping his arms she said, "That will be all."

Katherine hesitated, her eyes bright in the dimness, her face haloed by the light from the hall. Queasiness compelled her and her jaw locked tight.

Marian repeated more forcefully, "Mrs. Koryn, go now!"

On the stairs Katherine trampled Suzan in a frightful flight to the door. She spilled from the house into the night and staggered through the sandy snow of the beach, the icy air piercing her lungs and her hair trailing in the wind behind her.

When she reached the water's edge she dropped to her knees where the tide dispersed across the sand. Her breath expanded in a white cloud, her arms tingled with the chill, and tears rushed from her eyes like the seawater sliding down the shore.

In the bitter air, as frozen breezes rolled off the water, Katherine let her head fall back, closed her eyes to the sky, and clasped her hands before her lips in prayer. A wave of emotion broke over her heart, which leapt in her chest and spread its heat throughout her body like a lightning bolt. The thrill that had slept for eight long years was revived, as though resurrected from the grave.

Through sobs, a laugh escaped. Inside a heaving chest her heart both rejoiced and grieved. In disbelief but assured recognition she cried to heaven, "I've found him!"

2

Spring 1900

I t was an unlikely venue for poetry. The audience might have been considered the least likely to welcome fine art, foremost in the view of those who avoided the public houses that dominated The Hard in Portsea. A raucous symphony was the amalgamation of many voices, each one competing to carry over the next. As the door opened in from the street, the sonic barrage spilled out, polluting still night air for an instant before the clap of the door pulled the revelry back inside.

In darkness, smoke, and flickering lamplight, a faithful population of dockyard workers, sailors, fishermen, and others belonging to the work-worn class gathered. Relieved from the duties of the day, they labored here to relinquish their cares.

Coarseness of speech and roughness of manner did not preclude the assembly from an appreciation of balladry. It was customary to find some lad or another gracing the small platform of The Bedford in Chase with excerpts of Keats or Edward Lear and somehow, over the noise they would be heard, and cherished.

A young man, still a boy in many respects, took his turn at sharing verse from coal dust covered lips, as black as the skin of his face and hands.

"They went to sea in a sieve, they did;

In a sieve they went to sea;

In spite of all their friends could say,

On a winter's morn, on a stormy day,

In a sieve they went to sea.

And when the sieve turned round and round,

And everyone cried, 'You'll be drowned!'" His eyes alone shone clean to the crowd, his clothes hung rumpled and coal laden. "Ah." He scratched his head and shrugged. "That's all I know's the first part!"

When his fellows applauded with glad encouragement, he smiled and flashed his remaining three teeth at them proudly. As he bowed, a lanky figure assumed command of the piano at one side of the stage to assault the keys with wide, heavy hands. Another cry was raised in appreciation, and the few women were pulled out onto a scarred wooden floor to dance, with the exception of one.

From behind the bar, she monitored the dancers with a twinkle in her eye and the clap of her hands. Her white, lace ruched blouse had been altered, the sleeves rolled up to her elbows, the top four buttons undone from her collar down. A plain, straight skirt of brown batiste fell flatly from her hips to her feet. Dark chestnut hair spilled over her shoulders half swept back from her face into an unruly knot.

"Fine turnout this evening, hey Katherine?" The publican straddled his stool.

"Yes, it's fine, Wilkins," Katherine replied. "A beer for you?"

"Always!" was his reply.

"And the entertainment is top notch!" Katherine filled a pint.

Wilkins, the publican, nodded as he set his mouth over his glass.

A scraggly man raised his face from the bar. "Oi, but what'll ye do, Kathy, when yer married off and can't have yer fill of wonky Edward Lear?"

"Who's getting married off, Peter? Surely not I, sir!" She waved her hands.

"Yea, none would have her," laughed Wilkins before playfully punching her arm.

"They would so if I had a mind to *let* them! It's I who won't have them, the dull snobs."

"Oh, the martyr! More than a thousand pounds per annum is anything but dull!" Peter argued.

"So says you! You can marry them if you're so eager," she said.

"All right!" Peter shimmied to his feet and they laughed.

"Pete, you're not exactly their kind," Wilkins reasoned.

As they gave in to fresh laughter, Katherine caught sight of a tall stranger passing behind Wilkins and Peter. At the far corner he took a stool and laid his elbows on the bar. The smoky atmosphere made it difficult to be certain, but she suspected that she had never seen him in the tavern before.

He arrested her attention long enough for the others to notice and call her back with a cackle.

"I'll have another gin," Peter ordered.

"You've got two chins *now*! One more won't make you any more appealing," Katherine said before taking her eyes off the stranger.

Wilkins's eyes popped before he spit beer across the bar and slapped Peter on the back. Peter tipped off his stool from both the force of the slap and the power of his own laughter.

"See?" Katherine stared at them with passive amusement. "Why should I want to be married off and miss a moment with you lads?"

"What'll ye do, Katherine? Sling beer in this slum 'til yer looks are gone?" Peter asked, climbing back onto his stool.

"Why quit then?" She winked.

"Ye won't be able to afford living when the tips dry up!" said Peter.

"What, Peter! You won't pay twice as much to see *my* double chin?"

"Na! I can see that at home! Anyway, pour another gin for me already!"

"I thought you'd never ask." Katherine slapped the bar.

The stare of the stranger followed her and when she took a bottle from the shelf behind her, she allowed her gaze to wander toward his direction and catch him.

He casually lit a cigarette and in the flash of light from the match his brown eyes were deep. Their gazes held even as she poured a drink for Peter and passed the glass to Wilkins. Katherine approached the newcomer, who appeared dismal compared to the cheer that filled the taproom. He was entirely adorned in black, from his overcoat to his trousers, with black hair hanging at his temples and black sideburns tracing the line of his jaw.

"Good evening to you, sir. What'll you have?" Katherine mustered the customary words, despite a sudden tremble that broke the usual ease of her confidence.

His hand fell heavily on the bar and with red-stained fingers he pushed two pennies toward her.

"Are you *bleeding*?" she gasped, taking his hand.

He pulled it from her grasp. "It's paint."

"I'm sorry," she said and picked the coins from the bar. "A pint it is."

He accosted her, clasping his hand around her wrist. "No. A glass of milk, if you've got it."

She laughed, thinking that, in such a place as this, he must be joking, until the weight of his stare impressed her duly. With a nod, she said, "Of course."

He released her but held her steadily in his stare.

The general mood of the place fell while another speaker

claimed his moment. Katherine listened as she poured the glass of milk and handed it to the stranger.

"Nor certitude, nor peace, nor help for pain; and we are here as on a darkling plain," quoth the gentleman who sat at the edge of the platform while crushing his hat against his breast. Sweat glimmered from the forest of his whiskers. "Swept with confused alarms of struggle and flight, where ignorant armies clash by night." He concluded his recitation of Matthew Arnold and appeared ready to faint.

Wilkins urged Katherine, "Go up now girl and bring some charm back to this place 'for we have a suicide!"

"Yea, go up, Katherine!" Peter chimed in, and a handful of others joined the persuasion, crowding around the bar. Their cause soon reached the piano player, who waved and called from behind the sobbing reciter, tipping over to lay his face on the floor.

She glanced back at the stranger, assured of his tentative gaze, before rounding the bar to leap at her chance on the platform. Through the playful wails of rowdy patrons, she jumped up next to the piano player and his bench.

"All right!" She snickered as they jumped on one another, whistled at her, and teased. A smile spread wide across her face and her cheeks blushed in the heat.

From impish exuberance she transformed. She evolved as the cheers died and she calmed the crowd with a whimsical wave of her hand. With eyes that swallowed them in indigo, she glanced from face to face.

Her eloquence drew them in. "Gentle and *not* so gentle sirs, heed now as I impart to you a definition, a useful reference to guide you, if and when you are overcome." She relished their attentive expressions.

"And I tell you that you may benefit from such a lesson, especially in our cold, modern world today. It's a lesson in remembrance. A lesson I believe proves itself to be true time and time again," Katherine smirked and added, "Or, so I've read."

A spatter of chuckles spewed forth.

Her smile departed when she began:

"We seek from birth whatever is appealing; that which is desirable.

And one thing that inspires inclination above all else, is *love*.

This dangerous word is a delicious mystery,

For those that possess it cannot adequately describe it,

And those without it prey on these attempts,

Hoping, dreaming, and wishing to fall.

The dreamers aspire to be as the tentative lovers,

Who, as a result of loving, understand the truth of mortality,

Causing them to be eagerly aware of all indications of life;

One's pattern of breath, every word held sacred,

every heartbeat, and every touch.

Once enamored with the object of their love,

This sought-after emotion is pure, unavoidable entrapment.

Two become one, forcing them to need one another,

And alone without the *other*, one is stricken with aching,

Bound by chains of indulgence and branded with weakness.

It can be fickle and when ended, demolishes the severed soul with crippling dependency.

This beautiful addiction, so truly irresistible, affects us all.

It originates within us, ready to engulf the mind, body, and soul." She met the striking gaze of the stranger in the corner before she continued, "Love is a sickness, an *unmatchable* high...

It's an indiscriminate killer...and a gift from God.

Love is the world's greatest disease."

Katherine's gaze remained locked with the dark eyes across the room. They clapped as the stranger stared silently, as if to memorize her face. She was convinced that his eyes bewitched her, sending lightning sensations through her nerves and urging her knees to give way beneath her.

The piano player nudged her and hollered above the returning noise and motion, "I want a copy of that one, Katherine!"

She laughed, leaning against him for support. "Sir Jeffery, you know I'll not reproduce any of it. One copy I have and one copy I'll keep."

He chuckled and began to play a dancing melody with delightful quickness on his piano. Straightening, Katherine glanced back to the bar, straining to see over and around the heads of bouncing, spinning men, and the women tossed between them.

The corner stood empty. The gloomy stranger had vanished. She searched the room but didn't find him. Were it not for the empty glass he left behind, she would have believed she imagined him.

☸

The journey from The Bedford in Chase on the corner of Clock Street and The Hard, to her family's home in Festing Road, Southsea, was one that Katherine had come to know intimately. Instead of going directly to Portsmouth Harbour Station, she preferred to pass through Portsea in Kent Street on foot, and after cutting across Victoria Park, board the tram at Portsmouth Town Station, and ride to East Southsea Station.

The hour was young, and she narrowly preceded the sun. There would be no servant to greet her in the front hall or alert her parents of her arrival. As quietly as she was able, she crept inside, removing the boots she had unlaced on the tram. She tip-toed along the plush damask runner through the hall, a space as wide and twice as long as the tavern she had left.

The glass doors of the drawing room remained open. Lamp-light illuminated her path with a fiery splatter. Katherine crept to the entrance and peered into a room filled with white buxom furniture, rich blue drapery, and deep shadows. A silhouette moved among them. From a high-backed chair, it turned up the lamp, revealing a stern-faced young lady. A lace nightcap covered her hair and a scrap of embroidery laid across her lap.

"Well, just look at you!"

Katherine grinned and reclined against the frame of the door-way. "Just look at *you*, Dorothea!"

"I am perfectly dignified. You on the other hand, aren't you coming in astonishingly late?"

"I should think I am astonishingly early!"

Dorothea snarled. It was the one thing she did without fail, at least in the presence of her elder sister Katherine.

"But I wonder, little sister, did you rise particularly early or stay awake all night to revel in your favorite sport, that of lying-in wait to chastise me? Don't you have a husband to look after, or up to, or *down* on, anyway?"

"Am I to be vilified for attempting to look after you?"

"You needn't pretend to be concerned for me. I know you spy on me in order to make my comings and goings known to Father. And if you were actually concerned, you needn't be. I don't require looking after."

"If that were true, you might not be so utterly lost," Dorothea asserted.

"What you call lost, I call free."

"If that is freedom, I should say freedom is foul." Dorothea scoffed in one short breath. "You smell offensive! You're a disgrace! Your cheeks are red! What have you been doing? What goes on in that sinner's den where a lady has no business?"

"I would not expect a lady such as you to understand. And as you have always been so keen to point out, I'm not a lady, there-fore I may go where I please."

"For *now*, perhaps. Father's tolerance of your fool-hearted rebellion will not last forever. One day soon you will be forced to face reality."

"Not if I have anything to say about it." Katherine lifted her chin. She pushed away from the door and left Dorothea before another word might be said.

※

Myra MacGregor had been Katherine's friend since primary school. Both grew up in Southsea, and both had been favored with the privileges of family wealth. More than Katherine, Myra dressed and acted the part of a lady of their class. Having married a respectable gentleman, and settled into a comfortable domestic routine, she secured a place for herself well within the expectations of her family and peers.

They strolled along the pavement winding through the Rock Gardens near South Parade Pier. Scatters of alpine shrubs and flowers gathered around blocks of limestone, creating a sheltering labyrinth. Katherine dragged Myra from the designated path to trod across a patch of grass and away from a group of women who chattered loudly beneath the shade of their parasols.

Myra was dressed in a silk foulard dress, the print in varying shades of pink. Her toilette was topped with a voluptuous chapeaux which was home to a stuffed pigeon, nesting in ruffles of black taffeta and tulle. A pale pink parasol served to protect the petrified bird from the heat of the sun. Myra's auburn hair, in natural curls, filled the shade of her hat in the fashionable pompadour style.

In her costly tailor-made suit, Katherine determined to defy order, with her starched shirt collar unbuttoned and her cravat hanging undone like a scarf. She carried a straw sailor hat in hand and let her hair down to dance in the breeze. It reached below her shoulder blades, soft and fine like silk when not teased, ratted, and piled high to fulfill the popular fashion.

"Shall we allow your Denis to catch up?" Katherine asked, glancing at Myra's husband, who was securing the carriage and tethering the horses.

"He will get on, eventually. He may not find us though. Where are you taking me?" Myra squinted her green eyes, even beneath the double shade of her hat and parasol.

Katherine continued to lead them further from the paved path. "This way is far more interesting. But Myra, I must tell you... well first, you tell *me,* have you ever seen an angel?"

"Only in my dreams, dearest. Let me know if you find one," she laughed. "Why, you think you have?"

"Why would you guess that?"

"You are the sort who *would*. Besides, why ask such a question?" Myra propped her hand on her hip and stopped.

Katherine took her arm and directed her toward an assortment of yellow tulips. "I *think* that's what he was, what he *is*."

Myra clasped her hands together. "Was he bright and brilliant?"

"No. This angel, he was dark and brooding, he was beautiful and mysterious."

"Devil then, *not* angel." Myra curled her lip and dug her heels into the ground.

"I don't really care *which*." Katherine ushered them forward again.

"All right. Who is he?"

"I know not. He's vanished."

"Ah, a habit of angels." Myra shrugged.

They neared the seafront, where the sand was covered with mingling gulls and the sun set the water ablaze in a white-hot glow.

"You see, Myra, I have on a number of occasions since I first saw him, heard someone close by, so close I can *feel* it, following me, or watching from across the street, or above me from the sky. And every time I look, a figure walks away, disappearing before I can make truth or fiction of it!"

"Someone follows you," Myra declared.

"It would seem so, yes."

"You are mad, Katherine."

"You would judge me mad rather than believe that someone follows me?"

They looked at one another with humor and contemplation.

"My Darling!" called Denis, jogging breathlessly. He extended a red handbag, his fragile bones shaking and his boyish face wide with exhaustion.

"I am *talking*, dearest!" Myra snapped.

"I brought it for you, you forgot it in the carriage," Denis insisted.

"Denis! Is this parasol red?" Myra asked, turning on him.

Katherine sighed and shook her head, pitying Denis immediately.

"N...no—" he stammered.

"My dress, the dress, dear, is it red?"

He scratched his head, dislodging his bowler hat and briefly juggling it.

"No!" Myra answered for him. "I require the *pink* one! Or are you color blind as well as slow? You never, *never* pair pink with red! Go get the other one. The one that is not red!" Her face, defying the fashion rule, changed from pink to red.

"Yes, darling." Eagerly, Denis bolted for the carriage in a raggedy run.

The red in Myra's cheeks faded back to an appropriate pink. "Men are merely a blundering failure."

"That's *your* unfortunate opinion," Katherine said with a disapproving frown. Myra's haughty sneer was the only response.

Then, with mischief in her eyes, Katherine wandered away from the flowers, whispering, "Watch, Myra."

She raced, with a burst of unladylike speed, to the seafront. She threw her arms up, tossed her hat, and called out.

Intruding on the edge of the flock, the gulls lifted in a frenzy. As she ran into their midst, they took flight, each one rising after the one behind him. They beat their wings on the air and waves of rhythmic drumming thundered above. Their shadows darted across the beach below and then dissolved away.

Katherine sensed that she was being watched. An additional shadow loomed behind her, one somehow distinct from the crowds of people that were ever present in the streets of

Portsmouth. This shadow was purposeful, faithful, and though not her own, it was attached. After several days, she would have no more of this mystery.

It was evening when she strolled Queens Street with a purpose in mind. She rounded many corners and repeated many routes, and still the shadow remained. The footsteps were faint but certainly faithful in following. Katherine stopped in Camden Alley, and took a chair at the front of a public house to simulate amusement in the unscrupulous vendors that cluttered the street.

Twilight descended to calm the borough before dark and those left outside were subdued under its persuasion, moving lethargically under the spectacle of light allowed by the setting sun. Merchants peddled trinkets from booths in the street. They babbled excitedly and harassed the passersby. Katherine smirked at one who, clinging to a prospective buyer, danced after him a good way down Havant Street before admitting defeat and returning to his cart with sagging shoulders. She remained acutely aware of the shadow over her shoulder, seated on a bench not far off.

There he reclined, his face concealed partially behind a book. His hair, his coat, and trousers, all black. A cigarette burned, pinched between his fingers. He tapped the toe of a worn boot with a steady rhythm against the pavement.

She turned her head away, her gaze traveling the heights of the brick buildings with a well-placed smile on her face. His eyes traveled from the book to study her, yet when she looked back, he moved ever so slightly, just enough to hide once more behind his book.

He straightened abruptly, the book falling in his lap when she appeared, standing boldly before him. He looked up, startled as she appraised him with guarded severity, the same solemn face she burned into her memory from one evening at The Bedford in Chase.

3

"Sir, are you *following* me?" Katherine asked in accusatory fashion.

He seemed stricken by the sound of her voice. "I…well—"

"You *are* following me. You have been."

He looked from her lips to her eyes. Persecution burned from her stare. Seditious strands of hair fell loosely in her eyes, while the rest was bound obediently in a low knot at the nape of her neck. The blackberry, tailor-made suit she wore made her blue eyes piercingly bright.

"I am not sure I…" He seemed surprised at the accusation, yet mildly so. With a persistent stare, and so little to say, he made her uneasy.

Katherine raised her chin a bit higher. "In Kent Street, at the Town Station, and even in Southsea I've noticed you, I *know* it, watching me. Do you think you are so clever? I've felt you near." She could speak no more and failed to uphold the hardened facade.

With a grave expression he sat forward to declare, "Yes."

He was more magnetic than she remembered as the word dropped from his lips, affirmative and unapologetic. Her heart smashed against her ribcage and she swallowed, trying to imagine something more to say. An inexplicable force stole her breath.

Finally, a smile cracked the austerity she had set in place, and she asked, "Then, why haven't we properly *met*?"

His face did not change. Instead, he analyzed her quietly, compelling her to continue.

"You see, the proper procedure is you ask my name, and I tell you, 'Hello, I'm Katherine Madison,' and we shake hands." She held out her hand.

He kept his eyes on her face and closed his warm hand around her cold fingers.

She shivered. "And you tell me your name."

"Trayten Basel." He kept her hand.

"And where are you going, Trayten Basel? That is, when you're not following *me*?"

"Home. Sun Street."

"Shall I follow *you*? Walk you home?" She did not wait for his answer before pulling him to his feet.

He was tall and slender with a lean build. Katherine, standing so close to him, had to crane her neck to look up into his face. In what seemed like a dream, she walked beside him, a distinct impression tugging at her heart unlike any previously known.

The street was a dark narrow crevice littered with refuse and lined with brimming buckets. Rats scampered for the cover of night and stray children sprang from one alley to another. Overhead, dingy linens waved from lines connecting flats on either side of the street to one another. From somewhere ahead a howling shadow sprang and bolted down the lane.

Like many cramped streets in Portsea, the ripened odors of humanity inundated the senses, hanging heavy in the air. Neither the degradation of the lane nor its stench could distract Katherine from the wonder that surrounded Trayten.

"Now, you must talk with me. What do you *do* with yourself, Mr. Basel?" Katherine threaded her arm into the crux of his.

"I paint."

"I'm an impassioned *adorer* of art! Do you like Aivazovsky? His use of color is exceptional, even radical, one might say! And I like John Constable and John William Waterhouse. But you must show me your work. Will you do that?"

"Yes."

His silence, like a storm, stirred wonder within her. Trayten was remote and undisturbed, as if there was nothing peculiar about their encounter or his admission of following her.

"Doesn't the city seem more honest at twilight?" she mused.

He directed his eyes to the ground when she looked in his direction.

"Yes."

"Don't you think honesty comes more naturally, under the deep, rich light at the end of the day, when there is neither the harshness of the sun, nor the cold of the dark to irritate the senses?"

"Perhaps."

"Am I very foolish to you?" she asked, laughing shyly. His reserve made her wonder if she might be a ranting lunatic.

"No," he replied, and she smiled.

She searched the windows of the buildings as they passed. They reflected the sunset in glaring golden splendor, concealing dismal interiors.

"How is it you found me as often as you did? Am I predictable? We can be honest now. Twilight and all."

He was mute, as though he did not hear her. At last, after several paces, he replied, "I cannot say."

"You *cannot* say? It's unusual that someone admits to following you and then you walk them home. Why have I sensed you so often? Why have I *felt* you when I couldn't see you?"

"I cannot say." Trayten's hand slid over the top of Katherine's and pressed it against his forearm. His arm was necessary, in order to steady her, for when he touched her, her knees tried to buckle.

"You are mysterious, Mr. Basel."

They came upon Sun Street and at the bend of the road, a slender brick building appeared, identical to its adjoining neighbors.

"Shall we go up?" Trayten stopped at the door, which stood open to reveal a staircase ascending into blackness.

Katherine had thought little beyond walking him home. Escorting him was audacious enough, but to follow him alone into his room was simply scandalous. Propriety warned her to turn around, yet he had brought her to his door upon her own insistence, and her curiosity was not yet satisfied.

"You wanted to see my work," he reminded while she considered the stairs.

"Yes. I rather demanded it, didn't I?" With a nervous laugh, Katherine chased the notion of shame away and stepped forward.

Trayten's fourth story flat was small, derelict, and primitive. It was, under practical considerations, no more than a hovel. However, the moment they crossed the threshold, Katherine was dazzled by the unexpected revelation of an artistic shrine. The single room was long in one direction and short the other, with a scratched, splintering floor. The ceiling of open rafters peaked in the middle and sloped downward toward the door along one wall and toward a window alcove on the opposite.

Canvases cluttered the room, piled clumsily in corners. Across the floor, strangled paint tubes strayed. Open jars of inky oils and brushes in heaps littered a roughhewn table. Papers covered with sketches lay like fallen leaves on every surface.

A powerful essence was here, the sharp smell of oil paint and dampness, the palpable sense of artistic toil. The window stretched low to the ground, set in an alcove with an arch at the top and a wide seat at the bottom. The casement stood open, allowing a high breeze to animate a pair of red curtains who swept into the room and back out again like indecisive visitors.

Fiery dying daylight magnified particles of dust in the air and spilled over an easel by the window. The easel was wide and flat, a tilted table, and was papered with drawings. Katherine imagined Trayten seated there, weaving shadows and colors together.

The other furniture in the room consisted of a solitary chair in the center, an icebox, a little stove, and extending from another deep, windowless alcove, a bed.

He lit a lamp, for darkness prevailed. Their shadows decorated the canvases at their feet. Art surrounded them, his creations calling to her. She heard them at once, a symphony of epic scenes, pulling her attention in every direction.

The walls were crowded with his work; sketches of people at different angles and poses, oil paintings depicting dramatic landscapes and perfect pastoral places. They beckoned her with luminous sunsets, imperious mountains, and mist-shrouded gardens. The colors were rich and alive as any vision or dream or Aivazovsky. The eyes of sketched portraits watched her with lifelike glances, their bodies perfectly proportioned. Trayten lingered in the shadow, considering her expressions as she examined the contents of his soul.

"It's amazing! These are all yours?"

He did not answer.

"You are truly a wonder! It's fitting that I picked you out. I have excellent taste."

A hint of a smile grazed his face.

Katherine moved along the wall and even though it seemed an impolite thing to do, she traced a river, the markings of paint dried, yet appearing wet. She felt the relief and movement against her fingertips and drew closer still, studying a cloudy forest. Her breath brushed over it like the wind. Trayten brought a lamp and poured the light on her.

"I've heard of the majesty of paintings, the emotional connection to the artist, the depositing of an artist's soul into the work," she said whimsically. "There was once a man who painted scenes so moving that people were in a frenzy to obtain them. Using drops of blood, his *own* blood in his crimson, he sacrificed part of himself and immortalized his pain in the absence of his lost love."

She checked his face for a reaction, her eyes shimmering. Nothing. She turned back to the painting. "Collectors across the Continent scrounged and fought, and paid thousands, *thousands* of pounds for his work! He not only put his soul into them, but he put his own blood!"

Trayten lit another lantern. An orange glow warmed the air around them. She smiled a contagious smile. Trayten lit a cigarette, aloof in his composure.

"My new, somber friend is *your* life a tragedy?" she asked playfully, pacing along the wall.

He stared after, monitoring her every move.

"Trayten Basel. *That* is a good name." She turned to him suddenly and asked, "Why did you follow me?"

He sat down in the window alcove and let the last of that day's light tint his face vermillion and wash his hair with red. She waited in the line of his gaze.

"A lesson, you said." He smoked, pausing between phrases. "A lesson in remembrance." He raised his eyebrows at her. "I remember every word."

"Of?"

"Your verse. The one you recited in the tavern. I heard you and I knew."

"Knew?"

"I thought." He tapped his temple. "'I just fell in love with her.'" He smiled, gold twinkling from the rich depths of his eyes.

Intrigued, she was unable to reply.

"Is that all right?" he asked.

"I…it *must* be."

"Yes, it must. And now I shall escort *you* home."

৩৯৩

The drawing room of Madison estate was a palace, with a copper dome ceiling and hand-carved marble columns lining the walls.

Daylight displayed it gloriously, streaming in through five enormous windows on three of four walls. Here the family gathered, including Katherine's parents, Theodore and Winifred, her younger sister Dorothea and Dorothea's husband Caleb Edson, and her youngest sister Eliza with her husband Arnold Sumner.

Caleb Edson and Arnold Sumner guarded the fireplace, which was open to the floor and faced with swirling white marble. They were regal gentlemen, both in satin waistcoats, silk cravats, and fine tailored jackets. Arnold rested his elbow on the mantle near a crystal-faced clock and Caleb held a glass of scotch in one hand. Arnold talked about his shop while his brother-in-law showed more interest in his glass of liquor, which was dark like his slick, waxy hair.

Across the powder blue oriental rug, on a settee with her mother, Eliza held a cup of tea between her hands and watched her husband Arnold with an ethereal expression on her round face. Eliza's fawn hair was neatly tucked under a lace cap except for two spiral curls that framed her neck. Her lilting frame was draped in white lace, and her small feet rest on the settee, curled under the hem of her skirt.

Winifred propped on the arm of the settee, arguing with Dorothea in an exaggerated whisper. She appeared an older, fuller image of her youngest daughter Eliza, her face heavily powdered and her cheeks slashed with rouge. Her silver hair had been parted severely down the middle and was combed back to meet with an oversized chignon of a much darker shade. It was no doubt an attachment of false hair, long ago purchased to keep in fashion. She refused to relinquish it, even as her hair turned gray. The Mary Stuart collar of her dress was fastened tightly, squeezing her double chin to the top. She sat at the edge of her seat, for the enormity of her bustle prevented her from meeting with the back of it.

In a plush, white armchair, presiding with his ever-present mask of shrewdness, Theodore Madison smoked his pipe. He was thick through the middle, broad-chested as well as tall. Even more imposing than his size was his scowl, affected from thin, sharp features that Dorothea tragically inherited.

Dorothea sat across from the settee in her own chair, emitting short, dissatisfied hisses in response to her mother's impassioned speech. At the edge of the familial circle, Katherine sat disdainfully, leaning on the arm of her chair and propping her temple against her fist.

The serving girl, Ally, arrived with a tray of fresh tea and biscuits to the collective delight of Theodore and most of the ladies. Katherine turned up her nose when the girl attempted to hand her a cup.

"For the shop, Arnold has decided to include more goods," Eliza announced. "He thinks it will please many to find the things they cannot get anywhere else in our shop at lower cost."

"Ah!" Winifred raised her thick eyebrows as she accepted a cup of tea from Ally.

"Revolutionary," Katherine declared, picking at the hem of her canary yellow skirt. Against the brightly colored fabric, her hair appeared richer and darker, twisted into a high coiffure.

"Hey, Arnold, you might consider selling Caribbean Cigars." Katherine stepped in front of Caleb and poured herself a glass of scotch from the bottle on the mantle. "The boys at the pub grieve for a lack of good cigars around Portsmouth. Imagine their excitement if they knew someone carried Caribbean cigars so nearby. I could easily pass the word along and you'd have yourself a bit of new business."

Caleb narrowed his glassy eyes at her.

"Sounds right smart, Katherine." Arnold winked.

"Ugh! The disgustingly *corrupt* manner of you, Katherine! It's offensive and shameful to say the very least!" Winifred squawked. "Come over here!"

Katherine went to her mother, rolling her eyes at the chastisement she knew all too well.

"Thank you, Katherine," Eliza added. "It's wonderful that you would advertise for us."

"That's exactly the trouble! You're *too* eager to advertise!" Winifred groaned, and in one deft swoop, had her by the collar and yanked her down.

With disrupted balance, Katherine nearly fell on her mother, and lifted her glass before it spilled. Winifred fastened each of the buttons at her throat, then roughly pushed her away.

"I can hardly stand the smell of that drink!" Winifred fanned her nose. "Really, *must* you Katherine?"

"You won't be near your daughter with it, but you'll embrace and kiss your son-in-law, who would bathe in his drink if he could."

"Forgive me, Mother Madison," Caleb pleaded. "It is but a small drink. Nothing excessive. Quite medicinal in purpose."

"Ha!" Katherine laughed, returning to her chair. "And what would be excessive to you? To consume the barrel? Do you believe that, Mother?"

"Well I—" Winifred stammered.

"If you watched his cup, you might notice it refills every ten or twelve minutes. Mind you, it's not a matter of gradual consumption, either."

"Katherine! Mind your own habits!" Dorothea defended. "He drinks very little and for his health alone!"

"Not for health." Katherine laughed again. "It's his crutch, his shield. But it's quite common. That's how I know. I see it all the time in the tavern. It's in the eyes."

Despite the behavior of his eldest daughter, and regardless of his opinion, Theodore was decidedly absent, for he sat with his eyes closed, smoking his pipe undisturbed.

"Child, you have a disagreeable tongue, and I should like to hear no more if it," Winifred reprimanded. As she did, Katherine unfastened the top three buttons of her collar.

Arnold smothered a laugh into his shoulder. Eliza's pale hand grazed her mother's arm with intended appeasement. Winifred fumed.

"Mother," Eliza called gently, practicing her skill at redirection. "Didn't you and Father mention that we would have a visit from the Koryns?"

"Oh, good heavens! How I forgot such pleasantness in all this ugliness." Winifred lovingly kissed her husband's hand as she looked at him. "Tell them, tell them about our new *friends*!"

"Have they any daughters?" Eliza asked.

Caleb and Arnold retreated once more into their separate conversation.

"I raised my rents indeed, in order to fund the construction of our summer cottage," Caleb said. "And why not?"

"Ah yes, fox hunting at the cottage! We will *go*," Arnold affirmed.

Caleb grunted through his nose, gulping the rest of his third or fourth glass.

"Augustus Koryn is a business competitor of mine," Theodore announced. "He comes from a line of stately landowners and I believe there is noble blood in that line. He has tenements and businesses in Hampshire *and* Dorset. We've come to an understanding, that is, in joining our genius for business we are finding greater opportunity for investment. He has a villa in the North End, in London Road. His son has a fine villa there also, expansive and sprawling, yes very fine indeed."

"And we have invited him and his family to be our guests for supper!" Winifred smiled.

"But do they have any daughters?" Eliza asked again.

"No, a son," Winifred replied.

"Yes, a blessed son. How I almost forgot *that*," Theodore stated, looking at Katherine. "The son is mature and established, with thirty years to his credit. And as I hear, he is a most honorable and apt minded fellow, following his father's footsteps in business. A real gentleman."

Presently Katherine sat on the floor, entertaining Oscar, the family's border collie. As she rolled him from side-to-side between her hands, he playfully nibbled at her. The weight of her father's stare caused her to glance up, even as she had determined to ignore his promotion of the latest potential suitor.

"Your story is so *exhilarating*," she said dryly.

Dorothea sneered at her.

"They must be absolutely charming." Winifred ignored her. "We shall have a feast to envy!"

"That does sound delightful. Arnold, doesn't it sound delightful?" Eliza beamed.

"—with one shot and I was completely—" Hearing his name, Arnold returned Eliza's sweet smile. "Yes, delightful, love."

"When is this supper, or should we be more accurate and call it an uninvited, desperate display of your unmarried daughter?" Katherine asked.

"Four weeks from Sunday! We shall have an early supper and after, much stimulating conversation and games!" Winifred replied.

"Ah, Sunday, but I should be sorry to miss it. I have to work." Katherine feigned disappointment.

"You do not *have* to work!" Winifred clutched her teacup with spidery fingers. "You will spend the day at home!"

"Oh please, Katherine," Eliza begged.

"No, I don't presume I can afford to."

"You will!" Theodore ordered, stamping his foot. His patience having dissolved.

"Quite right you will. If it were up to me, you would have no *job*. Nonsense and wastefulness!" Winifred huffed.

"Indeed, Wini," Theodore continued. "It is nonsense and wastefulness. It is also a proof of my lenience, an evidence of my indulgence to our firstborn, to allow her fancy of 'independence.' However, there is a limit to everything and the limit on this will be met when a husband is secured to marry her! And for all of my lenience and indulgence, I am repaid in smug ungratefulness."

"Ungrateful," Caleb sneered.

"I am not ungrateful," Katherine defended. "Father, I *do* appreciate your selfless efforts to care for your poor, husbandless firstborn. But wasn't it *you* who insisted that while I cannot agree to a husband, I would have to work? Is it indulgence to allow the conditions you yourself set forth? Was it not you that professed it fitting that I should toil among the worst part of humanity, as you called them, in order to learn to appreciate my rightful place? Be patient, Father, for I have not learned my lesson yet." Her willful tone brought the heat into his face. "And, if it will do so much damage to be absent this once, I will endure this supper for your sake."

"Oh delights!" Eliza clapped her hands. "Arnold, we can bring some of those delicious cakes I've been making for the bakery! Can't we, my dear?"

"As you wish, Eliza," Arnold said.

Katherine hopped to her feet and casually sauntered toward the mantle, eager to leave the subject of another suitor behind. There she set her empty glass, and as she narrowed her eyes at Caleb, she swiped the bottle of scotch away. Before striding toward the window, she dropped the bottle into the front pocket of her skirt.

The east windows faced Festing Road. Between it and the house, a manicured green expanse stretched to the russet brick wall. A parade of great old elms threw their shade on the enclosure and the sidewalk beyond it. The voices of her family faded, and Katherine gazed over the wall into the street. She was surprised to see Trayten over the top of the wall, standing on the other side of the road and sending an anxious thrill through her.

He leisurely appraised the house, and Katherine smiled at the stirring of her heart. His dark features made him unmistakable from the distance, with his worn black coat, and a coil of smoke trailing from the cigarette between his fingers. Katherine glanced back at her parents, now engrossed in the subject of landscaping behind Dorothea's and Caleb's wing of the house.

Behind the couches she strode directly out of the drawing

room and into the hall. Passing Ally, Katherine held the bottle of scotch for her to take and said, "Keep this out of there."

"Yes. Oi, Miss Madison, where shall I say you've gone?" Ally clutched the bottle to her chest.

"Do not." Katherine proceeded to the front door with a mischievous smirk.

❦

She passed through the gate and he met her in the street. Footsteps that had been hurried to escape the house, now slowed as she approached him.

"I have a mind to ask how you found me, but I suspect you must have used your extraordinary tracking abilities."

"I couldn't stay away for long," he said, flashing a brief, enigmatic smile.

"It hasn't been long? I've been wondering where you were for hours." Katherine giggled and took his arm when he offered it.

"I've been engrossed." He escorted her beneath the shade of the elms, walking slowly and with his eyes cast down.

"In what?"

"The pursuit of the perfect picture." He opened his hands, revealing fingertips and palms stained with many colors.

"Haven't you already painted more than one perfect picture?"

Trayten stalled his step and turned to inspect the house. She waited, watching his face closely for signs of a response.

"I have painted many pictures, that's true." He pulled his attention from the house and resumed their walk. "I even believed I had already painted everything worth looking at. And yet, I know what my masterpiece will be now, if I can command enough skill to execute it."

"What? Town Hall? Ships in the harbour?"

"You," he affirmed, and she tripped.

When she met the fervor in his eyes, she was stricken with the realization that Trayten Basel was the first and only person that ever truly affected her. At once, she understood the fear she had articulated, but not before experienced, regarding love. For, although she had been a fortress of impenetrable guile, safe from weapons wielded against the heart and protected with disaffection, she now stood disarmed before her conqueror and trembled.

❅ 4 ❆

1909

Marian crammed heaping forkfuls of fried potatoes into her mouth without the least concern for good manners. She glanced at Katherine, seated across from her, who took a cup of tea and drank it sparingly.

"Tell me, if you would please, Miss Boley, when was he found at sea?"

Marian postponed her chewing, counted on her fingers, and proclaimed past the food in her cheek, "About eight years, almost *exactly* eight years ago this season." She dove back into her plate.

"And what other injuries did he have, specifically. What else apart from his…his memory loss?"

"His legs of course! They're terribly bad-off. He had no use of them. They were, well, I don't like to discuss *that* over breakfast."

"No use of his legs? Were they broken? Can…can he not walk?" Terror weakened Katherine's voice.

"Paralyzed he is, in his legs. The doctor saw no disease in them. Said perhaps it were some destruction of nerves, actually.

And of course there are his fits, usually they happen when he dreams."

"Paralyzed…" Katherine stared at the table, shadows darkening her face. She pushed passed the unease bending her stomach. "What sorts of dreams does he have?"

"*I* don't dream them, and he doesn't say."

"What *does* he say to you?"

"Not very much, Mrs. Koryn." Marian took a loud drink of water. "You go ahead and ask him for yourself, soon as I get his breakfast dishes cleared."

❦

It required more strength than before to enter his room the second time. As before, she entered and immediately closed the door behind her. This time, she faced him. He gazed at her inquisitively from his wheelchair. The clarity of his eyes, glowing in the morning light, quickened her pulse. She waited, hoping to find a spark of recognition there.

His expression, blank and disaffected, cut through her.

Standing in the line of his vacant gaze, Katherine made a silent commitment to hide from him whatever may stir in her heavy heart. It was Trayten Basel who had known her better than any living soul, and she was compelled by sentiment to believe that he could know her again, in time. Approaching him as a stranger, Katherine donned a mask and vowed to breathe evenly and proceed with guarded caution.

"Good morning," she said. Every second that she refrained from weeping, her confidence increased.

"It's morning. That's a fact."

She concentrated on the whiskers littering his chin, jaw, and neck. His face appeared rough, eyes hardened, the hair hanging in them sketching shadows on his cheeks.

Noticing the way she stared, he grunted, "Who are *you.*"

"Don't you know me?" She held her breath.

"No." The sound of the word fell as unwelcome and resolute as a guillotine's blade.

"My name is Katherine. I hear *you* are called T.B.. Is there no *actual* name you are called by?"

"No."

"Then you wouldn't mind if I picked one for you, I'm sure. We must call you *something*! Initials are so impersonal."

He stared at her and said nothing. Katherine sat on the couch across from his bed. She fought to keep her gaze from his legs. He wheeled back away from her and turned toward the window.

"I have one. The name Trayten. That starts with a 'T,' so it can't be too far off. We can call you Tray for short. It suits you I think. Very modern."

"Who is Tray?"

"I suppose *you* are now." Her eyes traveled beyond him to a stack of boards in one corner of the room. A wooden box sat on the floor nearby. Along the wall from his bed and night table, there was a low desk, accessible from his wheelchair.

With quivering hands, she approached the corner. "May I have a look?" she asked, although she bent down to pick up two of the color splattered canvases anyway. He glared.

The technique evident on each canvas was uncertain, with painted images that were hazy, shaky, and apparently abandoned.

"So, you're an artist," Katherine said.

"Am I?"

"I can't do anything like this," she said, tilting one toward him.

Instead of looking at the painting in her hand, he stared through the window. His silence pervaded for some time between them. Although she attempted to engage him in small talk, he gave no responses, refusing to participate. He kept his eyes away, staring beyond the window as though he waited for something to arrive on the sea.

Katherine offered to read to him. He grunted. She offered to let him read to her. He ignored her. For hours she sat with him, catching herself falling asleep several times as she reclined on the couch. He neither moved from his chair nor in it.

At last Katherine asked, "Do you wish to be left alone?"

"Yes."

"I will come again tomorrow. I will stay and talk with you more. Would you like that?"

He did not glance at her. He did not make a sound. Katherine withdrew, weary and saturated with silence.

※

Over the next several days little changed as Katherine attempted to engage Tray in conversation. Each morning she waited for Marian to clear his breakfast, entered with her usual greeting, and extended her usual inquiries about his welfare and his sleep the night before. Most of what she said was met with the same apathetic hush. He barely moved, staring across the snowy beach to the ocean.

Each time she visited he was no more alive than the day before. He conversed no more, he moved no more. Tray was a solemn statue, a vacant shell. Though she screamed at the silence on the inside, she kept her mask firmly in place.

Katherine behaved as though his silence did not concern her, as if she did not mind that he never greeted her, or bid her farewell, or asked her to come back. She continued day after day, talking to him as if he cared.

※

Katherine sat in the gaudy front parlor, writing in a red, leather-bound journal. There was a busy charm that attracted her to the parlor, crowded with all of its knickknacks. The bustle and variety reminded her vaguely of Portsmouth, a comfort amid the empty quiet of Alderney. When Marian stole in and startled her, Katherine ran her pen off the page.

"How has it been?" Marian asked. "You haven't said much at all. Since you came, you eat and stay hidden in either your room or his. Are you getting anywhere?"

"He says nothing. He is indifferent to me."

"What did you expect of him? He doesn't *see* strangers. He hates *Suzan*." Marian stood over Katherine.

"I suppose I thought I might be different." Katherine closed the red book around her finger.

"Pah! Of *course* you did!" Marian huffed.

"I'm not through. I will break the quiet. I talk to him often, so he can't call me a stranger forever."

"What do you talk to him about?"

"Nothing at all important. But I do it," Katherine said.

"Well, Mrs. Koryn, he talks to *me*."

"Does he? I am sure that he must."

"He does. And though I hate to give you reason to feel proud, I suppose you should know that he has asked—"

"What?" She nearly kicked Marian, uncrossing her legs to sit up.

"He has asked me about you. He asked me where you were today. You didn't go up."

Katherine's heart leapt into her throat and she gripped the book against her chest. "Did he?"

Marian shrugged. "Where *did* you go today?"

"I went walking," Katherine said.

"All day?"

"Most of it."

"You're not *very* old. Why should you go wandering about like a sad old person?" Marian dropped her weight into the settee with an exaggerated thud.

"I was thinking."

"You can't think in one place?"

Katherine opened her mouth to reason with Marian, then decided against it and waved her hand. "Never mind. Goodnight."

Gathering her journal, quill, and inkwell, she started for the stairs, asking, "Miss Boley?"

"What."

"He really did ask about me?"

"No. I lied." Marian dropped her chin. "Yea, he asked."

Katherine hugged her journal and breathed a sigh of relief. There was a chance. She still had a chance.

❦

A new day arrived, and Katherine sat on the couch in Tray's room. For hours he sat silently, rocking his wheelchair back and forth within a short distance. He ignored her as usual, refusing to look at her. Katherine stared toward the window, her eyes losing focus in the white light from the pale sky beyond. He became a blur in her peripheral vision, a gently rocking form causing the floorboards to creak.

"I do not paint *really*." His grainy voice surprised her, "I can't keep a steady hand. I only thought it might amuse me."

Katherine blinked to clear the haze from her eyes. He returned to rocking in his chair, rolling the tops of the large wheels with his open palms. Katherine held her breath, hoping to hear him speak again. With no further indication of his liveliness, she commenced to pacing the floor.

His gaze followed her. "Who are you?"

"You don't know?" With hope she asked.

"Why would I ask, if I knew?"

"My name is Katherine Madison-Koryn." She placed herself between him and the window and waited.

He stared blankly through her before asking, "And why are you here?"

"To help you, Tray."

"I need help?"

"You have no memory," she said softly.

Immediately he wheeled away from her. "You can't help a thing that doesn't exist."

"Can you tell me anything? *Anything* that you recall?"

"Is there something you want? I have no knowledge of my past. I only know that I'm here, shut away from a world I don't remember, homeless, forgotten, alone."

"That's the most you've said to me yet!" she exclaimed with a sigh.

He swiveled around to look at her.

"I'm not looking for anything in particular, that is, other than you, *yourself*," she said. "I *do* want to help you. Tell me, is that what you think? That you are alone?"

"If you want to, count Marian. She's my only history, pathetic as that is."

"There must be people who love you, and search for you. Why don't you try to remember them?"

"No. There is something about *you*." Tray narrowed his eyes at her.

"There's nothing about me."

"You tell me about *yourself*. Then I'll decide if I should talk to you."

"But I—"

"It's the only way I'll be able to tell. And if you're anything like Marian, I'll have to turn you out straight away. Understood?" He said it seriously, but she laughed, recognizing his humor in a glimmer. A fleeting tenderness passed over his face.

"I'm sure I'm not much *like* her. Still, you won't find me very interesting."

"If you're not like her, you're already infinitely more interesting."

"I can imagine. How you must suffer." Katherine smiled. "So, your silence to me is finished?"

"That's open for debate. You still haven't told me anything about yourself."

"Will you at least agree to acknowledge me when I come hereafter?" she asked.

"We'll see. I don't yet know," he stated, straight-faced.

Her smile faltered in hearing him speak curtly. She shoved her heartache down and said, "About myself…I'm a wanderer. I've been lost for years, much like you."

"How?"

Katherine took her time speaking, careful with her words.

"Years ago, I lost someone important to me, the only person that ever mattered, actually. Since then I've devoted myself to finding him. My soul has not been at ease without him. In losing him, I lost a part of myself. Some said I lost my mind." She inhaled deeply. "People say what they want to. The truth is, I haven't been free, and I haven't rested. I'm crippled *myself*, Tray."

He flinched.

"I too am wounded," she said.

He waited, letting the resonance of her warm voice swim around the room.

"Marian says you're a widow," he finally said. "Was that your loss? Was his name Koryn?"

"No," she said, watching the sea through the window. "His name is Basel."

1900

"How shall I trust a man I don't even know?" Katherine asked.

The row of trees supported a canopy of green high overhead. Shadows and light danced across their faces as they passed through Craneswater Park. A considerate breeze cooled them against the heat of the sun.

"Decide to trust me. You know me. You've seen my art. That's enough."

"Where is your family, Trayten?"

"I left them when I was young," he said.

"Why?"

He reached for her hand and entwined her fingers with his. "I understood that my calling was someplace else." He focused on her hand as the playfulness left him. "My older brothers and I went to work young. I was five when I started at the cotton mill in Todmorden, Yorkshire. I worked as a scavenger, clearing the fluff from the wheels under the spinning mule, because I was the smallest."

"At five years old?"

"It's common to start as young. Yes."

"What of your parents?" she asked.

"My mother worked as a piecer in the mill, until she died of a fever. My father worked the coal mines, my brothers joined him. We spent our days, each of us alone, waking before sunrise to begin, working until after dark, laboring to eat.

"I watched my mother die. I saw my brothers and father disappear into blackness, in body and in spirit. I watched others die living deaths. Lives *unlived*. Lives sacrificed to feed the forward motion of the machine. I saw children disfigured, their clothing or hair caught by the wheels, hands caught in machines. We fell asleep on the mill floor. We were punished for falling behind. When I had enough, I left. I decided to take my chances scavenging *beyond* the factory."

"You're a long way from Yorkshire. Did you mean to come to Hampshire?"

"No. I lived in many places before *here,* lending a hand on farms to earn my keep. I spent years in Oxfordshire, where I had the good fortune to work for a professor from the university. He taught me to read, and when he discovered my drawings, he encouraged me to try my hand at painting. I fell in love with painting landscapes, and after a time I continued south. The scenery grew more interesting the farther I traveled."

"And do you intend to travel on from here?"

"If I travel any farther, I will fall into the sea."

Katherine smiled, patches of light warming her cheeks. "And how long *have* you been stranded here?"

"Not long enough, if you've always been here."

Her smile widened, but she hid it away and pressed a finger to her lips before asking him, "Do you like music, Trayten?"

"I don't know."

"You do?" She nudged him. "Oh good! You'll take me dancing."

"Dancing; a pastime for the wealthy."

"I'm not wealthy," she asserted.

Trayten surprised her with a dry laugh. "I've seen your castle! Here, we can see it yet, looming over the trees. We walk in its shadow."

"It's not *my* castle. But it certainly is impressive. Did *you* ever imagine a prison so finely crafted?"

"I know a few hundred unfortunates who'd prefer your prison to their workhouse."

"You think I'm spoiled." Katherine let go of his hand.

"I didn't say that. It's a fact that you come from wealth, and that I do not. And I despise money. I despise it because I have none."

"Don't you sell your paintings?"

"I can't part with my work. Instead, I do what I must to scrape by. I work in the dockyard, when there's work to go round."

"The dockyard is fickle," she said. "If you won't sell your paintings, you will remain poor. Is that what you want?"

"If I remain free, I do not care what I am."

"If I were you, I *might* survive, if I had books to read and enough paper to write on."

"Katherine?"

"Trayten."

"Have you been to the library?"

"The public library?" she laughed, charmed by his severity.

"No. Follow me."

In Old Portsmouth, a mansion once impressive as a cathedral stood condemned. A tower pointed to the sky, with broad stained-glass windows decorating the cupola. The masonry appeared blue in the shade and pale gray in the sunlight. A fire had consumed the greater portion of the house, and its owner boarded up the doors and windows of the lower level, leaving it to rot, at least for the time being.

Trayten led her by the hand over the loose gravel and tangles of weeds that littered the yard. Katherine could imagine the fire's fury, how it poured from the windows to singe the stonework of the outer walls, leaving black stains like the lashes of an ink coated paintbrush. She searched the windows above the second story, some of them unbroken, glazed and foggy with grime.

"Come, this way," Trayten whispered. They passed through the immense shadow of the tower, and Katherine felt the warmth of the sun depart.

In the back, where the garden wall at the alley cut the lawn short, a wing of the house appeared, a gargantuan extension rising three stories high. There were no signs of fire here. Trayten crouched to a small window at ground level, covered with an iron grate. He felt along the edge, nudging until he worked it free and set it aside.

With the flash of a mischievous smile, he said, "Through here."

"Through…there?" She stared at a black abyss in the foundation of the house.

Trayten lowered her feet first into dusty oblivion and followed after. In the blackness she clung to him, her hand on his chest. He took hold of it and guided her forward six paces before directing her up a narrow staircase.

From a cellar they emerged into an impressive hall, a magnificent library that filled the unscathed wing of the mansion. Katherine was silenced with awe. The walls stretched to a vaulted ceiling at the topmost story, with balconies on the second and third levels, their black iron banisters creating circles that wound toward a skylight. The glass of the skylight was muted with weather and wear.

The floor was a masterpiece of mosaic tiles, laid to form a path that ran through a forest of towering bookshelves so tall they required ladders to reach the top shelves. Six rows of bookshelves divided the hall and lined the walls. Two shelves in the farthest row, opposite Katherine and Trayten, had toppled down and lay against the wall, their books piled in reckless mounds beneath dust, cobwebs, and shadow.

Little light managed to pry through the gaps where the windows were not fully covered with boards. It altered to a pale moon-glow through the mossy mildew covering the glass. Nevertheless, the narrow shafts illuminated the dust fluttering in the air.

A desk sat near the cellar, cluttered with open books, dust caked candles, quills, and a small wooden inkwell. On either side of the desk, tightly coiled iron stairs wound to the second level, and continued winding to the third.

Trayten strolled along the middle aisle separating the rows of bookshelves. His footsteps echoed, ringing across the vast, live space. Along his path, eight candles were enshrined in wax on the floor, four on one side and four on the other. He took a match, struck it, and carried the flame to the first wick. Katherine observed his movements as he continued, lighting each candle in succession. The wax, which had melted and molded to the floor, glowed golden around the fresh light, and together the candles created a luminous tunnel.

At the end of the lighted path he met her gaze. Drops of amber glimmered in his eyes. Dazzled by them, she quickly looked away and slid her fingers along the spines of the leather-bound books filling the nearest shelf.

"Now I understand." She smiled slyly. "Here is *your* wealth, Trayten Basel."

He grinned and leaned casually against a shelf, putting his face into shadow.

"It doesn't belong to me. It's a wealth merely borrowed." With reverence he regarded the storehouse surrounding them.

"Does knowledge belong to anyone? No, indeed we must all share it."

"Some are gifted with greater shares. Some with scraps. I wish that all had the chance to learn," he said.

"We were fortunate, you and I." Katherine gently turned the pages of a book. "To have been taught."

"You had a fancy education, with all your family's means, no doubt."

"I would've had the basics only, with a heavy emphasis on domestic duty, were it not for my tutor. Much like you, I was educated by chance. Mr. Gaffney made me his unofficial protege. There's a cafe in Queens Street where he and his associates used to gather to debate many interesting things like the effects of industrialization, the social strata, and aestheticism. Mr. Gaffney was a talented scholar of Edinburgh University, you see. I used to go to the cafe to read the papers and was admitted into their circle, listening and learning. He loaned many books to me and referred me to many more."

"And what did your family think of your outside education?" Trayten watched as she inspected another book and moved gradually toward him.

"They didn't think of it. I've had the unusual privilege to wander about virtually unobstructed," she laughed.

"Thank God," Trayten said. "I would never have known you otherwise."

"But I'm certain we would've met, even if I'd been kept cloistered and strictly managed, if you believe in fate."

"I don't," he said. "I believe in choice. Everything is the result of choices, not some predestined plan, as the notion of fate would suggest."

"And yet you thanked God for my wandering. Did He not govern my path?" Katherine asked.

"God blesses, guides, and protects. He grants us the will to make choices. He allowed your freedom, and directed my path, leading us to meet. Still, we both made many choices which, had they been different, could've prevented us from finding one another."

"So, you believe a person is entirely in command of their destiny?" Delicately, Katherine turned another page in the book.

"Yes."

A thrill raced through her at the idea: to be in command, to wholly govern the course of one's life. She wanted to believe such a thing was possible, even for her. For, even though she tried to ignore its reality, Katherine lived with the imminence of being married off to fulfill the expectations of her family and her class.

"Well, you must allow that sometimes there are forces that dictate our path, forces beyond our control," she offered, testing his notion.

"I must hold that we always have a choice."

"I don't know." Katherine closed the book she had been holding and searched the shelves for another.

After several quiet minutes, Trayten said, "Tell me something. Something you do know."

"Something I know?" she asked. Her gaze climbed the heights of the tower rising overhead. She smiled. "I happen to know that names are very interesting."

Still, Trayten said nothing. She caught his amused smile and paced as she spoke. Her movements were fluid, like a dancer meandering daintily over the tiles. Stretching her arms high to wipe dust from the titles of books, she allowed her fingers to travel along the shelves.

"Names were once chosen only after extensive, careful thought. Parents chose for their child a name that held a meaning, or one that might fit a personality, or fulfill a hope. Unfortunately today, we aren't as careful with the choosing of names. For example, I am Katherine, which may be related to the Greek word *aikia*, meaning 'torture.' My middle name is Dayna. It means 'parched, dry.'" She whirled around to face him. "Do they suit me? I like to think not. And yet, some names happen to be suitable, even in this age of carelessness. Trayten, for instance, is a good name. It means 'god of the sea.'

"Some meanings depend entirely on the origin you study, but from one culture to another, many similar names hold similar meanings. Ask me a name and I will tell you what it means." She inhaled the musty aroma of a leather-bound book, cracked open the stiff pages, and thumbed through the aged paper.

"Hector?" he asked.

"Hector, the poor dear! It means 'restraint.'"

"And Cyril?"

"That is, 'lord.'" Katherine performed a stately bow.

Trayten emerged from his shadow and drew nearer. "Damian?"

"Daman, meaning 'to tame.'" She caught his gaze and shyly diverted hers.

"What is Basel?"

"Basel is 'royal, kingly.' I told you it was a good name. *Royal, god of the sea!*" When she glanced over her shoulder, he stood a breath away.

"George?" He nodded and his nose grazed her cheek.

"'Farmer.'"

"Calandria?"

"That is, 'beautiful one,' but Calista is 'most beautiful,'" Katherine whispered.

"Somehow that was overlooked for you, 'torturous' and 'parched.'" A chuckle bent the tone of his voice.

"Injustice surely. Meanwhile, my unpleasant sister Dorothea is, 'gift of god.' My name matches their opinion of me."

"I don't share it." His hand brushed her cheek, scalding and inviting her at once. "What is the meaning of Angel?"

"Angel, of 'angelus,' is 'messenger.'"

"I rather like that for a name." He searched her eyes as though they held an enchanting secret. He set out to decipher her. With careful fingertips he explored the curve of her cheek, traveled the line of her neck, and pulled her tightly against him.

In the moment between that gesture and the next, time stretched and waited. The universe narrowed. All that existed beyond the slight space between them faded from focus. She knew that he would kiss her. The look in his eyes boldly told her, with a language that, although new, was remarkably easy to grasp. The knowing thrilled her and she wondered if his kiss would do as much.

There was nothing left to ponder when he closed the space between them and pressed his lips to hers. No thought possessed power to remain. No power remained to resist, for she was spell-bound in his arms. The fervor of his touch weakened her knees and she staggered, yet he caught her, lifting her off the ground with ease. She held him tighter, determined to match the passion of his tenderness.

5

1909

"How long have you been a doctor?" Tray asked.

"A doctor?"

"Suzan called you as a specialist and Marian called you a psychoist."

Katherine choked on a laugh at the invented word. "Well, my interest *is* your psyche."

In customary fashion, he faced the window in his chair. She expected him that way, with his gaze averted from her. Beyond him through the window the ocean churned, driven by relentless winds. Together, they stared at it, although they remained apart.

"Have you no feeling at all, in them?" she asked.

"Them?"

"Your…your legs."

"Nothing below mid-thigh," he answered tightly.

"I heard of a man once who had no legs at *all*, they had been amputated, but he could feel them, feel pain, as if they were there." She laughed dryly. "I don't know what would be worse, to have legs without feeling or feeling without legs."

A sliver of amusement pulled at the line of his cheek. He grunted.

"I once sprained an ankle when I was very young. It still hurts sometimes. Injuries are strange, the way we don't always entirely heal."

"You can walk on that ankle."

"True." She glanced at her hands, which would not be still in her lap.

Another heavy silence filled the room, and she could not bear it. She departed with as much composure as she could collect.

1900

"There, look there!" Trayten pointed across the park from where he and Katherine lay in the sun-soaked grass.

"What is it?"

"Observe the wastefulness of the wealthy. That woman, she has a tear in her purse, see how she inspects it?"

A refined gentlewoman, with a parasol on her shoulder and a gentleman to escort her, picked at the little hole in her handbag and trilled a distant laugh.

"She noticed the shillings that dropped behind her on the ground yet leaves them where they landed," Trayten said. "She's so sufficiently supplied with riches that three bob are of no value to her. She's too proud to bend down and take them back, too wary of appearing in need."

The lady disregarded the shillings in the grass and laughed as the gentleman placed the purse in his pocket.

"There is a perfect illustration of the excessive prosperous few, whom I loathe, who taunt poverty. I would gather it after her, poor scrub that I am; lowly enough to *bend*. I could buy more than a dozen tins of tobacco! I'd be lost to lose such fare," he said. "If I ever had as much!"

"You're right." She laughed at the way his forehead wrinkled and he threw his hands about.

"Would *you*? Would you bend to retrieve them?"

"I would." Katherine buried him with grass, plucking handfuls to cover his legs.

"Ah, but you can't fully appreciate it. Not only are you well-off by birth, but you have your own wages to replenish—"

"They are not my wages to keep. They are my father's. He puts them into his own accounts," she clarified.

"What good is that?"

"None at all, really. I can't take the money. He won't allow it. Until I marry, he says, I have everything I need while he supports me. It isn't for the wages that I work. Because my father ordered it, I should be opposed, but it affords me the opportunity to stay away from the house."

"Until you marry? And who will you marry?" he asked with eyes aflame.

"You? Is that what you want me to say?"

He only stared at her.

"I don't like saying what other people want me to say."

Trayten's face darkened, however he smiled through the pain. "I would only have you say what you truly think and feel."

"And so I shall." Drawing her cheek against his, she felt its coarseness before meeting his troubled gaze. She touched his cheek and sprang to her feet. "I'll see you later."

"You would leave me this way?" He held her hand.

"I have wages to earn, if not to keep." She kissed him quickly and let go of his hand.

He did not move from the grass where she left him, propped up on one elbow. Instead, he watched her move off into the distance, until she was swallowed up in the foot traffic of the street. He lit a cigarette and imagined that he needed to know her better, not only her shape and the features of her face, but her heart and her soul also. Only then could he paint his greatest masterpiece.

As before and evermore, Trayten was mesmerized by Katherine. He cared to do little else but remain near to her. In order to breathe, in order to feel alive, he needed to be close, to gaze on her, to hear her voice. He was determined to watch over her. An intimate guardian, he often eluded her, keeping to the shadows when she believed she was without him.

To leave her alone, unprotected in city streets, was unthinkable. If he were unable to paint, he sought Katherine. The remarkable skill and ease with which he tracked her was an unexpected surprise. Finding her came naturally to him, as though he were drawn to her by celestial forces, pulled to her by the tides, as if she were a wandering piece of him.

In the tavern, he could easily evade her from a corner. He listened to her laugh. He memorized her smile. If she drew near to his table, he would shift swiftly to another, content to remain unseen. In the moments when she was oblivious to his presence, he discovered more about her, and loved her all the more deeply.

As on the streets, through the park he followed behind her, his gaze fixed on her form. In the night, when she wandered home and the streets were clear, she was freer than anywhere else. Seeing Katherine, liberated from the rest of the world, thrilled Trayten.

In dark avenues, with no sound beyond her echoing footsteps, she would sing the bawdy bar tunes gleaned from the pub and laugh to herself. Sometimes she spouted verses, reciting poems she had written or carved into memory. To windows, as their lights extinguished, she would grin and blow a kiss.

When the night air was cool, she exhaled energetically to see her breath, and in the streetlamp light she laughed at variations of her shadow on buildings. He loved the way she hummed, trotting down the stairs, or treading light and fast along a low garden wall in Southsea.

When he was without her, Katherine occupied his dreams.

Visions of her drifted through his mind, stirring him and consuming him like the disease she had described. Often he awoke, believing her to be beside him, hearing her voice, feeling her touch like a feather. He would light a lamp, delirious with sleep, and discover the empty room around him.

The sickness weakened him, troubled his rest, and enlivened a relentless ache. Katherine was the only cure. The sorrow and yearning that crushed him in her absence was lifted and evaporated the moment he could hold her and breathe the scent of her in.

The affliction woke him again and he sat up, acclimating himself to the dark room before moving barefoot and shirtless to a canvas on the floor. Agile fingers carried oil paint to its surface and shaped her contours, her skin, her hair. With a brush he labored over the fine details of her face. Trayten slipped into a state of pure focus, working with both intent and frustration, from memory, from his constant study of her.

Long arms propped on his knees as he crouched on the floor, hands hovering above his work, visualizing the shape of her face as he remembered it between his hands. He envisioned her alive and animated before him. He anguished over her eyes, working to render their exact color, their dimension, and light. He feared he would go mad, should he be unable to recreate her image.

He lay back on the hardwood floor and closed his eyes, summoning her features, determined to capture her justly. At the early hour, exhausted and frustrated, Trayten fell asleep on the floor beside her rough depiction. Paint stained his arms and forehead where he had rubbed them in agitation.

Footsteps fell quietly, careful to maneuver around tubes of paint, brushes, and cans. Knees lowered to the floor beside his body, and Katherine's hair dusted his cheek in the dulcet glow of morning. She brought her face close to his, feeling the warmth hanging in the air around him. He wore a faint red smear of paint on his cheek.

Trayten surfaced from a dream of Katherine to the scent of her hair. She sat back on her heels. For an instant he blinked his eyes and waited for her image to vanish from before him. When she remained, smiling impishly, he observed the canvas and the morning sun highlighting white, sepia, and red on the floor.

She too studied the wet painting, unfinished, violent and wild, the lips crimson, the eyes striking.

"This is me?"

"You are being recreated."

"I see." She rubbed his cheek. "And I have kissed your cheek here. Aren't I forward?" She took the paint onto her thumb.

"It's not finished. It's merely an attempt."

"Well, you shall have time to work it out. I must leave you soon. Come with me to breakfast before I am taken today." Katherine reached out her hand.

"Who steals you?"

"The Madisons."

৪৫৯

He followed her to a bakery in Kent Street and Katherine purchased a box of biscuits to share as they passed through the lane. The air was enlivened by the heat of the sun. Over the bustle of people she said, "It's an early supper. One of my father's great rivals and his family are coming to eat our food and drink our wine. They're completely preoccupied with preparing for the event, so I slipped away so you would know that I remembered you."

"I nearly missed you," he lied.

She glared and shoved him.

Trayten carried the box, biting a biscuit as she pulled, swept, and twisted her hair and pinned it into place. When she finished, she caught his stare and smiled sweetly.

"It's nothing to look forward to. I rather dread it. But there are obligations." She fastened the top buttons of the blouse under her jacket. "What?"

A grin revealed the dimples in his cheeks, and he admitted, "I'm watching you transform."

Katherine grasped the collar of his shirt. In the sunlight, his eyes revealed greater depths, pools of sepia light swimming rich russet chasms. "How have I done?"

"A stranger might be fooled, but I see you. I would recognize you *anywhere*." He kissed her tenderly and sent her on her way.

⚜

The carriage arrived with a clamor, bringing the long-awaited guests to Madison Estate for supper. With a noisome approach the driver, his whip, and the horses he afflicted made their presence known. Even if they had been noiseless, they would have been immediately detected, for Winifred stalked the front hall and kept diligent watch through the window. At the sound of the horses, she shrieked with glee, alerting her husband to assemble the family and ordering Ally to attend the door.

When the call to action came, Theodore abandoned his armchair to shuffle the family into line alongside the dining room table. He took each one by the shoulders and set them accordingly for proper presentation.

Eliza, frail under her smile, relied on Arnold's supportive arm. He glanced compassionately toward her, the paleness of her face apparent even in the subduing glow of lanterns and firelight. She dusted at her skirt and fidgeted with her hair.

"You're perfect," Arnold whispered, taking her flighty hand and laying it on his arm.

Beside them, Dorothea thumped Caleb's shoulder, shooting him a disgusted sneer that dissolved into a frightening smile as Theodore tapped her chin and kissed her forehead. Flustered, Caleb searched for a place to extinguish his cigar.

Winifred charged into the room, waving her hands. She shoved Katherine gracelessly into line beside Caleb. "Shh! They come in! I hear the door!"

Katherine crossed her arms. Caleb's cigar sizzled as he dropped it into the water glass she held. She flashed him a fiery glare, but he stiffened when Theodore passed and slapped him on the back.

Katherine prepared to address Caleb, however Theodore roared, "Welcome, come in, oh welcome!"

The company entered and Katherine dropped her arms, draining the ashy water from her glass onto Caleb's shoe. His mouth hung open and he was prepared to shout. Dorothea, too embarrassed to scold him, clutched his arm, encouraging restraint with the digging of her fingernails.

Augustus Koryn's figure filled the doorway, and he shook hands heartily with Theodore. He had dark converging eyebrows and a feathery Kaiser mustache. In a silk shirt and velvet waistcoat, he was exquisitely dressed. Gold chains connected pocket to pocket, gold tips adorned his shoes, and gold plating covered his buttons.

"Good to see you outside of the ring, old mate!" Augustus bobbed a bulbous head that was balding at the crown.

"Oh definitely, definitely!" Theodore turned his attention to the son who, with hulking proportions, was taller than both of his elders. His features were thick and his eyes a sallow blue. He looked down on everything around him and stroked the end of a full goatee beard. Stiff, blond curls extended his height an additional three inches at least.

"Reuben, welcome," Theodore gushed.

"Marvelous house here, sir, yes indeed I was quite impressed on the way down from the North End, and if I may say, that is speaking much for I am not one to be easily astounded by houses other than our own houses, but here sir, the variety you know, quite cozy really, it is a delightful prospect. Your room is so very quaint as well. I have been able to genuinely call but few rooms as quaint as this, even so lived-in as yours." Reuben paused to breathe. He expressed himself with a rounded accent that sounded as though it might have been invented. "Ah, well it's a *dog*!" he exclaimed to Oscar, tugging his trouser leg with a growl.

Katherine, scowling with disenchantment, narrowed her eyes at Reuben Koryn. Of all the hopeful suitors who had been paraded through the dining hall of Madison Estate, Reuben's presence aggravated her the most. She wondered whether it was his personality that made him so repulsive to her, or if it was simply that he was not Trayten Basel.

A lady in a wheelchair emerged, small and frail, from behind and between Augustus and Reuben.

She squinted her eyes at them. "Where have my boys gone! Oh!" She wheeled into Dorothea and exclaimed, "Oh here, here you are Reuben."

"Gracious!" Dorothea squawked, looking at her mother helplessly.

The lady jumped in her chair. "Well that, no, that's not you, Reuben!"

"Here, Hilda." Augustus clapped his flabby hands twice. "Here we are."

Reuben bent down and clapped several times. "Mother, here we are."

Hilda wheeled abruptly around, lifting two wheels. She rolled forward with great speed and Augustus stuck out his boot to inter-cept the front wheel and stop her. Her hair was flaxen blonde, her eyes were faded, and her skin was translucent, as though she were an old woman. She was, in fact, little more than fifty years along.

"Mr. and Mrs. Koryn, Reuben, may I present my family," Theodore announced.

Winifred shook hands with Augustus and Reuben.

"Our youngest daughter, Eliza and her husband Arnold Sumner. He owns a shop in Bishop Street."

Eliza beamed a radiant smile. "Pleased to have you join us!" she exclaimed. "We've brought cakes from our bakery."

"Well, I do like cakes." Hilda grinned.

"Yes, and my daughter Dorothea and her husband, Caleb Edson, whom of course, Mr. Koryn you have met before," Theodore continued.

"Ah yes, the apprentice," Augustus hissed.

Caleb raised an objecting finger, stammering with a wobbly mouth, "Actually, I—"

Theodore moved past the Edsons and with an elaborate flutter of his hand revealed, "*This* is our eldest daughter, Katherine. Yes, I am sure you will find her to be appealing company. She reads *books*!"

Katherine laughed, unable to hold it back. Reuben yawned and after, raised his eyebrows at her suggestively.

Awkwardly the families scattered to sit around the table. One chair was left open across from Reuben. Augustus sat and clapped twice in the direction of his wife. "Table's here, Hilda. Come on."

Hilda wheeled vigorously, ramming her chair into his leg.

Supper was a tedious blur to Katherine. Reuben's attention vacillated from her to his father throughout the meal. She sat as withdrawn as she could manage to be, however keen to the irritating behavior of her parents. They boasted shamelessly and forced peals of laughter, extending great effort to be agreeable. They discussed the advantages of merging Madison and Koryn properties in nauseating detail.

Theodore, Augustus, and Reuben bragged of their holdings, fighting each other to speak and filling the air with a chorus that increased in volume with every refrain. Caleb continued to drink, sliding steadily into such a state of slurring that he relinquished his efforts to join the song. Dorothea smiled mechanically, lost from the conversations around her. Eliza attempted to keep up and occasionally sat back. Arnold handed her a glass of water and whispered in her ear.

In the drawing room after supper, Winifred played the gramophone and insisted everyone dance, except her. Katherine designed to avoid the activity and had nearly escaped the room when Eliza begged her and demolished her resolve with whimpering and guilt. The sanctuary of galloping hand in hand with her sister was not to last. When Arnold reclaimed his bride, Katherine was left exposed to Reuben's waiting arms.

Even as she protested, he encompassed her with a forceful embrace and waltzed her in wide circles. His face hovered somewhere overhead, apparent only by the labored breathing that moved her hair like a hot, unwelcome breeze. She saw nothing beyond his waistcoat and the frame of his imposing arms. His chest, like a wide, high wall, impelled her blindly backward. After he twirled her, she was cinched more tightly against it.

In desperation and contrary to her natural grace, Katherine fell out of time. At the risk of causing Reuben to fall and the possibility of being crushed beneath him, she tripped, one foot on the other, and hoped to break his hold with the weight of her body falling.

To her dismay, she was sustained by his grip, and hung from the fortress of his forearms. He did however suspend the next twirl to peer down at her. As his arms enlarged their enclosure, she put her hands against the barrier of his ribcage.

"If you'll excuse me, sir, I'm in need of a rest." She swallowed hard.

"So soon? After all I've heard about you, I expected more endurance—"

"Never mind anything you've *heard* about me. Your sources have a skewed perspective, no doubt." She took two strides back to alleviate her craning neck.

"What? Are you *not* beautiful, charming, and vivacious?" Reuben smirked.

"Not in the least." Katherine folded her arms and looked around the room.

"Well, they didn't boast of your candor." He smirked.

"Is candor a characteristic bachelors are concerned with?"

"They *did* exalt your spirit though, your exuberant energy and zeal." Reuben seemed pleased the more she bristled.

"I don't know who *they* are, so I doubt they know me at all."

"Playing the little shrew? This explains why you haven't been snatched up yet." He closed the distance of her two steps with one.

"Perhaps it is my abhorrence of being *snatched* at all." With a warning glare she attempted to deflect him.

"Don't be frightened, Kathy. I will handle you gently." He snaked his hand the length of her arm, from shoulder to elbow, and his fingers enclosed and constricted her there.

"I shouldn't like to be handled at any rate." She twisted her arm from his grasp. "If you will kindly let me go, sir."

"I am nothing if not kind." He bowed, bringing his face down to her level and winking at her with lustful eyes.

She took the opportunity readily and retreated from the room, unwilling to glance back. The icy flutter that raked her spine revealed that he watched as she went.

❧ 6 ❧

K atherine pulled the chain at the door of the MacGregors' row-house. It reached two stories high, adjoined to five other houses like it in St. Peter's Grove. The MacGregors' house was distinct however, washed with a salmon pink hue, unlike the brown, sepia, and white that characterized the neighboring homes. As if the siding were not individual enough the fascia, shutters, and porch had been painted bright canary yellow; a tint known to cause blindness in the glare of a mid-day sun.

She squinted and shielded her eyes with her hand to guard against their incandescent gleam. No sound issued from within. Her eyes burned and no movement suggested the door would open soon.

From the step she received the discrimination of a pair of women who strolled the sidewalk in her direction. They were dressed finely, as finely as Katherine had been taught to dress, complete with hats, gloves, and parasols. With superior eyes they ogled her. They scrutinized her manner of dress and were at work forming scathing assessments to share with one another beyond her range of hearing.

Katherine smiled at them stunningly before they passed entirely. Her hair remained free from any convention, laying loosely down her back. In her comfortable fashion, she rolled up the sleeves of her blouse, left the top buttons undone, and dared to stand bare without gloves, hat, or parasol.

She pulled the chain again and again. Over the porch rail, she peered through a window, hopeful. The glass was white, her eyes too overwhelmed with the light to see inside.

Overhead Myra's voice echoed through an open window. "Denis! What have you got into that you cannot hear the door?"

Katherine let go of the chain, sighing with pity for the plight of Denis MacGregor.

Finally, timid and apologetic, Denis opened the door. "Couldn't hear it. I been in the kitchen all day, and when you rang, I didn't hear you as the kettle was shrieking. Very sorry I am, sorry." He bowed his head before shuffling aside to let her pass.

A narrow hall led straight through the house, first to the front parlor, next to the dining room, and farthest back to the kitchen. Denis ambled in that direction, returning to the sound of perhaps another kettle. Katherine climbed the stairs.

"Your 'Denise' is hard at work," she teased as she entered Myra's bedroom. "You're a slave driver."

"Oh, Katherine! He's not a slave, he's a husband." On her hands and knees Myra hunched over a heap of rags near a vanity-table. She wore a dark pink, bengaline gown with navy blue lace trim. The skirt appeared to be decorated wildly with dashes and spots of white.

A sharp perfume assaulted Katherine's nose, and offended at its strength she cried, "Good gracious! You don't smell so bad as to need all that, Myra."

Wiping her forehead with the back of a white powdered hand, Myra sat on her heels and sighed. "Of course I don't. No, observe." She allowed Katherine a view of the floor, covered with powder turned paste from the spilled perfumes and lotions that mixed with it. A pile of broken glass lay shamefully to one side.

"My shelf has failed me." Myra glared.

"How dare it!"

"I should say! And someone said he put it up right," Myra screamed loud enough to be heard throughout the house. "Yet if he had done it right, I would not be up to my nose in an aromatic mess!"

"I'll help you," Katherine laughed and carefully knelt down. She took a fresh rag and scraped together a pile of perfume powder sludge.

"I have been hearing news concerning you recently."

"News of me? Is it scandalous?" Katherine smiled darkly.

"The least scandalous. News of a union of the Koryn and Madison families."

"What nonsense are you hearing?" It was the last piece of 'news' Katherine wished to hear, let alone accept, and the idea that it had already spread, sickened her.

"You, the Koryn heir, a marriage contract. Oh yes, my dearest, that is how it happens. It is arranged. Plotted. It is quite similar to how it happened to me."

"They are rumors."

"Something true provoked such rumors. My advice to you is train him well, hard from the beginning, so there won't be problems later. You remember Julia? She has not even been seen since she married Michael Preston and I tried to tell her to do as I had done, but it was too late and look at the result. She is a servant to him. But you have a chance to succeed. Take control, and you will have him under your thumb. My life might have been an arranged nightmare, but I chose to take control first and fast."

Katherine stared blankly, dizzy with the perfume arresting her senses and Myra's dispassionate matter-of-factness.

"What is the matter? Hasn't your father mentioned it?" Myra attempted to catch Katherine's troubled gaze.

"When isn't my father mentioning marriage for me?"

"Right, but in particular, the Koryns have been coming to visit often, yes?"

"They've come for meals, a picnic, and church …" Katherine

forcefully scraped the carpet with her rag, knowing how the evidence only served to legitimize that which she desperately wanted to be a harmless rumor. "Ted has brought suitors around before and I always send them away."

"Oh, I see," Myra said flatly. "You *actually* think you can avoid it."

"Can't I?" She truly wondered whether or not she could.

Myra laughed in response. It was obvious she didn't think it was avoidable.

"Sometimes, Katherine, you make no sense to me. You act like it is the end of the world to be married and you deny what is right in front of your face! Even I have made peace with it, as long as Reuben stays here and does not take you away from me, I will be satisfied. And you will have the comfort and wealth you require—"

"I require wealth?" Katherine asked, the blood rushing to her face at the insinuation.

"Dearest, admit it! Despite what you *say*, you require wealth." Myra dusted powder from her skirt.

"I don't know what you mean."

"Of course you do! Women like us cannot survive without the comforts we were born to appreciate. Embrace it. Stop taking it for granted! It affords you freedom now and will afford you freedom as a wife. Could you be happy without wealth, having to scrape for a living in a factory? Or taking some service job because you have become a spinster?" Myra laughed and tilted her head. "Ah, but you are joking with me, are you not?"

"I am not. I'm insulted, rather." Katherine threw the rag down. "I thought you understood. I have more imagination than that."

"You misunderstand *me* if you are insulted. You asked what I think."

"Remind me to never make that mistake again."

"Right." Myra took the lotion-soaked rag Katherine had thrown and handed her a clean one.

Katherine sighed mournfully. "I'm actually set on quite another path than the one you've all designed for me."

"And what is that supposed to mean?" Myra carefully folded a towel full of paste and began scrubbing the floor with a clean, damp rag.

"Do you know why I came here today?"

"Why, is there a reason other than to grace me with your elusive presence?" Myra resumed scrubbing the floor.

"There is. A dark, brooding angel. The man I suspected of following me. His name is Trayten Basel, and we are no longer strangers. He is the most intriguing man I've ever known, more than I imagined he would be, and there's more. I've been meeting with him alone."

"The stalker?"

"Not *just* a stalker. He's an artist, a mysterious gentleman. Myra, I can't deny what binds us together. When I first set eyes on him my heart ached. His beauty is painful to behold. I can't even describe it to you! I can only say that when he looks at me, fire travels through my blood. Have you ever felt that? Have you ever wanted someone so much it hurt?"

As Myra shook her head, reeling from the passionate declaration, Katherine continued, "It's a stabbing feeling striking deep in my palms when I see him! Have you had a sensation like that?"

"Pain? Fire? Stabbing feelings? I do not want to have such feelings. They sound terrible."

"Oh, but you miss so much, Myra! He's a singular person, yet he welcomes *me* into his solitude. And his stare!" She grabbed Myra by the shoulders. "My resistance is extinguished, slaughtered every time he looks at me that way!"

"Sounds very dangerous indeed. Do you hear yourself? Slaughter? Good heavens. But remember not to ask what *I* think." Myra worked to pry Katherine's fingers from her arms.

"I'm not asking. I only need you to listen." She held Myra more firmly. "I only need to say it aloud before I burst. I'm dying to be near him. I'm tormented. Do you even understand what I'm saying to you? Why are you looking at me like that?"

"I understand that you have romantic ideas about love, Katherine. It has never been *my* sort of character to grovel over any man. I only hope you know what you are doing. A lady such as you, such as any of us, is wise to abstain from affairs with seedy characters and better off marrying safely with her reputation intact. Have your fancy if you must, but do be discreet about it, or do not expect to hold onto your comfortable lifestyle. Katherine, you must be financially secure."

"What do I care for financial security when love provides so much more?"

"Does it indeed provide?"

Katherine held her tongue. Instead of arguing, she let go of Myra and calmly said, "If you will excuse me, Mrs. MacGregor."

"Katherine, I want you to be mindful. You have this delusion about romantic love, and you can't imagine being taken advantage of, but it happens to women who put their trust in desperate men. If I were poor, I could say and do anything for someone who might alleviate my situation. People are not always what they seem to be."

"That's true. *Poor* people aren't always the moral deficient leeches they are believed to be."

"For once I hope you are right," Myra sighed.

1909

Before entering, Katherine knocked, and after hearing no protests she opened the door. "Has the warden left?"

Tray wheeled around to observe her. She had returned from St. Anne with a package under one arm. After closing the door, she sat on the couch.

"I imagined you might appreciate these." She unwrapped the

package in her lap and revealed a tin case, watching closely for his response.

He hesitated, then wheeled forward to take it from her hand. Tray opened the lid and inhaled the fragrance of the cigarettes. He gasped. "These are…inexplicably appealing to me."

Katherine savored the trace of a smile on his lips.

"I don't even know, but maybe I *do* smoke."

She passed him a box of matches. He sat back in his chair and expertly struck one to light a cigarette. He took a drag and relaxed.

"Well, *that* is very nice. You do get out more than I do. Thank you." He stared at the trail of smoke ascending from his fingertips.

"It was no trouble. I had to post a letter, and I thought I could get you something while I was out."

With a deep breath he closed his eyes and asked, "To whom."

"I have a daughter at home."

"What do you call your daughter?"

"Her name is Angelle."

Were his eyes not closed, he might have noticed the glaze covering hers, and the departure of her smile. He nodded blindly, exhaling smoke through his nostrils. "Angelle. I like that for a name."

Sharply, Katherine gasped. When he opened his eyes, she wiped the hopeful haze from her expression. "You are rather agreeable with one of those between your fingers. It's rather nice."

He remained preoccupied with his cigarette and she waded through his familiar silence. Finally she asked, "What does Marian do for you? What is it you need?"

"You're the expert. You tell me what I need."

"I will, in time. But I want to know what she does for you?"

"Aggravates me." He glanced at her lazily. "She cooks my food, washes my clothes, keeps my room, and from time to time she puts me out of my misery with a little morphine." He flashed a smirk. "That's about all."

"Are you discontent, Tray?"

"So, you *are* going to call me that."

"I could go on calling you by two letters as she does."

"Never mind it." He wheeled back and forth shortly, cigarette hanging between his lips as he talked. "Am I discontent you ask? What *else* would you have me be? What would *you* be?"

"I have known discontentment, perhaps as much as you."

"Apparently." He surveyed her from head to toe and back again before he unleashed a furious rant. "This is my life. This is what I do. There is no interest, no meaning. I can't go on walks or go and buy cigarettes! Go on please, tell me how your life is terrible, and I will laugh at you. *That* is an exquisite ring you wear. How awful life must have been to you. Discontentment? You cannot know *my* kind as long as you can walk! Do you know what the first floor of this place looks like?"

"The first floor?" she asked.

"I haven't seen the first floor since, well years anyway. Even *that* short journey would be an adventure!"

"There's a balcony on this floor and a ramp leading to the beach. No stairs, and you could take in the air—"

"The air would be no different. It's as dead out there as it is in here. It's still Marian's beach," he spit.

"All air is the same, would seem the same, if you believe you have no meaning. I'm certain there was and is a purpose for you. You just don't remember it."

"And I won't."

"How can you be so sure?"

"How can you be so ridiculous? What kind of a doctor are you? Do you see this chair? These scars?" He slapped his leg.

"I must be ridiculous. Maybe you weren't anyone before. Maybe there is no purpose for you. You tell *me*. What kind of a person can you imagine you were?"

"One who walked."

"More than that."

"And wore shoes." He rocked back and forth by the wheels of his chair, smoking fiercely with the cigarette between his teeth. "Oh yes, I remember it now, I was quite ambulatory. I walked *everywhere*!"

"Please."

"I'm serious. You think I was crippled then? No, I tell you the truth. I walked."

"All right." Katherine slouched back into the couch.

His wheels creaked and whined as he rocked. "I know, I know what I feel inside, what I believe. Sometimes I dream it and it's very real."

She listened closely, her heart quickening.

"I get a notion, like I could remember. In dreams it's like I'm outside, looking in on someone else. I can't claim it's me. I was an artist. I painted great masterpieces. I see them in my mind; color and form." He stared into the distance, to some place beyond those four enclosing walls.

She caught a whimsical expression on his face. Anticipation tightened every muscle as she willed him to remember.

"I was a fortunate man. I had it all. A house so grand all the neighbors stewed with envy. Wealthy and cruel, on top of it all, I was. I wore only velvet and imported silk." With an arrogant flick he dropped cigarette ashes on the floor. "I had a harem of adoring women and carriages trimmed with gold! I was a king actually and I ruled everything and everyone."

Clenching her jaw, the blood rushed into her cheeks. The satirical gleam in his eyes cut through her. He laughed and she asked, "You really believe that?"

"No. Not really. If I were wealthy and adored, would I be stranded *here* on Marian's cursed isle?"

Katherine rested her burning cheek in her palm, still cool from the sting of winter air. "It must be frustrating to not know what happened to you."

"I was supposed to die," he said bleakly.

"Why do you think you lived?" Katherine concentrated on leveling her voice and extracting all emotion from it.

"For this torment. My life, or what remains of whatever it was before, is wasted."

"How can you say that?"

"Easily. My life is wasted. Hear how it rolls off the tongue? What about you? Is your life wasted, Mrs. Koryn?"

"Call me Katherine, and not *that*."

"Oh, I didn't forget. You aren't fond of your name."

"It's my cross to bear."

"Like my paralysis," he offered.

"Exactly."

"So why is it your cross to bear? Does it have to do with your lover?"

"Perhaps it does." Katherine avoided his eyes, breathing through the pain in her heart. "You say that you should have died. Sometimes I wish *I* had. Are we really so different, you and I?"

Tray ceased his rocking and noticed her ghastly expression, her hands held in fists, and her fingernails digging into her palms.

"What happened to you?"

"It's not what *happened* to me." Katherine swallowed and lowered her gaze. "It's...what I have *done*."

The shadows deepened her eyes. They lingered in silence for a moment as she retreated within and he examined her face, searching for clues to the nature of her burden.

The door flew open, and Marian crashed into their discomfort with a platter of food extended before her. She squealed, "T.B.! Smoking? You'll destroy yourself! And in my house? Mrs. Koryn," the cords of her neck twitched, "this isn't the intelligent behavior of a doctor!"

"We are calling him 'Tray' now," Katherine replied.

"The lady has given me a name." He reclined his head against his chair.

Marian slammed the platter on the desk, causing the meal to leap before regrouping with a wiggle into the bowl. "I'll have *that*!" She twisted the cigarette from Tray's fingers and fumbled with the window, laboring to unlatch it.

"Don't worry. His lungs aren't crippled, Miss Boley. He's quite unharmed," Katherine said.

"Not crippled. Not *yet*!" Marian finally coerced the window to slide open. She flicked the cigarette outside and jammed the window shut. Her thin lips pursed, and she scowled at them.

"And another thing, this bright light is too much for you!" She yanked the drapes shut. "How many times have I, oh!" Marian ground her fingers into her temples. As quickly as she spouted off, she recovered. "Mrs. Koryn, you must keep to my methods." Covering her mouth, she murmured as though Tray would not hear her, "He is a delicate creature."

From behind Marian's back, Tray smirked at Katherine, who held a staid expression.

"Now," Marian flopped her arms dramatically to her sides. "Come and have your lunch T.B., but eat slow and don't gorge! And don't be doing too much talking! I leave that precaution to your responsibility, Mrs. Koryn." She threw her shoulders back and with her chin raised, trotted from the room.

When she had gone, Katherine raised her eyebrows at Tray.

"I don't know what she thinks I have, but she acts like the world aggravates it." He lit another cigarette. "Quite all right though. I suppose I should expect it. What do you think? Maybe I did something terrible to end up like *this*? Maybe it's the price for me."

"I can't say for you." Her stomach was bound in knots. "*You* could have been wronged."

"This badly? Have you seen them? My scars? Maybe you'll believe me when you do."

He tugged at his trouser leg, raising the hem above his ankle. Katherine knelt to help, rolling the fabric up to expose one leg below the knee. Her heart stilled and her breath fled.

The length of his shin was defaced by a crosshatching of deep white scars, a half-inch wide, long enough to cut across the front of the leg, and at various degrees diagonally. The severity of the wounds left the unscarred skin, of which there was little, deep and purplish in color. Katherine stared, even as her vision blurred. The shock in her expression was impossible to hide. She struggled, breathing air that was like water.

Tray studied her face in bewilderment, finding not the brave unflappable reaction of a professional. He did not expect the terror in her eyes. The life faded from her cheeks, and they were white as snow. Something he could not define, a kind of heartache, darkened her eyes.

Only when she reached for him, did he pry his gaze from her face to watch her cover his scars with her hands. Katherine pressed her palms against the cold flesh of his shin and closed her eyes as if she might reverse the affliction from him. She held the tears behind closed eyelids. Tray was mesmerized by the sight of her hands touching him. He suffered, imagining how it might feel. Though he concentrated, though he willed it, his failure to feel remained.

Before he allowed the frustration to dampen his eyes, Katherine opened hers. Apologetic, she removed her hands and glanced at him sheepishly.

"I'm sorry. I didn't mean to…" To say anything more without bursting into tears was impossible.

Clearly, she was losing her composure and Tray was keen to it, although he did not understand. She pulled his trouser leg gently down, trying to hide her face as she staggered to her feet. Though he sat as still as stone, his gaze followed her, fixated, and his heart beat fiercely, echoing the terror of her own. Her need to shatter was too great to manage and clumsily, hastily, she rushed out, leaving him paralyzed with wonder.

❧ 7 ❧

1900

The rain fell richly that lonely evening, and Katherine left the tavern early. She swam the streets of Portsea, unswerving in her purpose. Under the barrage of rain, she stole to the library, assured and unhindered by the deluge.

Upon arrival she crawled down into the darkness through the small cellar window. She climbed the stairs to the great hall, drenched, and scarcely able to catch her breath in the driving anticipation to see him. She knew in the marrow of her bones that he would be there.

At the sight of Trayten, Katherine stilled, relinquishing her senses to the elation heating her blood. The warmth of the hall impressed her immediately. The candles flickered brightly, stretching shadows on the walls toward the ceiling.

And he sat, faintly illuminated with golden candlelight at the end of a row of bookcases. Smoke coiled from the cigarette in his left hand, resting on the frame of a canvas. Eyes, black in the dim, looked up as she entered his tunnel of light.

Katherine combed her fingers through damp, loose flowing hair. His gaze remained on her face. She gently leaned against a bookshelf and stepped out of her boots.

Trayten crushed his cigarette on the floor and presented the face of the canvas. "Finished."

As she neared, she confronted a vision of herself, translated from his memory, as seen through his eyes. For hours and days in her absence he had articulated her beauty with care, in oil paint on canvas.

"Now you have *truly* captured me." She sank to her knees.

"Have I?" He tilted his head.

Trayten studied the line of her neck as she glanced at the windows, their shoddy concealment revealing partial hints of the misty blue, night sky beyond. In the stillness, the rainfall created a symphony, shaping the peaks of the roof as it hit and reverberated, chasing the rest of Portsea's citizens into home and refuge, and quieting the borough around them.

As her gaze wandered away from him, Trayten abandoned the canvas and buried his fingers in the damp strands of her hair. With eager hands he drew her closer; her gaze returning to meet with his. Katherine read the passion in his eyes and blushed in their sight. When he sank his face against her neck to inhale the fragrance lingering in her hair, she gasped and closed her eyes, thrilled by the jolt in her heart and the heat traveling to her palms.

Trayten lingered, pressing his cheek into the cradle of her shoulder, as though he were taking refuge, hiding from the world. It inclined her to hold him fast, her arms locked tight. A shudder passed through him, caught by her embrace. He raised his head and brought his lips to hers, leaving only a breath between them.

He stared into her soul until he moved there, communicating what was beyond words, and it frightened her. Tenderly he traced the contours of her face with his lips, gliding over her cheekbone, the gentle slope of her brow, laying a kiss on her forehead. There his lips held still, his hands smoothed the hair from her face, and abruptly he released her.

Katherine opened her eyes, dazed as though shaken out from under a spell.

In response to her questioning stare he announced, "Now you will capture me."

"I'm not the painter *you* are, Trayten."

He stood in the slivers of light that fought through the planked windows above.

"You wished I would take you dancing," he clarified.

"I suppose I rather demanded it, didn't I?" She smiled.

Standing, Katherine stared into his eyes. She took his hand, raised it chin level in the air, and threaded her fingers into the warmth of his hand. His other hand she directed to the small of her back. She rested her hand on his shoulder.

Her breath caught as he pulled her firmly against him. With one step to the side, she directed him into a waltz and immediately discovered that he led well, confidently guiding her with capable hands. His focus remained on her eyes while he swept her down the aisle. Like the rain, light and steadily dancing across the roof, their feet floated easily over the tile floor.

They danced along avenues filled with volumes of history, through the aisles of fiction, and into the chronicles of war. He carried her, as though she were light as the wind. He twirled them fervently and deliberately through rows of philosophy. Trayten pivoted and swept Katherine low into the cradle of his arms beneath volumes of poetry and fable.

A rush of heat covered her cheeks. He kept her close, until she could feel his heart beating more fiercely than her own. He spun her away, the air billowing her skirt like a cloud and throwing strands of hair from her shoulders. Although weak in her knees, Katherine was determined to keep up with her profoundly talented partner.

Storms mixed in the dark of his eyes. The shuffling, sweeping pattern of their tread created music to complement the dance. The rhythm of their breathing, echoed by the distant mutter of rain, weaved a song without instrument to sustain their delight.

In a whirlwind, they swept against one another, lips grazing, hands joined by tight fingers. He tilted her back again, her hair sweeping the tiles, and his lips dusting her collarbone before he lifted her. Holding her hand, arms extended overhead, he twirled her around, and brought her firmly into his hold.

Through the aisles and alleys they danced beyond the candle-light. Their shadows were thrown at the ceiling, like pairs of silhouette dancers mimicking them in the air. Their palace was ablaze with the burning of their passion. A glowing sanctuary hidden from the rest of the cold, wet world beyond.

※

"It is my prediction that you will find my daughter is well suited to you." Theodore sat back confidently in his armchair, swallowing the last of the gin from his glass.

Rain streaked the darkened windows, veiling the lush green night beyond. Theodore observed the thick mass of Reuben Koryn who stared back with what appeared to be indifferent disinterest.

When he responded to Theodore's declaration, his words filled the air in much the same tone as the dull expression on his face. "I hardly doubt she is, sir, for you have brought up a fine, respectable family. Though Katherine is well into her prime, she maintains a fair complexion and a firm figure, not at all disagree-able. I daresay it is rare to find so exceptional a beauty in such an attainable match.

"She seems to be educated and steady, not comparable to a woman of frivolous thought and naïve incompetence. Her manner of independence is of some concern, yet not enough to dissuade my intentions. I surmise that the influence of a firm hand deliv-ered by a confident provider will domesticate her to her proper station as wife and mother. It is, of course, my honorable inten-tion, sir, to be that provider and to take her as my wife.

"For you, Mr. Madison, such an arrangement promises benefits twofold. You will be removed from the burden of supporting an adult dependent. And, this alignment insinuates a powerful union between our wealthy estates. As you have no sons to inherit your lot, the son born of your eldest child will carry both the heritage of your estates and my own, promising continued wealth and prosperity to our mutual descendants.

"This union, sir, is not just a gift to your legacy, but for me it promises to complete the life that is otherwise perfectly fulfilled. I have scarcely seen such a refined beauty in all my travels. Those few I have beheld that may compete in fairness with Katherine, have not the added benefits of so abounding a dowry and so agreeable a father; as you are most agreeable in my opinion and like-minded as I, to say the very least of it, a businessman like myself to whom I can easily relate." Reuben paused to draw breath with a great yawn. No sooner had he quieted than he continued lazily, "My offer is the best that you could hope to find, not to mention *receive,* at any rate. I am aware that something of her manner has reserved any other suitors from her trail, and I am willing to accept the challenge of whatever her impediment might be, as I am confident in my powers of persuasion and ascendency to correct her. Thus, I have settled my mind and am not a man of great patience. Your agreement to my taking her hand will suit me better the more expediently it is made.

"You understand a man such as me. I intend a simple cere-mony without delay, for I see no utility in wasting capital on the vows. There are other, more important investments that require finances, would you agree?"

"Oh, of course!" Theodore said. "That would be entirely your own decision; what you do with your finances and that which you acquire. I am in agreement that no better a match will Katherine find or will be offered. Still, I must insist a courtship of a respectable three months precede the wedding vows. I believe it only proper to allow the opportunity for Katherine to adapt to the ensuing change of station.

"The impediment to which you have alluded relates to her

reckless, somewhat willful nature and I would encourage you to familiarize yourself with it, in order to most skillfully correct it, as you say, when she becomes your wife."

Reuben was discontent with the idea. He sulked from the comfort of his couch.

Theodore's eyes darkened and he added, "It's only fair and proper, unless you fear the unreliability of my agreement, in which case I assure you that a courtship will not dissuade my offer. It is kindness for my eldest daughter that inspires me to permit her a little time to become better acquainted with her future husband."

"I'll make certain she is acquainted. Time has facilitated acquaintance already, sir. To your mind, will she be agreeable?"

"She will. She must," Theodore confirmed.

Reuben smiled and raised a glass to toast the sanction of their accord.

❧

The dance had ended, yet the rain persisted with its silken serenade. Tireless candlelight painted their faces in gold and crimson splendor. Katherine rested her head on Trayten's abdomen. Across his chest her hair spread damp and dark. They lay on their backs staring at the vastness overhead. He held her hand, close against his cheek, and the vibrations of his words were caught with her fingertips.

"You will marry me, won't you, Katherine?"

How deeply she felt the words. How desperately she wanted to welcome them yet feared the reality they would bring.

"I promise nothing," she said with a small laugh, choosing whimsy over candor.

"You stun me with such a blow. Is there another you expect to give your hand to?"

Katherine wiggled her fingers before his face and announced, "I'll consider giving this hand when I have a ring to put on it.

Until then, there's no assurance. Promises, words, are seldom reliable things."

"Don't you trust me?" He kissed her hand. "I tell you this: nothing can match the depth of my love for you. There is nothing more pure than what I hold in my heart for you."

Those words matched the depth, for Katherine felt them more deeply than his proposal.

"You're so confident of your feelings. But I've done nothing to deserve your devotion and you haven't known me long at all. Only time can prove whether your love is real, or not." Katherine felt the rough stubble on his cheek.

He smiled faintly, sadly.

"How can we leave our sanctuary? I'll stay out the rain."

"*Our* sanctuary?" he asked.

"I mean to say *your* sanctuary."

"Because I love *you,* without doubt or reason, I surrender it, I offer it to you, to be your sanctuary, as I offer *my* heart without contingency."

"Don't penalize me for caution in declaring my devotion. I've spent my life penalized for recklessness and the moment I exercise restraint I'm dashed as well." Katherine moved to withdraw her hand from his, but he held it tighter.

"There's no one here to penalize you. I'm as patient as the sun is constant, and even though I may be tormented, though I may crave that you open every corner of your heart to me right now, I will never demand it of you."

"That's good, because I don't respond well to demands."

Her hair hung like a veil to one side of his face and he threaded his fingers into it to kiss her. He held her as though he could bind her to him with the strength of his arms. Candlelight, even in its meager portions, danced and warmed the air to guard against the drizzling chill.

They hid together in sacred refuge, safe from the knowledge of forces at work to part them, oblivious to anything beyond each other.

A picnic was hosted on the manicured lawn of Madison Estate. The spring air was alive with busy insects and ripe with the smell of damp, awakening earth. Although the day was radiant, Katherine slumped as reluctantly as one held prisoner in a wicker armchair.

Eliza, Dorothea, and their husbands played croquet between her and the fringes of the lawn. They frolicked, their lightly colored frocks fluttering like the plumage of showy birds. Their laughter expanded in the open air. Caleb appeared to be, or was in fact, sober enough to play deftly in the game. His involvement no doubt contributed to the freely smiling Dorothea who giggled like a child at his every move.

Around the croquet game, Theodore, Winifred, and Augustus Koryn strolled. Hilda Koryn sat alone, like Katherine, her wheel-chair parked half concealed in tall grass near the garden wall. Though apparently restricted to her chair, Hilda bent and arched to examine its rear wheels. The lace cap covering a thin knot of flaxen hair atop her head flapped in the wind like the wings of a white butterfly.

"I intend to one day have a serious conversation with you, Kathy," the pompous intonation of Reuben startled Katherine.

He planted himself on one knee behind her chair to one side and held a glass to his chin. Reluctantly, she shifted in her chair to look back. An annoyed glare preceded a snide response, "Do you think *so*, Mr. Koryn?"

"Indeed, I am certain of it. It will be perhaps the most important conversation of your life," he opened his mouth as if to ramble on, however he was temporarily stalled by the hostility in her eyes.

"I hardly know how to respond to such a presumptuous declaration," Katherine began. "Other than to tell you that you know nothing of my life's conversations and are rather bold to assert your superiority *over* them. Have you been generally rewarded for such self-exaltation?"

"Why, yes." Reuben threw his shoulders back.

"Proof of the degradation of society: the absolute devaluing of humility."

"Well," he shrugged. "I tell you that the degradation of society concerns me very little, especially in my frame of mind as I am close to you at last." Reuben composed himself. "Perhaps today is that day?"

Katherine had returned to wandering the thicket of her thoughts, wholly occupied with a man as opposite Reuben as day from night. The question startled her, frustrated her. She wished to be left to her fantasies, yet was irritatingly compelled to ask, "What day?"

"The day you and I consider a most important agreement." He grinned strangely.

The sharp terror struck her inwardly.

"I'm not aware of any reason that you and I should have an agreement. You must be mistaken."

"In that case, Kathy, it is *you* who are mistaken." Reuben shrugged, drinking.

His conceited nonchalance infuriated her. "Why do you and your parents come here so often?"

"You must be utterly distracted." Reuben chuckled. "Our fathers are longtime chums!"

"As much as two bulls are chums." She laughed. "They are competitors. More precisely, they are rivals, disguised as chums."

He took another drink and said with a gurgle, "Forget matters of syntax. Delight me, Kathy and tell me what interests a feisty little vixen like you?"

With a deep breath she restrained the impulse to slap him. Resolving to save her energy for more worthy exertions, she smiled sweetly instead. "Surely nothing that would interest a man of *your* density."

Reuben, too thick to be deflated or affected by her comment

asked, "Are you certain? I hear it said that you fancy the music and the dancing. I myself have been known to—" and he swiveled one leg promiscuously, "—dominate the floor if a worthwhile partner has the energy. Been to a few wild parties. I tolerate the opera as well. A regular renaissance man am I."

"I never would have arrived at such a conclusion concerning you." Katherine eyed his leg with disgust.

"Ah, so very much you have to learn about me. Yes, yes, yes. What else? Oh, I hear you fancy working as well, among the *rogues* your father says. How unusual, quite radical really. I said to myself, tis a shame and a pity that so fine a female would relinquish her hopes of finding a mate and resolve herself to a laborious spinsterhood. You have given up on the promise of fulfillment, until *now* I daresay. I assure you, there is no need for you to toil anymore. Where you have given up your dreams of being wanted, I have rescued them and intend to invest in them with the greatest care."

"I remain in awe that you presume to know my dreams, let alone be invested in them. Perhaps you've lost your sense and confuse me with some *other* female, with whom you have a relationship, an agreement, a future, for I assure you that this *female* you speak of is not me. I, Katherine Madison, choose to work for my belief that there's no need to depend on others."

"So you believe you are independent?" Reuben asked, grinning with clear condescension.

"Whether it is that I actually am, or as you hope, merely *think* that I am independent, you will believe what you want, I'm sure."

Reuben regarded her answers with little consideration.

"As for myself, why Kathy, I am the captain of independence. Greater still, I am the captain of my finances. I mean that I have done smartly for myself as a businessman, my ownership is expanding, and I accumulate the envy of all of my peers." He raised his eyebrows in self-fascination. "You must come and visit my estate sometime soon. You will not be able to grasp the extent of my prosperity until you have seen my house. I have a villa so splendid you could fathom it only in your deepest dreams. It would please you beyond reason. Do you know how much it costs me to keep it up? Why, easily more than that tavern job could earn you in one year."

"What a shame." She stared at the top of the garden wall, considering the appeal of everything beyond it while Reuben's hot breath touched her shoulder.

"I travel extensively as well. Tell me, I am interested, as I'm sure you are inexperienced with travel, have you ever been to Scotland? Well, have you?"

"I haven't."

"There it is!" When he hollered, she jumped in her seat. "Why, how can you dream to expand your satisfaction in life without stepping beyond these bounds? What about Italy? No, you needn't bother answering for I know you have never been there either. A lady suited to your position must realize there is a fine world to be explored beyond Hampshire. You cannot know history until you have visited the Malatestiana Library in Cesena! You would drool over the scrolls from the sixteenth century kept there, manuscripts from the leaders of history themselves."

"Sir, even though you are likely to disagree somehow, I actually possess some lady-like qualities, one of which being that I would never drool over a book, or any sort of *thing*. Besides, there are enough books to suit my curiosity in Portsea." Katherine closed her eyes and hoped he might be gone when she opened them.

"Ah, in your father's study perhaps, but still, there is no grand library in Portsea."

"Of course, you've never been there. It only admits a select few, the humble, meek, and unpretentious sort with whom you would have no sympathy. You would think it beneath you. But I can tell you this sacred ground holds more excitement, more adventure, more *meaning* than your tour of pretence could offer. Therefore, Mr. Koryn, if you hope to entice me with the promise of traveling the world, you hang upon an empty aspiration. For I must insist that I prefer no other place but Hampshire generally, and Portsea in particular."

"I suppose, unfortunately you wouldn't know what you miss." He shrugged.

"Indeed you may, but I suppose I miss *nothing*."

"Your incompatibility for suitors thus far has made you bitter. Your sisters are happily matched and settled in their places," he said and nodded toward the pair, laughing with their husbands on cue.

Katherine turned her chair away from him.

"I understand it very little. How you turn away from happiness." He laughed at her.

"I turn away from you."

"Kathy, you are very simple sometimes." Again Reuben laughed at her as he explained, "I am your happiness. If you turn away from me, you cannot be happy."

She inhaled slowly through her nostrils, taking the time to shrug off the pest of his superiority. "Your proposal is nothing more than words to boast and glorify *you*."

"What words shall I use?" he asked, standing up in front of her.

"None! There is nothing you can say that will make me turn to you." She did not await his response but arose and sauntered away from him toward the garden.

Reuben plopped into her empty chair and stared after her.

❧

He left his door cracked open, so that she would know he was home. Katherine entered. Silent, as if she crossed holy ground, she drifted across the paint-scarred floor. Wan moonlight fell in a halo around his bed and the breeze from his open window wafted through the red drapes, disturbing the trail of smoke from his ashtray.

Katherine removed her coat and laid it on the only chair in his flat near the bed. She could not take her eyes from his dark featured face. Trayten lay, sleeping on his stomach, wearing a sleeveless white tunic and crumpled trousers.

She lowered to lay on his back and covered his bare shoulder with a warm hand. Gazing at him, eyes wide in sleepless dread, she laid her cheek against his back. Her body formed against him, holding him tightly, as if he might otherwise depart.

Katherine nudged his cheek with hers and sleepily he groaned, otherwise undisturbed. In moments when he was unaware, she lingered awake to bear the throbbing of her terror. Every moment in his presence seemed fated to be the last. While she could hold onto him now, Katherine struggled to imagine how she could hold him forever.

❧ 8 ❧

Trayten and Katherine sat in the window alcove of his flat.

"Do you suppose it's jealousy that makes you bitter to wealth?" Her face was white as they bathed in the morning sunlight.

He leaned back against the window frame and waved a dismissive hand. "Certainly not!"

"How can you be sure?"

The sounds of Portsea echoed below them. "Offer me one thousand pounds!"

With a small laugh she asked, "Would you like a thousand pounds?"

"Certainly not!" He waved his hand again. "Now, see how simple that was for me? How natural?"

"But I didn't have a thousand pounds!"

"But you do," he said.

"I believe you are convinced without proper experience." She reached out and straightened the collar of his shirt. "You don't understand it, the kind of temptation when it's in your hands. You can't know how you'd react, what you would compromise, do or not do, unless you held it for yourself."

"You may be used to people who make compromises for

wealth. I'm not that sort. I would never risk my peace of mind, not for any amount offered. I know it's where you come from. But you're not like them. You've got a soul and I believe it's one like mine. You'd *never* compromise your peace of mind and your heart for wealth."

☙❧

1909

Perhaps it was a dream of the past, of the days when he remembered her. Perhaps it was the vision of happier times, or the reality of the things she had compromised, or her own frightful fabrications of what actually happened the day she lost him. Whatever the impetus, Katherine woke with a start to hard falling tears.

She had fallen asleep on the couch in his room, curled and cramped into a corner. Unable to retract the tears, she smothered her face into a pillow to contain the sound. She wished to smother the dream, sweating with memory and remorse.

From his bed Tray witnessed the quaking shoulder across the room in the vague light. Her sobs dragged him from his dreaming and echoed through the room like haunting, magnified screams. He wondered at her, the strange and inscrutable *specialist*, crying in his bedroom in the night. The sound of her sniffling stung his heart. He lay still, unable to understand or ignore it.

☙❧

Marian's house was invariably chilly in the morning. Mist gathered beyond the windows, obscuring a gray sky. The hardwood floor shocked bare feet and squealed as Katherine descended the stairs. Pinkish hues colored the swollen skin under her eyes. Her hair hung disheveled over the shoulders of her robe.

The stimulating aroma of tea called her to the kitchen where Marian stood at a table in the center. Flour covered the table and parts of the floor from the mass of dough she beat with dry fists. Steely daylight filled the kitchen, colorless and bright. Assaulted, Katherine drew back from it.

"Would you like some assistance?" she asked, rolling up her sleeves to wash her hands.

Marian gazed past the sprays of hair floating in her vision and wrinkled her nose. "Would a fine upper-class lady stoop to do such work?"

Katherine smirked and took a handful of dough from the bowl. She coated it in flour.

"How's progress? I see no change in him," Marian said.

"No, you probably wouldn't. Not yet anyhow. I'm still trying to get him to be comfortable with me."

"T.B. is a stone. He won't get comfortable with you. He can't get comfortable. Suzan tried taking him out back a while ago for some fresh air. He resents her for it *still*. I mentioned taking him to the Continent for some new experimental treatment, but he wouldn't have it. I told him it would be so good for him, the doctors there knowing a thing or two about mind troubles, and memory. He refused to consider it. He begrudges me for even mentioning it."

"How do you treat him?"

"What do you mean? How do I treat him? I take care of him. I do *everything* for him," Marian boasted.

"Somehow, somewhere along the way, I think you mistook his handicap for childishness. He is a grown man."

"I don't treat him like a child. I treat him like a man who is helpless." Marian punched her fist into the dough. "He acts like a child entirely of his own persuasion."

"He thinks he has no one, no one who loves him in all the world. He is alone and abandoned. He feels trapped and frustrated," Katherine said.

"See how childish he is?"

"I don't think suffering is childish." Katherine stretched and folded the dough between her hands. "I think it's human. And it's maddening for him to be the way he is and not remember what happened or why."

"And he told you all of this."

"Not exactly."

"Then how do you know?" Marian asked.

"It's in the way he talks. I would like to presume that he was once loved very much. That he was wounded, inside." Katherine touched the flour covered heel of one hand to her heart. "And now he is rough, more than he once was perhaps. He is aggravated with life and its terrible treachery."

"There you go with the *psychoist* babble."

"My focus *is* his mind." Katherine set balls of dough on the table and Marian filled a pan with them. "My intention is to help him retrieve his past." Before Marian could offer a cynical remark she asked, "Where are your guests?"

"Oh, I am between guests at the moment. I placed a new ad in the newspaper, made it sound fantastic with a few too many adjectives. Maybe it'll draw more guests in. Why, you lonely?"

"How could I be lonely in the same house with you, Miss Boley?" Katherine received a sharp grimace in response. "So, he is really that temperamental, to *hate* Suzan and begrudge you for suggestions?"

"Can be, yes."

"It's something I must work on."

"Watch your *head* while you work. His aim is not crippled," Marian advised.

"Get up!" Katherine entered his room abruptly.

Tray stared at the wall from his bed.

"You aren't staying *there* today," she insisted.

"Sorry. Can't seem to get my legs to move."

"Not a problem." She pushed the wheelchair near. "I'm taking you out so you can absorb something other than this stale air."

"I must decline. I'm sorry but I don't enjoy long walks."

Katherine yanked his arm until he sat upright, staring at her indifferently. "You're quite funny, but please help me a little. I'll walk, you'll roll."

"No."

His apathy made her laugh. They stared at one another for a moment until she pulled at his hand again. "You're coming with me."

"Ah, no," he confirmed. "Did you hear what happened? To Suzan? She wanted to persuade me—"

"What happened, did you fall and sit on her until she passed out?"

"No. I despised her for it."

Katherine brought her face close to his. "Oh no!" Her voice held the same mocking monotone he often used. "Good thing I'm not Suzan. The air is crisp. It might sting the memory back into you!"

"Do you think so? I'll go out, and suddenly remember my father and mother, the rulers of our faraway kingdom? Will I recall my harem as well, and each of their names? Why, I'm sure the sting will electrify my nerves and I will dance circles around you, like I used to in my palace?"

"It's as possible as you being a prince," Katherine allowed.

"Pure fantasy. Exactly! Leave me here. Go walk yourself."

"I have walked by myself and am bored of it. I would rather have your sarcastic company, your gloomy voice. Do me the honor."

"No." He crossed his arms.

"I will help you, come."

"I don't need your help. Leave please."

"You're a bit stubborn." Katherine sidled the chair up to the bed.

"So are you."

"Tray, come with me. I'm not giving you a choice."

"Go on, try and lift me," he challenged.

Katherine took a step and he thrust the tray from the bedside table. She dodged the spinning cup and leapt over the clanging plate.

"Very well! I understand Marian confiscated from you a certain indulgence." She slyly withdrew the tin of cigarettes from her pocket.

His eyes sparkled and he pressed his lips together. "You wouldn't deny a tired and tense old cripple those comforts, would you?"

"I certainly could. You know they're not good for you. I can't justify the risk unless you agree to take the fresh air with them. You must come out. There's the condition. She'll smell it in here with that keen snout of hers, so best we go out of doors."

"I haven't the stomach for sea air."

"I can lean you over the water if you need to vomit." Katherine raised her eyebrows.

He glared at her fiercely as she waited. Then, he put his hands on the arms of his chair and with agility, lifted the rest of his body down into it. She found him a warm flannel coat, wool-lined slippers, and a pair of riding gloves from the closet.

The docks lined a stretch of the beach. Sea and wintry air brought the wind to life, biting, briny, and wild. The waters furled and crashed over the pale sand. Above them gulls called. They flew against the gray sky, which made even Marian's dim house appear bright. The golden strands of grass wafted and bent in perpetual motion.

Tray's trail of smoke mingled with the white cloud of Katherine's breath.

Buttoned securely in her black coat, her boots were caked with snow that lay in clumps on the glistening dock.

His weight was allayed by the enormous wheels of his chair. The wind disturbed his hair, and Katherine drove back the urge to smooth it into place, as she would have done eight years before.

"Miserable here," he grumbled.

"Miserable, perhaps only in the winter."

"No. It's always too quiet, too empty…lifeless."

"You must have come from a far more interesting place." Katherine stopped to watch the smoke float around his head.

"Probably. Well, as I mentioned, the rich kingdom of my spectacular parents."

"Of course."

He smoked with gentle satisfaction.

"It wasn't too arduous getting you out here after all."

"You're not exactly Suzan or Marian." He glanced back and saw her smile. "They didn't find my weakness."

"You're almost pleasant sometimes, when you allow yourself to be."

"A real ray of sunshine," Tray scoffed. "But wait, here I sense it."

Katherine rolled him listlessly along.

"I was on a beach once, walking, if you can imagine that. A beach like this one. I might have been with someone, and…I think I was happy." He tilted his head, gazing distantly.

"Really?" She slowed.

He paused for a drag from his cigarette and confirmed, "No."

She jerked him back into motion as he laughed dryly.

"Don't hate me for it," he said.

"You might like *that* too much."

"What is your age?" he asked.

"That's an impolite question," she cried.

"What is your age, *please*."

"Thirty-one." Katherine giggled. "And yourself? Do you know your age?"

"I don't. Unless perhaps you could cut off one of my legs and count my rings. I wouldn't feel it." He laughed. She was silent. "You know, like a tree."

"I understood you," Katherine said. "It didn't strike me as funny."

"Do you want to keep me from hating you? You ought to laugh at me when I mean to be funny. It might help your case."

"Is that the condition for getting along with you?"

"Yes. One among many." For an instant, he closed his eyes and reclined against the back of his chair with a subtle smile.

"I'll try to remember that," she vowed.

"Why am I speaking to you, anyhow? You're a complete stranger! You tell me little of yourself." He opened his eyes suddenly.

"Is it so bad to speak to someone?"

"It should be. But this air should be bad also, according to Marian. It isn't so awful," he admitted with a sigh.

"Ah, Miss Boley. She only wants to help you, right?"

"Ha! If she only knew how to help. I don't think she does, or I think she chooses not to help." Tray flicked his cigarette over the edge of the dock.

"Didn't she try to help you? Didn't she want to take you for professional help?"

"What?"

"Didn't she offer to take you to the Continent for experimental treatment?" Katherine asked.

"What experimental treatment? No, Marian never offered to take me anywhere."

Katherine went numb and the sound of the waves filled the silence. She considered the house, then the open waters. He bore her silence, like she often carried his; heavy and laced with thoughts that would not be shared.

1900

The candles burned in their rows, illuminating the dust of the air. Katherine tore through the columns of light, her feet shuffling against the tiles. She wove around the bookcases, trying to find him, running swiftly and pushing against the corners of the shelves for speed. An echo climbed skyward from both her laughter and his heaving behind her.

He dashed after her through the maze she navigated, gaining speed as he caught a flash of her blue dress disappearing around another corner. She playfully wailed, glancing back, as he drew near, following in her wake. The abandoned hall was disturbed. She charged through spider webs, through the broken streams of light tunneling down from the boarded windows.

He called to her, and laughing she leapt into another row of shelves, weaving in a new direction. Trayten plotted and switched his course, taking a different path as well. Their legs carried them through the shadows, into the light and back again. Bare footed they raced, expelling exhausted yet energized breaths.

Katherine slackened, panting, and noticed the silence beyond her own gasping. She called for him, but he stalked silently. She stopped, searching behind, in front of, and around her, squinting through the hazy dimness. Her chest heaved and she gazed at the high ceiling.

Trayten stole along the bookcases, sneaked up behind her and with a roar, lifted her as she shrieked. He whirled her around, high above the ground, spinning her, suspended on his shoulder. The dark shower of her hair splashed her face and blinded him in their collision. Their laughter filled the gloom, reverberating and escalating.

Trayten stumbled, dizzy from their twirling. Between a bookcase and the wall, with her arms outstretched, Katherine caught the edge of the shelf to prevent them from falling. He lost his balance, bumped into the giant tower of volumes, and she fell down, caught in the cradle of his arms. A rumble issued from the high shelf when it tilted. The shadow loomed, Trayten lost his footing completely, and they collapsed to the ground.

Pages, loose and leather-bound, bounced violently down. As the shelf toppled, they ducked in the downpour, covering their heads, tangled with one another; Katherine shrieking with panic and Trayten hollering. The shelf creaked, they bellowed, and the books dropped down on top of them. One loud, hollow thud exceeded them all. The bookcase smashed against the wall, braced at a sharp angle above them!

Trayten's heart raced, and he breathed heavily. He landed on top of her, and her arms strangled him until she felt the pulse in his neck. They lay in a mountain of books, exasperated and shaking. The narrow tent of wood above them spilled streams of dust and they coughed.

They surveyed with amazement the mass of the shelf that could have crushed them. With sweat on his brow and choking on the dust cloud, Trayten crushed Katherine defensively. She, disregarding the assault of the leatherbacks, laughed and pinched him, drunk with adrenaline. Through sighs and laughter she kissed his face hungrily.

⁙

Katherine was not expected at the tavern. Still, she escaped Madison Estate, claiming she was needed there anyway. Her mother had tried to stop her, proposing to have something important to speak of, but when Katherine dismissed her with a hasty 'goodbye' Winifred abandoned the attempt.

The journey into Portsea and subsequently Sun Street was eternal. Katherine wore a satin town dress, elaborately designed, in a pearly cream shade with pale orange trim. There were orange flowers woven into the curve of her straw hat and she wore her hair in an intricately braided bun.

Trayten surprised her in front of the flat, seated on a quaint green carriage drawn by one horse; a vehicle built for maneuverability with a slim structure and tight wheels.

"What are you on about?"

He tipped his bowler hat. "A ride, milady?"

"And you're going to drive?"

"Why not?" He reached for her hand and pulled her swiftly up beside him.

"From whom did you steal this wagon?"

"A good friend. Ready?" he asked.

Instantly Katherine was thrown back as Trayten whipped the steed, urging it ahead with a shout. They were off in a blast of delirious speed as he cut right into the traffic of Sun Street. Madly he drove with unyielding velocity, the horse running scared at the suggestion of his whip. Trayten's toes tucked beneath the cover board at their feet, and he stood, veering the horse by a hard tug of the reins to turn a sharp corner.

The carriage leaned on two wheels. Alarmed, Katherine yelped and gripped her seat. "Tray!"

The hooves clattered against the pavement, and the little carriage gyrated and blasted along behind. Although frightened witless, she had enough sense to grip her hat before the wind could tear it from her head.

The heaving steed flexed muscular shoulders and raced onward. They dashed into Kent Street where traffic thickened and Trayten directed them behind another cart. Katherine's stomach flipped. She held on, fearful they would collide, but in the moment before they might have, Trayten tugged the reins. He whipped the horse and wrenched the reins to maneuver around and ahead of the carriage obstructing their path.

At the maddening pace, Katherine observed Trayten, calm and relaxed. Maintaining the same devilish speed, he lit a cigarette and conversed easily.

"I sold a painting this morning. Oh, but don't worry, not my portrait of you. He gave me four shillings for it. I'll have a little beef this week." They bumped and swerved, but he was unfazed.

Katherine gripped her seat and hat, wide-eyed in disbelief. She choked on the rushing air, each breath shoved back up her nose and down her throat.

Trayten veered around another obstacle and cleared a fast corner. A horse and cart came close to colliding with them, and the driver nearly strangled his horse at the bit to avoid them. People fled toward the walkways as Trayten sped through the street. Other horses reared up, letting out fierce brays as they rumbled by.

After riotously racing around two more carriages, Katherine broke into a nervous laugh. With each near miss, as she deemed them, her heart would jump into her throat, her body would flush numb with fear, and her blood would rush alive. One driver shook an angry fist, rattling curses after Trayten nearly ran him onto the sidewalk. Katherine called as they zipped ahead of the fist-shaker, "He's not sorry for that!"

Trayten laughed, smiling brilliantly. He cut around another corner, tilting them on two wheels and spilling Katherine on her side in the seat. Sitting back, he sang, smoking his cigarette between phrases.

"Under the moonlight there, your fire dancing hair..." He cracked the whip and weaved in between two carriages. "Throw away your stockings dear, dancing close but never near. Tip the cup, spilling tea, glide on a river of sugar with me." He glanced at her, light radiating from his melting, elusive smile.

Katherine could not help but smile back, in the wind, at their terrifying speed, and amid the fear, her heart lifted like two wheels of the carriage around another tight corner.

ॐ

They came to a small house in the middle of Whites Row, a street where squalor sank to a new, deplorable low. Years had reduced what was once a practical, livable house into a weathered, rotting shack. The stones composing the foundation were crumbling in places. The roof had been warped by wet weather and cracked by heat.

Trayten knocked and took Katherine by the hand. As they waited, she surveyed the cramped community; the ragged shacks, the muddy lane strewn with rubbish, a gaggle of shirtless children playing in the mire.

"Basel!" exclaimed the man who opened the door. "I knew I'd be seeing ye soon in the light of day! Come in, yea?"

The balding, pot-bellied man stepped back. His wrinkled trousers hung from suspenders over a dingy yellow shirt. He invited them into the tiny abode; no better on the inside than the outside. A drip of water called from one corner and a mouse scampered across the floor at their feet. The table was covered with dishes and morsels of rotting food.

Embers glowed beneath heavy soot in the fireplace. Without a roaring fire, the solitary lamp on the table provided little light. There were two doors on the far wall, both closed and secured with chains. A ladder, which they ducked under as they entered, led to the loft where he slept. Their host brought two chairs into the center of the room; a stool and a wicker trap riddled with holes.

"Katherine, meet Jack Conway. Jack, this is Katherine Madison," Trayten announced.

"Hello." Katherine shook Jack's hand.

"It's Jack's carriage we have borrowed," Trayten explained.

"Oi, I didn't expect it back so soon," Jack said.

"Wasn't quite finished with it yet, but I thought it worthwhile to introduce you to my...preoccupation," Trayten gazed at Katherine and explained. "Mr. Conway helped me find my feet when I arrived in Portsea. Got me a job in the dockyard. He was a shipwright."

"*Was* is the operating word, to be sure," Jack said. "So, this darling gem's the reason ye haven't been helping me out lately, yea?"

"Well—" Trayten shrugged.

"A pretty reason to be sure." Jack laughed.

Trayten smiled smolderingly at Katherine. She blushed.

"So what's yer story, Miss?" Jack asked her.

At a loss for a clever narrative, she said, "I work at The Bedford in Chase. Do you know it?"

"I've passed the place, but never been inside. Not much for drinking, am I."

"There's nothing wrong with that." She smiled.

"What else?" Jack plied.

"What else?" Katherine asked.

"Her father is Theodore Madison," Trayten announced. "He owns a number of properties around Hampshire."

"Ah, my boy, what ye doing getting involved with a rich girl?" Jack laughed to break the tension arising in Katherine, then slapped his leg and grinned. "Ye think ye can deserve her?"

Katherine continued to blush with Trayten's arm around her shoulders.

He smiled impishly before replying to Jack, "I know I don't deserve her. But I'm selfish enough to pursue her anyway."

"If I know'd anything about ye, Trayten, it's that yer a dreamer through and through."

❧ 9 ❧

1900

Beneath an endless sky Trayten promised, "I will take you higher than you've ever been before, to the top of the town, in Old Portsmouth, where the buildings stand tall and cling to one another. You'll see everything from there, and nothing will see you. A bird on a ledge. An angel in the air."

The day faded out in flashes of fushia. Trayten drove them to Old Portsmouth into an alleyway underneath the great overhang of a building.

Katherine studied his profile and his long dark eyelashes. Catching her stare he said quietly, "We'll leave it here. Come, follow me."

She studied their shadowy location. From under the awning where they parked the carriage, the narrow alley jutted left and right, cutting between a procession of five-story buildings, rising adjacent to one another.

At the rear of the buildings, Trayten tethered the horse and Katherine gazed around beside him. Across the alley, a fire escape hung from the back of one building, constructed of iron stairs that descended from the rooftop to a landing approximately seven feet above the ground. Underneath it, a rusty door was framed with rubbish bins. Gathering her sense of direction, she estimated that they were at the rear of a tavern called the Club Cigar.

"I worked here for a while, scrubbing dishes. They serve something like food in there." Trayten nodded toward the building.

He held her hand and looked from one end to the other of the alley before crossing toward the back door. Trayten stopped at the door and looked down at her. "How are you for climbing?"

"Climbing?" She lifted her skirt to reveal her boots and their high, narrow heels. "Tricky shoes for that."

Trayten was intrepid. He reached up, and as a result of both the length of his arms and the height of his stance, he was able to grasp the edge of the iron landing overhead. He pulled himself up and swung his weight forward to throw his torso onto the landing before crawling up on one knee. Down in the shadowy dim, Katherine's eyes searched widely, from his high perch above her to the rest of the alley around her. Trayten knelt on the landing with an expectant eye.

"I can't do *that*," she said.

His brilliant grin lit the darkness. He extended his hand, his arm like a strong limb, bracing himself around the rail. With uncertainty, Katherine raised her arms, and he closed his hand around her slender wrist. There was neither a ledge nor any other solid place to put her feet in order to climb, and she dangled clumsily, unable to pull her body weight up as he did.

Trayten raised her until she could grab the edge of the landing with her other hand. As if she weighed nothing at all, he drew her straight up to where she could crawl onto the platform. Inwardly Katherine was in awe at the feat and admired his agility.

He initiated the next task, climbing the first flight of stairs. Katherine hurried after to catch him, the heels of her boots clicking against the iron grating and here and there getting wedged between the gaps. They climbed one story and the stairs met with another landing. They turned to ascend, facing the opposite direction. Glancing at the growing distance below, she followed.

Four more stories they conquered, and where the last landing ended, a thick concrete wall loomed, little more than five feet high. Trayten pulled himself up and balanced on the edge, which was only two feet wide, before dropping to the actual roof, four feet down on the other side.

She looked up at him, his features striking against the pale orange of retiring daylight. Once again, he extended his hand, and she took it firmly. She slipped and climbed the concrete wall. With her stomach laid on the edge, she encountered the decline on the other side. Trayten, with his hand abruptly against her backside, hauled her to the top.

Katherine was awash with sweat. Despite the rush of fear, she marveled at their height above the town, a vast roof laid out before them like a concrete field. It was flat and framed with walls on each side, like the one they had just climbed over.

She took his hand and let him lead her into the center. The roof at their feet was covered with a pattern of concrete slabs standing a foot high from the flat roof and were positioned with another foot of space between and around each one. They hopped from square to square, the surfaces under their feet incandescent red under the twilight sky. Katherine watched her footing, leery of catching a heel in the space between the squares.

At their height, there was nothing beyond the sky and a sea of rooftops tinted red. They navigated a minefield of deep cracks. With ceilings beneath their feet they were like birds, above civilization. Without a word, Trayten led on, his hand warm around hers. They drew nearer to the street side.

The faces of the buildings across the avenue glowed in the gas lamplight as the darkness strengthened. From the height they looked like a painting, or a model. Fake, miniature, a figment depicted in a story book. In ginger and rose tones, quiet and quaint far below, the otherwise noisy street was instead a peaceful picture.

They maintained a safe distance from the edge, sinking against the wall to peer carefully down. People and carriages moved below, minuscule and distant, their sound scarcely more than a hum. Katherine could hold them in her hand.

"It's like a dream." She gazed across the other roofs, stretching to pink and red clouds, undisturbed. "It's like the view from a cloud, or from heaven."

In the air of his stillness and with a breeze between them, she smiled. "Is this where you come to spy on me?"

He threw words into the wind. "No, only to spy on other people."

Her laughter echoed after him.

Katherine followed him back across the square field toward a high barrier in the middle of the roof. Three walls with a recessed floor created a shelter, where the wind could not antagonize them. Trayten hopped in. A dark chimney pipe rose from the center of it. He put his hands near the top of the pipe as though warming them and admired the sky.

Katherine stepped into the shelter and sat down. Wind pulled her hair into the air around her shoulders, and she swept it from her face. "Have you brought others to the top of the city?"

"A friend of mine called Seamus, he's climbed up here. He's not around anymore."

"What happened to your friend, Seamus?"

"He is…serving his sentence." Trayten scratched his head with a wry smile.

"He must have come down from the rooftop."

Trayten cleared his throat. "No one can stay hidden on rooftops forever. Sooner or later, we all come down."

"Well." She clapped her hands together. "It's a first for me, at any rate. Never climbed so high in my life."

Trayten drew closer and his eyes were deep and serious. Words left her as he knelt down. The wind worked to wedge between them, the night suppressed the light. He stared at her with such intensity that Katherine was breathless. His warm hand swept across her cheek, his fingers traveled to the base of her throat and lingered there.

Though his striking beauty pained her, it was impossible to look away. As if she could keep the memory of them forever, her fingers moved to follow his features, sweeping his brow, following the lines of his cheekbones, tracing the square shape of his jaw. They explored one another's faces, cast dark and light in the simple shadows and pale contrast of night.

With tender motions, Katherine drew near to him, her eyes searching his, her lips a breath away from his, the warmth radiating from him. Taken away by the thrill of him, Katherine was lost as his kiss consumed her. Its heat and the height, with the cool night air sent shivers through her body. Closing her eyes, she savored all that she could feel; his one hand on her neck, his other sweeping the hair from her face, the smooth warmth of his lips.

His fingers weaved through her hair, pulling gently. Opening her eyes, she caught his gaze, deeply transfixed on her, eyes like coal. As stars appeared in gaps between the clouds, she was convinced that she held an angel, his beauty unworldly. The sensations he inspired sang of divinity.

Shouting erupted from the distance, and a crash below startled her sensitized nerves. With a sigh, she snuggled her cheek against his neck and his arms closed around her. He lovingly placed a hand on her hair at the crown of her head and breathed her in.

The fear was there to whisper, amid her greatest exaltation. The premonition revealed itself no more distinctly than a forgotten dream, impressing a resonating impact; a dread of losing him, a faint notion that he would be lost. She held on, unable to speak of it, unable to define it.

"I left my cigarettes below," he said.

"And?"

"Wait here." He kissed her again.

"Where will I go?"

He smiled back and went to the opposite end of the rooftop.

Under the stars Katherine waited, stricken and nervous, although uncertain as to why. Anxiety twisted inside. For what felt like many hours she sat, grasping to hold the sensations he created and fighting against the voices of foreboding that warned of their futility. When Myra's warnings crept in, when the implications of her parents came to mind, and the face of Rueben Koryn presented itself, Katherine brought forward the impressions of Trayten and covered the unwanted words and images.

She was shaken from the warring of her thoughts by the sound of a whistle. Trayten crouched inside the concrete wall where they had come up at first. He crept across the open roof toward her.

"What is it?"

"We need to go, now," he whispered.

Katherine met him half-way across the roof. "Did you climb down?"

"I did and nearly was caught on the way back up. Shh!" He motioned with a finger to his lips and waved for her to follow him.

Heart beating, she concentrated on leaping across the gaps between the squares as darkness challenged her. They drew toward the ledge and far below, a hazy glow leaked from the back of the building where the door under the last landing was open. "He's in there, the barkeep, right inside the doorway. Shh!"

She grabbed his arm. "How am I going to do this?"

"We have to be quick, down the stairs, then jump and run."

Katherine shot him a grave frown, provoking his laughter, although she was not amused. The sudden obstacles, coupled with a sense of urgency, were entirely unwanted. Descending was an unnerving prospect, far more than climbing up had been.

"Ready? Quietly." He was on the edge of the concrete wall in one swift leap and lowered himself stealthily to the first iron landing.

She hesitated, observing how in the darkness, the five-foot concrete wall appeared at the edge of the earth, with nothing more than a void of space beyond it. She placed her faith in Trayten's leadership, put her hands on the edge of the wall and maneuvered her body onto it. Sitting on the wall, as high in the sky as ever she had been, Katherine held up her finger. "Maybe I should take off my boots."

Trayten examined the high heels and helped her off with them. She held them between her teeth by the ankles and Trayten lifted her onto the top landing.

The stairs proved to be no challenge at all. Quietly they descended one flight after another, Katherine's stocking feet silent as she held the rail and trailed after Trayten. When they reached the bottom landing they froze, suspended above the open doorway. Distinct light shone from within, and the frequent shadow of the man Trayten noted alerted them of his movements, piling crates outside the door.

He explained their plan without words, using instead the motions of his hands and fingers. Katherine narrowed her eyes, not entirely understanding his peculiar sign language. She held her boots between her teeth again and prepared to go with whatever came. He indicated a 'jump and run' strategy and it appeared reasonable, as any other option had failed to present itself.

The doorway darkened. His arm swung across to force their backs against the wall. The man shuffled out under their feet, he kept his arm against her. Katherine closed her eyes, as if it could make them disappear. Their hearts pounded, both gripped with the anticipation to act.

It unfolded somewhat disjointedly. The man below briefly withdrew, and although Katherine was not ready, Trayten determined it was the best time to leap from the landing. At his release of her, Katherine opened her eyes and panicked to find herself alone.

The idea of leaping twisted her stomach! During her hesitation, the distance stretched between the landing and the ground. He held his arms out to catch her, glancing nervously at the open doorway in front of him.

She sat and hung her legs off the edge. Awkwardly she stood on his shoulders, and released the edge of the landing, grasping for his head and neck. Trayten fumbled and snickered. Katherine slid down the length of his body, and they toppled and teetered until her feet met with the ground.

The shadow returned in the doorway, and in a flash they were off; Trayten dragging Katherine, shoeless and dizzy, across the alley toward the waiting carriage. After scrambling onboard they escaped into the dark of night. Katherine's laughter echoed through the alley in their wake. Trayten whipped the horse and drove them wildly into the unsuspecting streets of Portsea.

<hr />

In the shadows of the hall, Winifred was entirely concealed, except for a slight glow tracing the line of her face from the study's fire. She held Reuben's arm. They could see Katherine's hair spread over the arm of the couch in the study where she lay.

"You go in there." Shadows pooled in Winifred's wrinkles. "She can't claim she's too busy now. Make her understand. We shall wait in the parlor." With her back straight she nodded gravely and strode away.

Reuben arched an eyebrow and ducked through the doorway of the study. He leered around the couch to behold her fully, as she lay back absorbed in a book. Katherine wore a white night-gown under a long brown combing-jacket. The firelight danced on her cheeks and with as much heat, her eyes raised to glare at Reuben. She scooted up and closed the book around her finger. "What do you want?"

"Sorry. Did I frighten you?"

"Dreadfully. Actually," she sneered in a low tone. "You have no idea."

He batted his eyes and perched on the edge of the couch near her feet. "You have been hard to track down, my dear Kathy."

"Does that matter?"

"Actually, yes. My mother has been asking for you. She says you are the only sane person she's met. My mother is…a bit *off*."

"I should like to look in on her. I think I understand her suffering."

"She's quite comfortable actually. But do you know, in this light, one could almost mistake you for, serene. A gentle maid."

Katherine glared at him.

"What is it you are reading? Could it be Mrs. Beeton's *The Art of Household Management*?"

"I wouldn't be caught dead!" Katherine exclaimed in disgust. "No, but it's Christina Rossetti's poetry."

"Poetry yes! Why, if you wish to read poetry you must keep to the masters. Now Wordsworth is something, and Robert Browning, Hopkins and Meredith. That is true poetry. I should be helpful to educate you! I've not heard of a female Rossetti, or any female equipped for the art."

"I completely disagree! And here is evidence of our differing tastes. For I find your masters to be pompous and verbose, dragging on and on. Give me Emily Bronte, John Clare, Christina Rossetti, Elizabeth Browning, and Carroll who, in far fewer words, accomplish more meaning and generate more emotion than the volumes of verses cherished by the popular majority. I find that your favorites are so intent on domination that their poetry is like an assault. My beloved are the writers whose subtlety is powerful, who know true cadence and the value of space."

"Emotion. Yes, well of course female literature is driven by feeling, and therefore would appeal to you." He shrugged. "It is, however, flimsy and flawed. The high emotion of the weaker sex is not suited to the work. As for Clare, he might as well have been a female, weak and given to mental instability and madness. And Carroll was entirely nonsensical!"

"If you came here intent on charming me, you're moving in quite the opposite direction."

"There is that contentious spirit you are infamous for. Of course, I am not going to play these little games forever."

"What games?"

"Come along, Kathy. You act removed from reality. You act preoccupied, yet you *must* hear, you must know."

"I'm afraid I find *you* entirely nonsensical," she said with no trace of warmth in her tone.

"Imagine, if you will, the finest couple in Hampshire, riding in carriages trimmed with silver. Can you picture a beautiful villa with flower gardens and marble statues, such as would make the whole of England envious? Wouldn't it be marvelous, a staff in crisp white uniforms, hallways decked with art and mirrors and marble—"

"Why am I imagining this?" she interrupted. "Is this supposed to mean something to me?"

"Yes, are you dull, Kathy? All these things and countless more I offer you."

"I am beginning to feel ill." Katherine held her stomach.

Reuben sprang to his feet and paced. He stopped and stared. She retained her apathy and he resumed pacing.

"I have spoken to your father." He gazed at the walls, stuttering with a wavering pitch cutting his voice. "He respects me. He and I, we hold, we hold an equal exchange of respect, the two of us. I respect him."

"It isn't clear. Do you speak of *respect*?"

Reuben appeared flustered as he ran a sweaty hand through his hair. Although previously slicked back, it now stood like a rigid fin atop his wide head. Katherine held onto her laughter.

"Yes, anyhow, he values my worth. He thinks that my proposition is a noble and practical one. The details have been arranged, extensively; plans, arrangements, finances—"

"Really, what's your point?" She cut him short, his stammering like the sharp nuisance of a thorn in her side.

"Yes my point! It's, well, it's—" He fell on one knee before her. Katherine's eyes filled with fear and she sat back.

Eloquently, with his hair spiked high, he proclaimed, "I ask for your hand in marriage, Katherine Madison."

The dread that had been hovering for weeks finally clapped down on her. She could only stare with no expression on her face, much less in her heart. He swayed on his knee as if unsteady and waited. Her lips twitched and Katherine spilled forth a symphony of laughter. It struck him in the face, for he drew back.

Still, Katherine laughed, and clutching the book to her chest and bouncing in her amusement, she sounded dreadful to him. A tear escaped her eye and traveled down her lifted cheek.

Reuben asked gruffly, "Is that an answer?"

"I don't know what else to say," she gasped, the laugh lingering in her throat, aware of how it punctured his ego.

"I don't understand. Are you telling me no?"

"Yes. I mean, no. I *am* saying no."

He was both crushed and ready to explode.

"I thought you would have taken my previous signs as your answer," she explained. "I didn't imagine you would go so far as to *ask* me."

"Why no?"

"Does it even matter?"

"It does! How can you tell me no?" He towered over her.

Though she exuded indifference, his raised voice sent a frightful thrill through her. Through a careful laugh she said, "We don't even like one another. Truly Reuben, what are we, not even friends! What sort of life would that be? Strangers married? It's madness. Besides, you aren't what I had in mind."

His mouth opened, desperate for words he could not find. "Not…not exactly. *What* exactly do you have in mind?"

"Not you." There followed an intermission and Katherine yawned within it.

"And you laugh at me," he accused.

"Yes. I do, but you must forgive me. I have been influenced by those uncivilized rogues in the pub. I must have forgotten how to behave as a lady." She fanned her neck with her hand.

"We shall see, Kathy. Your options aren't as broad as you may imagine."

"It's obvious *you* think so. Or at least you would like to."

"I more than think. I know. So sleep well, my dear, on one of the last nights with your laughter and your haughty 'independence' intact!"

Katherine glared at him as he gathered his shredded pride to parade from the study. When he had gone, she stared into the shadows of the hall with no smile on her lips and no laughter in her throat.

1909

Katherine stumbled into Marian's front parlor gasping, "Did you see the gulls out there? They took off in one gallant—"

A man sat next to Marian.

With her cheeks flushed from the chill, Katherine smiled and said, "Hello." On her arm hung a basket of shells.

"Mrs. Koryn, this is my new boarder," Marian announced.

Katherine greeted him.

An amusing spectacle, he was skinny with a large bobbing head on a wiry neck. He had drooping, glazed eyes, and wayward stubble speckling his chin and cheeks. His clothes appeared too large, and his knobby hands twitched, clutching the brim of his crushed sailor hat.

"Tarl Frangul." He shook her hand.

"Katherine Koryn is a psychoist," Marian said. "Here to pester my permanent resident, T.B.."

Katherine rolled her eyes, ever amused by Marian's insistent use of her own made-up word, *psychoist.*

"Is there T.B. going round?" Tarl reeled with alarm and his voice rattled in the back of his throat.

"What?" Marian squawked, then waved away the idea. "Good heavens, no!"

Katherine smirked.

Tarl wobbled, as if his head might dislodge from his neck and roll onto the floor.

"It's nice to meet you, sir," Katherine said before retreating for the stairs.

⚜

She arranged shells along his windowsill, on the shelf above the bed, and placed a few on his nightstand. They were pale and sandy, some shiny and pinkish, a few orange, and even purple.

"What do you think you're doing?" he asked as she invaded his space.

Katherine finished placing a small, jagged shell on the chest of drawers.

"You think I want corpses cluttering my cell?"

"They aren't corpses. They're homes. Aren't they lovely?"

He did not respond. She went into the closet and strained on her toes to reach the high shelf. "Here we are." Spinning around she revealed a wide wooden box. "Chess. Would you play?"

"No." He laid in bed.

"Ah, don't make me plead." She brought the box to his bed and sat on the edge. As she set the sandstone pieces in place, she said, "It would make us feel more intelligent, don't you think so? When in doubt of intelligence, play chess."

"No. It would make me feel quite the opposite."

"How do you know?" She tilted her head. "Play with me."

"I won't be motivated, and I can't share your excitement."

"Please try." Katherine turned the chess board. "Which do you want to be, black or white?"

He only glared.

"Then what *shall* we do?"

"*We* shall do nothing at all. *You* may leave me alone," he replied.

"May I? And you'll what? Sulk?" She swept the pieces inside and snapped the board shut.

"Precisely."

"You don't *want* to get better, do you?"

"How can it be that you continue to think I'll simply *be* better?" Tray challenged.

"Allowing happiness into your life, a little *joy*, might be a start." Katherine replaced the chess board in the closet.

"Don't I look happy to you?"

"Not now!"

"Exactly!" he snapped.

"Yes, exactly, and you *can't* be happy unless you try!"

Tray ran a hand roughly through his hair. "Who are *you*!"

"What do you mean?"

"To demand I be happy, who are *you*? I don't even know you!"

"How can you be sure?"

"I'm not," he admitted. "But I believe I would know if I knew someone!"

"Really?" she asked.

"Really."

Katherine dropped her clasped hands and before she might speak regrettable words, departed.

1900

Katherine slid drinks onto the counter. Her hair had been reck-lessly tossed into a ponytail, and loose hairs had worked free to hang in her eyes. Catching orders from patrons and retrieving bottles and glasses from the bar, she pivoted with incessant rota-tion. Shouts, cackles, and music created a lively din.

Jeff played his piano like a man possessed, his knees bouncing up and down, his head swiveling to the rhythm of his music. A man perched on the stage, stomping his foot and pounding his hands on the piano top. Dancers filled the floor, circling round and round one another. The Bedford in Chase was packed full of bodies, sweating liquor as they downed pints and shots. Katherine perspired as well, hurrying and shuffling to serve the guests as efficiently as possible.

Come the hour of midnight she would be free, and to Sun Street she would run to meet Trayten, certain she would find him at home. Until then, she labored, her arms sore, the pain climbing across her shoulders. The motion of the dancing crowd filled her head with a pulse. Heat filled her cheeks from the high tempera-ture of the atmosphere. Still, Katherine kept moving to meet the demands of the carousing, intoxicated tavern.

⊙✹⊙

"Yes." Jack Conway inspected the carriage.

At the rear of the cart, crates filled with tin boxes were stacked tightly. Trayten swung another onto the pile. Jack hoisted two more crates, brimming with wax encased cheese rounds, to where Trayten positioned them over the first packages protec-tively. Crickets called into the darkness blanketing the length of Whites Row.

"Should be all of it." Jack helped Trayten cover the contents of the carriage box with a black, velvety tarp.

"Then I'm set."

"And ye'll be all right?" Jack asked.

"Yes."

"Can ye make it there and back in one night?"

"I ought to. I've done this before. Why are you worried now?"

"Pat's got a bunch of nasty fella's with him." Jack scratched the back of his head.

"We have no quarrel with them. I'll get there, make the drop, and be on my way back."

"Ye watch going over the bridge, they like to stop ye."

"I know." Trayten cleared his throat. "Yes sirs, it *is* late and quite dark, but the sun spoils the cheese. All is well under control, Jack."

"Well, see ye in the morning. Be careful."

"Always." Trayten climbed into the carriage seat.

With a snap of the reins, the horse jerked forward, and Jack Conway listened to the huffing, the hooves pounding the pavement, and the creaking of wheels as the carriage sped off. The sight of Trayten's slender form lingered as a silhouette against the night.

❧

When a squabble became a brawl, Katherine jumped over the bar and wedged herself between the rumbling bodies. She screamed for them to stop, drowning in their commotion until Wilkins came romping through the crowd to relieve her. His wide arms were enough to pry the starters of the fray apart and his raised voice shot them to opposite corners. Once it ended, Wilkins threw an arm of camaraderie around Katherine's shoulders and laughed. Together they were jostled by the billowing tide of the bar.

Wilkins was more amused than concerned by the wild atmosphere. Katherine wiped the sweat from her brow. "Payday, yea?"

Wilkins nodded, observing the tireless dancers as they resumed; sweaty men and breathless women, guzzling from cups and glasses between jigs.

"Crazy buggas." He tilted his head, his arm heavy on her shoulders as they moved back toward the counter. "I'd rather they spend their wages here all at once!" He put his hands around her waist, hoisted her up in one easy swing, and lifted her back over the bar. "Keep them coming, Katherine!"

Katherine was promptly back to work. "Yea, Wilkins!"

In the raucous mutter, the ever-escalating midnight rumble, laughter reigned. They were the best nights, and Katherine was wide awake in the rush of it all. Her smile illuminated the dim, warm and constant as she was bombarded with the latest stories and jokes. They drank away sorrows and the challenges of their poverty. They danced despite their woes and made her own worries fade beneath the volume of their energy.

⚅⚅

Trayten was shoved, blindfolded, into an unknown enclosure. Several solid thuds sounded amid the shuffling of hurried feet. Heat lingered in the musty air, and with what sounded like the closing of a door, he sensed the darkness around him deepen. The handkerchief was ripped from his eyes. His vision soon adjusted after a momentary blindness to see that four figures encircled him.

He recognized Pat as the one who removed the blindfold. Under a hanging lantern, Pat's face was jettisoned with scars. "Check them. Him too," he ordered the other three, indicating the crates stacked around them which had been on Trayten's wagon.

Trayten was set on his feet by Pat's cronies. His pockets were searched, and his limbs were patted. One among the three turned each of his pockets out and found them empty. The other two opened tins and searched their contents; bricks of dark brown matter. They held it to their noses, sniffed it, and squeezed sticky bits with dirty, gnawed fingernails. Pat shoved Trayten down on a crate and joined the others to inspect the delivery. "Isn't even pure!" he assessed.

"Yea? I was told it was pure," Trayten said coolly.

"Jack can't pay a debt halfway. What'd he mix in to make quantity, eh?" Pat narrowed his eyes.

"I know of nothing being mixed." Trayten clasped his hands, his eyes steel and impenetrable. "Nothing has been touched on our end."

Pat returned to count the tins and crates and mutter under his breath. His brow furrowed, he shoved the man next to him, and swiping a revolver from his belt he pressed it to Trayten's temple. "You think I'm an idiot, boy?"

Sweat trickled down Trayten's forehead. The others stared with vicious eyes. The bead of perspiration forming on Pat's sharp upper lip was distracting.

"What's the problem?" Trayten asked.

"The problem? So you're going to play the idiot? I'll tell you one thing Jack knew once and shouldn't have forgotten and it's this; you don't play games with me. When I'm owed something, I get it. All of it. I pay my debts in full, and I don't tolerate sluggards who can't do the same!"

"And so what is the problem?" Trayten asked.

Pat cocked the gun and Trayten felt the vibration of the action against his skin.

"The problem *is,* this isn't everything he owes me. It's less than two thirds!"

"That problem," Trayten breathed with restraint.

"Yea, what's the deal?"

"Sir, listen please," Trayten began smoothly. "Jack is waiting on the last third. The shipment was short but is coming to be sure. He means for me to come back to you with a second load. Jack didn't want you thinking he was trying to stiff you. So he sent me on with what had come in. I have to go back, but I'll return."

"It's expected?"

"Next boat in." Trayten put up his empty hands.

Pat remained silent.

"I'll return," Trayten said.

Pat chewed his lip, retracted the gun, and tossed it to one of his men. He extracted a wad of banknotes from his pocket. As he counted he eyed Trayten. "I'm sending the full amount. If you don't bring the rest, I'll come and get it myself and then I'll get you and Jack."

"I'll tell him. You have my word." Trayten flashed a confident smile. He was lifted to his feet once more by Pat's men and the notes were smashed into his palm. He retreated slowly at first, exiting into the night air and striding warily toward the carriage. When he arrived at the end of the road, his speed increased, and he drove the horse wildly onward.

⚜

The second hour after midnight, Jack waited in the street, leaning against the wall of his house. He snapped forward at the sound of the carriage cutting through the stale air. Trayten was breathless, leaping down as he drew the horse to a halt.

"He's demanding the rest." Trayten handed the money to Jack.

"What did ye tell them?" Jack squinted.

"That it's coming."

Disillusionment covered the face of his grievous old friend. "Oi." Jack breathed finally. He cleared his throat, a terrible sorrow in his eyes as he slapped Trayten's shoulder. "I'll take care of it."

"And he paid the full amount."

"Ye done well." Jack handed him a couple of pounds. "But ye look weak, gaunt even, my lad. Get some red meat in ye. Ain't ye been eating at all?"

Trayten took his wages and returned a humble shake of his head. "Still saving for that ring."

"The lady, yea?" Jack smiled sadly. "Well, I'll see if I can't work round the others and fix ye up with a few more night errands."

"I won't turn down the work," Trayten said. Despite the

danger that accompanied such opportunities, he sustained a meager existence on the fruits of such risk.

When he returned home, Katherine lay asleep on his bed, holding the pillow close against her. He set the last of his earnings, a few pennies, on his easel. Fatigue from the scare, the wind in his face, and the weary darkness made him languid as he moved to open the icebox. Inside, an insect scattered across the empty space. He filled it with two pitiful potatoes.

With awe he took her in, patient and faithful to wait for him, even after he vanished with no implication of his whereabouts. He tenderly brushed aside the hair that fell across her eyelids and felt the warm, silky skin of her flushed cheek. Katherine sighed in her sleep and his eyes filled with anguish.

He removed his coat, imagining all he wished he could provide for her as he laid it beside her expensive, velvet jacket. At the bedside he knelt and brought his face near hers, searching her features with a longing gaze. His heartbeat was heavy, doubtful and terrified. It thumped in his throat. He revealed a face full of fear, not unlike the expressions she hid from him. They both had secrets.

Sleepily she opened her eyes, groggy, on the fringes of a dream. "Where were you?"

"I'm here now," he said, sweeping her hair from her eyes again. He offered a smile. Katherine scooted back and he crawled in next to her, spreading his arms. "Come here, milady."

She nestled into his embrace, fitting in the frame of his arms and chest perfectly. Sighing, she returned to the dreams from which she had not fully emerged.

Trayten kissed her hair and breathed her in confessing, "I love you."

1909

Tray sat in his wheelchair, hands firm on the wheels. Katherine sat on the small couch, a finger against her temple. No movement issued between them. The lantern threw shadows around; gigantic behind each of them, but neither were distracted. The sound of his breathing echoed across their mutual hush. Katherine set her eyes steadily upon him. He stared back as firmly. Between them transpired a battle of wills.

He would reveal nothing beyond his mask. Her face was impenetrable as a steel wall. Minutes passed, and they remained in the same postures; like statues, eyes fixed and set. Perhaps truth would be extracted under the weight of a stare, perhaps fault could be realized.

Neither would yield, neither would glance away. Both determined to remain unread, both were stubborn and prideful. A creak sounded from the hallway. Tray cunningly lifted one eyebrow and Katherine, mouth tight, tilted her head slightly as though challenging him. Neither glanced away.

When the door opened, and Tarl Frangul stumbled in, his neck rubbery and his bulbous head wobbling upon it, they continued to stare intensely at one another nonetheless. Tarl stuck his gut forward and puffed out his lower lip with a loud sigh. Intuitive to at least the thick tension filling the room he entered, Tarl glanced from Katherine to Tray with confusion. Caught in their staredown, they ignored his presence entirely.

It would have liked to drive a sober man insane, the heavy focus between the occupants of the room. Tarl was anything but sober and in a slurred mumble he rambled, "Sorry, interrupted a bit of a session. Obvious hard work happening here. Well yes, merry on, carry evening!" He fumbled a bow before retreating and closing the door behind him.

Tray's nostrils flared. Katherine took her hand from her temple, crossed her arms, and lowered her chin. The silent stare continued.

"You can't leave me! I won't let you go." Trayten grabbed Katherine around the waist in the doorway of his flat.

"It's troublesome enough to leave you without open protest!" She squirmed. "I have to make an appearance at home. The parents, you understand." She touched his lips gently.

"I don't understand. I hate them. You can't leave me for them."

"Would you like to come?" She laughed; her eyes bright. The golden morning spilled into the hallway beyond his door.

"I'd really rather die." He grinned.

"Well good because I won't take you anyway and I want you alive. So shut up your windows, toil and brood over a painting to make the most of your gloominess." She kissed his lips and was clutched by his enclosing arms.

Though she squealed, he refused to release her or allow her to speak. Instead, Trayten attacked her with kisses. Finally Katherine gasped, "I must go." She pried herself from his arms. "Will you miss me?"

"Of course not." He lied.

"Say you will," she commanded, jabbing him in the chest.

"Never. Not unless you stay."

"You can't miss me should I stay. Say it!" She clutched his collar, announcing dramatically. "Or I'll never kiss you again!"

"Torture." He wrapped his arms around her once more. Finally, he relented. "I will miss you." Sorrow cut through his voice. "I will miss you every moment you're away."

Her eyes glistened. "Thank you." She kissed him.

Before she broke away, Trayten kept hold of her hand. "I hate you."

"Of course you do, just like you won't miss me."

He savored her coy smile last, before she parted from his grasp and disappeared around a corner toward the stairs.

◈

"My daughter! Where are you going?" Theodore demanded in the front hall. He caught her rushing intently toward the door. The sky had darkened, and it beckoned her.

"To the tavern. Pardon me, Father."

"No." He blocked her path. "You are not needed there."

"Rather, I am."

"I went there, to that God forsaken den of filth, and I told this Wilkins fellow myself that you will not be back."

"I beg your pardon!" Katherine snapped. "You did what?"

"You have resigned, it is finished."

She grappled for words and finally stammered, "What right have you? What's the reason for this, if not to hurt me? Don't you know who I am? What makes me thrive? You take it from me? Why?"

"I forbid it."

"Why now? Suddenly *now*? What has changed?" she cried.

"You may forget that I am your father, and there are things I can do, including revoking your privileges. Your presence is required elsewhere here on. The last place for you is among those vagrants."

The gravity of his news took hold, weighing her down. She breathed heavily, attempting to quell the anger that climbed like a flame through her body.

At last she asked, "Have I gotten in your way with my shred of independence?"

"It's not as though you keep *out* of the way. I heard what you said to Reuben Koryn!"

"That isn't any of your—"

"Business? Yes! Yes, it is my concern, my business! You refused his proposal?"

"Of course I did!" Katherine yelled.

"When did you arrive at the conclusion that you have a choice? Unless you consider living on the street a viable choice. I refuse to support you further. Do you understand me? Your last chance has arrived, your last suitor, capable of providing everything you are accustomed to and more, asks for your hand.

"I thought you would have more sense, and I would not have to tell you to obey. You will marry Reuben Koryn, because he is the only person who will have you, else you shall be on your own entirely with nothing in the world to your name."

Katherine stared back, separate from her body. "I...I can't marry him."

"You will find that you can, and you *will* marry him. It has been decided. It is final! One week from today," he concluded and locked the front door.

"It is not final!"

"What did you say?" His voice carried a threat of volume.

Katherine suppressed the shudders that shook her frame. "I said, I cannot, I will not marry him. Not for you, not for myself, not for anyone!"

"You are deluded, daughter. Your options have run dry. Unruly child, no one else will tolerate you. Do you understand? We have extended our best efforts to find you a suitor and most have retreated from your disagreeable demeanor! None want an uncivil woman who would rather languish away in a tavern, with the roughest sort of tramps, than to tend a house, husband, and children! You do not cook, you cannot sew, you refuse to learn the skills required of a wife!"

Katherine's eyes burned with tears.

He circled her, scolding, "You have contributed nothing to this household apart from grief, worry, and argument! Now, despite your faults, you have managed to attract and secure a husband who stands to inherit both the Koryn and Madison holdings, for both of your positions as heirs. Through this union you will inherit and without it, you are destitute."

"You would cast me out, without mercy, should I not comply and marry?" Katherine trembled.

"Yes."

"I have a right to my wages! I've earned them with my own efforts!"

"You have no rights. The wages are your dowry to Reuben, and that is your only access to them. Should I have to disown you, the dowry ceases to exist. You take nothing with you if you go."

"You're an animal! You have no more affection, no more loyalty, or love than an animal! I hate you!"

Theodores's eyes filled with rage, and he slapped Katherine across the cheek. The smack echoed sharp across the high, dim hall as she sank to her knees, powerless against the flood of tears spilling forth.

"Enough!" he hollered. "This is how you repay my care, your lenient upbringing, your expensive things, your easy life? Listen here!" He seized her forearm and dragged her to her feet. "If you are not his wife, you are not my daughter!"

"Father!"

Theodore tightened his grip on her arm. "You are selfish, ungrateful! You want too much you do not deserve! Do you understand what I am telling you? Not my daughter. You are penniless, you are no one with nothing, unless…" he released her with a shove, "you go to your room and pray that God give you the strength to stand at the altar in one week to marry Reuben Koryn!"

He departed.

Removed from herself, Katherine was fearful to proceed into this cruel new world. Broken, she waited, hoping to wake from the nightmare. What she had attempted to avoid, was inescapable. She considered the narrow paths that demanded her choice, and both appeared riddled with pitfalls and snares.

To leap into the arms of love, would be to plunge into privation and struggle, improving the odds of meeting with an untimely death by sickness or starvation. To follow the course designed by others, would be to trade her heart for her subsistence and was an affront to her romantic ideals. Katherine sank to her knees, placed her palms on the floor to try and steady herself, and washed the floor with helpless tears.

After the first day and night passed that Katherine failed to come to him, Trayten invented excuses for her, in order to forswear his worry. He could not locate her in the streets or the markets. He lingered in the library and loitered in front of the bakery. When he woke to discover that she had not come to him by night, he considered that she might have been swept away on a family excursion to the countryside, as families of her sort seemed likely to do.

The second day went by much as the first; empty with no sign of her. He had roamed Portsea for hours on end as fear and frustration invaded his awareness and the world altered to a hostile place. In the evening he guarded a corner of The Bedford in Chase, willing her to appear by the force of his desire.

When he asked a man behind the bar whether she had been or would be in, the bartender shrugged. "As I don't know her, she must not be employed here." He returned to wiping the counter.

Trayten returned to his flat, hoping that Katherine would be waiting for him. She was not there and still she did not come.

A third day without her arrived and Trayten, though wary of leaving Portsea and missing her there, made his way to Southsea to spend the day surveying Madison Estate from the safety of shadow and shrub. While over the course of many hours, he caught sight of several persons coming and going, he spied no indication of her presence. It seemed as though Katherine Madison had vanished entirely.

Before the onset of his present suffering, Trayten always found her easily. He was guided to her, able to track her with little conscious effort. She was ever existent. Into the world he would plunge and follow spontaneous paths leading straight to where she was. His divine gift, the talent for locating her had failed him for three days.

More disturbing than the conclusion that his supernatural powers had departed was the overwhelming premonition that Katherine chose her obscurity. The stark reality remained; she was gone, and he could not find her. He feared she might never return. A sensation like drowning consumed Trayten while he searched his memory of their last encounter; for signs, for clues, and he found nothing.

※

A murder was reported in the papers on the fourth day of Trayten's depravation. The city streets were crowded with people. Wandering by a newspaper stand, Trayten's gaze caught the headline that chilled his blood: Authorities Identify Victim of Homicide as John "Jack" Conway.

He stopped dead in his tracks and snatched a copy, reading hungrily before the attendant ordered him to, "Pay or scram!"

It happened in open daylight and several witnesses related the crime with identical testimonies. Four men stalked Mr. Conway down North Street. They called his name and as he responded, they opened fire on him. Two nearby women were hit with debris from a lamppost that was struck by a stray bullet. The victim collapsed in mid-turn, seizing under the hail of multiple shots.

Before bystanders could react, the assailants escaped through an alley. A North Street resident identified the shooters as Pat

Rooney, Alex and Dorf Callahan, and Michael Sayer. The residence of Mr. Conway in Whites Row, when searched by officials, housed an astonishing supply of refined opium. Alleged residences of the assailants were searched as well in Langstone.

Though the assailants remain at large, officials confiscated several crates and tins, packed with the same substance in Mr. Conway's possession. Appalled and aghast at the idea of an opium trade and its related implications circulating their midst, the people protested with disgust and reproach in the streets.

Trayten dropped the paper and moved on before the attendant demanding payment could apprehend him. Though he walked, he felt as though he stood still. Guilt and dread constrained him. When he blinked, idling at a corner, he imagined Jack's face, troubled, worried, and striving to hide it.

Though he mourned his friend, Trayten chose to abstain from the funeral service, lest a connection be made that might jeopardize his own personal safety.

The fifth day also failed to bring Katherine to Trayten. The weight of his world anchored him to the ground. Misery saturated him, bitterly obscuring his environment. He stared into an empty icebox and at paintings cluttered, stacked, and haunting him around his room. The landscapes she had touched tormented him. He stared at them, fixated on the river she traced, as though it could reveal where she had gone.

※

Pleased to see three of the four shooters who killed Jack Conway brought to justice, a crowd gathered around Kingston Prison. After an expeditious inquiry, Pat Rooney, Michael Sayer, and Alex Callahan were charged and convicted collectively for Mr. Conway's murder. Punishment followed accordingly and the convicts were escorted by officers from the prison into a steel barred transport carriage. They were to be hanged.

Many people clustered along the walkway opposite the jailhouse. In perfect disgust they waited, anxious to witness retribution in action. When the first terrible face emerged from the shadow of the prison door into a passage lined heavily with guards, the jeering began.

Alongside the concerned representatives of the working class, several stately fellows judged the degradation they perceived surrounding them. The guards marched the prisoners out, each clothed in gray, flannel jumpsuits. The steel door to the wagon bed was opened and for a brief moment they would pass.

The volubility of the crowd increased, and infiltrating those who spit curses, Trayten shoved his hands into the pockets of his black overcoat. A cigarette dangling from his lips and his hair covered his black eyes. The energy of the people hustling and clustering around him, contrasted his staid, motionless stance. Despite his placid posture, great storms raged through the heat of his stare as he glared at each convict in his view. Anger consumed him.

Reuben Koryn, accompanied by two comrades, joined the bustle to survey the crowd and the prisoners through the gate. They hung back from the shoving mass nearest the fence. Pompous and effusive, Reuben pontificated about the laziness of the lower-class and the shameful opium use that illustrated their innately flawed nature. Reuben laughed while the prisoners writhed against the guards.

A sharp-eyed Pat Rooney identified Trayten, the pillar of calm among the movement, and exerted to break from the grip on him. "You lying bastard!" he bawled across the parkway of the jail. "You're dead, Basel! You're dead! You worthless—hey—" Pat was kicked and prodded by the two guards who maintained control of him.

Trayten kept a solid stare straight ahead. Those nearest glanced at him with curiosity and scrutiny; Reuben being one among them.

As Pat was shoved and tugged into the enclosed carriage box, he continued to yell, "You lied to me! You'll get it like Jack did! I told you, Trayten Basel!"

The back door of the carriage slammed on him and an officer secured it with a chain and lock before the horses were driven forward. Trayten, shielded in gloom, turned with the dark clouds thick on his shoulders and a trail of smoke following after him through the thinning crowd. He passed Reuben Koryn, who sneered and rammed his shoulder, muttering a snide, suspicious judgment to his fellows.

Katherine read about the death of Trayten's friend. She was too consumed with mourning for the living however, for Trayten and for herself.

Eliza entered a room that was terrible in darkness, a vast cave of hardwood floors, high ceilings and massive, looming furniture. Katherine lay on the floor, an arm under her cheek, her knees curled tight against her chest. She had not moved, as though waiting to die.

With her gentle presence Eliza drew near, in a dress hanging loose from her thin shoulders. Her fair hair was bound in a plait. Two spiral curls rested at the base of her small, frail neck. Eliza knelt and touched her sister's shoulder carefully. "Are you ill?"

After a brief silence, Katherine replied listless, staring straight ahead into the dark, "They do so love you, your naïve tenderness. I can't be ignorant, and it scares them."

Eliza remained still, impervious to Katherine's sharpness. She smoothed the wild, loose strands of hair that Katherine had neglected to comb.

"How much more difficult it is to fight? I cannot fight as you do. I cannot have a child, but I do not get angry about it. I cannot fight it. Do you see? Grace, acceptance, these will sustain you."

"I can't accept what I can't even like."

"You will learn to," Eliza said. "Won't you try? You are needed."

"I'm not."

"I need you. You have been in here a very long time. Please try, you have to get up. Do not cry."

Constant and without sound, Katherine's tears fell to the floor. Her face glowed white in the dark, sallow and lifeless. Her stomach heaved, and she clenched her fists. The agony in her expression revealed pain inexpressible.

Eliza combed the tangles from Katherine's hair with her fingers. "Why do you cry, Katherine? You look like you have lost something."

The mere contemplation of articulating what she had done brought anguished tears, fresh and boiling to burn her eyes.

"What have you lost?" Eliza repeated.

Katherine could not answer. She could not allow herself to admit to reality, unable to acknowledge it for herself. How could she say aloud that she had betrayed her own heart for fear of poverty?

Both Madison and Koryn families gathered around the marble dining table in Augustus's villa. The unofficial occasion first centered on the lavish supper they shared however the content of the conversations revealed its true purpose as the meal progressed. Winifred and Augustus engaged in the exchange of ideas for the wedding, an event that increased in lavishness the more wine they consumed.

The leading voices, busy with preparation, were accompanied by the excited agreements as well as the unaffected grunts of the company around Katherine, their sounds combining to create an unnerving clamor. It echoed and stretched to the skylight, arched above the table.

"Oh, darling!" Winifred laughed, clapping her hands together.

"She'll wear my dress of course, as soon as the alterations are done. My Katherine and her wide hips." She flashed a delirious smile at her daughter. "And you must get the carriage with the silver trim from Miller as you promised, Ted."

Theodore chewed his food and listened to Reuben, who rambled on beside him. Across from Reuben, Katherine had been placed. The atmosphere being enough to sicken her, she refrained from looking at him, for fear of losing control of her stomach. The nauseating chatter ran strong. She kept her red-rimmed eyes and her pale face directed to the tablecloth.

Like Katherine, Hilda Koryn ate quietly, and when finished, she wheeled inconspicuously away from the table and out of the dining room. Soon after, Katherine followed. As she attempted to pass Reuben's chair, he slapped a hand around her wrist. "Where do you go, my love?"

Katherine scowled and searched his thick cheeks and his dull, small eyes with an element of cruelty in her own. As curtly as possible she said, "To find your mother."

"Oh extraordinary! Bonding!" he exclaimed, flashing a wide, despicable smile.

Katherine pried her arm free. "And I'm not your love."

"You broke away," Hilda observed as Katherine entered the den. "Come, sit here."

Near the settee in her wheelchair, moonlight blanketed Hilda. The window behind her provided a perfect aperture through which the full moon could shine on them. Across the grand, endless room, Katherine drifted through the shadows to sink beside Hilda like a listless spirit.

"I'm glad I will see more of you." Hilda patted Katherine's hand. Her eyes seemed unable to focus and she stared through Katherine. "You do not look at me the way they do."

Despite the depths of her own depression, Katherine was able to sense the suffering in Hilda's countenance. The heavy sorrow hanging in the air around Hilda softened her heart against the callus that had been forming. For a moment, her own hurt quieted beneath the hopeless, hapless aura of Hilda Koryn.

"Such a pretty bride!" Hilda shrugged her shoulders. "We shall have a lovely time yet. You will learn to weave tapestries with me. Yes! Oh—" Hilda sighed deeply. "But do not be sullen. Took me a bit to master it as well. Much like croquet, or horse-shoes ... something."

"Hilda, did you love Augustus?"

Hilda stared into the shadows of the room. At last, she let her mouth fall open. "We ought to arrange a party afloat. Reuben has a quaint, but elegant ship. That would be romantic. What's your best color dear?"

Dizzy and drained, Katherine sank into a lonely void. Hilda promptly struck up a new topic entirely wanting of substance.

⚜

1909

In winter on the island of Alderney, sea air often married with warm western winds to create snow as fluid as rain. The endless gray sky broke, spilling freezing showers. Water streaked in thin, snaking rivers down the outside of Tray's window. Locked deep in secret contemplation he kept his back to her. Katherine sat with her legs curled up on the couch, writing by candlelight.

"Read," he breathed.

Startled when it broke the longstanding silence, she was uncertain of the word at first.

Surprisingly, he repeated, "Read, will you?"

She stretched her legs and held the journal with trembling hands. "What shall I read?"

"Whatever you are able to."

Her fingers flipped nervously through the pages of time and

her pulse quickened. Katherine strained to perceive the words clearly for her vision blurred. She scanned and searched, but had trouble comprehending anything.

Softly she inhaled, considering. He fell in love with her once. Perhaps he would remember the moment. From memory, she recited the verses that had arrested his attention years ago in The Bedford in Chase.

Near the end he tried to catch her expression and she cast her gaze to the book, pretending to read from it. "A sickness, an unmatchable high, an indiscriminate killer...and a gift from God."

She caught his gloomy look. "Love is the world's greatest disease."

She waited and drank in his silence. His eyes were dark wells of mystery. Katherine set the journal beside her and clutched the fabric of the couch. "What do you feel?"

"Suffocation." He widened his eyes, as though it might help him to see through fragments of dream and nightmare.

1900

In a crisp red coat and clean black trousers, a garb customarily donned by couriers, Trayten approached Madison Estate. The uniform would likely be reported stolen soon, although he intended to return it after conducting his business. At present, he carried a thick envelope that guarded an imperative correspondence.

The estate loomed, enclosing him in shadow as he neared. Sunlight gleamed against the windows of the castle-like turrets, glittering like gold. He climbed the front steps to the portico, further into her world than he had ventured before.

Taking a deep breath, he pounded the door knocker. He detected voices at the side of the house and stepped across the lawn to catch sight of a broad carriage surrounded by servants loading trunks and boxes. Busily they carried baggage out of the house from a side door and to the carriage. The front door creaked, and Trayten quickly returned to the porch.

Ally, the young maid opened the door slightly and smiled. "Hello? Can I help you, sir?"

He gathered his courage. "I have a message for Miss Katherine Madison." He studied the envelope for affect.

The maid's cheeks fell, and her smile faded. "Who sent it?"

"An anonymous person. I was only sent to deliver it. Is she at home? Doesn't she live here?"

Ally shook her head. Before she could speak another word, she was nudged aside, and Theodore appeared in her place with an unsightly glare. "What's this?"

Trayten displayed the envelope, tight between his fingers, and forced the words, "I have been sent to deliver a message to Miss Katherine Madison."

"And you cannot say from whom?" Theodore challenged.

"Anonymous."

Theodore forced his eyebrows together and barked, "No. She won't have it."

"I have orders to deliver this, sir."

"Tell your employer that Miss Katherine has relocated, and I don't pass messages from anonymous senders." Theodore slammed the door shut.

Stunned, Trayten stepped back. He glanced up to a second-story window. Curtains moved and voices issued from above, yet there was no sign of Katherine. He turned away with heavy heels.

He continued to revisit the places they had been together, hoping to find her again. He spent a night in the library, watching ghostly hallucinations of them dancing down the aisles. He stared at the shelf, toppled and braced against the wall and saw her beneath it screaming, then laughing. He sifted through the books laying piled on the floor where they had fallen.

Passing time, he paced the aisles, finding tracks of her footsteps on the dusty tiles from when she ran from him in the dim. He waited beside the candles, seated on the floor and staring at the portrait he presented not long ago. When a faint glow through murky glass above indicated daylight, Trayten blew the candles out, and drifted from the sanctuary as bleakly as the smoke that curled and vanished in the air.

He sat by the bakery, tortured by the aroma of bread. He searched faces in the street, desperate to find her again. The continued failing of his powers wilted the wings of the guardian angel, who languished with unfulfilled purpose and impoverished existence.

⚜

In Southsea, St. Bartholomew's Church was surrounded by violent winds and many stately carriages. Within, the aisles were packed with members of Portsmouth's most esteemed class. None of them knew Katherine, or cared to, apart from Myra MacGregor who watched from the back row with Denis on her arm. She wore a pale pink gown, and her hat stretched wide on both sides, shading her small husband.

The altar was lit with a profusion of candles, the wax melting down the length of their tall brass stands. Their golden gleam haloed the priest. Though like a saint in white, with Bible balanced on clean hands, Katherine perceived a dark demon before her.

A choir sang solemnly in Latin, their melancholy voices echoing from the balcony of an upper level. Katherine was covered in white lace, her hair arranged in a bushel of exquisite curls dripping over a white crown atop her head. A veil attached to the crown covered her face, lifting as she breathed. Brightly rouged lips wore a frown. Her eyes revealed an empty expression.

The train of the gown stretched behind her, satin shining in the candlelight. The sleeves of the gown and the tension of her corset mercilessly constricted her. Reuben took her hand, and at the priest's request, presented the ring to place on her finger. The glittering band of diamonds blinded the eye. As it slid past her knuckle, she held her breath. Her fingers betrayed her as they put a wedding band on his finger in return.

Her eyes remained faithful to her soul however, refusing to glance at him, though his plain gaze burned her, and his voice agitated her as he repeated his vows. When she articulated them, she was sure she was possessed. The words flowed through her without meaning. As the priest read the blessing, and asked the final affirmation of their union, she looked at the congregation and her family in the front pew.

She scorned the smiling pair, with their hands locked together, faces cheek-to-cheek. Theodore was pleased as a king and Winifred waved a hand at her nose, feigning to suppress tears. Eliza's eyes were fixed on Arnold, gleaming with love. Dorothea was busy knitting, her elbows jabbing Caleb, who sneaked a swig from a tiny flask before returning it to his jacket pocket.

Hilda Koryn wept, sitting with her back straight in her wheelchair, her hands set under her chin. Meeting her eyes, Katherine saw her more clearly than before and the sorrow driving her tears. Beside Hilda, Augustus wore a stony expression.

Reuben declared, "I do," and in the stillness all eyes pierced Katherine's back like tiny daggers. She little noticed when the two words fell from her mouth, as foul as any she had uttered. The choir sang as for a funeral. An echo of swishing skirts and shuffling boots murmured when the congregation stood. A grueling heat encased her body.

He was an unwelcome stranger, the man who lifted her veil, and she beheld him with rising hostility. Katherine did not close her eyes or move her lips to accept him as he leaned in and kissed her lightly. The congregation roared, clapping and crying in celebration. The pipe organ struck a chord, blasting abruptly and Katherine almost collapsed, hit by the waves of sound. The church doors opened.

They were directed to face the congregation, Reuben lifting

Katherine's hand to wave. Mr. and Mrs. Reuben Koryn were announced, and the husband bowed. With her emotions forcibly sedated, head high, and face solid, Katherine advanced down the aisle, each step erasing more and more of the person she had believed herself to be.

Into the fierce wind they burst, Katherine dragged by an energetic, galloping Reuben. Petals slapped them, released by the congregation into the vengeful air. A carriage with pale yellow sides and trimmed with silver awaited.

Apart from the celebration, a dark coated figure set his gaze on the bride beneath her veil, rippling in the air like the wings of a falling angel. Though his expression seemed placid, his eyes smoldered with torment and shock. When he glared at the groom, he crushed a burning cigarette in his fist and threw it on the ground. Rage stole the air from the atmosphere. Asphyxiated, he watched her disappear into the carriage.

঩৵৵

The horse's hooves clattered against the street and the movement of the carriage rocked Katherine within.

"Glorious ceremony, truly it was, and oh, for the sum I paid, well done. We have a worthy reception waiting, and you shall become well acquainted with my villa. Your things have been brought and prepared and I have set to the remodeling of one of the guest rooms for a nursery! My dear Kathy, aren't you completely exhausted with joy?"

"I want you to understand something." Her words were blunt and heated. "Foremost, do not think that my vows were truly mine by personal desire." She gripped her lace handkerchief, her eyes fixed to the opposite, blue velvet seat.

"I never told you I would marry you. Of course, you're a man like my father, you get whatever you want because you believe you own the world. Well, I don't care for you," she said hotly as he stared at her with humor in his raised eyebrows. "And I'll never love you."

"I am surprised my dear, that you do not cut yourself with that tongue," he remarked with an unabashed chuckle.

❧

Trayten's skin was splattered with crimson. The canvas before him stared back with taunting eyes, like the other works that had mocked him for days. His brush slashed the face of it and the torment increased. He released paint without care, across the walls, on the floor, wasting and bleeding through it with one fist tightly clenched.

In a hasty temper he dragged color across the work. He wiped his sweaty brow with the back of his wrist. Paint smeared into the line of his hair. Abruptly he recoiled, unable to look longer at the face he had recreated, the face he memorized and now destroyed him.

He opened his fist and a slender gold band lay in his hot palm. He starved; his ribs distinctly visible when he gasped. One diamond chip represented his impossible dream. Disgusted, he thrust the ring across the apartment and it clanked along the floor, resting near the empty icebox.

Defeated, Trayten plopped down, and propped his elbows on his knees. He sat with his head in red-stained hands; barefoot, shirtless, in worn-out trousers. Paint ran like a current through his desolate room, dragging his mind through rivers of anguish. Paint was his only possible means of survival.

The stacks of canvases presented the only option left to help fill his stomach, short of surrendering himself to the servitude of the workhouse. He recognized that in order to go on, he would have to sell his paintings. Bitterly Trayten decided to cut his works from his possession, just as Katherine had cut him from her heart. He could do it to survive.

12

1909

Melting snow transformed the streets of Alderney into a slushy marsh. Katherine held up the hem of her skirt, maneuvering around ruts and mounds of mud toward a walkway. Against the bleak of the scenery, she shielded her eyes with a gloved hand. On each arm she carried a basket, filled with the grocery items Marian requested after Katherine volunteered to make the errand. Besides the sloshing of her boots through the wet snow, all was quiet along the avenue.

"There! There she is!" A cheerful voice cried.

"Well, catch her! Oi, yoo hoo!"

The Saunders sisters waved from the entrance of their shop. Louisa poked Mary, who called, "Mrs. Koryn! Come and visit us a moment, won't you?"

"How is your work with that shut-away?" Mary asked excitedly. "We don't see you about town much at all. Must be interesting!"

"I'm still trying to get comfortable there," Katherine said.

"Of course. It takes time. But we have come upon a revelation in the meantime!" Louisa jumped.

"Oh?"

"We swore we knew you before. We couldn't believe we overlooked it then!" Mary cried.

Louisa grabbed Katherine by the arm and said, "Come with us, we must show you, we figured you out at last!"

Confused, she followed when they took her baskets from her teasingly.

Bombarded with sensations from the past, Katherine faced the painting. The light made it glisten, and the eyes in the portrait focused ahead, large and blue. The woman in the painting stared back at Katherine with a striking likeness. The technique of the work, and the way the brush strokes formed the lights and darks of her hair, returned her to the flat in Sun Street, filled with art.

The sisters were amazed at her expression. Louisa smiled as Mary elbowed her. Katherine gasped for air, trying to put together adequate words. She could not resist and raised her fingertips to touch the rough surface of dried oil paint, the curves and ridges, the smooth shining lines.

Other works occupying the museum hall vanished, completely unimportant. The lantern burning above the piece illuminated the wonder in her eyes. "He never sold any…I thought."

Two curvy initials on the bottom right corner read: *T.B.*.

"Looks just like you," Louisa said.

"It certainly does," Katherine admitted. "Do you know the full name of the artist?"

"The artist is unknown to us." She shrugged.

"This one has been our favorite, so real and striking. When you came, we wondered why you were familiar to us," Louisa said.

Katherine backed away. "I must get back with the groceries."

"You are startled! Did Marian never mention how familiar you are?" Mary asked.

"No, why would she?"

"She's seen the painting herself and the resemblance is so amazing, I'm sure she's noticed it too."

"Marian has seen this?" Katherine asked, shaken.

"Yes," Louisa confirmed. "Marian and the doctor both."

Katherine took her baskets from Louisa and Mary. "Thank you, ladies."

⁕

Katherine could detect Marian's laughter, strange and unnatural, as she entered through the kitchen door at the back of the house. She put the baskets on the table, removed her coat, and followed the sound into the enclosed patio that extended from the dining room.

Tarl sat beside Marian on the wicker couch, her feet up on his knees. Her face flushed red, and his eyes were glassy. He held a drink in one hand. Startled, Marian viewed Katherine and immediately put her feet down, covering her ankles, and moderating her breathing. Tarl blinked slothfully, a belch congesting his throat.

"I need to ask you about one thing, Miss Boley," Katherine asserted.

"What one thing?" Marian's face returned to its standard fierceness.

Katherine sat across from Marian as Tarl wiggled to his feet and started for the bar.

"Do you know about the painting in the museum?"

Marian drew her chin to her chest, her eyes lazy. She opened her mouth faintly. Tarl poured himself another drink.

"The museum is full of paintings, Mrs. Koryn," Marian said.

"Let me be more specific. There is a portrait that looks like me."

Tarl tripped over a stool and his drink splashed down one trouser leg. Wobbling his head, he was the least surprised, and he crouched to pluck the slippery ice from the floor.

"Sorry, what?" Marian's gaze lingered after Tarl.

"Do you remember it?" Katherine demanded. "The artist is not well-known. It's a portrait in oil, right at the end of the front hall. It looks like me."

"Well, *you're* conceited, aren't you? Yes, I've seen it. And?"

"Is there anything you can tell me about it?" Katherine tried to slow her breathing.

"Why?"

"It's important," Katherine answered vaguely, determined to protect her true connection with Tray and give him time to remember her on his own.

Tarl was lurching back to refill his glass.

Marian yawned. "You are the strangest doctor I have ever met."

"Do you know something about it? Anything at all?" Katherine asked, testing to see if she would admit to seeing the resemblance. It had not escaped her awareness that Marian did not want Tray to remember his past.

"I don't." Marian chewed her bottom lip. "I'm not an art connoisseur."

The wet fronted Tarl slid in beside her, bringing a fresh glass to his lips at last.

"Please do not lie to me, Miss Boley," Katherine pleaded. "I need to know more, anything more, and I'm convinced you're holding something back."

"Didn't you say, sorry, uh, say he can't go out 'cause of a, a painting?" Tarl stammered.

"Maybe." Marian leered at him. "There is one small thing."

"Tell me, please," Katherine asked.

"I won't speak of it." Marian uncrossed and recrossed her legs.

Katherine dug her fingers into the cushion of the chair and

swallowed. "There is another physician in Alderney, is there not?"

"There are a few. And so?"

"A physician informed me that Tray was here. He must either be the one who treated Tray initially, or he would know who did."

"I don't see why it matters," Marian dismissed. "The doctor couldn't do anything for him. That's why he's the way he is now. Besides, I thought you were the specialist? Why should you need the help of a lower physician?"

"I never said I was a specialist," Katherine admitted, and before Marian might ask her to clarify her mission, she sought to retreat. "I'll see if the doctor knows something and is willing to help me."

⚜

The odor circulating through hospitals, a collage of stale, sick air and sharp medicinal stenches, woke dismal sensations in Katherine. The first wave of the smell brought her back in time. She entered the small clinic to wait in the empty lobby and when she sank into a chair, she closed her eyes and the hopelessness of years past returned, carried through the mournful memory that entered her consciousness with a jolt.

⚜

1903

Katherine fell across the counter, her eyes pale with dark sagging bags beneath them. The woman on the other side gasped, frightened at the sight of her. Like the living dead she appeared in the crowded waiting room where children coughed and elderly men huddled, some infected, some bleeding. Wind, rain, and darkness outside made the waiting room the lesser of two evils.

Soaked through, her clothing clung to her, stale and reeking unclean odors. Mud was caked halfway up her skirt from the hem and her boots tracked the mire in. The nurse disdainfully noted the water spots forming on her counter from the strands of greasy, damp hair hanging in Katherine's face.

"Miss, you must wait like everyone else."

"No please, I have—" Katherine panted.

"Do you have any money? This is no charity hospital, there's a shelter down the street, if you—"

"I don't want to be admitted. I—"

"Look, please take a seat and wait." The nurse swiveled around. "Dr. Bruce, could you—"

"Listen!" Katherine pounded her hand on the counter. "I need—"

"Miss! I told you, go have a seat and wait. Next!" she called.

Katherine blocked her view. "I walked...where am I? From Bristol I walked here and—"

"Listen, please! They have food and blankets at the shelter, you can stay there, and you don't have to pay. I can't help you here."

"No!" Katherine yelled. "You can't possibly help me when you won't listen to me! I'm cold! I'm tired, but I'm not destitute! I'm not *poor*!"

"What's this about?" A brawny attendant appeared beside the frightened nurse.

"Will you hear me, sir?" Katherine pleaded.

"Do you have an appointment?"

"I...no, I don't have...do these people?" Katherine swept her arm back toward the people crowding the waiting room.

"Yes, and I am sure that somewhere else—" He pried her fingers off the edge of the counter, but Katherine jerked her hand away and gripped another place more firmly. The diamonds on her left ring finger were caked with grime.

"I have already been somewhere *else*! They told me to come here! I need to check your records! I need to know if you have accepted, treated a patient, please—"

"You'll have to wait," the attendant said. "I think you do need help."

"You're going to need help, sir, if you don't listen to me!" she growled. "I want you to go through your records. His name is Trayten Basel. Do you have that? Trayten Basel."

Two additional attendants joined the first to take Katherine forcefully by the arms. She continued to fight against them. Her urgency became desperation and her determination escalated into hysteria as they acted to remove her.

"Trayten Basel is his name! Was he here? Let me check the records, the morgue! Listen to me, let go—"

The volume and aggression issuing from the commotion quelled the once rowdy atmosphere of the waiting room, and the people gasped and gossiped at the scene. She hung onto the counter while they pulled her.

"Anything from the last two years! Two years he's, please you have to look! His name is Trayten!" Neither pride nor dignity existed. Tears poured down, attempting to wash her filthy face.

Unable to fight against them any longer, she was pried from the edge of the counter, swiftly dragged across the room, and shoved through the door into the rain. She wailed in desperation, "Trayten Basel! Please look!"

In a state of shame, depravation, and self-loathing, she ambled back into the elements; unprotected, raving like a lunatic, and regarded as a blight against humanity by all those who encountered her.

1909

His name rushed through her mind, shaking her until she blinked away the glaze of dark remembrance and focused on the empty waiting room around her. Katherine's pulse pounded, sweat dampened her brow, and she felt illogically muddy and sore, tired and dirty. She observed her hands. They were clean and the diamonds on her left hand shimmered piercingly. From the window she felt the white light. No rain and no darkness threatened her here.

"You might be lost. I don't think I can help a lady as apparently well as you." The young doctor startled Katherine.

He smiled warmly in the hall with teal eyes and gentle features. When she arose, she discovered his stout stature. Although his face blessed him with a youthful appearance, his voice sounded low, aged, and deep. He wore his brown hair cut short against his head.

"Are you Dr. Danby?" she asked.

"Russell Danby. Pleased to meet you! And do call me Russell. Come, you may follow me back."

"Yes, thank you."

He held a door open for her and moved ahead to lead the way. She followed down the corridor to a little office at the end. He offered her a chair and seated himself opposite the desk. The window at his back was draped with white curtains, ballooning from the outside air.

"Would you like me to close it? Are you chilled?" he asked, noticing her eyes on the window.

"I'm quite all right." She smiled.

He picked up a quill and a sheet of paper. "You are new. I know because so few people here *are*." He winked. "Allow me to take some general information first."

"Actually, Russell, I just want to speak to you."

"I didn't think you were ill." He smiled, setting the quill on the desk. Sitting back, he casually asked, "What is your name, Madame?"

"I'm Katherine Koryn, from Portsmouth. I'm here about the patient at Marian Boley's."

An amazed light streaked through his expression before sadness subdued it. He choked humbly, "Koryn, that is familiar."

"I wrote to your clinic, asking if you had treated anyone

called *Basel*. I received a response about a mysterious man living on Alderney who no one knew—"

"That's right! Well, it's a pleasure to meet with you! I was curious about your inquiry. Have you come to work with him?"

"I suppose you could say that." It was more difficult than before to peddle her lie.

"Wonderful! It's *remarkable* really that you are working with T.B., especially in light of my own failure to help him."

Katherine was compelled to correct him. "Tray."

"Pardon?"

"I'm calling him 'Tray' instead of 'T.B..'"

"And he is allowing it?"

"His protest was futile. I continue to call him 'Tray' and he doesn't dispute me." She shrugged.

"You must truly be a miracle worker! That he should be agreeable. I wonder what I can possibly do to help you?" Russell's manner of speech was comforting, kind, and conducive to putting one at ease.

"I wanted to ask if you knew anything about a painting, a portrait in the museum," Katherine said.

Russell's eyes filled with knowledge, and he folded his hands seriously on the desk. Patiently he waited as she continued.

"Miss Boley wouldn't tell me anything, although I could swear there was *something*."

"Yes...yes." He shifted upright in his chair. The gravity in his eyes made her sorry to have driven away his easy smile. He sighed, speaking earnestly, "I will tell you one thing about Marian right now. I will never understand her. She doesn't want to help him, and that's why I am truly, utterly shocked that she is allowing you near him. I never thought, well," Russell took a deep breath. "I wanted to begin evaluation and treatment with him. Of course, they called on me when he was first brought in, when he was so badly—" he looked at his desk. "I was there in those critical hours when he was merely hanging on. He was unlike anyone I had treated. Of course, when he finally returned to consciousness, he didn't know anything about himself or what happened to him. He was a complete mystery.

"And I was there every day, ensuring that his wounds were cleaned and wrapped, trying to help him with his memory. Though it frustrated him greatly, he tried. He wanted to know, he ached to. Before the incident, I was always there. After it, Marian wouldn't allow me to come and see him. She refused to answer her door. She doesn't want him to remember. It wasn't just that she was angry about his relapse, which she blames me for, but she doesn't want him to recover, ever.

"And I believed he could recover. But she has staked her claim on him. She's enjoyed the attention. Having him makes her special, gives her something to tell the guests, and she's concocted elaborate tales regarding his condition. If he's *well*, he's not interesting. With him as an invalid, she has control of him. Did you know Marian was engaged once?"

"She was?"

"Truly." Russell smirked.

"Apparently it didn't last."

"No, she was far too possessive. When he wouldn't be tied to her side, she would rant, jealous and suspicious of anyone else he knew. Although he loved her, it was too hard to live with so much mistrust. She was fearful of being lonely and she drove him too far. He left her. Just got up and sailed away without a word. She never heard from him again."

"That's very sad."

"You can't force people to love you." Russell reflected. Then his smile returned as he laughed. "I am sorry, but you asked about the painting, didn't you?"

"Yes."

Russell invited her to the small house that extended from his clinic and into the sitting room with a modest fire on the hearth. Katherine sat on a well-worn couch and he brought her a cup of coffee. He stoked the fire to keep it alive and she sampled the coffee, the rich flavor sweetened with honey.

Sitting across from her at last, he began, "That particular piece was bought from a dealer in Portsmouth about seven years back. I remember because it was during the remodeling of the museum. So, of course, by that time Marian had T.B.. He wasn't too bad off at first, after the wounds healed as best they would. Like I said before, I was working with him then. I did for nearly two years, before the incident. He talked constantly, little fragments of his life no doubt. Though, they were so obscure he couldn't expand on them, still—"

"Do you remember anything he said?" She sat forward eagerly.

"He mentioned libraries, I think maybe he loved to read. He would sing sometimes, part of a song, but only one line of it, over and over. That song, 'glide on a river of sugar with me.'" Russell danced in his seat and she laughed, her eyes stinging.

"And he mentioned poetry, but very abstractly. I think he remembered the people, or rather the *person* in his life. He could have led us to find her. He was doing wonderfully. He talked constantly and I was ready to help him find his place. He wanted to experience more than those same four walls, and so I pleaded his case to convince Marian that it would be to his benefit. Begrudgingly she agreed.

"So we went to the museum to look at art, since he was trying to paint, had an interest in it anyway. We took him in the chair I special ordered from the Continent. We saw the painting. The portrait," he examined her face, "and he was affected."

"How was he affected? Did he remember…I mean, did he know it?"

"It was frightening, like he was being suffocated. He stopped breathing, he closed his eyes, and jerked like he saw something horrid! He went into a seizure when we touched him. He completely collapsed. Fell from his chair and couldn't comprehend us, couldn't open his eyes.

"It took him two days to wake from it. All that time Marian was cross with me, worried about him, a complete mess. She decided outings created trauma for him, and so did the painting. She told me it would be best I never come back, that it be forgotten, and he be kept inside, where he was 'safe.' Something had sparked for him, but when he woke, he was changed."

Katherine sat twisted in knots, her heart skipping.

"He was quiet and gruff. His chatter ceased, like the things he had been recalling were wiped away. That trauma set him back. That was six years ago, and since then, Marian hasn't let anyone treat him. She told me he was peaceful after the relapse, and she would keep him that way."

Katherine stared into his eyes.

"Mrs. Koryn? Are you breathing?"

"You must tell me something more," she cried. "If you saw the painting, well you must have seen it, you must have made the connection, the initials."

"T.B.. Yes, I recognized the initials and I told Marian. I tried to talk to her about his response to that painting and how I noticed the style of the portrait was similar to the attempts he had been making to paint. She refused to hear any of it. She didn't want it mentioned again. And now, after all that, I am perplexed to see *you* before me."

"He *did* remember." A nervous laugh caught in her throat. "He was never completely lost! He could've probably even told you. I'm sure he knows more than he will say. I believe he's been silent and lost because he's had no one to tell, to believe him, to find him. I think he can be brought back. He *can* remember!" Her words spilled out between excited gasps.

Dazed, Russell asked, "Who are you, truly? The portrait *is* of you."

Katherine smiled through her darkness.

"Although I haven't seen it in a while, I can recall that portrait clearly with you here before me."

"Russell," she said, setting her cup of cold coffee on the table between them. "I have a dreadful secret."

"And so do most people."

"I think you know it."

"Why do you think that?" he asked.

"The way you're looking at me."

"Go on, tell me and I'll verify if you're correct."

"Russell," she said seriously. "I'm not certified, as a specialist, that is."

He leaned in. "Neither am I, technically."

Katherine raised her eyebrows and stifled a laugh.

"I never graduated from university. I attended, yet never graduated." He winked.

"Russell, I never even attended. I mean, I'm not trained at all. I'm not a specialist, or a *psychoist*, as Marian likes to call me. I'm not even a student."

"So, what are you doing here?"

"That man is Trayten Basel. Eight years ago he lived in Portsea where he was a painter whom I knew and loved. He painted portraits of me, and he sang that song, and he loved an old library, and then I lost him."

"You are certain T.B. is the same man?"

"He may be crippled, but he has the same face, the same eyes, and the same habits. I lost him eight winters ago. I've been searching for him ever since. But Russell, he doesn't remember me. He sees me as a stranger. Marian believes I'm a specialist and I've allowed it so that I can get close to him, to try and gain his trust and make him remember. Because he *has* to.

"We have a daughter. I promised myself I would find him, I promised her, although she's never known him." For the first time on Alderney, Katherine let her mask slip in the presence of another, and there sobbed. "I have to make him remember me."

"I knew that painting resembled you." Russell snapped his fingers.

"It's important that you don't say a word of it," she warned.

"I have no reason to."

"But do you believe me?"

Russell passed her a handkerchief and said carefully, "I do

believe you. But the way he arrived here, the state of him, you must know what happened to him!"

"I can't tell you *that*!"

"He nearly died."

"I couldn't…I didn't mean…" Katherine held the handkerchief to her nose, squeezing her eyes shut.

"Who is your husband, Mrs. Koryn?"

Agony crossed her eyes. "Was. You mean who *was*." She shivered. "Reuben Koryn. He's dead. He was killed. He died," she sounded cruel, "the day Trayten disappeared. And I looked for him, believing he must be alive somewhere, because there was no body. He just vanished!"

"It's all right, Katherine. I am sorry, calm down." Russell attempted to soothe her, but she was beyond consolation.

"It was my fault!" she wept. "If it weren't for me, he wouldn't be…as he is now. And I never even told him that I loved him!"

13

1900

"Is it such a curse to be taken care of? No, you will not work! Your place is here, to be a wife to me! You don't need to leave!" Reuben insisted.

Katherine stormed out from the privy, fastening the last few buttons of her collar.

"Perhaps I wish to work to get away from you!" She folded the blankets that made a modest bed on the floor.

He pointed. "One more night of that and you won't have a single pillow!"

"That's fine!" she said, throwing a pillow onto the bed. "I still won't sleep with you!" The bed chamber was enormous, and sunlight showered through the glass doors of an open-air balcony.

"Very well! Break your back on the floor, but you will eventually sleep where you ought!"

Katherine arranged the items on the vanity, shifting them back and forth. "I have been stuck in this prison for three days! Have mercy! Some compassion! I can earn wages. My talents are wasted if I'm locked within these walls to rot! Your servants, I am confident, are capable of managing your house! There will be no children to tend. There's no need for me to be here all the time!"

"It is your duty to be here, and yes, oh yes, there will be children!"

Katherine slammed her brush down. "That is going to be impossible when I refuse to share your bed. Let me develop a hunched back from sleeping on the floor! Perhaps then you'll toss me out!"

"Never. I've grown to love you so much."

Katherine whirled around, carrying her fit back to the vanity. "You have, really?" She picked up a floral vase. "As much as you love this vase?"

"And more!"

She threw it to the ground with full force and it shattered as she exclaimed, "Good!"

"You will not work, at all." His voice remained pleasant. "You will stay here, sleep in our bed, bear my children, delight me with the charm and grace I know you possess, accompany me in…"

Katherine moved to a cabinet and ripped open the doors as he muttered.

"…in parties and dinners. You will kiss my cheek, bow your head…"

She threw him a glare of warning before unleashing a tantrum. Item by item, plate by statue, by box, Katherine threw them all, hurling the ceramics at him. Another glass bowl broke into pieces inches from his foot.

Katherine's face burned. "Am I sweet? Am I gentle?" She chucked anything she could grasp.

Reuben covered his head.

"Go on! Be honest!" she demanded.

"Stop, Kathy! That, ah, that one was an heirloom!"

"Good!" She turned over a chair and stormed on, considering it *more* ridiculous to stop now. She ripped the silk coverlet off the bed and tried to throw it. It floated to the floor at her feet. "Do you love your prize, your wild savage?"

"Only further validation that you should not work beyond this house. You are not fit for the public! You cannot be trusted among civilized people!" Reuben laughed at her.

"I am more civilized than you!" she screamed with abandon.

Reuben thundered forward and seized her by the shoulders. "I will learn to deal with you!" His thick, mediocre face was furious and frightening. "I will learn to love you! And you will learn to behave properly!"

Stubborn tears leaked from her eyes. He let her go and she sank amid the broken glass that crunched beneath his feet as he walked around her.

۞

Somberly Katherine joined him at the breakfast table, in a nook surrounded on three sides by wide windows. Everything in the villa was high and wide, all pictures enormous, all spaces vast. She sank lower in the grandeur of it all. Katherine had powdered her face, covering the redness and attempting to mask the swelling around her eyes. She donned fine clothes like armor, a blue velvet tailor-made with a thick, stifling black waistcoat.

"So, you've finally decided to calm your little frenzy." He nibbled at the edge of a piece of toast.

She waltzed to the table, snatched a saucer, and flung it to the floor where it cracked. Reuben cleared his throat and pulled his shirt collar from the flabby skin of his neck.

He ate in the silent, tense air. Finally, after finishing his tea, Reuben said, "I never intend to stifle you. I can't understand why you will not open your heart to me. You have no reason not to. You shall never want for anything. I will ensure your comfort and health.

"Kathy, you are a queen in my palace. You will live far better than either of your sisters or any other woman in all of England! I am not a terrible man. I have never shown you unkindness. I never will. Ask me to take you to Rome to see the cathedrals, and I will, this very day! Ask me to bring you shells from the beaches of America, and I shall, promptly. If you are bored, I will bring you to the most talked about parties, and you will meet women who share your status.

"Everyone will be envious. You will have the finest, most modern fashions, if you would but ask for them. I do not wish for you to cry. I do not wish to hear you yell. Kathy, I am not your enemy, but I am your truest ally."

Katherine stared into her plate. The world spun quickly, and she remained trapped in place. A glaze veiled the clarity of her eyes. Bitterness filled her mouth. She shoved the perfectly designed breakfast away from her.

"Do you want something else? Fruit perhaps? We have the first of the season from the—"

"Nothing," she groaned.

Reuben moved toward her and put his heavy hand on hers before she could snatch it away. "You will find that resistance won't make you happy. This wall won't benefit you, it will only isolate and imprison you." He yanked the napkin from his collar and stood up. "I'm off now. I have to collect some overdue rents. If you need anything, the servants will direct you. Only until you are familiar withal. I have made it clear to them; they are at your service."

Katherine glared as he strutted off down the hallway.

1909

When Katherine climbed the stairs, she encountered Marian exiting Tarl's room.

"That was a lengthy visit," Marian huffed, restraining a bushel of stray hair, red faced. "You were gone what, all day? It's dark now!"

"Russell happens to be delightful company."

Marian searched her face, detecting the slight red tint under those glassy eyes for she said, "Been having allergies?"

"There's," Katherine dabbed her cold fingers against the skin under her puffy eyes. "There's a bitter wind making my eyes water."

"So you say. What did you and *Russell* speak of?"

"We discussed medical theories, university days and the professors and all. It has been a long time since I could talk about my passion with a fellow physician."

Marian nodded, either confused or disinterested.

"It was a productive talk, some of it in Latin, but you," she touched the back of her hand to Marian's brow even as she jerked back, flinching, "you appear flushed, Miss Boley. Are you ill?"

"I am fine." Marian's eyes flickered to the far corners of the hall before she awkwardly shuffled down the stairs.

◌⁎◌

Tray finished a cup of broth, seated in bed with a table over his lap.

"Thought you ran away again," he said to Katherine as she entered.

"I have an idea."

He slurped his meal and ignored her. Katherine gathered items he would need; a canvas, several brushes, and a small, fastened box. He drank the broth as she brought them to the nightstand, setting up a palette within the box and dipping one of the brushes into a glass of turpentine. She laid a rag beside the palette and held the canvas out to him.

Tray eyed her, setting his bowl down. "What do you want with all that?"

"I believe it'll be helpful to you. I believe you can paint. I want you to try." She took his bowl and put the canvas on the table.

"I stopped trying, *for* my health."

"For your health, you will start again," Katherine ordered.

"Is that your prescription? Expert advice?"

"You can do this." She put a brush in his hand.

"And what is it I'm supposed to render?"

"Whatever comes to mind." She dipped his brush in the paint and pointed to the canvas. "Just begin. Let it take over."

When he turned his eyes to the canvas, he appeared lost and helpless. He depressed the brush clumsily, and swept it carelessly, as if he had no control. Tension and sweat formed in the line of his forehead.

"I don't think you understand."

"I think I do," she argued, and folded her arms.

His eyes were fast becoming steeped with pain. He clenched his jaw, directing the brush in a rounded sweep, though it slipped, and he groaned. "No! You don't!" He jerked his head. "I can't. It's too—"

"Hard? You once knew how."

"It isn't that," he stammered and his hand flexed. "I'm…" He breathed faster still.

Katherine reconsidered her approach. He scribbled with the drier brush and punctured the canvas in his strength. His eyes closed, his head lolled, and he shouted as if seeing something terrible.

Katherine touched his shoulder. "Tray?"

He shoved her and swept the table off the bed. Katherine called his name until he cut her off, his face red, his voice breaking.

"You don't understand. I don't remember how!" He gasped for air and transformed, departed, entered a nightmare.

"Tray… please calm down. I thought only for the best!"

"For who?"

"For you," she cried.

"You don't know me! You can't know what's best! I can't do it. I can't take it!"

"All right!" she stammered, momentarily defeated. She chose to preserve her dignity and escaped from his presence forthwith.

Music wafted from the front parlor of Marian's house. In the red room crowded by antiques, Katherine cast away the walls with her venturesome melody. An annoyed thump resounded from the floor above, from Tarl's room, where Marian likely complained. Katherine drifted in another sphere, her eyes closed, her fingers dancing over the ivory keys intricately.

Mournful chords twisted the ardent emotions of the listener. She played a melancholy ballad, learned long ago. It began gently, unfolding toward a crescendo that climbed the scales like building thunder; powerful and tragic, in minor chords accentuated by the intermittent echo of higher octaves.

She rocked, seated on the edge of a little stool, her hair covering her back like a shawl. Katherine tilted her head to one side, her eyelashes dusting her high cheekbones. Behind closed eyes she saw dancing figures, she could sense lightning and thunder, rain and clouds, stars and darkness. She played Hilda's Song, imagining the absent breathtaking cello interlude that meant to accompany the refrain.

1900

"I'm pleased when you spend time here with me, my daughter," Hilda exclaimed. Her lace cap bounced on her head when she nodded. "I wanted a daughter, but of course Augustus wanted the boy only. Now he doesn't want me at all."

Katherine set down a tray of tea. The sunlit parlor of her new, strange home swallowed them both. Her white gown trailed behind, with a scarf fluttering behind her shoulders like wings when she moved. The silk skirt draped and moved freely, adorned with a diaphanous outer layer that shined in the light. In the bright, the diamonds on her finger glared, glittering as brilliantly as the gemstones dangling from her earlobes.

"Such a lovely wife you make," Hilda admired. "A lady, indeed!"

Across the extensive room Katherine glanced to a mounted mirror and observed how she was changed, appearing vacuous, defeated. Her dark hair was piled elegantly on top of her head and her expensive clothes covered her to paint a different picture. Although she dressed richly before, Katherine was no longer a daughter, and her new attire cloaked her in the sophistication and stateliness of the wife of a wealthy man. To herself she appeared distant, older, like an actress in the role of an aristocratic matron. The transformation was impossible to escape, as mirrors filled Reuben Koryn's villa, lining halls and climbing to ceilings in dining rooms and parlors.

"Four weeks married, my daughter, and my boy treats you well? He loves sugar on toast, does he not? Never run out of sugar."

"He treats me well," Katherine said. "The house is mine alone all day, and I have too much time to ensure everything is in order. The servants listen well."

"That is good! A sign of a powerful, successful lady. But you are unsteady. You pace anxiously."

Katherine twisted her fingers together and sat on the sofa across from Hilda's chair. "How do I stand still? The walls are immovable enough."

"It is sweet weather, is it not? I fell in love once, some time ago, in the summertime."

Katherine's attention was snared.

"I met him in a hotel." Hilda closed her eyes and conjured the memory, "In the lobby there was an ensemble. They played the saddest, most sweeping song I ever heard. I love the cello, and there was an interlude, where the other instruments hushed, and the cello played a brilliant refrain.

"He worked there. I dropped my handbag and he retrieved it for me. Oh, if ever there were eyes like those. It made me sick inside. And he asked me to dance with him, there, right there in the lobby, to that beautiful song." She hummed, her finger counting in the air. "Like that. He called it Hilda's Song and I couldn't have loved any other song more. And we danced under the balcony, on my feet…when they were strong."

Her smiling chin pointed, her fair hair gleamed richly in the light, and she laughed again. "I fell so fast, you'd think me a fool in some romantic poem. I couldn't … I couldn't catch my breath! He smelled like clean summer laundry."

Katherine laughed with a small breath, a tear rising to her eye.

"They were the best three days of my life, in the park, under the sun. We stole away to see each other. It was so exciting. I was there with my family. They searched for me constantly. I was young, but I won't forget him. I haven't yet." Hilda poked through her pearl handbag and revealed a primitive, sepia tinged and deeply creased photograph.

She passed it to Katherine, who was shocked to behold a man other than Augustus Koryn. A handsome young man in plain, unremarkable clothes stared back, frozen in time.

The tone in Hilda's voice dropped. "He had nothing, and I had to have more. No father of mine would hear of such a match. I went along. I did not protest. I let him go. I saw him cry. Have you ever seen a man cry? One of the most tragic marvels. It's a wide-open wound for a man to cry before a woman. At the hotel he was a baggage boy, paid less than the doorman. He lost his job during the days we spent together because he neglected his work, for me.

"In the end, he told me I deserved to be taken care of and he left. I was married to Augustus two months later. And my only love…he died a year after. That's what I heard." The loss returned to Hilda's face. Katherine drew back, eyes full of empathy.

"He was brave, to let me go. He told me he could not be enough for me, and he died in the street that next winter. It was too cold. Too cold without shelter for him. I could have lived with being poor, to be loved again. I can't recall another sensation, after he left. Do you know my song, the one like this," she hummed more of the melody. Despite wobbly legs, Katherine moved to seat herself at the piano.

The slick black instrument reflected the dimensions of the room. She felt out the melody, remembering the tune from when she took lessons as a little girl. Glancing back, she watched Hilda's expression melt. A faint smile wrestled beneath years of loveless solitude.

Katherine shivered on the floor of the bedchamber. Reuben removed her blanket and opened the window as soon as she fell asleep. He stared at her, the hair rising on her arms, discomfort pinching her face as she slept. A somber howl was carried in on the wind. Shadows played among the empty shelves and across the bare dresser top.

With a wince, Katherine awoke. He watched her, waiting. Sleepily she glanced around her, the blanket and pillow gone. She glared at Reuben. Quietly he peeled back a corner of the quilt on the bed.

She stomped to the window to pull in the shutter. "I hate you." She passed through the bedchamber door and slammed it behind her.

Katherine ambled tiredly down gold carpeted stairs, concentrating on keeping her balance. Her robe trailed two steps behind her, blue in the dimness, white in light. Once at the bottom she proceeded through a hallway adorned with hundreds of clocks, keeping time together in a clamor of tapping, chiming, and click-ing. From the hall, she entered a warm study.

The tomb that was the study, before Katherine began to frequent its sanctuary, had been left neglected for years. Unused, unopened leather-bound volumes packed rising shelves. Katherine crept inside and lowered herself onto a leather couch. It was the only room in the house that she did not despise, for Reuben never entered the study.

For Katherine there was comfort among the books. She dragged a fur rug from the floor to cover her body. Before she fell asleep, her cheek sticking to the slick leather, she allowed her vision to slip out of focus, staring at the spines of books, soon imagining the old library surrounding her instead. She could picture his face clearly, as always, before drifting into dreams. His sad eyes rarely made for pleasant dreaming.

❧ 14 ❧

Upon arriving at Madison Estate for a picnic, Katherine was caught unaware by her parents' targeted eccentricity.

"Oh! Honey!" Winifred exclaimed. "Look at you, so grown!" She squeezed Katherine's confused face.

Her parents eagerly dragged her across the lawn. Reuben greeted Arnold and Caleb, who smoked their cigars on the porch. The lawn stretched brightly around the house, the garden flowers that lined it waving in the breeze. Hat strings and coat tails fluttered in the wind.

"Look at our darling eldest. Ted, isn't she such an accomplished lady!" Winifred gasped.

Theodore put an arm around his wife. Winifred hugged him while he approvingly surveyed Katherine. "Marvelous! What change a wedding brings."

Katherine rolled her eyes in disgust. They strolled with her to a table and chairs set on the porch and Winifred took a seat next to Katherine, clutching her hand and grinning ridiculously. The first excruciating hour or less, Katherine sat listening to Reuben drone on and on about the maids' unanimous adoration of her and her skills at remodeling the bed chamber.

At that elaboration she glared and snapped, "I broke it all and you say that's remodeling?"

Winifred's mouth dropped open a moment until Reuben laughed.

"My sweet dear." He smiled at his mother-in-law. "She likes to make such jests!"

Theodore and Winifred erupted with phony, broken laughter.

Katherine's head throbbed. The more they leaned in, interested in Reuben's babble about soil and properties, the more Katherine slipped away into another realm. She withdrew to stare at them, laughing stupidly, bragging about her happiness and theirs.

"Oh, my boy, what say you of our extension? With the names combined, Koryn and Madison, a new branch of our enterprises, we drive up from the south edge of Portsea island," Theodore suggested with his glass in a wispy hand. "Up into Cosham. Lovely place for summer homes."

Winifred grinned, gripping Katherine's hand and nodding as if attending a most interesting conversation.

"What a wonderful idea, of course! We shall be expanding tremendously," Reuben asserted.

"Come along, son. I'd like to show you one of my plans." Theodore directed and Reuben followed.

Winifred leapt after them. "What plans?"

"I thought of planting hedges and walls to create a maze of a garden," Theodore explained.

"A maze! Good heavens, joyousness!" Winifred grasped her husband's arm. They frolicked away, and Katherine was glad to remain in isolation, savoring the fading of their voices.

Eliza slid into a chair next to her. "He's not as handsome as some men, but I believe he cares for you very much." The flawless innocence and sincerity in her face challenged Katherine's determined aloofness.

Leaning her cheek on a fist, Katherine stared at her sister, the breeze nudging the neatly rolled curls against Eliza's neck.

"I came to love Arnold for his care of me and we grew in love together." Eliza waited, but Katherine said nothing.

Eliza patted her hand. "Oh darling, won't you brighten up?"

"Of course, let me transform myself." Katherine smiled cynically.

Drawing her chin to her chest before rising, Eliza said, "Try and relax a little. The stress of a new marriage seems to be wearing on you."

In a life based on charades and empty feelings staged as full, Katherine could not be certain whether the glows on her sisters' smiling faces were genuine or not. Still, she was envious of their joy, and silently lamented over her own.

The family gathered close and Dorothea, with the assistance of her mother, announced that she was with child. Eliza shrieked, releasing what appeared to be pure elation. Reuben toasted with Arnold and Theodore. Their laughter reached Katherine, who roamed the edge of the garden, distant from the rest. They drank in celebration, speaking at once to promote their plans.

Caleb took solitude from the party as well, pacing the grounds with a bottle of bourbon close to his mouth. Katherine strode toward him and snatched the bottle from his grip. A good portion spilled on his unexpected face. She whirled around and thrust it into the trees.

Caleb stiffened, a shocked and pitiful statue with bloodshot eyes, his hands spread empty before him in disbelief. Katherine gave him no further regard and advanced toward the house.

"Well, this is lovely news isn't it?" Katherine slipped into their midst.

Eliza and their mother paused, holding Dorothea's blessed stomach.

"Yes it is!" Eliza smiled. "A baby! We shall be aunts, Katherine! And Grandmother, and Grandfather!" She held her father's hand in her small white fingers.

"Yes," Katherine said. "Most certainly it's miraculous. Such a blessing." Their smiles faded at the confrontational tone of her voice. "And don't you deserve it."

"What is it you imply?" Dorothea cried.

Eliza looked from one to the other. "Why, it implies nothing, dear."

"Eliza," Arnold said. "Shh." He backed her away from her sisters.

"Poor little thing," Katherine said. "If he's a boy, we can only hope that he'll be as wise and sober as his father. What a happy, cursed life to be born into! But let us celebrate as though he will *truly* be loved, as though he will truly be free and happy."

"Katherine!" Theodore barked.

Reuben dropped his glass and seized her by the arm in one swoop. He dragged her off the porch. As they went, Dorothea stammered, and their mother squawked.

"You've got no more manners than a barbarian! What is the matter with you? Have you lost your sense?" Reuben yelled.

"I'm fine, nothing's wrong with me! It's you who have no sense!" Katherine sneered.

He turned her roughly and tapped her cheek with a light slap. Her eyes burned with heat.

"You will be controlled!"

The family hushed. Reuben ordered, "Don't you speak another syllable. You will go back and respect your sister, and apologize to your father and me, who you have completely disgraced!"

"I disgrace *you*?"

"Yes! You're not behaving as a proper wife! Now you come back and behave," he yowled, red and flabby in the face. "We'll all have a bloody wonderful time!" His voice cracked at the end.

"You go back," she hissed. "And have *yourself* a wonderful time!" Katherine slapped him back and shoved past him to stride toward the street. Reuben bristled, yet allowed her to run for a while.

They were excited at first, as well as intrigued to see Katherine return to the tavern. When she slumped onto a stool and ordered scotch from the young-faced bartender, they noticed the alteration in her manner. Her eyes were shrouded with brewing fury, and her formerly fanciful hair hung disheveled, tendrils fallen in her face. A contradiction she was, in fine, expensive clothing and muddy boots soiling the hem of her light-colored skirt. She drank as smoke encircled her.

"Are you unwell, Katherine?" Wilkins asked.

"Look at me!" She snatched his cigarette and pulled a drag from it.

"You didn't quit, did you," he declared.

"No. I didn't quit." She took another drink, and the blood filled her cheeks.

By the stage, Jeff leapt from his bench as two scrappers rumbled into the piano. Wilkins, taking no notice of the fray, propped an elbow on the counter for a closer look at Katherine. "I wish I knew more. No one's seen you."

"Wilkins—" She downed the rest of her scotch. "I'm a prisoner ... in a cage." She waved her clammy hand like a white bird in his face.

"Katherine!" Jeff dodged the dancers crowding the floor. "Katherine, we need a verse! Calm our riots!" He was flushed and panting.

"Come on, Katherine." Wilkins smiled. "Have you forgotten about us?"

"I have it..." She slumped against the bar, slamming the glass down. "I have it!" As she moved toward the stage, Wilkins called for quiet, raising his arms over the heads in the crowd.

When she climbed onto the stage, the patrons stilled. The room however, spun around her. She blinked tearfully. The hush fell as soon as she began, impassioned and despondent:

"The air has thickened now

As if the dark clouds above,
Vicious with scorn,
Descend much lower than they've dared before…
And I am pressed to find
Something to replace what ought to be,
The presence I cannot feel, although
I've detected it like an elusive visitor.
In my enclosure, the air is merciless.
I'm drowsy, elsewhere, and whence I move,
I am heavy and prevented,
Melted by arduous air.
Haunted by an empty ache,
That cannot be relieved.
Caught in my own destruction,
Yet he holds me in a dream.
And I close my eyes." Tears slipped down her cheeks, cooling them. Smoke floated in the air and the audience listened with pity. "I think I have him to hold again,

But no. Memory is a tormentor.
Tranquility crushes, a prolonged death,
Little by little, in thickening air.
I am no longer here.
I do *not* long for him.
I am not crippled. Not broken." She staggered and caught her balance, wiping her face with the back of her hand. "We lie in dreamlike states.

We lie in emotional death." Katherine collapsed as Wilkins reached up to carry her down.

They hesitantly clapped, raising eyebrows and scratching heads. Someone whistled and was duly smacked. Wilkins assisted her back to a stool, where her head dropped onto her arms and she spilled bitter tears on the bar.

Jeff touched her shoulder asking, "What can we do?"

"Deliver me from the one who has soured my existence! Can you do that?" She slapped her hand on the bar and the bartender, taking it as a request for a refill, poured one swiftly. The glass scarcely touched the counter before Katherine snatched it from his hand and tipped it back at her mouth.

"I can't live like this!" Her glazed eyes pleaded as she wept. "What meaning is there to anything now? What have I done?"

Wilkins took her firmly by the shoulders and asked, "What's happened? What's wrong with you?"

The door burst open, and a tall, chubby figure entered with his nose in the air. Wilkins eyed the well-dressed man who waltzed in behind Katherine, and he protested when Reuben took her by the arm.

"Home, Kathy! What do you think you're doing here?"

"Who's Kathy? She's not *me*! And you get out! You're not welcome here!"

"I have had enough!" Reuben barked. "We're going!"

"Take your hands off me!" she slurred and the men around them closed in.

"Take your hands off the lady!" Wilkins demanded.

"She's my *wife*! I shall insist the lot of you stand back!"

"Get him off her!" Jeff rallied and they rushed in. The constable and ten policemen poured in, clubs out and arms tearing between the angry drunks and Reuben.

Reuben managed to wrestle Katherine outside, leaving the officials to control the tavern. On the way to the carriage, Katherine hit and elbowed him, weeping and cursing.

"I won't tolerate this!" Reuben shoved her into the carriage, jumped in, and ordered the driver, "Home!"

She kicked him until he pinned her and locked her wrists in his fat hands. Her screaming echoed through the streets in the wake of the shaking carriage.

1909

Katherine crouched on her heels before the smoldering fire in her bedroom. Hopelessly, the black smoke billowed into her face and coughing, she stabbed and stirred at the charred log. Darkness ruled the house. Shadows stretched along the walls like Katherine's dark hair down her back. From across the hallway, she could hear Tarl in his room, banging into furniture as it sounded. The sparks snapped at her hand. She held the poker in the embers, her eyes watering from the smoke.

"Trayten…" Katherine rubbed the back of her neck, staring at the black mass of charred wood. Merely a wall away, he was farther from her than ever, even though she had found him. She stabbed the poker into the fireplace and went to the window.

A dismal assemblage of turquoise clouds hovered low over the inky sea. Wind rushed in the shivering grasses between patches of electric white snow. Her stomach flipped when she perceived a seated figure on the end of the dock. A halo of smoke encircled his head. Immediately she snatched her coat.

❧

As Katherine jogged down the dock she tried to call out, yet she could hardly speak. Frosty air struck her face, which appeared like a moon in the murky night. Her eyes were wide and fearful, and deeper than the sea.

He sat in his chair on the edge of the dock, smoking. Katherine delayed her approach, although her heart raced on. She bit back the impulse to hold him and choked on calling him 'Trayten.' Instead she forced herself to stop behind him and attempt to catch her breath. He muttered something lowly, lifelessly, and hauntingly.

"Under the moonlight there—" he took a drag.

Katherine drew back, clinging to her coat while the wind pulled at her hair. "Was it another dream?"

"Why. Do you think you would understand?" He waved her away. "Go on back, I'm staying here."

"It's so cold." As tightly as she might, she embraced herself.

"Wouldn't want me to catch a fever? Wouldn't want me to be incapacitated?"

She exhaled with exhaustion at his tone.

"A fever would be exciting at least." He laughed and with the cigarette between his teeth began to roll toward the ocean.

"Tray," she stepped after him instinctively. "What are you—"

He stopped.

"Did you think I was going to roll myself off the edge and find my own end?" Turning, he looked at her.

"No. You're smarter—"

"I wouldn't give anyone that satisfaction!" was his short reply.

"You're not even making sense."

"Yea, I'm not. Well, you don't make sense to me. So, how do *you* like it? What do you want from me?"

"I don't want to fight with you," she whispered.

His eyes were red-rimmed.

"Are you afraid to sleep?" she asked carefully.

"Don't even try. I warned you—"

"Tray, do you fear your nights because of the dreams?"

"Just stop!"

"You see things, things you knew." Her throat tightened.

"I don't know anything, I don't! You never stop when I tell you to stop!" He wheeled around to face her abruptly. "I can't put anything together and what's the point? Eight years! No one has found me. And what happens if I *do* remember, and the life that I left has nothing to offer but consequences? What if I discovered the truth of loneliness graver than this? I'm better off in darkness. I have no one, no one who cared. If I did they would've found me, and since they haven't, I'd rather never know for sure."

As calmly as she could, she sat on the dock and grappled with whether to confess herself to him. Yet she feared he would not yet receive the truth, he was still so far away, so cynical and removed. More than that, after eight years of searching for him, she wanted to be found. Katherine hungered for it. Long ago it was he who sought her out and knew her better than anyone. She wanted to believe that the same passion that drove him then could restore his memory now. He eyed her in her contemplation.

Finally she asked, "Do you think no one cared about you?"

"What should I think?"

"Think that, hope and pray that, there was someone, *is* someone who loves you, who is trying to find you. If it were me, I would hang on to that belief." Katherine shivered and rubbed her hands over her arms.

"How easy it is for you to say this. But hope runs dry after so long, and prayers spread thin until eventually, years pass and you're still alone." With stiff, bluish fingers, Tray lit a fresh cigarette from the end of the one that was spent and took a drag. "No one has come for me. And even if someone came, what good am I now?"

"You're alive! God must have something planned for you," she submitted.

"I'm not really seeing any possibilities in my life."

Shades of night passed between them in variations of blue, and Tray implored with lifeless words that floated as white clouds out to sea, "So, what is it you want from me? Really. I have nothing of worth for you. I have no story to tell. Are you trying to prove yourself? Are you so arrogant to believe that your talent and skill can cure me? What is it?"

"I want to help you." A tear escaped down her cheek.

"Why do you cry?"

She smeared the tear with the back of her hand and exhaled without a word.

"Is it pity?" he asked.

"No."

"What? Stop!" He lowered his voice. "Stop crying. Please."

Turning her face to the sea, she willed herself to stop, and continued to lose the battle. Katherine wished the dark were deeper, in order to hide. She sat vulnerable and embarrassed at his feet. Inelegantly his hand extended, and his rough fingers grazed her cheek. Her heart seized and her breath stopped short. When Katherine glanced at his face, he left his fingertips lingering against her skin, until he wiped the tear away.

After a moment of insufferable silence, Tray breathed carefully. "I would say," he hesitated, caught and held by her stare, "that a lady like you should never cry."

Katherine swallowed, although her throat was dry and she sat still, lest he should retreat. For Trayten sat before her, recognizable by the warmth in his eyes, appearing as the man who knew her, his touch still charged with electricity.

"You *would* say, but won't?" she asked shyly.

Trayten slipped away, however gentleness lingered in the face that viewed her as a stranger. "You, Mrs. Koryn, Katherine, I'm perplexed by your interest in my lost cause."

"It's reasonable for you to question my intentions," Katherine delivered from the script she had written herself, falling into the part she decided to play. "One day I'm sure you will understand. Only, not now." Icy wind climbed over her skin. "Shall I take you in?"

"Please. Leave me out here alone."

"But it's so cold."

"It helps to face it." He stared at the water. "That which brought me here, my enemy, the one who delivered me into captivity. I want to face it. I need to face it for a while."

Katherine forced a smile through the invading tears and arose. Unable to resist, she swept the hair from his eyes and kissed him on the cheek. Her hair waved warm against his face fleetingly. When she reluctantly walked away, he directed his eyes to the sky.

1900

The steamship was crowded with guests, clustered on the polished decks beneath lantern glow and twinkling starlight. It drifted gently and languidly through deep night waters in the harbor. Laughter and wine, fine food, and the sounds of the Portsmouth Symphony enlivened the floating event.

Diamond earrings dripped from her earlobes, shooting sparks of light against the graceful curve of her neck. Her hair was swept up smoothly and tangles of shiny curls fell down in back. Katherine moved under the mahogany arch that served as a gate into the dining room. Her white silk gown accentuated her figure and dragged the floor after her footsteps.

Aware of the many gazes following her, she carried herself with poise and confidence. Under the twinkling gas lights, the band of diamonds glittered on her hand. She smoothed the front of her gown. Her dazzling eyes reflected bright indigo hues in the lanterns' warm luminescence. They darkened to black as she caught sight of a figure approaching. She breathed in dread.

"Ah! There's my jewel!" Reuben extended his hand, calling her toward his gathering of landlords. "My wife, come and greet my associates!"

Dutifully Katherine neared and the bearing pressure of his fat hand closed around her elbow. As he introduced each person, she would force an interested lift of an eyebrow or the parting of her lips and a smile. She shook sweaty hands and suffered a few awkward, customary kisses on her cheeks. Beneath her performance, the torment ran deep.

Hours entrapped by such showing and greeting provoked Katherine to seek escape. She went through the dining room, fingers rummaging in her handbag. Focused on the task of searching for what she needed, and not finding it, she neglected to watch where she was going. Nothing slowed her. A waiter in crisp white livery dove from her path. She would have run right into him otherwise.

Outside on deck, she breathed in deeply and released white smoke into the night air. A cigarette clutched tightly between her knuckles. With her back against a wall, she stared at her fingers, acknowledging how she had gleaned his habit and taking some measure of comfort in that. She bit her lower lip, lost in anguish and regret.

The world had faded to the volume of her thoughts until an echo rang sharp through her ears. Clean and exact. Footsteps. They pulled her back from tormented deliberation. Katherine lifted her eyes to stare into the face of a phantom.

Trayten, attired in a white shirt and white trousers, uniform-like in fashion, faced her with nothing to say. He appeared sharp, the contrast between his smooth, clear skin and his black hair enhancing his beauty. His eyes gleamed, as black as his hair, and they cut her in two. Without a word, Katherine understood the anguish and ire they held.

Paralysis gripped her at the sight of him. A glacial demeanor replaced the warmth she once knew. Perhaps he intended the silence to unnerve her. She desired to speak yet could not.

Standing up from against the wall, she took a nervous drag of the cigarette and searched his grave face. He was more dashing than she recalled, and painfully so. Still, the sharpness in his eyes dispatched her. Foolish and desperate to break the silence she muttered, "I heard about Jack and I'm sorry."

His eyes narrowed, harshness in them. Under the perpetual stare she was chipped away and fidgeted, trapped, and gasping for air.

"Trayten, please."

As if it were not his name, as if she had no voice, he was unmoved. Were they strangers? Did he hate her? Katherine groaned and flicked the cigarette over the rail.

"What am I to say?" she pleaded, her voice faltering and her composure failing.

"How should I know that?" he answered gruffly.

"Do you wish me to explain?"

"Will it change anything? I know…about *him*. I know you are another man's wife, a man like your father, a man with power and money. What is there to explain?" The ardor in his tone and the fury of his eyes burned.

"You don't know anything."

"I know *you*. And as much as I hate to say it, I guess you are where you always belonged." He appeared cruel and unfamiliar.

Katherine chewed on words she was reluctant to speak.

"I haven't seen you in so long." She stepped toward him.

He moved beyond her reach. "You did not see *me*, but I saw you!"

Katherine's mouth opened but before she could form a word, Reuben called, "My wife, where are you? Kathy?" His footsteps followed.

She whirled around, compelled to disappear. Trayten caught her by the arm.

"Go to him! I need no explanation. All is clear." He released her.

Desperate fear clutched her, and she was regretful to hear Reuben call again. "I *have* to."

She ran down the hall, rounded the corner into the dining room, and Reuben blocked her path. "Ah, come along. There's dancing!" He blinked rapidly and caught her wrist.

Dragged behind his giant strides, Katherine jogged, unable to glance back. Ahead of them clamored the banging of drums and fervent fiddling conducive to a heated dance.

Into large and forceful arms Katherine fell subject. Terribly awkward to accommodate and not at all graceful, Reuben spun her violently and trampled her feet. Foolishly they tripped into other couples. As artfully as Katherine could exude dignity, she could not find enough diligence or balance to make dancing with her husband appear graceful.

"Smile Kathy, this is your celebration!" He swept her around and dipped her back, cracking her spine.

Amid the chaos Katherine caught sight of Trayten from the corner of her eye. At the outer edge of the dancefloor, he dragged an unremarkable scullery maid by the hand. Katherine was filled with alarm. He danced closely with her, his lips hovering near her ear.

For a song that dragged on incessantly, Katherine suffered to witness as he charmed another, close in his embrace. His hands moved along the other woman's waist and the small of her back. His eyes met with hers and lingered on her confused, yet hopeful expression.

Trampled by Reuben's dancing, and battling to turn them where she could see, burning jealousy ripped through Katherine.

"Hey, Koryn, you old dog! She's lovelier than you said."

An old man tapped them, and Katherine beamed an insincere smile as Reuben exclaimed in mid twirl, "Of course. I am worth too much to settle on mediocre. Isn't the boat well designed? Why, everything she's near takes on a flush of elegance. You should see our home. It is definitely transformed by the touch of Katherine."

"Brilliant! Mrs. Koryn, my wife Edna would love to have you pop round for decorating ideas." The old man waltzed a young lady in his arms. Katherine could understand the suffering behind her eyes.

"Brilliant," she said, unable to resist. "Perhaps, Edna could invite me over, if she wants ideas."

"Good deal, Mr. Bucking, that would be splendid for my Kathy." Reuben ignored her. "You telegraph and I'll send her when it is convenient for you."

Katherine's eyes flickered back toward Trayten. He met her gaze and his lips pressed against the other woman's mouth. Mr. Bucking's chiding tone eclipsed somehow the rage filled reaction welling up inside of her and she was twirled out of view of Trayten.

"Edna, did you not thank Mr. Koryn for his invitation?" Mr. Bucking said to Reuben, "Forgetful."

When the young Mrs. Bucking timidly bowed her head, Katherine nudged her. "Edna, you telegraph *me* and I'll come take you out, whenever you have need and it's convenient for *you*."

Mr. Bucking twisted his face bitterly. Katherine smiled gently, with hostile lights in her eyes. Before Reuben could dangerously dip her back once more and chide her for her outburst, she stood firmly in place and with her wrists rested at his neck said, "It seems as though a pair of caterers are slacking and taking advantage of our celebration!"

Her eyes were fierce. Reuben glanced around to catch a glimpse of Trayten from the back in uniform. With firm fingers she forced his chubby face back in her direction. "You carry on and tell Mr. Alfred and Mr. Cosage about your newest investment. Let me herd them back to the kitchen!"

The moment she broke loose from him, he seized her wrist. "My love—"

"Yes?"

"Make sure their wages for tonight are cut, by half!"

Sighing in relief Katherine said, "Of course."

Trayten was rudely struck by a hand on his collar, gripping and tearing him from the maid swooning under his charms. Katherine dragged him from the dining room and down a small flight of stairs. He staggered momentarily, then followed fast behind her. Once into a small galley she slammed the door behind them. Hot eyes pinned him against a wall, and she shook her finger. "You tell me what that was supposed to mean!"

"You've got your husband." He adjusted his collar, calm except for his disheveled hair.

"Are you blind? You say that you have seen me. You haven't seen anything! Can't you understand? Can't you try?"

"Listen to you! Understand? How can I? You wake up one morning and decide to cut me from your life, Katherine! Or had it been your plan all along? I waited, and I waited for you, for nothing! I was ready to sacrifice everything for you, and I *did*! But I'm not enough for you. And you couldn't even tell me you were finished with me. Instead you disappear and leave me in the dark!"

"Please, stop! You don't understand!" Her mind raced to collect her thoughts, struggling to see clearly, to breathe.

"Oh, I think I understand you now." He looked at her in disappointment.

"I've been driven mad without you, unable to reach you. How could I tell you? How else can I explain it to you, it wasn't my choice!" she cried, desirous to believe it.

"Not your choice? After everything between us, you're going to stand here and lie to my face? I've watched you smiling on his arm in the streets!"

"This isn't *my* choice!"

"Even if that were true, you don't seem to be too unhappy with it. Look at you: new clothes, priceless jewelry." He looked her up and down.

"Trayten, I had no other choice—"

"Not in your mind, no. I guess you wouldn't see me, *us*, as a choice. How could you, when you have become, or worse, you always were a shallow, soulless materialist?"

"I'm not! You don't understand!" When she tried to catch his gaze, he turned away.

"Why else couldn't you say no?" His sharp gaze stabbed her. "If not for the money?"

Katherine answered, hating herself as she admitted, "I would be completely cast out."

"From the comfort of your riches! Right?"

"From my family, from the only life I've ever known." Even as she said the words, she knew they could not justify her betrayal.

"I can't even look at you." He closed his eyes and stepped back.

"Please!" Desperate to stop him from walking away, she begged, "Tray, stop there!"

He hesitated.

"You have to know that I never wanted it this way for us." Katherine's heart beat furiously.

"So walk away, Katherine." His eyes glistened. "Now! Just *be free*!"

"It's not that easy!" Her knees locked, her eyes filled with fears and then tears. "I can't just *be* free!"

"Then you are exactly what you said you hated." With finalizing words, he crushed her.

"Wait, please! Don't leave me!"

He left her, for she had already left him.

The echo of his footsteps faded from the stairwell. She wiped her eyes while her body vibrated from the force of their collision and the agony of his displeasure. There was no mask, no armor, and no amount of acting that could cover her disgrace. Katherine sank down and placed her hands on the floor, her vision fuzzy, her head spinning. The only way to prevent blacking out entirely was to release a flood of bitter tears.

1903

Dear Trayten,

Oh, how frightful is the night, and the impression of death that it brings. If your fate is equal to this, I might find your resting place. In the churchyards of Portland I began roaming, calculating, reading every weathered headstone; each one in dread that I may find your name.

With ample rain, I'm ill from tromping about drenched and alone, inhaling miasmic air. Fresh graves stir my empathy for the ones they left behind. It overwhelms me, and I wonder whether I am one, left behind.

I plucked a branch and laid it on the freshly tilled earth of a new grave. I closed my eyes and saw you, stiff in a casket. I fell and was covered with mud, the earth pliable and damp. This is how I am all the time now; cold, soiled, and trudging through the mire.

When I did not find you in Portland, I scoured the peninsula, traveling to small hamlets one by one, roaming the graveyards. And I miss our Angelle beyond words. Yet I do this for her as well.

I arrive most often at night. I carry my lantern through quiet darkness, taking refuge in the shadows to avoid the ridicule and questions that accompany the light of day. I fear my appearance repels other people.

'A beggar,' 'a mad woman,' they taunt when I am seen. Though it stings to bear any insult, I understand they can think little else, seeing me in my wrinkled, filthy clothes trimmed with mud. In the daylight, in travel, the mud hardens at the edge of my skirts. There is nowhere to stop and restore myself, and no resources to spare.

All money is kept with Eliza for the care of our daughter. I could not bring myself to travel in luxury, in search of you, when *you could be suffering. So there is no time to rest, and I have not stopped. I maintain perpetual motion.*

I lost my carriage in the town of Yeovil and have been traveling on foot. In Yeovil the cemetery caretaker reported me as a grave robber, dirty as I am, and lurking about the graves as I was. The constable detained me directly. I was locked up for one night.

I would have slept I suppose, if it weren't for the constant lecturing and scolding I received from an overzealous jailer. When I had enough, I affirmed that I needed no lessons in morals from a backward simpleton and had I not been clutching the bars at this time, he wouldn't have struck my knuckles. Bruises blend well under days worth of dirt and grime.

In the morning they released me, which proved to be less liberating than I had hoped. It was daylight, harsh daylight, a perfect viewing ground for the townspeople. I stumbled out of that jail like an old drunk, blinded by the sun, and utterly grotesque. I felt pity for those who saw me, yet their hostility quickly turned my pity to distrust.

Their taunting criticisms stripped me of any compassion. I'm sure in the noise and confusion I may have remarked something along the lines of them being 'ignorant and pathetic for having nothing to do but persecute one outsider.'

Never call the citizens of Yeovil 'ignorant and pathetic.'

They took my carriage and of course my horse along with it. Then they expected I should leave immediately.

I cannot begin to explain how I am changing. My darling, so many things your absence has done to me and the newest discovery is humility. Perhaps I'm losing my wit, my edge. It may have been stolen. When one realizes they have lost all that ever mattered, pride is baseless.

I know pride led to my downfall.

Nevertheless, I go on searching for you because of the constant thought that revolves in my mind; that you are near, that tomorrow I may find you. Each and every hour, I must think: tomorrow we may finally begin forever.

Waiting for forever,
  Katherine.

1909

Tray sat gazing through his window. In patches throughout the grass, the recently fallen snow gleamed, wet and melting slow. His chin and jaw were swathed with a thick shaving lather, and he held a mirror in one hand on his lap. Katherine draped a towel around his neck and knelt at his feet, a straight razor in her fingers.

With a coy smile she asked, "You're not going to have a fit once I begin, are you? You'd put your neck in jeopardy." A playful light streaked through her eyes.

"Get on with it. I am trying to trust you." He remained serious, his posture rigid.

Katherine bent over him, hesitating to touch his forehead and gently tilt his head back. She carefully shaved upward from the base of his neck. The razor scratched against his coarse stubble.

She withheld all praise of him. Were it not for the deep chasm between them, she would have complimented him easily. Instead she silently appreciated him, her eyes feasting on the forms of his face; she knew them well, the smooth feel of his skin, the firm corners of his jaw. Smiling she said, "This is a leap forward. This trust."

"Don't get too excited," he said through clenched teeth. "I'd surely slice myself with these shaky hands. You'll have to do. Go on."

"There's a safe, clean man behind these wild whiskers. Your eyes are already clearer."

"Where did you find a razor?" he muttered. She paused to wipe the blade on a towel and continued working, concentrating on the curve of his chin. Inch by inch, more of the man she remembered was revealed.

"I took it from Marian's sleeve while she was sleeping. One of many."

Tray scoffed and she corrected his face with her hand. "Be still. Actually, she's gone today. I went into Mr. Frangul's cabinet."

"Oh yes, the dipsomaniac."

"What a word! Do you even know what it means?" she giggled.

"Of course, I do. I can smell him before he passes my room. And I've seen him," Tray paused as she shaved under his bottom lip diligently, then as she wiped the blade he went on. "Out on the grounds, bottle to his mouth. He's a useless man. I wonder how he pays his board."

"Marian appreciates him."

"What?" Tray released a short laugh, much like a cough.

"They are always together in various rooms and who knows where they are *this* early in the morning. It's obvious there's something between them. She's always flushed. I've been a hapless witness to their attraction one time too many."

Tray cringed. She cleared the last of the shaving lather from his face and paused, gazing at him with a nostalgic gleam in her eyes. He noticed her laughter melt into sorrowful silence. When his gaze finally struck her, Katherine shrugged and sighed. "You're almost tame."

"Almost." He laid eyes on himself as she brought the mirror to his face.

"Yes." She bit her lip. Crouched before him, she rested back on her heels and after sitting in the silent air, bundled the towel and took up the basin of soapy water. "I'm glad for Marian though."

"Why?" Tray lingered in the mirror, pinching his cheek and studying his smooth skin with a frown.

"She's distracted lately. It makes my work easier."

"And her cooking has improved." He set the mirror aside.

"She hasn't cooked for days. I've been taking care of that." Katherine smiled sheepishly.

"Why weren't you cooking from the start?" he asked, acting enraged.

She laughed, flattered.

He glanced at the window. "Look at that wind. This place is desolate."

"And what sort of place would you prefer?"

"I can't be sure. Somewhere inhabited at least. Busy. More people. Here it's too quiet, too forsaken."

She sat in the chair beside him. They kept their eyes on the sea beyond the window. It trapped them, ever moving and never leaving.

"Of course, what else do I know but here?" Tray uttered.

"What *do* you know?" Katherine glanced from his face to his hands, which twisted together in his lap. She imagined he would never speak, until distantly he murmured, as if from a dream, with eyes locked on the sea.

"It sounds ridiculous, but I think I know that the name Hector means 'restraint.'"

Katherine held her breath.

"Terrible name," he laughed. She bit her tongue and he added, "And George is 'farmer.' I'm sure that Marian must mean 'crab-by'… or 'crone.'"

She could not muster a laugh at his joke, too shocked to breathe. Tray searched the window as though pulling sparse knowledge through the thick glass. "And Calandria is 'beautiful one.'"

Katherine slid to the edge of her chair, heart thumping. Wide eyed and breathless she asked, "Do you know my name?"

"No…I cannot think of Katherine. I don't," he scratched his

chin, "I don't know why but sometimes names circulate in my mind."

"What about Angelle?"

"Messenger."

When she said nothing more, he finally looked at her. She was caught in the throes of apprehension.

He asked, "How about that, Doctor?"

"It's, it's wonderful."

✿ 16 ✿

Until long after dark Katherine paced the cluttered front parlor. It was not an easy feat, as crowded and cramped as the room was. With sweaty palms and unfurling angst, Katherine could not sit still.

"Hector!" She snapped her fingers. Pondering, she glanced at one of the many clocks adorning the gaudy walls.

When Marian finally emerged from the night, her hair puffed and frizzing in every direction, she startled Katherine. Her freckles were dark due to the color in her cheeks. She sighed heavily. She threw her head and shoulders back, swaggering in alone; coat buttoned askew and resting crooked down her front.

"I'm a bit surprised to find you up, Mrs. Koryn," Marian commented.

"Evening, Miss Boley." With great restraint, Katherine pulled back her elation, wary of how it might appear.

Marian cleared her throat. She plopped down on the settee, folded her hands, and asked, "Is he asleep?"

"He has been sleeping for a while, yes."

"Very well," Marian murmured, laughing with a squeak. She cast a tentative gaze on Katherine. "Is there something else?"

"Did you have an interesting day out? All day?"

Marian snickered again, wiping the corner of her eye. She kicked up her feet and reclined, her boots resting on the arm of the settee. The unruly blaze of red hair jutted from her white forehead. "You've waited up just to ask me about my day?"

"Miss Boley, I have some wonderful news. I've been waiting to tell you."

"Is that so."

"There's hope, Miss Boley, great hope!" Katherine burst, giddy as a child.

"Ah yes, I suppose maybe there *is* hope for you."

"Hope for Tray," Katherine said.

"T.B.?"

"Yes, Tray. I stumbled into a remarkable discovery today! Unexpected yet brilliant! I could hardly contain my joy!"

"What!" Marian groaned impatiently.

The front door sprang open and slammed against the wall as Tarl slithered over the threshold. His head teetered as he hissed at Marian, "Hi." He passed the hall and she giggled deep in her throat, snorting.

Katherine winced after a clatter resounded. The hall table must have disrupted his path.

"Miss Boley, please listen. Tray rambled off some things from his past. They were certain names, and the meanings of those names. He was concentrating, entirely focused. He's improving and there's hope!"

"I don't know about that. Eight years and he has had no clear recollection of a single thing other than what he's seen or heard here." She dismissed Katherine's testimony with a salute of her hand.

"I believe it was a memory. He's coming back! We may discover him after all!"

"He must have read them in a book, Mrs. Koryn. Simple as that." She rubbed her temple, closing her eyes and speaking firmly, "I want T.B. to get well as much as you do. But I object to any false hopes, especially if they may disappoint him. There's no need to be emotional and excite him, only to let him down. I can't have it."

"There are no books of the sort here."

"Excuse me, but that's a hasty assumption."

"There are none. I checked," Katherine confirmed. "Go on, be honest with me. You don't want to believe it, but he has a life out there, and it's trying to resurface—"

"Isn't your rent due?"

"I set the money on your desk."

"You went into my room?"

"While I was searching your books," Katherine added. "I'm doing you a favor. I'm helping him."

"You are pressuring him. You haven't done anything but bother his peace of mind."

"He hasn't been at peace here." All joy drained from Katherine's expression as she looked down at Marian. "And despite what you think, he is changing. He's remembering. Don't you want him to get well? Don't you want him to get back to where he belongs?" It was a test, for Katherine was certain she already knew the answer.

Marian grunted, pulling at her ratted hair.

"Maybe you don't. Maybe you'd be happy if he never recovered. But you can't stand in the way of what is meant to be, where he is meant to be," Katherine declared.

1900

"Dear, can I bring you anything more?" Denis waddled into the darkened den carrying another pillow for the aching head of his bride.

Myra's hair, like a fluffy beacon, caught the light from the low burning fire beside which she lay on a chaise lounge. With a hand pressed to her forehead she reminded him, "I asked you to leave me be. I am trying to recover from your racket, pounding about all day."

"I was fixing the creak in the stair, like you told me—"

"I don't care! I have a headache now and I want quiet!" she barked.

Denis bowed. "Sorry dear, sorry I'll—"

"What?"

"Myra, how can you yell, if your head hurts?" He shuffled near to bring her the pillow.

"I don't want to yell, but you make me!" She tore it from his hands.

"Sorry, dear."

The doorbell rang frantically. Burying her face in the pillow, Myra screamed through the stuffing, "Make it stop!"

"I'll show them in, dear—"

"No! No one!" Myra hurled the pillow at Denis, striking him at the side of the head. "It's after midnight for heaven's sake! I need peace and quiet!"

"Yes, peace and quiet. Yes, and no visitors," he muttered and collected the pillow to hand to her once again. "No visitors, not a one!"

Denis opened the door to the night and Katherine slipped inside, eliciting a shriek from him.

"Myra is not well. She'll see no one, please go away," he shouted in a whisper.

The fury in her eyes vanquished him and her shadow encompassed him. "Denis, I must come in!"

"Oh no." He held out his little hands. "You can't! She told me no one! You may not come past me."

Katherine narrowed her eyes, grabbed him by the shoulders, and whisked him aside. "You'll move!"

Myra groaned, overhearing the muffled confrontation. "Look, I am not in the mood for visitors—" She opened her eyes and met the desperate plea in Katherine's.

Wearily she entered the den and sank down on Myra's couch.

They could hear Denis, clanging and banging dishes in the kitchen.

"You don't look good." Myra drew back when she saw the tears forming. "My goodness, whatever is it?"

Katherine faded. She appeared ashen and gaunt. Her otherwise smooth, melodic voice was raspy and hoarse. "You've accepted it. Eliza and Dorothea, my mother, all accepted it; but there are things that make you different from me. You, none of you ever knew what you missed! I've seen it, felt it, and I miss it with my whole heart. I can't play this part. I'm not like the rest of you. I've tried to be. But I can't do it! How do I even survive?"

"Oh, is this about the stalker?"

"Myra. I'm serious! It's Trayten. I *saw* him! Tonight he came, he was there on the boat...at the party."

Katherine slid to the floor, drowning in a pool of her white gown. Her curls had lost their strength and hung in defeated waves on her shoulders. Tears smeared the rouge that painted her cheeks.

"He knows what I've done, and he hates me for it." She stared across the room, losing her focus to tormented contemplation. "And I hate Reuben so much! I can't even *breathe* anymore. I can't think. I didn't imagine I would despise the man I call my husband. I didn't imagine he would be *that* man!"

"Now Katherine—"

"I don't need your chastising! I need help. My world is a prison! I have no control in it, no say. What happened to me? What happened to freedom, truth, beauty and love? To dreams? I've lost the only man I'll ever love, and for what? To gain the only man I've ever actually hated? I do, I said it; I hate Reuben, and I can't stand to be near him. He's a slob! He's boastful, arrogant, agitating! I can't...it's not—" She attempted to catch the tears with quivering hands.

"Do you *really* hate him? Are you *sure* you can't love him? I mean, you can't grow into it?"

"Not even if I had never met the man that I *do* love,"

Katherine affirmed. "I have to get out. I never want to see him again or hear his voice."

"You cannot divorce," Myra said.

"It isn't possible; we both know that, especially with the power he and my father have."

Myra glowered with black eyes and pulled the pillow tightly against her chest. "Are you truly desperate?"

"Of course I am!"

"So desperate you would do anything?" Myra asked.

"Anything within my power."

"You would steal?"

"If it should somehow free me—"

"Could you kill?" Myra asked.

Katherine stared, fearful yet calm.

Myra's eyes burned. "Would you make yourself a widow for the stalker?"

"What are you saying?"

"Listen to me closely, Katherine. There is no way to leave him, he'd track you down, and your father would help him! And then, you'd wish *you* were dead. But you could make him leave *you*."

"You aren't serious—" Katherine wiped her cheeks, straightening up as a hot flame traveled down her spine.

"I am. If I could not have managed Denis," she glanced toward the hall, "and he was half as unbearable as you say Reuben is, I could have done away with him, sure."

The nonchalance of the statement should have chilled Katherine to the bone, yet from the distress of her entrapment she could only ask, "How?"

"However. You could be a widow, free to go where you please. In your grief, in your dolorous time, you could escape from the town that reminds you of your 'dear' departed husband. A respite, to shut out the sorrow. No one would stop a weeping widow. No one would suspect you for being glad. You could be with your stalker, away from here."

Katherine's eyes were shadowy, her mouth fell open as she searched Myra's face. Some irrational creature replaced her power of reason and navigated her responses, influencing her consideration with frightful ease. "I could get rid of him …and go where I please and be free from these families…my *own* freedom, forever."

"I follow convention and the rule of law, don't misunderstand me. But when it is completely destroying you, some formalities must be put aside. I won't have you miserable, Katherine. I thought you could find happiness with Reuben, but I see it isn't so. You need out. I won't stand in your way."

They exchanged a lengthy stare, until a gentle rapping at the door pulled Myra's attention away. She frowned, ready to holler for Denis, yet he swiftly entered with Eliza at his heels.

"Katherine, please." Eliza knelt beside her sister. "I came to take you home. Arnold has the carriage waiting for you."

"I will talk with you more, later," Myra said.

"Yes. Very well." Katherine arose and without protest, let Eliza lead her away. She stepped outside and reflected the stillness of the star filled sky in tearless eyes. With an eerie resolve, she climbed into the carriage, and as it took her back to the house she deemed her prison, she pondered the workings of a calamitous plot.

❀

Candles burned in the heavy, damp air. Rain pelted the boards covering a cracked window, then leaked and trickled down the wall. In the library, insulated from the rest of the world, Trayten grieved for the love he believed was lost.

The cigarette between his lips sent a trail of smoke to encircle his head like a halo. He gripped a quill in his left hand. His brow tightened and his eyes burned like the candles' flames. With love and loathing he wrote:

This is blackness, staining the purity of white

This is my hand, too unnerved to paint, too nervous to rest.
This is ink on paper, an attempt to find you, in what you love.
This is the absence of love, turning to hate.

He lowered his mouth to his shoulder and smothered it there, squeezing his eyes shut. Her words swam back to him through the sea of silent rage, *crippling dependency, severed souls, love, the world's greatest disease.* He inhaled deeply and wished to erase the words from his memory and suppress her image from his consciousness.

He sensed her presence when she climbed out of the cellar. She shed her coat to the ground and left her shoes behind her. Desperate eyes met his when he raised his head and her heart stilled. Rain trailed down her cheeks from strands of glistening wet hair, hanging like dewy black vines. The twinkle in her eyes struck him deeper than any blade possibly could.

He wondered, *is she truly here?* He was curious if she ached for his warmth, standing with her clothes soaked from the rain. It dripped from the hem of her skirt to form a ring around her. Barefooted and thin-skinned, she waited before him. Damp lips parted, without sound to follow.

When she perceived him standing, his intensity frightened her; the way he drew back his hand as if he would release it against her, the way he cast a cold breath over her wet face. Katherine could not allow the anger. She threw herself into his arms and clung immediately to his body.

They held each other, until the moisture clinging to her body dampened him, and their arms were strained with the pressing. Crying in relief, Katherine gasped for air, and took his face between her hands to kiss him hungrily, as if for the first and last time.

❧

"Tell me you won't hate me when I must go back." Her voice echoed to the ceiling. Her cheek rested on his chest.

"You will go back?" Trayten asked, stunned.

"I have to, for now. Don't think that because I escaped tonight that I'm completely free."

"I thought you were just another dream, when I looked up and saw you here last night. If you go back, you may as well have been one."

"My heart is with you. I belong to you and I *will* be with you." Katherine turned to look at him. "Give me time, trust me. I couldn't bear your doubt, your hatred. I couldn't bear the thought that I'd lost you."

"You'd lost *me*?" Trayten exclaimed, surprised by the idea.

The fair morning light crowned her hair.

"I die a little, every day that I can't see you." He sighed and reached up to tenderly smooth her hair with his hand. "I will die a cruel death knowing you are in *his* bed, *his* arms around you—" He spit the words in fury, but Katherine covered his mouth and pushed his head down, glaring.

"Trayten, I detest him! I avoid his arms entirely and I will not share his bed! If I could only stay here forever I would, but I can't."

"Couldn't you?"

"Please." She sat up, combing her fingers through her hair.

"You don't want to talk about it, but jealousy eats me alive. And you deny you have any choice or power."

"You've seen him, haven't you?"

"I have seen you *both*." Blackness filled his eyes.

"And how monstrous is he? How could I even begin to favor him over my love?" She reached out to touch his face.

"Your love? Who is he?" Trayten snatched her hand and held it.

"Trayten, don't be jealous. You don't even know what you mean to me."

"You're right. I don't," he said gravely.

Katherine stared back, unable to reply. Deep down she feared that, if he knew the perilous path she considered taking in order to be free from her mistake, he would cease to care if he mattered to her at all. In an instant of piercing dread, she had a vision of Trayten renouncing her and turning away. It strangled her strength for candor.

"I'm unworthy to you, *beneath* you," he offered his own explanation for her silence.

"Say such doubtful words and I'll start to agree with you."

"Then, you *need* me, you *adore* me, only me." Trayten wrapped his arms around her waist and dragged her back down to the floor.

"All right." She giggled, tickled by the rain of kisses falling on her neck.

He held her cheek in his hand and said, "You *love* me."

Katherine was lost in the warmth and tenderness pouring from his expression.

"Well," he prodded. "Say it."

"Of course." She teased him, yet in truth, Katherine was reluctant to confess her love to Trayten, not trusting herself, in her weakness, to choose that love over fear.

"Of course you love me? Say you love me if you do." He shook her playfully, or so it seemed.

"Yes! Of course," she gasped.

"I hate you."

"Not this again!" Katherine laughed.

"This time I mean it!" He pressed his frowning lips against hers.

"Of course, you do," she said, silenced by another kiss. She laughed against his lips and wrestled against his hold.

Before she would disappear again, Trayten gripped her by the arms, stared fiercely into her eyes and said, "You came here as though you were returning. And though I can't make you stay now, remember that you said you are mine. Engrave it in your memory. I'll carve it on *my* heart."

Katherine touched his face and her eyes glistened. Through tears she smiled gently. "I'll see you soon."

When she began to walk away, he stood behind her and pulled her close. He said, "Wherever you go, and whoever you will see, I am the whisper at the back of your mind. I am keeping the greatest part of your heart. I have taken up your soul and entwined it with mine, so you cannot forget me, lest you forget yourself. Even if you leave me, my warmth will linger like the heat from the sun, just as you will never leave me. I promise you. I will be with you, and I will see you ... when you cannot see me watching. I will find you. I will always find you."

Katherine swooned, his lips dusting the back of her neck. He held her in his able hands, and after she glanced into his eyes, he gently propelled her away, back out into the world.

❃

On her way home, filled once again with the hope his words, his eyes, and his affection brought, Katherine drifted on air. People passed and she moved oblivious to them. The wind scurried around her, scattering her loose, unruly hair and she gripped her coat tightly against it. Fresh rain puddles presented themselves along her path, and Katherine strode through them without slowing her step. While her mind raced with memory, she lost all regard for the crowds, and brushed the shoulders of passersby and ignored both the greetings and the admonitions that resulted.

Wistful eyes remained fixated on visions in candlelight and her dark-haired beloved with warm hands and deep eyes. She remembered his lips against her throat and turned into London Road toward her prison. Katherine gazed ahead at the quaking, wet leaves of elm trees lining the street and saw the candles flickering and painting his face with golden light. Her heart raced, and she stopped short. A roaring carriage sped across her path.

She blinked yet could scarcely focus. Her steps echoed the rhythm of his breathing and the cobblestones transformed into a vision of his eyes, focused and sincere. A young gentleman tipped his hat and Katherine stared through him before swerving around him. Transcending the noise and the crowds, she relived the night. His heartbeat reverberating, after holding him as tightly as her arms would allow.

Wind blew the hair from her face, revealing flushed cheeks. A smile spread wide and set her eyes twinkling. The air carried the fresh afternotes of rain and mingled with morning dew. She climbed the hill toward her internment, carrying him with her, savoring his memory that she might subsist from its afterglow.

Katherine brought the tea, carefully balancing the hot kettle between her hands. She passed through a corridor to the breakfast room where sunlight abounded and reflected blindingly from a trio of crisp, silk waistcoats. Reuben and his fellow property owners, Mr. Bucking and Mr. Cosage, hovered around the table, greedily devouring what was once an abundance of chocolate cakes. Katherine briefly glanced down at Reuben as she poured him a fresh cup of tea. "How is that one, dear?"

"Isn't she a marvel!" He sipped loudly. "What a magnificent little wife. Managing her duties!"

"How *is* that?" Katherine plied.

"Ah, too fair, I like it stronger, less sugar." Reuben evaluated.

"Of course, I'll fix it. More rum, Mr. Cosage?" She lifted the kettle.

"Surely," he replied.

Mr. Bucking lifted his teacup after her helplessly and said, "I like sugary tea—"

She was gone as though she had not heard him.

Throwing back her shoulders, Katherine climbed the corridor toward the kitchen. A steely expression covered her face. The blue of her satin gown amplified the indigo flecks in her eyes.

Polished and armored, Katherine appeared a model of poise and decency, even as she conducted her ominous mission.

Setting the kettle on the counter, she immediately plucked a tiny bottle from her bodice and looked over each shoulder to ensure that she was alone. Holding it to the light she gauged its volume; half-full. Katherine opened the kettle's lid, extracted the cork from the bottle, and tapped several drops of inky liquid into the tea.

She peered down the hall, the echo of their laughter and boasting in her ear. Katherine shook several more drops of the liquid from the bottle into the kettle, hesitated, and finally drained the entire vessel before tucking it back into her bodice. After a rapid stir with the spoon, she closed the kettle and swept it into her hands.

"Here we are." She filled Reuben's cup.

Mr. Bucking lifted his finger. "I'll take tea as well."

"Oh no, too bitter for you now, to be sure. I eliminated all sweetness," Katherine chided while she filled a glass with rum for Mr. Cosage. "It would knock you right out of your chair!"

"I'll brave it," Mr. Bucking insisted.

After guzzling his cup, Reuben coaxed, "Yes dear, give him tea if he wants it. It is excellent! Just right!"

She smirked at Reuben, a streak of wicked curiosity racing through her as he drank. The meek old Mr. Bucking tapped his finger at his cup. "Come come, do not be odd, Mrs. Koryn."

"Yes, Katherine. You have been flighty and odd since I returned from Southampton yesterday," Reuben resounded.

"I'm sorry, dear." She reeled from the bitter taste of calling him '*dear*' and persisted in her charade. "I'm sure I must have missed you *terribly*. But I'm all right now."

"Good. Enough of this childishness. Pour him a cup and let us proceed with our discussion," Reuben ordered.

"I truly believe you will hate it. It's pure bitterness," Katherine pleaded, her heart beating faster.

Reuben finished his cup and she rushed to refill it. Although he tried to cover it with his hand, he was too sluggish to prevent her. Still, she noted, Reuben's eyes were wide and pale as usual, and his voice remained irritatingly even.

"What is the trouble, Reuben? Your wife is certainly strange. Tea, if you please, madame!" Mr. Bucking insisted.

"I'm not strange," Katherine snapped. A scowl flashed across her face and she wrenched Mr. Bucking's cup away. "Enjoy your tea, sir." She filled it.

"Finally!" Mr. Bucking took a drink, wincing slightly but recovering smartly. "What were we discussing, aside from Mrs. Koryn's oddities?"

"Rents and the tenants who are trying to get around them," Reuben said.

"And these relentless farmers!" Mr. Cosage railed.

Katherine studied Reuben intently while he finished his second cup. He sat upright and talked expressively, endlessly. She observed Mr. Bucking's sour grimace before quietly leaving them.

That evening, as Reuben read his paper by the fire in the den, Katherine held her book open and unattended between her palms. She stared, mouth agape, eyes wide, as he smoked a cigar, stoked the fire, and laughed loudly at his newspaper.

"Kathy, why are you suddenly fascinated by me?" Reuben finally asked. "Why do you look like that?"

She stared grimly while he crammed several pieces of fudge into his mouth at once. Indefatigable he remained. No signs of instability. She was furiously, regrettably amazed.

1909

Katherine adjusted the gramophone she had placed on a table in Tray's room. He gazed distrustfully at the arched attachment, opening like a rigid lily in mid-bloom. As she placed the needle down and flashed a giddy smile, a scratchy buzz preceded the jaunty song that spilled from the horn. Tray jumped and held tightly to the arms of his chair.

"What in the world is it?" he asked.

"Don't be primitive!" Katherine laughed, adjusting the horn. "A gramophone! I borrowed it from the Saunders sisters."

"Extraordinary. From the what?"

She mused at his wonder while he listened in awe to the crackling recording of instruments. Katherine clapped her hands together and beckoned to him. "Come on."

Below them in the kitchen, Marian sat forward, balancing a mug on her knobby knee. "I must not charge enough to put up with such disruption!"

Her fierce glare fell on Tarl who lulled in his chair across the table. Rhythmically, a pounding thundered above them, accompanied by the hanging static of the music machine. Laughter permeated the walls.

Marian slammed her mug down. "It's late! She overexerts him constantly. Still I say," she shook her finger as Tarl blinked casually, "she's going to kill that poor man! When was the last time you saw such eccentric behaviors in a doctor?"

"Can't say I recall the last time I saw a doctor in *any* behavior." He scratched his purple, bulbous nose. In dim light, the bones of his face were pronounced.

Another thump resounded from upstairs, and Marian jolted, grasping her throat. "My nerves!"

More laughter was to follow from above.

Katherine swayed to the brassy music. She took hold of his hands. His eyes betrayed the wonder he attempted to conceal while she directed his arms to dance with her. She pushed and pulled him in order for him to roll along.

Tray chuckled as she pretended he was as mobile as she. Placing one of his hands on her waist, she held the collar of his shirt. Gracefully she held his other hand and using his arm as leverage to turn them, approximated a twirl. With surprising rhythm, despite his wheeled stance, Katherine managed to dance them around the little room. The jollity of their motion, fortunately for Katherine, aided in masking the pained and tearful expression in her eyes, for she was haunted by the memory of their last dance, when her feet scarcely touched the ground.

With determined focus, Katherine threw off her sorrow. "This is the finest ballroom gala in the North End, on a Tuesday night. I've never seen this many diamonds and gold cuff-links in one room!"

Tray laughed with her, a dry and rusty chuckle, but his smile was genuine, melting, and as vibrant as years before.

"And *you*, sir, what a fine crushed velvet waistcoat trimmed with silver twine," she complimented Tray and he nodded with a snooty expression.

"Look at that fellow! He must have come in off the streets! What idiot doorman let him into our elegant festival?" He put a hand to his wheel and took the lead as she flashed him a curiously proud grin.

"Am I a rich man?"

"A rich man need not question himself. You are if you must be, and powerful without a doubt, by my evaluation. You ordered me to dance with you and completely charmed by your confidence, I was convinced straight away."

"They're all staring at us." He forced a pompous accent.

He made an effort to twirl her. She giggled as he pantomimed smoking. When the music blared toward an exciting crescendo,

Tray took her with his hands, spun her once, and dipped her over his lap. She squealed as he dropped her low.

The door sprang open. Tarl leaned on the knob the whole way in. His head wiggled. For a moment he stared with indiscernible expression at Katherine, who was suspended halfway to the floor. He hugged a liquor bottle in the crook of one arm. The recording ended and a vacant hum persisted.

Tarl squinted, and looked as though he had realized something profound, and then he belched. "Sss sorry—" He slithered backward clumsily, trying to close the door on his foot.

Tray chuckled and Katherine joined him. Sighing deeply, she embraced him briefly yet tightly before leaping to her feet.

1904

My Darling Trayten,

I'm a great many horrible things. I know this now. I should have known it then.

To have done this to us. To have ruined our love.

Have I ruined it? Sometimes I wonder. I am longing for you so much that I am hollow. I am empty. Where have you gone? I'm frustrated by the mystery. I want to scream, where are you?

Forgive me, but the madness has settled on me. It has been circling for some time now. I am a wandering vagrant. I am a hapless shadow in places unwelcoming. How can it be that no one in this wretched world remembers you? Only I do. Maybe you were no one. And yet, who am I without you?

I am sitting at the edge of some God forsaken road. No road in particular, well if I knew its name, perhaps I wouldn't be lost right now. In some tiny hamlet on the Old Frome Road, they told me this was the way to East Horrington.

Well, I think they lied. I've been walking this road for days. I've seen meadows and sheep, and one carriage passed, occupied by some elite barbarians whose driver spat at me when I waved for him to stop.

God help me. Did I ever spit on anyone? The ways I once behaved are revisited upon me now.

What more must I endure? Shall I be punished first, for my actions, before I am permitted to find you? I cannot say if I would rather know you are dead, than to never find you alive. How easy we had it before. If only we knew the things we know now.

Trayten, I am waiting for some direction to strike me, for some divine wind to push me toward you. I'm writing letters to hospitals, town halls, and churches. I am praying to God. I close my eyes and see you with me, and I'm tormented. The simple things were extraordinary with you. I want them back. I want to watch you watching the world. I want to climb buildings with you. I want to tell you the things I was too afraid to say.

If I could change the past, I would. Then again, if I had the power to do something that grand, I would find you today.

Forever,
Your Katherine

1900

Myra held a flawless rose to the sunlight and wrinkled her nose. Delicate pink petals shined with dew. She threw it on the ground. "A wee little pathetic one!"

Katherine shuffled behind her and her proud basket of the largest roses. The garden behind the MacGregor's townhouse was small and narrow, enclosed by high brick walls on each side to conceal them from the neighbors' adjoining gardens.

"Maybe you don't believe me, but I've been trying, Myra."

Myra's wide-brimmed straw hat shaded her face, and she whirled around like a pirouetting ballerina to glance disappointedly at Katherine. She seized another rose and cut it promptly with her sheers.

"Aren't you listening?" Katherine asked.

"Sickly." Myra observed the deadened petals near the stem of her rose. She threw it aside.

"Why are you so finicky about roses you're going to dry and put in a wreath?"

"This is my art, Katherine. Don't criticize my art!"

Katherine sighed, shielding her eyes from the sun with her hand.

"Dear, I say that if you haven't been successful, you aren't trying hard enough," Myra suggested.

"Honestly I have! The one thing I can conclude is that he's inhuman! Inhuman! He consumed an entire bottle of rat poison in his tea, and the man had more energy and zeal than ever! He's a beast!"

"So, why *ever* would you want to kill him?" Myra laughed smugly and Katherine shuddered.

Denis emerged from the house carrying a copy of the Portsmouth Evening News, which he waved at Myra. "Honey, my love, I fetched your paper! And I only creased it once, as you like it. There are sandwiches as well in the kitchen."

"Lovely, dear! I hope you got the ones with roast beef and Stilton cheese, not that Gouda mess again."

"I think I got Stilton." Denis stopped and scratched his head. "They're practically the same color." He squinted against the sun, sneezed largely, and waggled his head to read the paper. Myra regarded him with a pitiless glance, and groaned, "He's allergic to the sun."

"And roses," Denis mumbled.

"Yes, tis a pity I love them so," Myra grinned at Katherine.

"And grass," he added.

"Enough, Denis," Myra said. "At least I get my garden to myself."

Katherine moved in her path to plead, "You were the one who suggested this insanity to me. So help me!"

"Fine, fine." Myra pressed her finger to her chin.

Denis sneezed and blew his nose loudly into his handkerchief.

"Now poison, Katherine, that is amateurish. There's never a guarantee with poison."

"And I'm sure you're an expert on matters of murder?" Katherine folded her arms. "What would you have me do?"

"Are you afraid of pain?" Myra snipped the bloom from a drooping stem. It rolled lifelessly onto the grass and she stepped on it.

"Of course not," Katherine said uneasily, eyeing the crushed bloom.

"Then you must use more violent, sure tactics."

"But I must be able to conceal it. That's why I tried poison." She lowered her voice to a whisper as they neared Denis. "What do you suggest? Should we take him into the woods and shoot him?"

"Oh!" Denis shrieked. He held the paper firmly in front of his face. "Look here Myra dear, on the social page, it says that, well, you know that little old man, Mr. Bucking? He took ill overnight it says, and doctors are perplexed. They fear it might be some terrible epidemic, for it's nothing they have seen in decades!"

Katherine's eyes were wide, and her voice was frantic. "No! That can't be!"

"It's what it says here." Denis tapped the page. She stormed at him and he ducked, throwing the paper over his head. Katherine caught it and fumbled to find the article. Myra narrowed her eyes.

"He is ill! Oh Lord, it's true!"

"What is the matter with you?" Myra asked.

Denis stared at Katherine with wonderment until Myra fired, "Oh, go in the house, Denis!" He scurried away immediately.

She threw the paper into the air and clawed at her face. "This is what I get! I'm murdering the wrong man! God hates me, Myra, and He's given Reuben immortality to torture me!" She fell back onto the step.

"I highly doubt Reuben is favored by God. Men of his sort aren't even warm blooded. They have to be snakes to be landlords, so that no one is in danger of liking them." Myra giggled at herself.

"What is it then? I'm cursed. I can't do this. I can't live like this. I try to murder my husband and instead kill off some poor old sweet-tea drinking man."

"Get it together! No more sobbing and complaining! If you're not happy, change something! Don't lose your mind over a casualty of war!"

"I killed Mr. Bucking. I know I did." She buried her face in her arms.

"Good!" Myra barked. "There's your start. *Now* go after the big animal! Think of your freedom, your sanity! Think of your dark brooding stalker!"

Katherine raised her head and the clarity, or what she interpreted as clarity, returned.

"You're right, you are. I can do this. No more whimpering, no more weakness." Katherine stood slowly. "I can do this, because I *have* to. There is no other way."

"Certainly not," Myra agreed.

"And I can't let anything stop me, not remorse, not guilt, because that would make me vulnerable. Myra, I'm going back." Katherine brushed off her skirt and headed for the back door with bleak determination. Denis dodged her in the hallway as she went through the house with a sardonic shadow covering her eyes.

❧

To Katherine he appeared an awful sleeping giant, sprawled grotesquely on the parlor settee. Reuben's pale brow glistened with sweat, and his nostrils flared. He lay defenseless and still, completely at her mercy. He could neither gaze at her with taunting, snobbish eyes, nor rattle on with incessant boasting. He could not assault her ears by calling her 'Kathy.' She cringed at the thought of his voice.

She brought the rifle around in front of her, ready and braced in her hands, the barrel aimed at his head. *Violent, but quick*, she thought. She stared down the metal shaft of the gun, twitching and again hesitating. Even if he woke, he would be too late to stop her. It would take one fast pull, for her finger grazed the trigger. Hair fell in her eyes. She shook it away and her breath bounced back from the body of the gun.

Frightened, she focused on her desperation to be free. She cocked the gun and the click resounded. She glanced around her to the open parlor. Once more she rehearsed the plan she contrived of the break-in she had staged. It would appear to be an attempted robbery.

The scene was laid before she took up the gun. The parlor door stood open to the courtyard, the path from there to the settee was littered with debris, as though strewn by a careless looter. A table lay overturned and the rug beneath it was buckled. Along the path through the door and into the courtyard, a trail of jewelry implied the escape route of the fictitious thief, as well as the empty oak jewelry case that lay broken on the ground.

She would shoot, drop the gun, and fall on the floor shrieking. Katherine would perform the role of a hysterical wife, her husband found dead; the victim of a ruthless thief after waking to discover the burglary. The plot reaffirmed, she nodded, and convinced herself it was plausible.

Her nervous system numbed, and her blood ceased to run. She closed her eyes. Releasing a determined breath, she bit her lower lip and pressed her finger to the trigger, bracing herself for the kick of the gun when wheels across the floor alerted her. Katherine's hand seized and she whirled around.

Hilda wheeled near, her face full of questions. Katherine lowered the gun to aim at the floor with tingling hands.

"I woke and you were gone, dear," Hilda said.

"I didn't know if…if this was my husband's gun, or perhaps Mr. Augustus Koryn's. I was going to ask him, so I could…clean it. He wouldn't…he wouldn't," she looked at Reuben and exhaled, defeated, "wake."

The eyes of Hilda Koryn were confounding, focusing as though she were deep in mental calculation. Katherine's knees locked, sweat dampened her skin, and she waited for Hilda to speak. The silence settled.

Eager to escape, Katherine staggered backward from the settee. "I'll ask him later," she said before retreating into the gaping hallway.

※

When there were neither lamps left glowing nor fires burning in the house, the grounds outside were more clearly visible through the windows of the villa. Light from the cloud veiled moon cast the world beneath in muted blue shades. Katherine stared into the foggy tones with worry stirring her blood. Anxiety barred her from sleep, and she gazed through the window, imagining Trayten's eyes glittering from myriad stars.

Without conscious will, her eyes were soon closed, and she hung on the notion of a dream, with his warm words against her neck. "I am the whisper at the back of your mind." With a whimsical expression she opened her eyes.

He was with her. She sensed him like a second heart beating alongside her own.

❧ 18 ❧

Katherine galloped down the stairs, the promise of a new day revitalizing her spirits. Though faint, she wore a smile, glad for the small pleasures that came fleetingly. Her mother-in-law had returned to her own estate and the villa was virtually empty as the servants took their monthly holiday.

Before breakfast she had opened the windows throughout the house to allow fresh air to comb through the many stale halls and rooms. Entering the center of the house, she noticed that the windows in sight were closed and the curtains were drawn.

Katherine stared at the heavy drapes, perplexed. Reuben went into Portsmouth for a meeting before dawn. She did not expect him to return until much later. Humming, she went toward the arched window across the open floor. Searching through the drapes she found a handle and jerked, unable to glide open the shutter. It was locked.

With narrowed eyes and a tight mouth, she pulled at the other windows along the wall, finding each one locked like the first. Although the locks caused her to itch with wonder she moved on. Down the corridor, beyond the numerous mirrors, she followed the musky odor of cigar smoke to the masculine chambers belonging to Reuben. The slick satin of her evergreen skirt announced her presence in the dead silence. Unsure whether or not she was alone, she entered into the dimness.

In the billiard room the furs and mounts of conquered animals adorned each chestnut paneled wall. Their glass eyes followed Katherine with stagnant gaping gazes. She turned toward the cabinets and gasped.

The gun racks, each and all, were completely bare and the glass doors were open. She clenched her fists and fell on the cabinets where his knives were harnessed. They too were empty. She exploded, ripping the drawers out and hurling them at the floor with a yell. Her temper boiled as she slammed and shattered each glass cabinet door and tore through the rest of the chamber to find the cupboards and racks empty.

Her distress could not be withheld. Nothing rational touched her mind as she scurried back through the corridor and beyond the taunting mirrors. Heat flushed into her face as she glanced behind her, convinced she heard someone following. The massive house mocked her. Claustrophobia closed in. The doors in another hall, formerly open, were shut. With increasing hysteria, she made her way to the front door.

To the door Katherine scampered, the air thickening, and the walls shrinking in to swallow her. When she tried to twist the doorknob, the rage caused her entire body to quake, for the knob would not yield. Frantically she withdrew a set of keys from her pocket and fumbled with them. She could neither find the right shape, nor direct one into the keyhole. She looked more closely. The keys were filed down. She threw them against the wall.

Katherine shouted threats at Reuben. She could neither see nor hear him and it frightened her. Vowing to find him, she pushed from the door with collected resolve. Desperate for a weapon, she crashed into the kitchen. Yanking drawers out onto the floor, she found not a knife, not a cleaver, not a fork. In the cupboards; no plates, no glasses, nothing glass at all! With increasing fury she slid across the marble floor toward the cellar door, which she found was bound in chains. Katherine kicked it in aggravation and whirled around to flee the kitchen.

After she scoured the villa, slamming into locked doors, racing across empty rooms, beating on every window and calling for Reuben, Katherine passed the last open parlor. A generous fire roared at the hearth, creating a hellish heat, given the high sun beyond the walls in its reigning summer season. Through the open windows warm wind blew inward, stirring the flames of candles perched on shelves, tables, and the mantel. Though the temperature of the room would provoke otherwise, a shiver rattled her, perhaps attributed to the stillness, which like the rest of the house vexed and confused her.

Her nerves hummed with dreaded wonder. What dubious hoax was this? She immediately suspected Reuben and she sensed that he hid somewhere, taking deviant pleasure in her panic.

She endeavored to rein it in. Having entered the last chamber and soon dizzy by the suffocating heat, Katherine stilled her temper to focus on the silence, listening to catch any movement that might present itself. The cadence of her breathing remained the only human sound decipherable. She poised for response, her senses stretched, alert. The house watched her, eyes tracked her.

Turning in a circle, Katherine surveyed the chamber. She studied the gold and burgundy damask armchairs, the milky-gray marble top of the card table, the blood-red granite hearth, and the rigid iron poker resting on its pedestal!

Neither the crushing weight of the heat nor the exasperation of defeat could hold her weary, and Katherine rushed to the item she viewed as her only defense, a sacred weapon carelessly left behind. With eyes lit by renewed empowerment, Katherine clutched the hilt of the poker and drew it from its stand like a sword, examining the sharp, pointed spire at its end.

The revelry was trampled, as a wall of stone crashed against her from behind. She howled, panicked, and was silenced immediately by a thick hand covering her mouth. Reuben wrestled the poker from her. It clattered ineffectually to the floor.

Katherine struggled under his yoke and attempted to yell through his fat fleshy palm. Terror filled her as her thrashing was met with his debilitating grip. He snapped her around as though she were a weightless rag doll, holding her tight by the shoulders and burning her with a cruel scrutinizing gaze.

"Tell me!" he hissed. "What have you been trying to do, my dear?"

At last, free to speak she spit hostilely, "Let go of me, you lunatic!"

"And what will you do *next*? Will you try to poison me again?" His words gurgled deep in his throat and anger tinged his corpulent cheeks red.

No amount of desperate wrenching would loosen his grip on her. Her bones felt ready to snap against his resistance. His strength surprised her, and she was fearful of him as never before. His jagged breath washed across her face. The intensity of his expression could not be escaped at such close range. He shook her until her hair fell recklessly around her shoulders.

"You're delusional!" she cried. "Unhand me!"

"I want to understand. I demand to know why. You are my wife!" A pathetic whine accented his tone. Vastly more pathetic, he held his sweaty cheek against hers, charging her with fresh, unbearable revulsion. "My love," he cooed. "Tell me, why would you want to harm me?"

"Stop it!" She shrieked through gritted teeth, pooling her strength to push away from him, though it amounted to no distance, only a reverberating ache through her strained muscles. "I can't—" Winded, she panted to catch her breath, arms throbbing under his grasp.

"What, you cannot what?" he pleaded.

"I—" she spit with cruelty. "I can't stand you close to me!"

For a moment they fell completely still. It wounded him enough that he let his hold slacken and Katherine jammed her knee into his stomach, breaking free to run.

Reuben bellowed and reeled, but with a groan was after her in mere seconds. He had her again by the waist with one swoop of his massive arm. They fell, his weight crushed her against the floor, and he jammed her wrists down. He kept her beneath him, and she bellowed, outperforming him only in that, until eventually he roared back, repeating for her to stop.

Wild, fierce light burned in her eyes as she fired, "Get off of me, you ogre!"

"What are you trying to do to me, Katherine? You want my fortune, is that it?"

"I want my freedom! I don't care about your fortune!"

"Your freedom at my expense? You want me dead! You're very sick indeed and you need help!" He squeezed her wrists tighter, and her tears responded to the pain. "My silly little wife, you can't *kill* me!"

"Apparently!" She tossed her shoulders to try breaking free, although the feat was hopeless.

"I am yours and you are mine! You're stubborn but you will be cured. I'll see to it you are put right. This current state of things will not continue!"

"A threat? From you?" She would have laughed, but he smashed his lips to hers, his teeth cutting her flesh. She squealed beneath the vicious kiss. When free again, she cried through the blood on her lip, "I hate you! I do! Let me go!"

"You love me!" he hollered. "You'll know it yet! Try as you will, fight and cry and toil, you won't kill me. I know your game now, and I shall be a more than ready opponent." He removed himself from her abruptly.

A blunt pain lingered where his heaviness had compressed her sternum and ribcage. Tear tracks lined her face. In his shadow she lay on the floor, hair disheveled. She surrendered to the fear, unable to move beneath its influence. An overwhelming sense of revulsion debilitated her.

"And Kathy," he said as he paused before exiting the searing chamber. "You will become a proper wife. I have been exceedingly patient with you thus far. Incredibly passive. No more. You will be agreeable, and I will not indulge your willfulness anymore."

Weakened, she could do nothing but lie still. Her hands were clumsy at her mouth, finding the blood where her teeth had pierced her lip. Even though it aggravated the wound, she tried to wipe away every impression of his kiss.

1905

Trayten,

I am becoming immune to these dreary places, the asylums that I haunt endlessly. For countless days I have roamed through hospitals, bombarded by the stench of sickness and blood, of chemicals and stagnant air. Cold walls and cold faces meet me faithfully. I imagine that the jarred expressions I inspire are the same that would welcome a true apparition, for it is candid to admit that I must seem like one to them in my neglected state of appearance; the emaciated exhaustion that has imprinted its deprivation on my health and figure at last.

Children cry in these foreboding establishments and the elderly ramble to deaf ears. I miss our Angelle, our precious child. I have traveled ever so long.

This eerie apprehension chokes me, every time I speak your name aloud, in order to have attendants search for it on registries and lists. I am tired; tired of them shaking their heads while I stare into their unfeeling faces in what has become a predictable reaction to my query, their indifferent eyes stirring my anger. Don't they know what you mean to me?

When efforts prove fruitless from the nurses and attendants in the lobby, I venture underground to the morgue, to wander among the corpses, drowning in my deepest phase of fear. It only feeds the nightmares, the ashen, petrified skin, the complete absence of life and light, facing the truth of mortality. No matter how weary, how anxious I am to find you, I dread that it will be in such a way as this; unguarded and undignified on a slab in some cellar. Each day is filled with such dread that my nerves are in constant agitation.

Still, my quest to find you drives me into places I never imagined I could enter, and toward deeds I would have abhorred to simply hear of. It is my unapologetic shame to confess that I have, on three occasions, broken into these wretched places. When they have refused to search for me beyond a current day's log, or to even look at all, I have resorted to transforming myself like a burglar, stealing under the cover of night into the eerie halls to creep and hide, and spend long hours scanning over records in search of your name. Trayten Basel.

I have scoured Glastonbury, Trowbridge, the hospitals there and in between. All I could think to do after that was send letters to clinics asking that you be watched for. I sent donations to towns, begging for their own city registries to be searched.

Trayten Basel.

Your name circles my consciousness, following my thoughts like a shadow.

On a train across Yorkshire, I closed my eyes in a state of exhaustion. I had been staring across an expanse of fields, blinded by the white heat that encompassed the sky. Parched as I have never known. The heat scorched my brow through the windowpane. Sweating, my hair stuck to my neck.

I recall these discomforts and then, in a flash, I existed in some ethereal place. A great meadow spread before me, alight with shimmering green, gold, and coral tones, set on a sea cliff where beneath, white sand glittered and hugged the grasses. It appeared like the scene you had painted, the one with the deep textured grasses that hung on the wall in your flat. A wind blew warm and wet from the south. I turned on impulse and drew a hand to gaze toward the sinking sun.

And there you were, floating on air, but I knew you were running. Even from the distance I was stricken by your features and I indulged to drink them in, weakened with delight, reverence, and desire. The beautiful character of your face transfixed me as always and ever; the confident gaze from your ardent eyes, bold and dark, filled with a depth of aptitude, virtuosity, and tenderness. The supple, perfection of your lips and the strong, sure curve of your nose, your chiseled cheekbones and jaw, features encoded with affectionate care in my brain, igniting at first sight this intense yearning, refined by concentrated adoration. In the light, the striking contrasts of your black hair against flawless skin emphasized your dashing appeal.

As you moved, I savoured the graceful motion in your agile gait, the towering, sculpted structure of your physique melted my sensibilities and I longed to be swept up and carried in your arms. A creation as beautiful as you is painful to behold, and your charisma left my heart wrenching, as it always had before, perplexed that one of such unearthly perfection would ever turn toward me.

As astonishing as holding you in my view was the appearance of our Angelle, four years in age, as she is now, dressed in the fresh blue of a spring sky and smiling her pure, childlike grin. She bounded through the grass, her black hair in shining ringlet curls, her laughter peeling after her like bells. And I beamed, the joy within me spilling out when I heard you call to her, and you caught her in your arms. You swung our little girl into the air, and I compared you together, your beauty, your likeness.

Salt spray from the sea permeated the air and I drifted toward you both, toward the promise of your smiles, your twinkling, deep brown eyes. But the train stopped in a squeal of steel and heavy momentum resisted, and most delirious I awoke.

I never felt so alone. The landscape was never so deserted. I could almost taste the sea air, hear your voices. I never reached you in that dream.

And the realization of that kept me awake long after.

Forever,
  Katherine

1909

Tray reclined against the pillows on his bed and closed his eyes. He lay with a quilt draped across his middle and his bare legs outstretched before him. Katherine had adjusted her reaction to their marred appearance; the deep gashes that cut the flesh and disrupted their formerly flawless length and the scars left behind, crossing what little unaffected skin remained in silvery streaks.

His legs appeared feeble, atrophied and routed with cuts and gouges. Katherine perceived the wounds as a haunting echo of the violence that created them, a violence she could scarcely fathom without fainting. As her fingers gently traced them, following carefully the deep marks in the flesh of his thigh, she withheld her questions, her tears, and her fury; unable to help imagining what kind of weapon had been wielded against him with such force, for the depth and breadth of the wounds dismissed any consideration of an accident. It had been rage— that brutal, primal emotion that caused these scars, glaringly evident before her.

Katherine sat beside him holding a clay jar in her lap and she dipped her fingers into it, bringing out a thick salve. She carefully spread it on one scar after another. The distribution of candlelight throughout his room harmonized in a warm, amber glow. Beyond his window the white waxing moon stood bold against an inky sky.

She could sense his discomfort and remained silent at first, unsure of how to ease him. At last she ventured to speak, "I can neither have Dr. Danby treat you here, nor can I take you to him; warden's rules. Yet he assured me that I can treat your skin as effectively as he would do. This balm will nourish your skin. He said it would help prevent even the scar tissue from cracking and bleeding, or worse deteriorating and breaking down."

"I suppose even if it did deteriorate, I wouldn't have to feel it."

"If it starts to rot, you'll surely smell it," she said.

Tray smiled and opened his eyes to reveal his delight. "Indeed." He cherished a notion of pride for her wit.

Katherine grinned, took more salve onto her fingertips, and spread it across his shin.

"I can't feel what you're doing," he said. "What's it like?"

"It's—" She concentrated on her fingers. "It's warm and smooth to the touch, like whipped butter. There's a tingle to it, a cooling effect following the warmth, as from eucalyptus or peppermint, perhaps. Your skin is very dry. It's a wonder it hasn't cracked yet. But it looks better, you can see it drinking in the moisture. It is quite changed!"

"It will transform my life."

She chose to let his dry comment drift unmet with a response. Startling her with an abruptness of tone he more accused her than inquired, "Are you keeping secrets, Mrs. Koryn?"

Breathless in the immense heat of his gaze, Katherine reproached his address of her, instead of exploring the nature of his question. "Why do you insist on calling me *that* when I've told you—"

"Ah, see? You apparently have something to hide. Your evasive reaction gives you away." A satisfied glint shone in his expression.

"Everyone has secrets. Well, everyone but *you*, of course." She winked.

"Think what you will." He smiled in such a wise and relaxed fashion that he was a vision from the past. She recognized light in his eyes that she had missed for eight years.

Amused yet masking it with severity, he continued, "I have one secret in my poor pathetic existence and I'm going to share it with you for two reasons, one of which just might be because I'm not wearing any pants, and there is some provocation to be truthful when one is well, pant-less."

Katherine laughed with a sputter of apprehension, unable to digest his off-handedness. With a wide grin illuminating his face and a twinkle in his eyes rarely seen, he watched her reaction, satisfied.

"And the second?" she urged.

"Oh, come on! Don't get fidgety on me! You're not in any danger," he chided playfully, pushing her shoulder with the back of his hand. He recovered his serious delight and said, "Katherine: *not* Mrs. Koryn. I will call you Katherine because once again, without pants, there is but a shred of propriety that remains. Let me confide in you this secret, Katherine: I have been holding onto something, for oh, probably seven years. I regard it as the last scrap of control I have in my managed environment.

"I found a key in the night-table drawer beside the bed, a year after I was dragged up those narrow stairs to my incarceration. It's the key to my door there, to lock it from the inside." Tray motioned toward the bottom of the bed. "Reach under the mattress there."

"Here?" Katherine searched blindly with her hand under the edge of the mattress where he pointed. At last beneath the weight of the mattress pad and resting in the coils of the bedsprings, she felt the solid bar of a large key.

"Is this it?" She withdrew her hand carefully and displayed an elaborate key between her fingers.

"No." He smirked.

Katherine glanced at him incredulously.

"Marian never asked about it and it suited me to keep it to myself," Tray explained. "After all, there were times in the early days when I wished I could keep her out. Sometimes she would come into the room and I'd be asleep, at least, to her knowledge, to avoid her rambling. For a miserable number of occasions, she would lean on me and cry. She soaked my shoulder with tears, muttering, holding onto me. Imagine!

"I was bothered to say the least, unable and frankly unwilling to move to defend myself, fearful of giving away my conscious state, not knowing what her trouble was. She called me George, and carried on for what felt like hours, chattering about the ocean and the tide stealing me away.

"She obviously believed, or wanted to believe, I was someone else. I've been convinced that my name is not, nor ever was *George*. It doesn't sit well with me at all. Adverse to her delusional rants, the key, once discovered, was an opportunity for protection. I began locking the door at night, and either she never noticed, she stopped lurking at night, or she simply never said a word."

Katherine's hands slipped over his kneecap, where there was far more unscathed skin than anywhere else below his thigh. She smiled gently.

"And what about you?" he asked. "Haven't you got a secret to tell?"

"Many I have, but none to tell," she replied, her eyes cast down.

"Oh, go on. *You're* not wearing any pants either," he chuckled heartily, and Katherine could not resist laughing with him.

"In the last months before my husband died, I—" she choked. "I accosted a servant, stole the key to *my* room, so that I could lock it at night and keep him out."

Tray's eyes widened with surprise and disbelief. "That's unusual. Why?"

"Ah well, never mind the details; none of it matters now." They stared at one another and the quiet sat heavily between them.

"Sometimes, I act out fits, to encourage Marian to leave me alone," Tray confessed.

"That's terrible! I should pinch you!"

"Go on, I can't feel a thing!" He laughed until his eyes watered.

"I tried to poison my husband," Katherine said quietly. "His associate took the tea, and then took ill."

Tray stopped chuckling.

Katherine returned to the jar, taking more salve for his thigh. "He didn't die."

"And I let you cook for me?" As Katherine giggled, he laughed again. "Well, don't tell Marian about my key. Promise?"

"I promise."

"I'll tell you *this* also," he solemnly admitted. "I haven't locked my door since you arrived."

Katherine lost the skill to direct her movements, as though transformed into a sculpture at the proclamation.

With an awkward hesitation, he continued, "So, I will ask you for one favor. If you would keep the key on my behalf, keep it out of sight. And if something should happen, and I have the door locked one night, you'd be able to get in and discover me, *before* I begin to rot if we are fortunate. Or, if," his laughing eyes darkened, "if you didn't hear anything from within for a while, at least you can get in. If I needed you, if I slipped into some kind of oblivion and lost my powers to communicate. I trust you with that."

Even the elation filling her heart, hearing evidence of some measure of trust in her, could not dismiss the sharp pang of witnessing the fear in him. He shared his hypothetical as though certain such a fate were possible for him, to lose what remained of his mind perhaps and be rendered helpless and unreachable.

Katherine smiled shyly, wiped her hands on her apron, and covered his legs with the quilt. "You might have a chill if—"

"If I could feel anything."

She set the jar on the floor and stared at it. Tray put the key in her palm and closed his hands around her fist. "It's all right. I don't get emotional about it. I don't *remember* feeling or walking."

"That's the tragedy: the fact that you don't miss it, because you have no memory of it." Katherine put her other hand over his.

"Don't cry any more tears for me, milady. Promise?"

His words took her breath away.

"That's not a promise I can keep," she said, trying to hide the weeping that had already begun. However, his dismayed expression, his furrowed brow, and his concerned eyes forced her to find a smile beyond her sorrow, and she winked. "But I will try, if only for you."

Tray reached out and swept his fingers under her chin, raising it to admire the way the candlelight softened its contours. It was more than she could bear with her eyes opened, for like a lightning bolt striking a raincloud, his touch sent her tears spilling down. Wiping them, she sought to hide her face from his view, and nervously laughed. "See, how glad I am that I did not promise."

"You don't have to be perfect at it. I'll take effort over perfection," he said with gentle assurance. Tray took her hand and removed it from in front of her face to catch her eyes and offer an affectionate smile from the past.

Instead of a hasty retreat, Katherine held still and savored the strength of his hand holding hers and the refuge she found in his eyes.

❧ 19 ❦

1900

Reuben Koryn abandoned all lenience and grace. A new monster formed in him, one more disgusting in Katherine's perception than she could have imagined before. His large hand held her elbow, goading her down the street.

"Come along, Kathy. No straggling off for dark plotting tonight. We are expected at this social event to *be* social."

Across Katherine's rouged and powdered face, a remarkable scowl spread, her crimson lipstick hard against the white of her skin.

"Dark plotting?" she questioned, her tone bitter. "Whatever do you *mean*, Reuben?"

"None would know better than you, my little villain. Ah, here we are. Turn." He steered her forcefully up the walkway of a glittering estate.

The home of Baron Wilford Teluse was a monument of industrial gain, nestled on five acres of manicured gardens, in the shelter of towering machine houses and mills in the center of

Cosham. Opulent iron fences served as a barrier to separate the Baron and his clean, immaculate house from the working-class drudges who labored in his factories from dawn until dusk.

Mr. and Mrs. Koryn were admitted through the gate and they proceeded along a lamp-lit promenade toward the house, with lanterns bedecking the veranda and the candlelight shimmering through pristine windows ahead. Their heels clicked hollow on the pavement. Katherine stared at the gathering crowd ahead with rising apprehension.

Clusters of guests passed through the front doors. In the entrance hall a row of servants in livery took hats and coats to hang them. Reuben flicked a coin to an elderly butler with snowy tufts of hair encircling his bald scalp. He hung Reuben's coat with a smile and reached for Katherine. "Your fur, Madame?"

Katherine clutched the front of her coat defensively and veered away from his gloved grip declaring, "I'll keep it on, thank you."

He glanced at Reuben who chided, "Dear, what *have* you? Pockets lined with poison bottles? A knife in your sleeve?" He plucked her wrist away from her body with an enclosing thumb and forefinger, her arm attempting to resist against him.

"Pipes from the bath?" he asked, making a show to inspect the inside of her coat. With a chuckle, more so a snort, he jerked the fur from her shoulders, and forced her locked arms from the sleeves. Reuben slapped the fur into the butler's stunned face before driving his wife by the small of her back. She clenched her teeth as he herded her along. Couples behind them observed with interest and alarm.

"You defy reason. I don't know what gives you license to behave with such distrust," she antagonized.

He pinched her side forcibly, determined to keep her in close restraint. They entered the grand hall, maneuvering among huddles of luxuriously clad characters holding wine glasses and artificial smiles under clouds of cigarette and cigar smoke.

"Have I done something to cause you to behave so warily?"

"Enough, Kathy. I am not blind, even if you would like to pretend I am. You may as well abandon your game and suffer the consequences of what you have done."

"I've done nothing."

"I don't believe you, of course. But it's just as well, my pet," he yawned, continuing as though not hearing her, "I love you, despite your foolishness."

A gentleman strode at them with his hand extended, piercing through the poisonous shell of their friction. "There you are, Koryn! Lovely, lovely!"

Reuben bent to shake his hand, for the man was strikingly short. "Baron, good evening." He returned his heavy hand to Katherine's side.

"Here is a new thing! I have not seen you with a lady." The Baron raised his thick eyebrows at Katherine and his silver capped incisor tooth gleamed when he smiled widely, whispering loudly, "Mistress?"

"Wife," Reuben confirmed, and Katherine developed an immediate distaste for the Baron. She rolled her eyes and a sharp pinch startled her.

"Hello, Baron. What a lovely home you have. So modest and humble." Katherine grinned. Her diamond earrings directed light from the glittering chandeliers to play across her cheeks like tiny stars. Like Reuben, she stooped in order to shake the Baron's hand and the sweat from his palm transferred to her formerly clean fingers. Katherine suppressed her aversion with incalculable strength.

"Reuben, you fiend! Have you introduced her to my friends yet?" asked the Baron.

Katherine calmly wiped her hand on her skirt, elbowing Reuben's arm as the pain set in from his fingernails.

"I have not." Reuben surveyed the room.

"Come, come!" The Baron danced in place like an exhilarated child before leading with waving hands toward the thickest ensemble of guests.

The people were much taller than he, not surprisingly. They towered like a forest of boisterous, chattering trees that parted to admit their generous host into their circle. Women with necks draped in gaudy necklaces blushed and complimented, as the men beside them smoked and fought one another to dominate the conversation. Into their midst the Baron disappeared, except for his little hand extending from their limbs to wave the Koryns over.

Katherine followed on Reuben's heels, dragged by the hand. From the center of the gaggle the Baron introduced Reuben, who puffed his chest forward like a penguin. Then he presented Katherine to the group, "His *wife*, Mrs. Katherine Koryn, of the Madisons I believe, correct, Madame?"

"Correct." She mimicked his cheap grin and all attention turned to her. One of the women, leaning on the arm of the dashing gentleman beside Katherine, crooked forward into the clearing of their group and exclaimed to another across from her, "Look Claudia, isn't that gown quaint? I wore the same, last spring, to the Gates's afternoon picnic!"

Katherine let a smirk break through her mask as the other lady, Claudia presumably, assessed her with an arrogant amusement.

Reuben tugged at her elbow and bragged idiotically, "My Kathy, one of sometimes unpredictable style. Come to think of it, unpredictability all around!" He laughed heartily, obnoxiously even, and proclaimed, "Until now, that is! Some things, though born wild, can be harnessed and controlled. However, Miss Violet, I would tread carefully. Gentlemen, be sure that in our presence you keep your pistols and blades safely concealed and secure, and mind your drinks as well, for good measure." He smiled, much amused with himself.

A roar of laughter went round. Katherine glared sharply at her husband.

"We must have a bit of marital dissatisfaction seeping through the cracks." Lady Violet laughed, being the woman who had regarded Katherine's dress and to whom Reuben saw fit to give warning.

Katherine slid the cigar from the gentleman's hand beside her, meeting Lady Violet's eyes boldly. They ceased laughing and took on a jealous light. Her dashing companion scarcely minded as Katherine put her crimson lips against the cigar and artfully pulled in her breath. Releasing a billow of smoke, she said, "Oh, it's much more than a *bit*."

"Ah," the ladies sighed with raised eyebrows, relishing the show before them.

"Koryn, are there problems? No, she must be jesting for certain," the Baron muttered. "Yes, indeed. They jest." He laughed in a rattling little cackle.

Katherine blew smoke across his nose and narrowed her heated eyes.

"I will not lie. Be cautious about my wife. She has dark intentions and deviant thoughts," Reuben proclaimed.

Katherine shook her head dismissively, the eyes of the group raked her with scrutiny. With a sultry smile she said, "It's true, you should beware, all of you. Especially *you*, husband. Most carefully should you tread." She was eager to leave them hanging in threatened unease, however Reuben ensnared her with a quick hand.

"Do not wander off, dearest. I don't want you developing any more deadly plots. I must keep these eyes on you at all times."

"Only because you feel threatened," she jeered.

Lady Violet's gentleman chuckled exuberantly, and Katherine winked at him, savoring his cigar. "You are threatened by a *woman*, by your own little wife."

The group snickered together, except for Lady Violet and her faithful Claudia, who would not be caught dignifying Katherine's behavior. Instead, they scoffed and demonstrated their disgust with matching sour expressions.

Katherine touched Reuben's forehead with the back of her

hand. "What has put this idea into your mind—that I should be dangerous in any way. You've had too much to drink, how indulgent you are!"

"I haven't even finished one glass." Reuben gritted his teeth, the humiliation he meant to impart falling back on him.

"Well, then, you haven't had *enough*! Something is off!" She snapped her fingers at a passing waiter. Katherine swept a glass from his tray and slung it against Reuben's chest. "Cheers, dear."

Spitefully he watched her over the glass as he tipped it back.

Katherine easily detached from his grip. "There you are. Your delusions will soon fade from your mind." She addressed the group, "I would apologize for his behavior, but I have no part in it. And, although standing here with you has been the highlight of my deprived life, I will leave you at its apex." Katherine smiled at the women. "Lovely to meet you fine ladies especially. I shall always be envious, lacking that which you possess in abundance, aware that I may never master such skillful self-representation and the emptiness that leaves your shallow souls free from the burden of meaningful passion." She nudged Lady Violet's gentleman, who could not contain his gleeful snicker as she offered him his cigar.

Lady Violet and Claudia flinched with pinched faces, inexperienced at receiving insults. Before the meaning of her words could saturate and an actual retort could be devised, she made her escape.

Reuben did not pursue her. Perhaps he was too embarrassed, the scald of her attitude burning him into inaction. Perhaps he remained behind to save his reputation and flip the scene around on her or encourage it as a jest. The Baron assuredly maintained the belief, still chuckling after she departed from them.

In a separate corner of the inner hall, Katherine consigned herself to sit alone, observing various troupes of guests with contempt and restless anxiety. She vanished from them easily, retiring to the shadows where she could observe them unobstructed. During her study she catalogued the places she would rather be. In the passing moments, she imagined Trayten beside her. She felt him under her skin, as though he kept her, the way she kept the wealthy party-goers in sight. Endlessly she wondered, *Where are you now?*

❀

1909

Another night transformed the rickety old house into an icebox. Cold tremors racked her body and Katherine hurried to pull a thick nightgown over her chemisette. She paused before the mirror to ponder her image in the flattering light of a flickering candle on the chest of drawers. She rubbed her arms and shrugged. In the forgiving light she did not appear as old as she felt. Daylight would return inevitably to shine on the truth.

Katherine glanced at her bed with a frown. She blew out the candle's flame and smoke swirled across her face, illuminated by the frosty blue light of wintry sea shining through the window-pane. The room was left to its solitude.

Entering his bedroom, Katherine discovered that the window was open, and the night air surrounded his scarcely covered, motionless body. She dashed into the crisp cloud at the foot of his bed and jerked at the casements, fighting the wind to shut them.

A wisp of white breath propelled when she shuddered. Her hands stung from the polar bite of the windowpane and rubbing them together she determined to catch her breath, gazing at Tray with concern. Katherine perched on the end of the bed near his feet. He lay outstretched and at rest before her.

At last she could breathe when his chest lifted. Nimbly, and careful not to disturb him, she gathered and replaced the quilt that abandoned him for the bottom edge of the bed. Kneeling at his side, she tucked the covers against his legs, her first thought to be careful and not wake him, her second, realizing that he could not feel her. Her hands pressed on the bed beside him.

He slept as they say, like the dead; in perfect stillness, serene inactivity. He breathed soundlessly through his nose, his lips resting sealed and composed. She studied his cheekbones, brow, and temples; consolidating each with memory, validating that she remembered them accurately. His was the face that haunted her dreams, and they were the features carved into her subconscious. He was often present in her mind, his image fresh throughout the years when she closed her eyes.

She resisted the inclination to trace the delicate skin of his eyelids, the dark, full length of his eyelashes, and the warm curve of his lips. A piercing sorrow cut through her, for she could summon the memory of the smooth heat of his kiss, the silken surface of his neck against her cheek.

Though the memory remained unforgettable, it could do little to ease the pain of longing in the face of such separation. Temptation exhausted her, riveted by his allure. Even with the secrets, barriers, and unfamiliarity between them, the ruse could not contain her prevailing adoration.

What would he do if I held him, she wondered. *If I lay down beside him the way I would have years ago*? How effortlessly she could fit her body against his own. It seemed possible that even the years between them could not change his tendencies in slumber and that his arm would respond to her nearness and draw her closer. At rest, as in wakefulness, he had known her the same; with as much attention and interest, aware of her every move and reacting to keep her near.

In the past they slept as entangled as two bodies could manage. When she woke in the night, she would turn and he would pursue, unconsciously reaching to hold her. He would not release her. He would hold onto her through the night. Awakening to present reality, Katherine recognized the length of time that she had been sleeping without him.

The stillness was disrupted, and she drew back, thinking she roused him somehow. Tray jerked. His eyes remained shut as he stirred. Deep rumbles were trapped in his throat, tension rippled across his forehead, his eyebrows converged, and his nostrils flared. His arm thrust out and hit the pillow. His body contracted and he curled inward. He whispered, "No, wait! No!" Sweat covered his face.

The seizure intensified and Katherine jumped back to avoid the swing of his fist. In pain and fury he shouted. He jolted and she leaped, crawling onto him with determination. As she straddled his ineffectual legs, he cried a broken gasp that resembled her name.

"Trayten, wake up!" She arrested him by the shoulders. Katherine kept her weight on him, shaking him. The urgency to rouse him increased each second he remained unresponsive. "I am here! I'm here, Trayten! Open your eyes!"

An instant of stillness surmounted him and remarkably he did as she asked. He opened his eyes. Katherine lingered, suspended over him. He startled her when he looked up and she drew in a breath. With bewilderment he moved his head, straining to acclimate to his wakeful state, no doubt aware of the sweat soaking his hair and the peculiar restraint of the 'specialist.' Disoriented he exhaled, "Wha?"

"You're awake, thank God, Trayten, you're all right now," she swallowed, although her throat was dry, and her nerves were frazzled. "And I'm here."

"Where?"

"You were tossing and thrashing. You were ensnared in some terrible dream! Can you see me? Can you concentrate at all?"

"I can't...I can't feel anything, my legs," he gasped, lost in the haze where inability was forgotten.

"You haven't felt your legs, not for eight years. Are you awake at all?" Katherine asked.

"I'm not sleeping! You're not supposed to be here!"

"Tell me, what was it you saw?"

He avoided the burning of her eyes, erecting a barricade.

Katherine would not retreat. "Tell me, what did you see? I know you saw something."

"I've seen nothing." Tray turned his face away from her.

"I won't accept that! You were dreaming!"

"No." He closed his eyes.

"Stop this! Don't lie to me! I heard you calling out. You said 'No.' You writhed in your sleep as though fighting someone. Don't you want to know? If you tell me I can help you to fit the pieces together!"

"I don't know!"

Katherine's voice cracked, more wounded and tentative than forceful as before. "Please, all I need is a glimpse, something you saw."

"A glimpse? A glimpse of blackness, darkness, nothingness? There's nothing relevant or real! Words can't describe what I can't even recognize!"

"How can you be sure unless you try? Something has to linger in your mind. Your memory of life before Alderney is lost, but not your memory of a moment ago, a day ago, of last night's dream, this moment's vision! You've seen things you don't forget, and you hide them, claiming to know nothing of anything!" She pushed his shoulders down. "Look at me!"

He turned his face away.

"Look!" She put a hand to his jaw and directed his face toward her. "I'm not going away! I'm not letting you get away with this! You're hiding! Trust me and *tell* me, don't be afraid!"

"I'm not afraid! There's nothing I can tell you! Let it be! You can't help me, so find another hopeless case to harass!"

Their eyes caught and held, and he drank in the transparent anguish flowing from her wide-open heart. Even his severity was thwarted by an injured expression.

She loosened her grip from his shoulders, her head bowed, and she inhaled with a quake. "You remember your dreams, but you push them down as soon as they surface, out of fear or hurt. These fragments are the keys to your future! You act like you *want* to forget, to *be* forgotten! You need to search! I have searched. I feared the worst, but I never gave up, because my failure only led to my loss. I know your black void, your darkness! I've felt it for years. And I refuse to leave you in it. It's why I'm here, it's why I *can't* let go."

"What! What am I? You need to solve me in order to somehow redeem yourself for *your* mistakes?"

"Oh, stop this!" She faltered in her composure. "We are battling, you and I. It can't end until you speak to me, look again, through the darkness and find it! What did you see? Is it the day you were wounded?"

"No."

"Trayten, please!" She pressed his shoulders again. "Was it winter, on a cliff? Tell me what you saw, you said a name. Who was with you?"

"No one! I can't!"

"Search the blackness. Who is she? Can't you remember her, Trayten? You said her name!"

He shook his head.

"What happened to you?" Katherine pleaded.

"I don't see anyone, I see white…I see rage!"

"Remember!" Her voice cracked with despair.

"There's nothing!"

"There is *me*! Trayten, remember! Please, *remember* me!" Her words were jagged with sobs and her speech cut short. She released him.

He too was stricken, eyes wide open and fixed on her horrified expression. Katherine covered her mouth as if she could retract the admission. He searched her eyes. He caught it as soon as she said it.

Awkwardly she slid from the bed onto the floor with trembling legs. His scrutinizing stare followed her. Katherine left him there with his mind circulating on the escalation of her temper, the fervor of her words, her pleading, and her hasty retreat.

The weight of her body, as it had compressed him, left another impression, under which it was impossible to move. Numbness set in, accompanied by shreds of insight from a dream, like those from other dreams, unforgettable and haunting from the past.

❧

1906

I had a glimpse of you
in a fickle state of dreaming,
so near, in seconds brief
yet I surely felt you breathing.

The warmth that's overdue,
of your lips' attentive praising
the eagerness of my skin
for their touch, surreal, amazing.

And I think I saw your eyes
out of darkness, sweetly hovering,
although you're nowhere near me,
I woke with your presence covering.

❧

When a sliver of electric pink marked the eastern horizon for the rising of the sun, Katherine had made it to St. Anne where she hoped to find a ticketing agent for the ferry.

"Where are you off to, Mrs. Koryn?" Mary emerged to obstruct her path in Victoria Street.

"Is that luggage in your hand?" Louisa appeared at her sister's side.

"Come inside and sit awhile by the fire," Mary insisted.

Excited and jubilant Louisa clapped. "Oh come, come in!"

Sunlight was filling the iridescent street. Katherine carefully chose her footing to avoid the slick patches of melting ice. She glanced at the sisters and their eager smiles cultivated by chronic loneliness.

"I haven't time, I'm afraid," she answered.

"Oh! No," Louisa groaned.

"Well, where are you going, dear?" Mary nudged her sister with a round hip. "It's very early! Not early for us. We are *always* awake, but early for you, and early for anyone at the Boley house, that lair. Indeed, much too early!"

"And luggage, Mrs. Koryn. I know a leather suitcase when I see one." Louisa inspected Katherine's bag. "Although, yours is especially fantastic in design, kind of like those numbers in the catalogs that Mary clips the return addresses from, so I can't order anything. Does it have embossed leather detailing on the top around a custom silver clasp?" She stretched her neck forward to peer around Katherine's gloved hand.

"Perhaps. I'm not certain. I'm on my way to catch the ferry. You must forgive me, for I can't stop and visit."

"Are you giving up on him?" Their smiles faded as Louisa asked. "Are you finding yourself outdone?"

Katherine moved to speak, bothered by the preciseness of the observation. She paled and before she could muster a response, Mary drew close to tenderly touch her arm. "Dear, you are all that man has for hope in the world. Would you really go and leave him to the likes of Miss Boley?"

"I can't explain. I have to go or I'll miss the ferry." She shrugged, guilty shadows in her eyes.

"But—" Louisa called after however further sound was smothered by Mary's hand over her mouth.

"Hush dear. We may pray, but all else is beyond our control."

❦

Narrowly, a shred of white daylight peered through the heavy drapes. The sunbeam fell in a jagged line across the rumpled blanket covering his legs. He stared at the wall, fatigued, for sleep evaded him cruelly. There were muffled footsteps in the hall and his interest was stirred. Curiously he waited, anticipation building after hours of silent contemplation.

When the door opened his face fell in disappointment at the sight of Marian. Her hair sprang from under her nightcap, her arm balanced his breakfast on a platter.

"Where is Katherine?" he demanded.

Marian hummed, disregarding his question and eyeing him like a wild bird of carrion for the fierce set of her eyes. She set the plate on his bedside table and stirred the gelatinous porridge that smelled like scalded glue. Her arm flapped as she beat the mush into submission.

"Where is Katherine?" A grave tone accented the second inquiry, accompanied by a pointed stare.

"Breakfast, T.B.," Marian said with a shrill inflection. She lifted a spoonful in his direction as if she would feed him.

"I won't eat that. What are you doing in here?"

"It is my house, or have you forgotten? I am your caretaker, am I not? No more unrest, no more disturbances. Mrs. Koryn has gone and if we are fortunate, for good."

"When?"

"Oh, must have been early. She was simply gone."

"And her things?" He investigated.

"Pretty much gone." Marian blinked slowly.

"Pretty much?"

Marian huffed, holding her hand under the spoonful, which she raised to his face and was forced to withhold each time he replied. "T.B., I have had enough of it! That's it! That's all I know! She's done nothing but disrupt your peace, provoke you to fits, and expect too much for anyone's good! I didn't like her personally. I don't know who sent her, but I've never heard of a specialist to be so unprofessional!"

"I need a cigarette," he grunted. "Get out."

"You need to eat this, that's what you *need*, and no more smoking!"

"I said get out!" he roared and sent Marian reeling. She dropped the spoon and clumsily tripped for the hallway. He thrust the platter at her heels and porridge splattered, and the dishes smashed against the wall.

Above the mercantile, at the top of a narrow staircase, Katherine passed through the door into a cozy flat. A blend of cinnamon, plum, and citrus saturated the air as she entered the parlor and set her luggage beside the faded blue sofa. A cast iron stove warmed the room, welcome against the frost clinging to her skin.

Stillness permeated the atmosphere. Quaint paintings with muted colors depicting country scenes covered the walls. Katherine removed her gloves and crossed the parlor to a paneled hallway. Past the little white kitchen and around a corner, she followed the faint murmur of voices.

Eliza, dainty and fair, appeared more advanced in years than in fact she was. Lines beset by worry and disappointment etched beneath her dimmed eyes. Thinner and more fragile than when she was blighted by fevers in her youth, her white gown hung from her frame like an oversized robe. Yet her mouth curved into a content smile at the child at her feet.

Late evening light filled the nursery, a twilight brightness soon to fizzle away with the approach of night. In preparation for the dim, several candles burned along the mantle of a minuscule fireplace. The room resembled a petite library more than a playroom. Books filled the shelves along each wall, and stacks of them covered two end tables beside a pair of gray brocade armchairs. A somber faced child, fascinated by the worlds found in books, read aloud to her aunt in a low tone.

Katherine removed her black feathered hat. The child raised a head of shiny black curls. The distance melted away. When Katherine beheld Angelle, her pain both diminished and deepened. Gazing at the child's large brown eyes, her round cherub face, and her mouth, with the same solemn set as her father's, the sting of his absence was magnified.

Angelle stared at her mother with an unchanged expression, with no animation at all. Her thin little figure curled over the book in her lap, her lily-white fingers pinching a page. Eliza waited patiently, careful to not disturb their reunion. Angelle sat up, head high in the manner of her poised mother, hair as shining, and manners as elegant.

Katherine sank to her knees before her daughter and gathered her little hands to kiss them through a deep sigh of relief.

Angelle's expression was compassionate, insightful. "Is it what we have feared?"

Katherine, breathing warmth onto her daughter's hands, said, "I don't know. It could be worse."

Eliza tilted her head and reached for her neck. Deep sympathy laced her voice, "Katherine, you're tired, most surely."

"More than I can say," was the weary reply.

"How can it be *worse*?" Angelle drew back. "Did we not find him?"

"We have found him and it's certainly him, I haven't any doubt."

"I waited very long this time." Angelle squeezed her mother's hands. "I read your letters, again and again."

"We have been praying for you, Katherine," Eliza offered, unsure what emotion to express, for the delighted sentiment of the news was dampened by Katherine's moroseness. "Even Arnold has offered his prayers. But honestly, I'm baffled to see you. We did not expect you back so soon."

"I'm afraid that through impatience, I have ruined everything."

A door closed from the front of the flat. "That's Arnold. I shall go and keep him company." As Eliza passed she touched Katherine's shoulder.

Katherine caught her by the hand. "Eliza, I thank you for all you've done, for taking care of her. Truly I—"

"No, Katherine. I thank you." Eliza smiled and drifted through the doorway.

Angelle pensively asked her mother, "Well?"

Katherine lifted Angelle onto her lap in the chair that Eliza relinquished. She endeavored to summon and organize her words.

"You wrote to me and said that we found him," Angelle prompted.

"Yes."

"He is not dead," the child declared with a frown.

"He is alive, dearest one," Katherine assured.

"And—"

"And I desperately wish I knew more. I wish I could have been there and seen what happened to him. I can't say what was done to him, but I *can* infer by the impressions left behind that it was…in fact—" she caught her breath and swallowed with difficulty, "—severe. Before he vanished, he was hurt very badly."

Angelle concentrated on her. Against sorrow, Katherine said hoarsely, "Let me tell you a story," and she recounted to Angelle what she knew of Trayten's condition and the process of her attempts to guide him to remember. The child listened patiently until she had explained everything, then nestled her warm, round cheek against Katherine's chest, her soft curls tucked under Katherine's chin.

There the heart beat sadly. Katherine sighed again, embracing Angelle with childlike vulnerability of her own. Her daughter's voice reasoned, resembling her father's simple, rational logic.

"We have found him. He's ours, Momma. He may not know it yet, but he belongs with us."

"He is not the same man, not the picture I've painted you. Time and anguish and cruel fate have distorted him. You must be prepared for this."

"I'm not frightened." Angelle lifted her chin boldly. "However distorted, he is *ours*. We found him and I must meet him."

"It's a risk. But, what else can we do?"

"Nothing." Angelle shrugged.

"Then you'll come back with me to Alderney. I'm confident you can handle the splintery Miss Boley."

A smile revealed the youth in Angelle's face. It faded and she said, "I missed you."

Katherine smiled brightly, kissed her forehead, and gathered her in a tight embrace, safe against the world.

Katherine was happily reacquainted with her sister's exceptional cooking. Eliza blushed while admitting to her accomplishments since having attended cooking classes at the Pembroke Road Bakery on Tuesday evenings. Evident by the rounding out of his figure, Arnold was reaping the benefits of her new skills. Though altered to twice his former size, Arnold remained as hospitable as ever. He was warm, jovial, and welcoming.

Katherine stared vacantly over the scraps of paper littering the table. Arnold held an expense ledger between his hands and pressed his nose into the spine of it, a pair of spectacles perched at the end. Eagerly he set about to balance her spending and evaluate what remained in her accounts. When he raised his face and removed his spectacles, he smiled to announce his conclusion, "All is in order, of course. Your expenses are well within your budget this month. In short, there is more than you should ever have need of."

In response, Katherine laid her head on her arm at the table's edge, her eyes cast down, vacuous and glum. "What empty comfort it is. Figures, numbers. The bitter spoils of war."

"How long will you stay?" Eliza peeked into the guest bedroom where Katherine unpacked blouses and skirts from her suitcase. She roughly beat at their wrinkles and folds after hanging them in the armoire. The diamonds on her finger flashed, glittering and bright against the dark colored fabrics, like violently falling stars in the night sky.

"I wanted to visit Hilda. Perhaps I'll leave after tomorrow. I've left some things in Alderney and I wouldn't put it past Miss Boley to dispose of them."

"This Miss Boley, she is his nurse?"

"She is his prison guard."

"I couldn't believe it," Eliza sighed. "When you wrote to me that you found him, *really* found him. I didn't doubt that you would, only it's gone on for years—your wandering, the searching. I couldn't quite imagine it ending."

"There is much to be done," Katherine said, pondering with her gaze fixed on the floor.

"And yet, your most fervent prayer has been answered! What a testimony!" Eliza smiled. "He is alive! It's remarkable!"

"He is alive," Katherine said meekly. Her eyes wandered to the window.

"I'll leave you to rest."

"Goodnight, Eliza."

From the darkness of her room Angelle slipped away and stole into her mother's chamber to crawl into her bed. Katherine held her close, humming the tune that lingered in her mind, Hilda's song.

The dark-haired pair traveled the streets of Portsea. The sight of familiar lanes and buildings brought a nostalgic gleam to Katherine's eyes. The parks, blanketed with snow, inspired memories of laying in the warm summer grass with Trayten. Recollections of her guardian lover, shadowing her through the crowd, filled the marketplace, where vendors stood beleaguered by interested consumers.

Even under the white rule of the winter sky and snow-covered trees, colors enlivened the season, carried on the garments of passersby and gleaming from store fronts, carriage sides, and motor cars. There had been changes in the years since Katherine frequented the streets; new shops replaced various withering businesses, young trees along the boulevards gained height, and new, brightly painted signs suggested the prosperity of several remaining stores. Katherine's usually determined stride was awkward, caught up with identifying the modifications, spinning around to take notice of each one.

No quiet, barren solace was here, like that which enveloped the town of St. Anne on Alderney. A lively chorus of voices billowed from the crowds. Breath hung as white clouds over their heads, like the smoke swelling from hundreds of chimneys. Not even the frigid air could dampen the busy goings-on of the town. Tires cut tracks in snow packed streets, young men and boys dragged carts and carried packages. On corners and in the alleys of the shops, artists in their poverty slouched or slumped, painting, weaving, and singing in the shadows of the wealthy who passed them under the sunlight.

The living, active multitude elicited deep sentiment. She was at home here, safe amid the commotion. In crowds she could easily hide. Unlike the wide-open spaces, the expanses across England she had traveled and the desolate stretch of Alderney, where loneliness was her cruel companion. Here in the crowd, she drifted unnoticed, apart, yet connected. She was content, secure, and concealed.

The massive main corridor of the asylum was paved in gray tile, imitating the high stone walls that consumed them.

"Do you promise to wait for me in this hall?" Katherine asked.

"Where would I go?" Angelle remarked with a serious face.

Katherine glanced back at the large woman in a green wool stuff dress who waited with tight lips and clasped hands. "I trust you won't wander away."

"I will be here," Angelle promised. Katherine touched her cheek before following the nurse toward the secure wing of the asylum.

A chair was brought in and placed remotely in the center of the bare cell. Colorless light sneaked through narrow, barred windows. The door slammed and latched behind Katherine and a slot in the panel pinched shut with a shrill squeal of metal.

Hilda Koryn, more than ever, was confined to her wheelchair. She wilted against its weary frame, draped in a dingy gown that once had been white, perhaps. Her hair hung in thin wisps on her narrow, bony shoulders. There were hints of color in her translucent skin and in her hair, however the rest of her had dulled to an ashen gray.

Hilda had aged rapidly. Illness, despair, and perhaps the exertions of psychological disability marked her face with weary lines. Her cheeks were gaunt, her lips pale and thin. Her hands testified of her age however, the skin as smooth and tight as Katherine's.

Fragile and feeble, Hilda's skeletal form hid in the chair that swallowed her. And yet sunlight penetrated the pale dusk of the room when Hilda smiled.

"You sly girl! Gone for days and now you appear, as if I sent you any invitation." Her eyes failed to focus.

Katherine smiled. "Forgive me?"

"I cannot forgive this *decor*, dear! I haven't warmed to it yet."

Katherine ran her fingers along the dusty concrete wall, collecting cobwebs. "At least it's not *mismatched*."

"Can't mismatch without color, can you," Hilda affirmed. She sank lower in her chair. "Where have they all gone?"

"Who, Hilda?"

"Everyone. They *all*. Is there no Portsmouth anymore? Did it depart? I can't see out. Is there anything left, beyond this? They've ceased to exist."

"The town is still there, Hilda. People have gone and changed, but Portsmouth remains."

"How many days since I've seen your face? Oh, no—" Hilda stilled, her gaze swiveling around the room. "—my mallet! Did you see it in the hall? Did that woman in the trees have it, the lady with the glass eyes? She's taken other things too. They've all lost something and told me about it. She took my rings, my shoes," she glanced deliriously at her feet. "But, no, not my mallet!"

"I'm afraid I didn't see any mallets," Katherine said.

"Blast! They took Miss Parsley's undergarments, didn't you know, so that she wouldn't hang herself with them."

"Oh my," Katherine gasped. "What ward is she in?"

"The cafeteria, dear. Of course. Can you imagine, hanging in your own under-things?"

"Hilda—"

"Though someone else's would be *much* worse!"

"Certainly, much worse."

"Good Heavens!" Hilda shuddered, revolted by the idea.

A sad resignation colored Katherine's face. She surveyed the primitive accommodation.

"Katherine? Dear girl, why are you so sullen? A new bride ought to be bursting with joy. Why aren't you celebrating?"

"I am not a bride anymore, Hilda. It has been years since then. Don't you remember? Your son is, he is gone."

Hilda could not hear her, and she continued, staring through Katherine into an illusion of the past. "There is no room for regret, or for tears. If you are not happy as a new bride, it is no one's fault but your own."

The words stung. The only way to reach Hilda was to slip into the past. "You must understand, Hilda. You made the wrong choice. *You* married where you did not love, and you suffered as I do. I didn't want this, and I never deluded myself into believing I could be happy with Reuben."

"*You* married him."

"I had no choice!" Katherine cried, yet it came as a reflex from the past.

"Of course you did! You could have told them no, only you couldn't stand the notion of being poor."

Once again she felt like a young woman standing on the brink of her greatest mistake, at the beginning of its consequence, heavy with regret and desperate to assign the blame elsewhere. The burden of the fault crushed her soul, for she knew it was her own.

"You might have dreamed about it; living on scraps in the arms of passion, yet you could never have gone through with it." It was possible that Hilda spoke purely from the perspective of her own experience, as she had also chosen security over love. "You know your limitations, the limitations of your dreams. Reuben is the practical choice. To follow passion would have led to a shortened life and death from starvation or disease, to be sure. Take comfort, Katherine. You may not love him now, but you will appreciate him as the years pass, you will see that he has *saved* your life in the end."

"I alone made my choice, and it was the wrong one." Katherine bowed her head. "But I cannot give in to that extent of acceptance, nor could you, despite what you say. I'm older, Hilda, and Reuben is dead. I'm sorry that I couldn't find it in my heart to care for him, even though he provided for me. But I don't blame him for my misery, because I brought it on myself. I *know* that now. And I live with it every day.

"Because of me, Reuben is dead. Because of my selfish fear, I set everything in motion for the ruin of us all. I broke the heart of the only man I love and sentenced him to a misery more unimaginable than my own. And I can never make it right. All I can do is own my part in it, which is *every* part." Katherine offered her tearful confession to Hilda, for whether or not she would be lucid enough to understand it, it begged to be said aloud. "I was terrified of poverty, regardless of my great passion. I couldn't bring myself to leap, to let go. The fear stunned me to inaction, and I clung to the life that fate gave me; my station and my comforts, which became my rightful prison. If I never live free from misery again, it would not be restitution enough for the damage I've caused."

Hilda snapped up straight in her chair and blinked. "Did you say something, dear?"

The well of emotion, broken briefly open, receded as she followed Hilda back to the present, leaving her pain behind for the moment. "I've got Angelle with me today. She is beautiful and frightfully smart."

"The bastard child, right?"

"My daughter, Hilda," Katherine said, disregarding the noxious label.

"Sweet pet, and how old now, she was only—"

"She is seven."

"No, she was tiny when I last saw her. She can't be *seven*! Good Lord! What is she, four? How long have I been *here*?" Hilda looked around her.

"She is seven years old."

"Looks like you?"

"Somewhat." Katherine softly, sadly turned her eyes to the ground, and envisioned Trayten's face.

"Lovely, lovely."

"She looks like her father, really."

"I couldn't say who *that* is, dear, aside from human," Hilda scoffed. "Did you close my window? It's gotten stuffy in here and if you closed my window my starlings can't get in."

The window was barred, the thick milky glass set between frames of iron. Katherine sighed, "Sorry."

"Open it up, will you?"

"I will, Hilda."

"Thank you, dear." Hilda tilted her head to the ceiling and smiled. "You are the only visitor I've had, you know. I was sure they would go away eventually and never return, leaving me here the first chance they got. Maybe it was because Reuben was gone and Augustus saw no purpose in staying, after all, most of the Koryn properties were passed on, and now of course belong to you. What would Augustus want with his widowed daughter-in-law's property? No, more wealth was to be made elsewhere, where the rumors ran out and none knew the stories. New lands and new tenants.

"He ran from the embarrassment. He doesn't have to know me, or *you*, anymore. I think he has bought himself a mistress to add to his decorations. I never made for a pretty one on his arm, stuck in my chair, indeed." Hilda kept her eyes straight and focused them on the barred window. "The embarrassment of you, most of all, drove him away. After my boy and you returned, him in a box, and you with child, it was your disregard for him, your preoccupation that drove those accusations."

"I promised you the truth, Hilda, always." Katherine's pulse quickened, recalling the aftermath of Reuben's death. "I did not kill your son."

"So you say. He was dead and you were a perfect suspect. I really don't care. They never loved me. And I don't pretend he was ever much to you. Maybe I'm trying to justify why my husband abandoned me. Funny, he should be the one burdened with justifying it, even if he wouldn't bother. He and Reuben were exactly alike. Why am I in a prison? I'd give anything for curtains, for grass and pretty sheets.

"Don't ever close your eyes. You do it for an instant, and when you open them again you have lost everything, or it's been taken, while you were off in your head, no more pelicans, no more music. They've taken your sanity and it's too late to say a word, to save yourself. You are already in the asylum, where no one wants your words, and no one can hear them, even if you could find the energy to speak."

Katherine contemplated Hilda in bewilderment and pity.

"Ah, I remember what I meant to tell you: you will." She wheeled toward her bed. "You will be free. And I too will be free, very soon. I'm leaving this place. But help me to bed before *you* go."

⁂

Released from the cell, Katherine stepped into the narrow hall of the locked wing with a dampness clinging to her skin and exhaustion bearing down on her. She gasped deeply, as though she had been asphyxiated. The oppressive gray walls closed in, disconnecting her from the outside world.

The thin ease of the winter air was never wanted more and a frantic compulsion to breathe it gripped her. The clicking echo of her footsteps skipped farther into the darkness behind her. Katherine strode toward liberation. Stress tightened the muscles in her neck, and she rolled her shoulders back against the strain.

Not even the rapid clap of her mother's heels could shake the child from her concentration. Angelle was seated on a stone bench in a window of the vast corridor, one leg curled under her, her elbow resting on her knee, diminutive chin perched on the fist of the same arm. The focus of her unflinching stare was the ivory chess board with pieces arrayed across it, set between Angelle and a man who could be mistaken for none other than a resident of the asylum.

The gentleman engaged in the game wore a stained nightshirt. He was extremely thin and birdlike, with a slim neck arching forward, a bald head, and a sharp jutting nose. He waited for his opponent to move and grinned widely, glancing from her to the board, his open mouth revealing a toothless, blackened territory.

Katherine drew carefully near, for his eyes shifted in their sockets and he rocked where he sat with his legs crossed at the knees.

Angelle was little, if at all, affected by his abnormal characteristics. She swung the leg that dangled off the side of the seat, her shiny boot catching the light that sifted through the thick, marbled glass in the window. She slid her bishop behind the white king, capturing the white queen and placing her opponent in check.

The turn of events provoked the gentleman to stretch his mouth wider and elicit a shriek, rattling and blaring. Katherine jumped, jarred and unsettled by it, however Angelle calmly glanced at her mother, dark eyes impassive.

The child slid from her bench and bowed properly toward her opponent, his mouth hanging open, a chess piece gleaming from within, swimming in saliva. "Don't forget that pattern," Angelle instructed with authority in her voice. "If you employ that, you shall be successful."

He bobbed his head rapidly and extended his hand. She shook his fingers, though they could not grip for the arthritis that stiffened and curled them. With her aloof, staid expression, Angelle said politely, "Good evening, Charles. And good luck."

"Shall we walk home, dearest?" Katherine asked, smiling pensively.

"Yes." Angelle took her hand, and they commenced the journey through the colossal hall to the metal doors separating them from the world beyond.

"Were you not frightened of that man?" Katherine asked, relishing a deep gasp of unsullied air in the evening.

"He was in desperate need of chess maneuvers, Momma. The large patient the nurse called Grommet was unbeatable and had been winning Charles' custard daily. It was apparent when I saw the fellow, he hadn't eaten any custard in quite some time. So I shared my strategy with him."

In happy amazement Katherine grinned at her clever, fearless Angelle.

❦ 21 ❦

1900

Trayten eclipsed the light from the window in the dim, dusty flat. Beneath his silhouette, streaks and splotches of vermillion, yellow ochre, indigo, and aquamarine darkened. He squeezed the handle of a brush in his fist. His latest work leaned on the far wall, caught in the light that escaped him, its glittering mixture of blues staring back.

He wore a ragged tunic, his arms unrestricted, and his suspenders hung uselessly from the band of his belt. With hair hanging in the line of his intense focus, he stared into the painting, losing himself in the mirage of it, exploring it from within. He dove into it, swimming through the technique he had executed and examining the strokes that comprised the hauntingly realistic image. It far surpassed his prior attempts. Something in it stirred his blood and whispered to his soul.

Katherine opened the door and entered, prying his attention from the counterfeit to the real. A mixture of eager relief and anxious disbelief deepened his eyes like black pools. The vision moved toward him and broke through the void dividing them. She locked her arms around his neck.

Trayten threw his paintbrush to the floor and clutched her to him, determined to crush her by the strength of his hold. She gasped. Her breath squeezed from her body. She kissed him ardently. He clawed his fingers through her hair. He surrounded her, enveloped her, towering over her, arms wrapping around her.

⚜

"I have to keep you. I can't lose you anymore." Trayten stared at the ceiling from his bed. He held Katherine in his arms, her head resting on his chest.

"Do you think you will lose me?" Katherine asked. She tilted her head back to gaze at his face.

His eyes were fixed on her. "When you are not with me, I'm left wanting. You're rarely, if ever, with me. I can't survive it. I need you too much."

"You won't lose me."

"So quick you are to promise. It's not easy to put faith in a promise so flippantly made," Trayten said, gently tossing her own reasoning regarding promises back at her. "And what about him? I watch you smile from his arm."

Katherine covered his mouth. "I'm trying to break free, to get rid of him. I've tried to kill him!"

"Brilliant plan." Trayten pulled her hand from his mouth and raised his voice. "If you succeed they'll lock you up, and what *then*? You would trade your figurative prison for a literal one. Be reasonable."

"Oh forgive me!" She sat up, flushed and erratic. "But I don't care! I've transcended reason! All I can think about is wanting him gone! I long to be *with* you!"

"These irrational ideas of yours! You long to be with me, so you say and yet you ignore the simplest solution!" His tone was exacting yet also tender.

"I am trying. You don't see it, but I'm trying!"

Trayten glared at the wall, letting the echo of her words fade before he suggested sharply, "And while you are *trying*, spending your time in his company, lavished with gifts, you can be sure you aren't growing to love him?"

"I should strike you for that!"

"Go on, strike me. I'm no stranger to pain. But I retain the right to wonder, to fear, when I remain here ignorantly waiting. Wasting away with nothing."

"Nothing? You had your art before me, it was enough to paint—"

"It was my own then! Now you're inseparable from it. You've infected it. I try to distract myself, but you are there, in everything I paint, and I can't make any money from them, I cannot *sell* you. So I starve while you haunt me."

The pain in his expression and his voice wounded her. She cried, "But I am not gone! How can I haunt you when I'm right in front of you?"

"You are gone most of the time. Even when I can see you from a distance, I'm alone, *more* alone then, because you're with him."

"So stop following me then! If you're always in agony."

"Yes, I'm always in agony," he affirmed. "How can I be otherwise as long as you're another man's wife?"

"I told you, I'm trying! Maybe it isn't enough for you but, what more can I do?" she cried.

Trayten shook his head at her, torn between his love and his frustration. The risk of driving her away loomed too costly. As he stared into her eyes, he wrestled with the suspicion that he was not enough for her, not worth trading her wealth for.

"You can make a real choice!" he said.

"And what does that mean?"

"You know what it means." It broke his heart that she seemed determined to cling to the assertion of her own helplessness.

"A real choice? What is that?"

"I'm more disturbed that you can't comprehend it on your own. There's no point in telling you," he said, disappointed.

"Trayten!" She squeezed his arm, his skin warm under her fingers. "Trayten, talk to me!"

He breathed steadily, and she waited. His reluctance was imminent. He refused to risk provoking her anger and declared himself a coward, cursing his weakness inwardly. "Are you trying to torment me? Do you even love me, Katherine?"

In years to come she would not be able to decipher the reason for that nervous, broken laugh, and that senseless reply. "You know how I feel."

His eyes shut tight to shield his pain from view. "I love *you*."

"And, I *knew* that, without you having to tell me." Her reply lingered in the particles of air between them, thick and obtrusive.

His eyes were firm and black. His voice sounded deep and heavy. "I would do anything for you. For the rest of my life, it's all I want. If there were anyone in the world standing in my way to you, in between us, I would go around them, or through them if I had to! I wouldn't leave you alone, not for one night. Wherever you want to go, I would take you, if I had to carry you on my back, anywhere, I'd carry you *everywhere*." He leaned in to kiss her and she turned her cheek to his lips.

"Are you not going to kiss me?" Tratyen asked. "Don't turn away from me."

Katherine wondered how she could face his devotion when his words exposed her guilt. She was too fearful to admit it and proclaim her selfishness, her weakness. The fear held her silent, and she withdrew.

He interpreted it as indifference. On his fingertip he caught the tear that escaped her eye.

"Am I hurting you?" he asked. "Because if I am, you should go away. I don't want to make you cry. I'm not worth it. Nothing would be."

"Don't tell me to leave!" she gasped. "I am agreeing! I haven't made a choice! And I need to. You want this to end? I'll end it! I'll let go of what I've known all my life. I will leave him. I'll tell the whole truth. I'll lose my family, my name, my home, but I'll do it. I'll do it for you if you can promise me that you will never leave me, that we will be together, because Trayten, if you left me." She released a storm of tears. "If I lost you, it would kill me. I would never get beyond it."

He could not contain his smile, even as it was ill-suited to meet her tears and her anguished expression. He held her face between his warm hands. "I promise you, against my life, which is worthless without you, that I'll never leave you. And if we fall apart, I will find you. A soul is pathetic cut in two, and we are one, Katherine. No matter what your family says, or his, you never belonged with him in that world! We've been fighting through a nightmare, but it will end! We can wake up now. We can make it right!"

Katherine closed her hands around his wrists, and he kissed each tear that traveled down her face. He held her again in his arms. "Here is where you belong! That's the end of it. I may be destitute, I may be lowly, but I love you with abundance, and that's all that matters."

Against the warmth of his skin, Katherine sighed a laugh.

⚜

There was no longer any regard for secrecy. Katherine had decided to leave Reuben, and she remained with Trayten to celebrate her liberation. They went about the town as they pleased. In the park they strolled beneath the gold and amber canopies of changing leaves. They took refuge from blustery winds in their library and danced again like ghostly shadows in the dusty seclusion.

Aboard a ferry they stood underneath the brassy autumn sun. The broad passenger vessel sloshed through the harbor as Portsea shrank and quieted behind them. Its mosaic of fiery hues, with the dying of the leaves, smeared and blended like an impressionist painting. Crisp, sharp moisture thinned the air, warning of the winter to come.

Wrapped in Trayten's black jacket, Katherine held his bowler hat against the breeze. Her hair danced wildly around her face and she laughed, resembling a child in adult clothing for her petite stature. He balanced on one foot atop the bench before her, bowed to the water, and wobbled with the lift of the tide. She squealed at his comical expression and beamed as he recited his delirious song.

Few other passengers braved the arctic gusts on deck, and they were taken aback by the raggedy pair. Trayten wobbled again, throwing his arms wide to maintain his balance and his voice cracked, lost in the wake of the ferry, carried on the traveling air. "Under the moonlight there, your fire dancing hair." He seized Katherine's hand from his perch, and twirled her, imploring, "Sing along if you know it!"

An old woman, apparently appalled, was not concerned with hiding her expression. Several other passengers stared at them with various scrutinizing glances.

Trayten attacked Katherine and embraced her. "Throw away your stockings, dear, dancing close but never near."

She drowned in his coat, his hat slinking over her eyes. Her laughter trailed after. Twirling around, lost in her own momentum, she stumbled and landed face to face with Trayten, for he caught her. Through her giggling she said, "Tell me something delightful!"

"You're beautiful and I'm quite attached to you. Is that delightful?" He spun her around and caught her again. "Tell *me* something true."

"You're a terrible singer."

"I'm offended!" He jabbed at her sides, tickling her as she playfully shoved him.

"As am I!" She appealed to the old woman, "Isn't he a terrible singer?"

The woman shrank into her coat, her frown contrasting with

the lively pair before her. She shrugged. "Better than most, I'd say."

"Ah, hear that? I'm not bad at all!" Trayten called, triumphant. He turned to Katherine. "And you're a miserable liar!"

"She's too kind!" Katherine broke loose to run from him. He caught her and pinned her arms behind her back.

She felt the words forming against her lips when he spoke. "You're right, in fact it's atrocious." He lowered his voice. "And it can be much worse. I'll take you to the busiest corner and sing to the masses, at an exceptional volume."

"Don't you dare."

"It's no trouble, really. Anything for you." He kissed her, cutting in on her laughter, stamping his lips across her face in a frenzy of exaggeration. He danced her in his arms. She rolled her head back and sighed. Trayten swept her tightly against him.

The old woman meant to withhold her attention from them, yet her gaze continued to wander back. They were indifferent to the world around them, unbound and carefree, dancing without a tune, drunk on the mirth of their love. Though the summer heat departed, they warmed the atmosphere as two halves of one burning soul.

When the door burst open, the gathering offered their salutations in a masculine billow of grumbling. Katherine visited The Bedford in Chase with Trayten at her side. Her smile divulged of her liberation as she greeted the patrons, clustered around tables, hanging from barstools, and raising their dirty glasses into the clouds of smoke.

Jeff bounced into view out of the throng and wrapped a casual arm around her shoulders. "It's been too long again, Katherine, how've you been?"

"Well enough. How about you, you old cat? Jeff, meet

Trayten. Everyone—" she announced, "may I present Trayten Basel, the painter extraordinaire!"

"Glad to meet you." Jeff shook his hand immediately, followed by a slew of men nearby, extending thick and work worn hands to be shaken and acquainted. Trayten politely nodded and suffered to be rushed with the greetings, although he was more inclined to remain unnoticed and unacknowledged.

Jeff was gone in a flash, hopping toward his piano bench. Two barstools were evacuated and Trayten and Katherine claimed them. A safe, familiar feeling enfolded Katherine and she inhaled deeply to relish the smell of pipe tobacco and cigar smoke. Trayten lit a cigarette and rested his elbows on the bar.

"Katherine!" Wilkins waded through the patrons to them, his wide mouth stretched wider into a welcoming smile. "Well, blow me down! Thought you'd never come back here after that ugly scene."

"Ah, that was nothing whatsoever! We've seen uglier, haven't we? Anyway, you honestly think I'd stay away forever?" She smirked, shaking his hand.

"That chubby feller following you? Want me to lock them doors?" Wilkins asked.

"Thanks very much, but we're safe now. Edward Wilkins, meet Trayten Basel, if you please."

With his cigarette between his lips, Trayten shook Wilkins's hand.

"Yeah, okay, I've seen you in here before," Wilkins said. "Get this gent and our lady Katherine a round on the house."

The bartender swiftly complied.

"You gonna treat the boys to a dance? We got 'mean-fiddler Mac' here tonight," Wilkins offered.

"I'm rusty, to be sure." She tilted her head. "But, if you're stomping too, I won't look so ungainly by comparison."

"I'm in! It's a full house tonight, a good night for stomping!" Wilkins threw his head back to drain the glass the bartender had handed him.

Katherine glanced imploringly at Trayten. "Care to have a stomp?"

"I don't stomp." He winked.

"Then, I will return." She whirled around as Wilkins dragged her toward the dancing crowd. He commanded the band to play. Jeff poised over the keys of his piano and 'mean-fiddler Mac' leapt onto the stage between two drummers who were perched on the edge with their drums braced between their knees, their hands ready to ignite the beat.

The music exploded, a fiery collision of passion and purpose, vibrating and climbing the senses. Driven by the cry of fiddle strings and carried on a heavy pulse of drums, the pounding song gathered all together in one collective rhythm. Wilkins waved his immense arms, forcing open a clearing in the center of the floor.

They tapped their heels and swept their toes to the music's quick cadence. Footwork clapped and snapped across the floor, percussion as dedicated as the drums and as brisk as the fiddle's four pounding chords. Katherine and Wilkins mirrored each other's jig, hastening in their dance as the tempo quickened. Legs kicking and feet stomping at an exhaustive pace to keep with the music, they orbited in circles, leapt in the air, and twirled back down to the vibrating floor amid clapping and stomping.

A contagious conviviality swept through the tavern. With fervor and delight, Katherine danced in the center of a galloping horde, a delicate flower trampled and tossed among charging bulls. They stole Katherine from one another to swing her in their arms.

In the dim heat of the smoky arena, sweat dampened shirts and foreheads. Katherine drowned in their riotous merriment and her face was dewy with perspiration. Her damp hair dripped in her eyes like strands of black silk. A careless sort of amusement illuminated her smile. She danced with confidence, grace, and the fire that embodied the essence of the music.

The surrender to music and motion had its effects, yet Katherine glowed from within, ignited by the worth of her decision. The freedom and ecstasy of choosing love was newly won; the satisfaction of the soul, the heart, was a surreal experience. Her senses still adapted to the foreign reality, eager to discern actuality from wishful dreams.

The few days spent devotedly bound together; feeling, seeing, and hearing Trayten, drenched her with the determination to keep him. Having tasted the experience, the wholeness, the complete fulfillment with another, the perfect peace, Katherine exalted within.

'Mean-fiddler-Mac' sprang from the stage and landed on a table, which tottered and nearly went over. He retained his balance and with his elbows to his knees, crouched and grinned. He drew the bow across the strings with imperceptible speed. His fingers danced on the frets, his heel stomped the tabletop to keep the beat.

The drummers were sweating to keep time with him, their palms red and pounding the drums ferociously. They bobbed their heads and shouted. Even Jeff could not keep still. Standing, his back arched and his fingers traveled up and down the keys.

Katherine was lifted in the air and passed into another pair of hands. She swam amongst them, tossed as though by the waves of the sea. Thunder erupted around her; the men with their boots thumping both in time and out of it, their knees bouncing high and elbows jerking about them.

Trayten caught sight of her intermittently, swinging through the bounding crowd, lifted above their heads, and plunging back down as swiftly. He smirked to himself, entranced by her and undertaking to hold her in his view. The bartender pounded the counter behind him with the rhythm of the music.

"Beer," a rough voice ordered. The man's face was shaded under the brim of a hat. He glanced at Trayten. The distracted bartender took some coaxing before he jumped and went to pour a fresh pint for his patron.

A rumbling holler reached Katherine's ears. From the muddle of bodies, she searched for Trayten. She caught him in her view briefly while lifted up, and her eyes filled with concern. Across the commotion and noise, beyond the smoke and stomping mass, a figure moved like a sinister cloud and Trayten unflinchingly faced it.

A portly gentleman prevented her view with his vigorous jig. With the whirling momentum of the dance, she swam against the current and strained to see beyond the men. Trayten's face was a grim, hot, furious flash. He threw a provoking nod toward the figure, who flung his jacket and hat to the floor.

"Trayten!" Katherine yelled, gripped with dread amid the commotion. The music climbed higher and faster. She stretched on her toes, submerged in raucous dancers and calling out his name, "Trayten!"

The music dissolved, except for Jeff's clumsy chorus of notes, pounding from the piano. A rumble vibrated against the crowd until it parted, and two bodies came orbiting from the bar into the center of the tavern.

Tables were shoved aside, and they created an arena to watch the brawl. It escalated with such alacrity that none had time to intervene. Those closest to the bar witnessed the exchange; a shove impressed on Trayten was returned with a mean left hook. The fervor unfurled without limitation. A glass shattered against an arm or shoulder, and Trayten was charged. He grabbed his attacker, lifted him, and slammed him against a support beam that ran from floor to ceiling.

The stranger recovered and charged at Trayten, spitting and cursing, swinging his fists. Trayten caught a fist in his grip and bent the man's arm backward, knocking him to the floor with the kick of his heel against the attacker's calf. There was little time to stand as Trayten loomed, kicking the man whose arms and legs flailed in retaliation. Trayten seized the collar of his shirt next and delivered several blows to his jaw and nose.

Even Trayten's obvious skill met its match in the fanaticism of his attacker's rage. The stranger would not accept defeat. Bloody faced, he managed to untangle himself, slip out from underneath Trayten, and knock him down. He scurried across the floor to a bottle, dislodged from a toppled table. Trayten arose and his attacker cracked the glass against his face.

Katherine tried to lunge herself into their midst. She was barred and held back by the men who cheered at the fight. Trayten sank unsteadily to his knees and felt the floor against his face. The stranger scraped at his back, tearing at his coat to pull him up. When Trayten pushed himself away from the broken glass that had fallen with him, blood dripped from his forehead.

With renewed ire he sprang at his opponent. He shoved the stranger several paces backward, latched onto and lifted him, then hurled him at a table. The stranger slammed against the surface and slid, glasses exploding as they smacked the ground, his body skidding after them, the table overturned at last.

Trayten breathed deeply, his nostrils flaring, his face twisted with wrathful derision. Blood ran down the side of his face, stained one ear, and tinted the collar of his shirt. A frightful iciness gleamed from his eyes. Stillness gripped the tavern. They stared at him with astonishment, as though he were a vicious beast.

It had lasted for a few aggressive minutes. Wilkins, indicating the stranger grunting on the floor, ordered the man nearest the door, "Throw him out. Latch the door too, will you?"

A pair of men took the stranger by his arms and dragged him into the night. His face was shadowed black, blue, and red, his shirt hung, ripped from his chest, and his coat and hat were left behind on the ground by the bar. Quietly, patrons shuffled around the broken glass and the upended tables; lethargic and seemingly unsure of how to continue after the disruption of their revelry.

Katherine finally broke through the towering men, her face white with confusion, her eyes wide and her mouth agape. She faced Trayten across the open floor, unable to catch his eyes. He heaved, blinked, and rigidly flexed his fists.

Timidly she said, "Look at the mess I bring, whenever I come back here." She fixed her stare on Trayten. He was scarcely aware as she snagged his coat sleeve and led him toward the back door, stepping around shattered bottles, a toppled table, and several stools.

Katherine twisted the rag over a basin of water. Blood tinted the water pink and stained her hands. Droplets trickled across the floor as she brought it to the cut on his temple. He winced and held her wrist tightly. Trayten sat on the edge of his bed, his gaze fixed on the opposite wall.

"I respect your frugality with words, in *most* instances. But this isn't the time for it." She held his head between her hands. "I don't understand it. Who was he? You know him?"

"Let it be, Katherine."

"I can hardly do that. I've seen brawls and they are never that intense for nothing. It's only fair that you tell me why you almost killed a man tonight."

"Kill is a bit dramatic."

"Dramatic was that scene back there!" Katherine snapped. She clutched the rag in her fist, and he tightened his grip on her wrist.

"Katherine."

"Tell me." She worked to dampen and clear the dried blood from his hair.

"His name is Dorf Callahan."

Her eyes widened as she recognized the name from the papers.

"I was friends with Jack, you know that, and they had a problem with him. That's the extent of it."

"All that because you were *friends* with Jack Conway? I don't believe it."

"And what do you believe?" he asked.

"You aren't somehow linked to Jack's troubles?"

He raised his eyes to look at her. They were black and guarded. "Katherine."

"Right, you only *know* Jack."

"Right!"

"But why you?" she asked. "Why would this man come after you?"

"Sometimes, people in the real world have enemies. Jack had enemies because he did some things, made some choices. I didn't initiate his actions and he did what he could to keep me separate from them. Dorf would target me because Jack is gone, and he needs somewhere to direct his anger. I happened to be a target this time."

"You were intent on damaging one another. It looked personal."

"They took his actions personal, to the extent that they shot him! I'm not thrilled with them either, especially because he's dead. The others paid for that, but Dorf is still walking free. His thirst for revenge is set after the only person they knew was close to Jack. Me."

There was finality in his tone. He would say no more. Though the dread sinking at her core made it difficult, she reluctantly withdrew her questions. The sight of his blood at her fingertips agitated her senses.

"I believe you." She tilted his face toward her and said with a wry smile, "At least you laid him out."

At last the grim mask shattered with the smirk that crossed his lips.

❧ 22 ❧

Three days passed before Katherine decided to return to the villa. In the dim of late evening, in the shadows near the lampposts at the front gate, she hesitated, attempting to quell her nerves and rally her courage.

Pensive at her side, Trayten watched her closely, a fearful glow apparent in his eyes. Each time she had returned to that house, he was cast into an abyss of apprehension, terrified she would never again emerge and return to him.

"I will do this," she confirmed, as much to herself as to Trayten. She shivered in the night air. "Don't stand there thinking I won't do this. I will. I'm going to."

Trayten rocked on his heels, glancing from the black silhouette of the house to Katherine's tense expression. He watched her, diminutive in stature and shrinking at the iron gates. The yearning to protect her compelled him.

"I don't want you to," Trayten reaffirmed. "I still say it's a terrible idea, and I don't think you need to go back."

"I'm not going back. I'm declaring my independence." She shivered.

"I thought we already did that. Katherine, this makes no sense."

"Maybe not to you, but I have to do this. I don't want to slither away into the night as though I am ashamed! I don't want to leave them with the satisfaction of inventing explanations for my disappearance. All this time, I've been afraid to follow my heart, to speak the truth, and now that I'm not afraid anymore, I want them to know it and to hear it from my lips."

"Then, let me come with you." He stepped toward her.

"No. The sight of you would only ensure the worst reaction. I'd rather not stoke his anger and risk a fight. We've seen how *you* handle attacks and I think we ought to leave him in one piece."

Her jesting tone disturbed him.

"You think he won't be angry with *you*? You think you're safe, alone with him, after you wound his ego and destroy his reputation?" A sharp edge cut his words.

"It can't be worse than if he should see *you* beside me."

He stared at her, the intensity of his gaze resembling fury.

"Please, trust me. Wait for me in your room. I'll come to you."

The arrangement could not satisfy him, however he conceded if only to honor her wishes. Reluctant he advised, "Tell him, leave him, and come back to me quickly."

With warm, calloused fingers he caressed her cheek, raw in the autumn air. The heat from his touch revealed how cold she was. It ignited the impulse to be free at last and dive into his tenderness forever, never to resurface. A stirring determination enlivened her, and she affirmed, "I'm going to tell him. It'll be fine. Most importantly, it will be finished. Say goodbye to me."

"Never." He swept a strand of hair from her eyes. When he kissed her with a firm, decisive pressure, his arms clutched her body and he lifted her from the ground.

The tension of his hold startled her. A desperate and fearful energy surged through his affection and it shone in his eyes when he gently tugged at her hair, tilting her head back, staring into her eyes for a brief but ardent moment. He would squander no more words.

Quietly, he left her at the gates. After he faded away into the night, Katherine faced the grand villa alone. One window glowed from its massive shadow, with sinister light. Before she would lose her nerve, she hastened toward it.

❦

"And where have you been?" The agitating voice confronted her. It halted her immediately in the hall, and she faced the aperture dividing the corridor from Reuben's study.

From the room an eerie scarlet luster flickered, spilling light and heat into the hall; the fire in the hearth roaring high. A wave of musty odor hit her as she dared creep nearer. Reuben was seated facing the mantel in a colossal wing-back chair, his fat arm hanging off one side, a glass of dark liquor dangling from the fingertips.

Katherine's eyes fixed on his hand and she was frozen in the dead hush that followed his strident inquiry. That hand had restrained her and infuriated her. It tested her courage in partnership with the feverish atmosphere that clouded her senses and weighed her down. Nonetheless, she decided she would not be intimidated by him. The infernal room alone was to blame for her physiological distress, for slackening her step, and challenging her confidence.

His breathing was evident as she inched forward. The desperation to be forever removed from its grating sound subsequently increased. When she quietly glided into his view, her hair silhouetted by a crimson aura, she was unable to shield her trepidation with pride. Pretending that she was unfettered, Katherine straightened her spine, raised her chin, and faced him; unshaven, shirt rumpled and soiled, sinking in his chair with his eyes lost in shadow.

"Have you an idea?" she asked calmly.

Reuben's eyes were small, narrow, and hot. Twisting his face to one side he gurgled deep in his throat and barked, "Have *you* an idea of the frantic state you've kept us in?"

"No," she answered curtly, staring boldly into his eyes.

"My mother's been in tears! Your parents are … *people* have been looking for you all over Portsmouth!"

"If they had looked at all, I would've been found. I wasn't hiding, Reuben."

"Is that so?" He appeared ready to spring from his chair, a storm brewing in his tense body, his angered face reddening deeper by the moment.

"I came to tell you something true for once, Reuben. It's time to do away with illusion."

His face revealed a threatening rage, yet she proceeded.

"It's important that you hear the truth. As a businessman, you must value honesty—" She stopped short and added with a shake of her head, "What am I saying? That's a poor association. You're going to be angry, but you must remember this: I told you clearly, the day I so ignorantly married you, I made my feelings known—"

"What are you rambling on about? Where were you for the last three days?"

"I've been with the man I love," she said.

With a spasm of temper he slammed his glass on the floor.

"Yes, Reuben, I'm in love. I've been in love and never with you! I will not stop seeing him. I'm tired of trying to please my family and yours! I'm tired of living in compromise, too weak to nullify my greatest mistake, marrying you! I can't stay with you here another minute. I'm leaving you. I'm going to be where I always belonged."

"You—" he gasped or coughed. She braced herself for the worst. Reuben did not move, only continued to gasp as though choking, venturing to speak but unable to get beyond his first word, "You—"

He growled like a bear and snatched her by the arm with a

merciless, crushing hand. Her blood boiled, flashing heat to her extremities, rising in her throat to choke her boldness with peril. Fragile and helpless against his strength, the undeniable shackles of fear clamped down to confine her resistance. She wavered.

Reuben roared into her face, yanking her closer to feel the scorching breath of his words, "Who is he? Tell me about your *love*! I want to hear the sordid truth from your own deceitful mouth!" His voice fell, low and gritty at the end of his demand.

Katherine trembled.

Impatient, he forced her into the chair he had evacuated. "Go on! What *of* him? Who is he?"

Indignant to be harshly shoved, she proclaimed from the flimsy shelter of the enormous chair, "He's a poor man! He may not have your kind of wealth but he's twice the man you'll ever be!" She would not spare him open ridicule. With her temper ignited, she was determined to knock him down.

"So you say!"

"His name is Trayten Basel! You might remember him. He was a server on your steamship once!"

Reuben was chillingly calm. Katherine panted, breathless and enraged. With a sinister smile twisting the corner of his mouth, he glared at her.

"I should know him, I daresay, even better than you yourself!" Reuben said.

"What do you mean?"

"You are quite right to say that you are leaving here, Katherine, only you will not leave as you expect, nor will you go with whom you anticipate."

"I will!" She sat forward as though she would rise resentfully. Reuben's forceful hand shoved her into the damp, sweat soaked chair.

"Your *love*, as you have so pathetically named this tramp, has been revealed to me, not only by your own hand, in the shameful confessions of your diary, but also by my own inquiries and observations."

"You've read my diary?"

"In the spirit of protecting my foolish wife from her own imprudent actions, yes! That, and I have uncovered truths about this vagrant that you have yet to realize!"

"You don't know anything!"

"I know a great deal. Trayten Basel is a criminal! Did you ever think to ask him how he gets on?"

Mystification engulfed her and she was without retort. Reuben delighted to continue with the steel edge of judgment cutting his words, "Trayten Basel is an opium trafficker. A filthy roach, spreading the disease of addiction through the streets of Portsmouth! And *this* is what you cling to!"

"You mistake him! He's an artist. He's a good man." Katherine felt the room turning with the confusion that circled her mind.

"I identified him with my own eyes! I discovered his association with my own ears when that smuggler gang threatened him and connected him to John Conway, the opium dealer they put down! I knew him, even before I saw his name in your diary and traced your unfaithful footsteps to his lair!"

Panic installed itself in her body, Katherine searched frantically for evidence to disprove such an accusation. Caught off guard by Reuben's claim, she was reduced to denial and pleading. "You're mistaken, you must be! He's not a criminal, you don't know him!"

"Not only is he responsible for bringing refuse into the lives of others, but he has also seduced you, once a good woman of status and reputation, into reducing herself to his deplorable level!"

"He is not a villain and I am not reduced!" The tremor in her throat displayed a less than confidant resolution. Her unraveling pleased him.

"He most certainly is! Poor, blind, fool! The tragedy is that he has tarnished you! And although, because you are stained you belong with the tramps and vagrants *like* him, slithering in the alleyways and leaching at the workhouses, I have the goodness of heart to rescue you!"

"Rescue me? How dare you!" Tears spilled from her eyes.

"Silence!" His fist reeled back, poised as though to strike her. When she cowered, Reuben continued his chastisement, "You were never worthy of the lifestyle bequeathed to you. Everyone knows that, even your own family would admit to it! You're reckless, wild, and vile! Still, I did you a favor! I took sympathy on you in your disgraceful situation, and I made sacrifices to bring you up out of the pit you dug for yourself. I was benevolent to you and I made you my wife! I gave you the opportunity to be better. I saved you from ruin, but you'd have ruin at any rate; your stubbornness demanded it! You gravitated to vulgarity and rebellion! You became the creature of a junkie! For shame, Kathy! For indecency!"

"I refuse to accept your scornful words!" Katherine wept. "You're bitter and jealous! You've concocted lies and twisted the truth to turn me against him! But you don't know him! You don't know what he is or isn't!"

"Enough! Kathy, wake to reason! You refuse to accept the truth. Has lust made you senseless? Do not answer, I know it is so. Hear me and attempt to understand the logic of my counsel. Do you not think it suspect that this poor urchin appears out of thin air, and claims to love you? Consider, what motivation drives the poor? Survival alone to be sure! He is a criminal; he survives by offending the laws of good society!

"What could he hope to gain by attracting the trust and admiration of a wealthy lady such as you? His love is the deception he uses as bait to trap you! Yet here you are salvaged, in that I will not allow you to be blindly disgraced, robbed, or murdered! You've fallen prey to the manipulations of a crook!

"Yet, I will forgive your naïve blunder and rescue you from his snare. The preparations have been made; your belongings have been packed and the carriages are ready. I have enough charity to save you from your indignity, enough grace to absolve your sin, and enough means to bear you away to where you may be free of its temptation forever!"

There was no chance for an argument here. His last words fell heavy. Reuben held her fast by the arm before she could crawl out of the chair and escape him. He yanked her to his side where she felt the rumbling of his heart and the driving wind of his breath.

The hysteria took possession, as insensible and ferocious as a riotous tantrum. Katherine threw her body against his retention. He dragged her, bearing her efforts to escape like the frantic flailing of a butterfly's wings against the power of a crushing human fist. His wrath and his mass were too great for her to allay and she was carried off to be contained.

Behind the estate, in the black abyss of a terrible night, the servants busied themselves with the carriages, preparing for their master's departure. Strangled, unearthly cries echoed from the house.

৩১৩

In the weakest, most hollow gleam of dawn, Katherine attempted to lift her swollen eyelids. Disoriented, she grappled for consciousness, aware of enclosure, aware of the sharp throbbing pangs that hounded her head. Feebly, as though she had been resurrected from death, she reached along the walls of her cage, feeling the texture of heavy brocade material and the curve of a low ceiling. The carriage box felt like a coffin except for the door, made apparent by the dagger of light that stabbed through a crevice at the top.

Hazy recollection could not explain her location. She was clothed in the same tailor-made suit that she had worn in the freedom of Trayten's company when they stood at the gates of the villa. The heaviness in her head made it difficult to straighten in her seat. Trying to withstand the stabbing light of the dim cabinet, she searched the blackness of her mind for answers.

First she recalled the frenzy of a great struggle, Reuben in his strength clamping her fighting limbs in his solid hold. The panic had given rise to guttural screams before she was subdued. The substance was unknown, however remembered by the sharp smell when he smothered her mouth and nose with a damp hand-kerchief.

Lingering stupefaction held her cowed. There were voices. They sounded cloudy, dizzy, and strange, as though under water. She strained her ears and reached for the door. With as little strength and as much helplessness as one rising from a casket, she coerced the door open a small space and leered forward as rigid as the dead, straining to see the living world beyond. For the lethargic semi-paralysis that ruled her body and weighed against the will of her nerves and muscles, she felt as though under the yoke of death.

She could not support herself poised at the open door for long. Katherine closed her eyes and slumped back against the cushions of the seat. The watery noises from without continued to baffle her until again she lifted her eyelids and was stricken with bitter anguish at the sight of Reuben in the doorway.

Katherine cringed instinctively as his massive form invaded the box, blacking out the early light from behind him. The hysteria returned, her heart fluttering like a bird in a tiny cage, however she had no strength to speak. Reuben said nothing. In fact, as she reeled from his presence, he gave no reaction, only kept his eyes to the door after shutting it firmly. He knocked on the ceiling and they jolted into motion. Katherine's erratic breathing soon passed her into a weary, protective sleep.

1909

"How shall I behave when I meet him?" Angelle inquired as she trotted alongside her mother at a brisk pace. Katherine carried a suitcase in each hand, leading Angelle up the winding, snow-packed road to Marian Boley's house. Before she could catch her breath to respond, Angelle pushed the dusky curls from her eyes and added, "I have not quite decided on my approach."

"It will come to you in the moment. Not every behavior can be prepared. But you must wait until I've gone in first."

"Will you tell him?" Angelle stopped walking. Against the vast white stretch of snowy ground and low clouded sky, they were like a pair of ravens. Angelle's wool coat reached her toes and its deep hood sat balancing on the crown of her head. Her face glowed pale as the landscape, except for her pink tipped nose and the blushing apples of her round cheeks.

"Would you advise that I do?" Katherine asked.

"He ought to remember us. I do not wish to hide from him. We mustn't lie, of course."

"But I'm afraid."

With conviction, Angelle charged into forward motion. "Do not be afraid, Momma."

"I shall try my utmost. Meanwhile, you will charm Miss Boley for me, won't you?"

"I will keep her occupied."

Katherine smiled, though her lips were laced with nervousness. The little expression could scarcely conceal the anxiety surging through her and tightening her senses in preparation for disaster. She inhaled the air, noting the dull sting of its bitter stab, mild compared to the sensation in her heart.

※

Katherine knocked her boots one at a time against the jamb and opened the door. Angelle mimicked the ritual precisely. Into the narrow, dimly lit hall they carried the cold. It clung to their coat sleeves and hung in the strands of their hair. Angelle cast a wide, sweeping glance from one side of the corridor to the other, and looked down the length of it.

Her imagination climbed the staircase, and she fixed her

wonder on the father she believed lay beyond their plain, surmountable steps. The immediacy of the opportunity, to meet the father she never knew, sapped her energy and she stood in suspense.

When Katherine set their suitcases down and removed her coat and hat, she found Angelle in an awestruck state; eyes averted to the top of the stairs. Katherine knelt before her, gently unbuttoned her coat, and assisted her from her bundling.

"Are you nervous?" Katherine asked quietly, aware of her pensive child. As Angelle wrenched her gaze from the top of the stairs to retort, Suzan tromped hastily from the kitchen toward them, and Angelle looked at her instead.

"Mrs. Koryn, what are ye doin' here?"

"Hello, Suzan. I've returned. Have my things put in my room, if you would, and put out another pillow for my daughter, Angelle."

"But—"

"Thank you very much indeed," Katherine concluded.

Suzan took the suitcases and trudged up the stairs. Angelle watched her ascend as Katherine smoothed her hair in the mirror hanging on the wall. Then she led Angelle to the kitchen.

When they entered the kitchen, they were neither heard nor seen, at first. Marian, with her back to them, stirred some concoction. A jittery kneed Tarl sneaked up behind her and pinched her sides. She wiggled with a snort and he murmured in her ear.

Katherine cleared her throat with force and announced, "Good afternoon, Marian."

Marian ceased squirming, even as Tarl continued to dance behind her, laughing. She whirled around sharply, slapped her hand against his chest to desist him, and laid cool eyes on the dark-haired pair. Her eyes narrowed and she tilted her nose to the ceiling with the snap of her chin.

"And how has Tray been getting on in my absence?" Katherine asked. She pulled out a chair at the table for Angelle to sit in. "I trust you haven't poisoned him, have you?"

"I was just making his lunch," Marian said. She spooned a lump of the mysterious matter from her bowl onto a serving dish and stabbed a fork into the elastic mound. "And who do we have here?" Marian pointed sluggishly at Angelle, who blinked solemnly from the kitchen chair.

"May I introduce my daughter, Angelle."

Marian gawked as though the child was a menacing threat. A dreaded, unwelcome presence. She stuttered, "Didn't you return to England to stay?"

"I went only to fetch my child. She has been without me a long time, and I'd promised to take her with me and return to finish my work."

"Your work." Marian stretched the words out as if they were difficult to comprehend. "There isn't any of *that* left! He's actually perfectly fine now. He doesn't want to see you anymore. Also, we have been getting along much better at any rate." Marian nodded and squinted her eyes until they were closed.

"Miss Boley, don't forget I'm a paying customer. I shall even pay you for the inconvenience of keeping my room while I was gone. You'll also appreciate an increase for the addition of my daughter as a temporary tenant. If you would," Katherine took the serving dish and braced it on one arm, "prepare her something to eat. Bread with jam should be incorruptible enough to manage. She can even help you. I'll be tending to Trayten."

"Well, but…" Marian spread her hands wide before her, searching the table where the dish had sat. "…who?" She threw a helpless look at Tarl, who scraped goo from the mixing bowl with his fingers and licked them, oblivious to the ladies in the room.

When Marian turned back, Katherine had slipped away and only Angelle remained. She fixed the child with a heavy, merciless stare.

🦋 23 🦋

Nerves wound tightly, Katherine passed through his doorway and drew back with surprise. Trayten sat in his wheelchair with a canvas across his lap. Canvases were spread across the floor, smeared with wild splashes of various colors. They were blurry distortions, savagely rendered. He gripped a paint brush and pressed it to the abrupt end of an indigo river that cut a round, pastel form on the canvas in two.

Slowly he raised his gaze through strands of dark hair. His concentrated expression unraveled. His arm ceased its motion, the forearm bare for his sleeves were rolled up. His fingers were darkened with paint, the blue appearing black against his skin.

His gruff voice broke her illusion of the past. "What are you doing here?"

No blade could cut as deep, no rush of ice water could chill her more thoroughly, than those words in that tone. The rejection was more immediate than she anticipated. Katherine searched her strength to check the ebb of tears begging to fall from his admonition.

To leap, in that atmosphere, from claiming to be a stranger to revealing her intimate attachment, was a plunge into certain devastation. The height stirred dizzy sensations in her stomach.

Yet, certain peril made her brave somehow. He already despised her, and with nothing left to lose, she held firm. She was not afraid of breaking, for she had been broken for years.

Bearing the heat, she stared into his eyes; their black and russet depths swallowing her whole. Her vision blurred; his glare burned. Katherine dared her weakness to glance away and withstood the cruel lights in his stare.

Throughout their days as strangers on Alderney, Katherine combatted the affliction of his impersonal, unfeeling gazes. She searched beyond the heartless looks, endeavoring to remember a time when he gazed at her with only warmth, with adoration rather than contempt. From knowing her to forgetting her, there was no middle ground. There were only the extremes of love and hate, which by contrast with one another, resulted in the bitterest grief changing from the former to the latter.

Despite his most scathing scowl, she was determined to fulfill her purpose. With dutiful diligence she carried the dish to the table beside his chair and properly set it down.

"Your experimental soup is served! Of course, if you *want* it. I would advise against it myself." Katherine attempted to remove the fork Marian had lodged into the lump of goo. His eyes had not left her face.

"Marian said you were gone."

"I did leave. I went home to Portsmouth. But I'm back, just as I intended." It was impossible to keep her eyes from wandering over the attempted works of art that decorated the floor and his lap. "Is that what you thought? That I was finished here? That I left without a word, never to return?"

"It's what she said."

"Never mind anything Marian Boley says. I'm not finished here. I won't be. Not until you are better."

"Better than what?"

"And you're painting!" She ignored his wry response. "It's extraordinary! What is it?"

He regarded the wild markings on the canvas he held. "No, I…I don't know."

"Of course you do. What is it you're forming there, something you've seen, when you sleep?"

"I said I don't know!"

"Don't get angry with me, *Trayten*, because you're only trying to hide it. And honestly, I'm tired of it."

At the scolding tone of her voice, he replied with indignation, "Trayten? Hiding what?"

"What you know. What you see!"

"I see a room, the same cursed room I see every day. And all I know is pain."

"It's deeper than this room, than your physical pain."

"I certainly didn't miss your interrogations." Tray shook his head.

"What *did* you miss?" she asked.

He focused on the canvas. "What good is a painter who can't paint? How could I have been one?"

"But you *were* one."

"You don't know that. Neither do I. My hands aren't crippled. Wouldn't the gift remain?"

"Whether you'll admit it or not, Trayten, you're finding pieces of yourself. They are fragments, but if you would put them together, we can find you."

"Tell me something, for once, Mrs. Koryn. When did I ever ask anyone, ask *you*, to help me find myself?"

"You're afraid, it's understandable. But I would be more afraid of going on until I die, alone here, and never *living* for the rest of my life."

"There is no life. It ended when I forgot. I've accepted that."

"Have I done nothing?" Katherine asked, the hurt cutting her voice.

"It's not up to you. It's not up to anyone. I can't create memories out of thin air, I can't find meaning in what I can't describe. I don't want to. And I don't understand why you *do*."

"You've seen things for years, only you don't recognize them. You choose to forget them because of fear, so again and again you submerge them. You cover them up, disregard the meanings that are already there! I'm only asking that you surrender to them, uncover them. Don't be afraid. Just tell me!"

"Why do you keep assuming I've recalled anything?"

"Because you've conveyed things that you knew before, you've sung songs you used to sing, you've dreamed disturbing dreams, you've painted abstract versions of what you once painted clearly!" Katherine set the canvas down.

"You're mad! You don't know what I said or sang or painted or dreamed!" Tray ran his hand through his hair. "You don't!"

"Are you so attached to this lonely existence that you won't let me show you your past? Don't you want your life back?"

"I don't *know* my life! Maybe I am afraid. Maybe it's best not to know because what fragments I do dream are terrible. What kind of life was it to remember? Why would I want to remember if I was hated, if I was poor, and alone?"

The pressure of a flood strained to break free, and her eyes glazed at the desolation in his voice.

"My past is as intangible as the glimpses in my nightmares, and for good reason, I'm sure. It isn't worth remembering. If my life had been worth anything, I wouldn't have survived just to be tormented and punished."

"You lived for a reason, for a very significant reason. You lived because you are needed." She lowered to her knees before him. Carefully she put aside his canvas, pried the brush from his fist, and held his paint soiled fingers tightly in her small white hands.

"Even to those who didn't think they needed you, you *were* needed. I prayed," she swallowed, "I prayed for you to live, for you to be alive."

"I don't understand."

"Please don't say a word. Only listen to me, I beg you." Troubled frailty and a glaze of tears slipped across her vision.

He listened, awaiting her words.

She had to reveal herself and tell him the story of their past. Though she wished to be closer to him by now, to have some assurance of his accepting the truth, the mismanagement of her emotions made it impossible to proceed from at a distance any longer.

Katherine struggled to begin. The moment spread before her, as brimming with potential as a blank page. She searched for the right words and the air to breathe them into life. Holding his hands firmly she said, "This isn't how I imagined it. I had a plan. And I thought I was clever, so careful in my scheme. I had my own expectation of how you would perceive me. I imagined you would know me, as you once did, that you would see me, as you saw me before, without any doubt. I used to be able to read how you felt and what you thought. I didn't have to say a word. I never needed to dig or pry.

"I was certain you would remember me on your own, that everything they told me about you not remembering who you were would disappear if I were near you. I believed you would recognize me and remember what you adored, and the spell would be broken, and you'd be cured, by me and my face alone, my selfish beliefs.

"From the start you didn't recognize me. And still, I believed in the power of my influence. I believed I could bring you back by my voice, my presence, maybe even my touch. I thought I could do that much.

"But you don't recognize me and I'm afraid you won't. If I don't *tell* you, you'll never know. And I'm tired of this place. I'm tired of denying who I am, endeavoring to be who I'm not, while the person I am should be the only one you remember. And you don't!" She closed her eyes and tears slid down both cheeks. She squeezed his hands and he stared at her with intense scrutiny.

"Trayten, let me tell you who you are."

He sucked in a breath and held onto it. She continued with a desperate inflection in her voice, "Your name is Trayten Basel.

Trayten Basel. If you dreamed it, it's probably true. You were not a wealthy man. You kept a flat in Sun Street, in Portsea, and you made barely enough to survive. You survived more than you lived.

"But you painted! Oh, how you painted, breathtaking works precious to your soul. You couldn't bring yourself to sell them." She smiled with a bittersweet mouth, closing her eyes. "You covered your walls with your paintings, and you transformed a rotten old flat into a majestic gallery."

He examined her face, full of pain and whimsical charm. He sat transfixed as her words crawled beneath his skin.

"The room, see it! The shadows, the arched window shedding light onto your easel. Can you imagine yourself there? You were a singular person, an island unto yourself. When you drove horses, you drove like a madman. You were incredibly quiet, but you had such a way with words when you did use them. You hated money and convention of any sort. You came into a tavern called The Bedford in Chase and ordered a glass of milk. You sat in a corner, so calm. So set apart."

"How can you know this? It sounds…it sounds…"

"Real? Because it is real," she insisted. "Can you remember? That song, the one you mumbled, 'Dancing close but never near,' you sang that song! I never knew where you learned it, but you sang it all the time. And before, when you told me the names you knew and what they meant, I told you those things years ago, I listed them to you, and you've remembered them."

Though he was captivated, his expression remained guarded. "Who are you?"

Her stomach was churning. Her throat went dry. She took a deep breath and said, "Can't you remember me at all? I was Katherine Madison then, and I worked at The Bedford in Chase. I recited a poem and you heard me, sitting in the corner alone one night." She searched his face for any glimmer of realization and found nothing.

With a heavy heart she plodded onward. "I introduced myself

after you followed me. You brought me to your flat and I saw your artwork. You let me into your world. And you knew me better than anyone. Trayten, we were in love!"

He drew back in shock, as though something passed before his vision.

"Please hear me, it's the truth," Katherine persisted. "Do you remember it? The candles melted to the floor in the library? We scoffed at society in the park. And, and you followed me everywhere, you painted my portrait."

He shook his head and she tugged at his hands.

"I lost you. I married a man my parents chose, and we tried to leave, you and I."

"No!" He broke her hold with one angry heave of his hands. He wheeled backward. "You're not real, you're dead!"

"I'm not dead. I'm here! I've been searching for you for eight years, relentlessly! You weren't forgotten. Even if there was no one else, you had me! There's a painting of me in the museum, you painted it a long time ago. Am I not familiar?"

"You can't be."

"It's all in there, the evidence is in your dreams!"

"You can't know anything of my dreams! You can't know what I've seen and done!" he screamed.

"I don't, it's true. I haven't known all this time!" Katherine shouted back. "I was shut in. I couldn't get out and then you were gone. You disappeared that day—"

"What day!"

"The day I lost you! The day my husband died! You were gone and I went out searching for you, I didn't stop searching until I found you here, and I knew it was you the moment I saw you. Trayten, you have to believe me!"

"Stop!"

"You need to hear it! This is your life!" Katherine pursued him, holding his neck gently between her hands. "You *were* loved! I loved you." She bit her lip. "I'll love you my whole life!"

Trayten ceased his squirming. He stared at her, stricken.

Mechanically, he raised his hands and closed his fingers around her wrists. "But I don't *know* you." He pushed her hands away, as he would shove back a reviled trespasser.

Katherine was lost. More troubling than being a stranger to him, was being abhorred and sent away from him. In the line of his horrible stare and in the echo of his denial she could neither breathe nor speak. Though the motion of retreat sent a scourge of fire through her heart, she backed away and fled from his sight.

◌❀◌

As Katherine delivered her confession to Trayten, Marian was deeply troubled one floor below them. The little girl had eaten, solemnly chewing her food and starting at Marian all the while. Then she retreated to the front parlor, took the only book she could find from a shelf covered with glass creatures, and slunk low in a corner to read it.

Marian wandered after to see where the little imp would go and found her engrossed in the book. Angelle's dark eyes set intently on her page. Her little legs extended on the floor in front of her, crossed at the ankles with the toes of her polished black boots pointing in opposite directions. Angelle didn't pay attention to the penetrating stare of Miss Boley. She remained focused on the events of some sentimental novel.

Marian withdrew to the kitchen. Her mind raced with peculiar thoughts and she narrowed her eyes, slinking lethargically toward the counter. Alone in her kitchen at last, she pondered the items recently presented before her. She reached her freckled hands for a dish on the counter and uncovered a slab of raw beef. The child's image was before her, with familiar eyes that had followed her for the greater part of an hour.

They were not the mother's eyes. She had seen eyes like the child's every day, for several years. Eyes like those would likely have been inherited from the other parent. Eyes as dark could be traced through heritage. Confronted with the notion, the resemblance, Marian searched her intelligence to figure a way around it, to deflect the sure blow of its blatancy. *It cannot be*, she decided, not in the way that she believed it was impossible, but she meant that she would not have it.

In her imagination, she placed the child between them, Mrs. Koryn and T.B., and the appearance of the three of them together sickened her. For she was keen enough to recognize the striking likeness between T.B. and the little girl.

With burning contempt, she assessed Katherine's face in her mind, the polished features that she loathed. She listened to her voice and scrutinized her mannerisms from memory. Her arm snapped forward and she smacked the defenseless roast with a tenderizing mallet. A wisp of frizzled hair bent into her eyes, her lips curled, her nostrils flared, and Marian whacked it again. "A psychoist!" she hissed under her breath.

Her thoughts traveled back to when the voices of townspeople and the doctor drove her mad, telling her what she ought to do with him, what must be done, barging into her business, instructing her on his care. Specialist! She could hardly believe it, although she narrowly believed it before.

For what had Mrs. Koryn done for T.B. other than harm him, disturb his rest, and carve a chasm between him and herself. He no longer happily ate what she prepared. He no longer depended on her. She had lost him to that woman, who was a liar.

Had she lost him? Marian served the roast another mean whack! *This is my house, and he is my tenant!* For she alone saved him and nursed him from the clutches of death! Marian could admit that perhaps Mrs. Koryn was prettier, with her rich clothes and her blue eyes, eyes like the sea she despised, but Marian sneered, *I am smarter*.

Marian had convincing arguments to expound, a few objections prepared, enough to stop the widow and her little girl from taking everything she worked for. They could not take him from her. With both hands Marian grasped the mallet and thwarted the meat with all her might, repeating the punishment with rapid force until her hair sprang loose from her chignon in several directions, her wild eyes crossed, and her hands reddened.

The thought of it boiled her blood; Mrs. Koryn and her face, upstairs with him, saying whatever she may say, and her child, with those beady eyes staring at her while she gobbled her sandwich like a miniature troll, watching, measuring her up for the attack! With a grunt Marian hurled the roast into a pan and the mallet hit the floor with a thud.

"Marian!"

She yelped when Tarl tugged on her sleeve. Whipping around she faced him, her cheeks red and her freckles dark. Her mouth hung open. He drew back. With a jittery mouth and wobbly neck, he searched for a pair of words to put together. Impatient, Marian bumped him from her path, yanked open the door, and shoved the pan into the oven. A halo of hair spread around her face, matching her internal fire.

"You beat the blazes outta that roast!" he exclaimed, a tinge of shock in his tone.

Marian wondered how long he had been standing there. Determined to seize control of her senses, she detected the faint escalation of voices from the floor above. Her eyes flickered to the ceiling. It sounded like shouting, muffled, but disquiet.

"Do you need some gin, yea?" Tarl slurred as he went for the cupboard.

"Shh!" she hissed and pointed. Her wild stare stabbed the ceiling as if she could pick out an exact word with enough focus.

"You want me to…" He pointed in the direction of the stairs.

"Why are you still standing there daft? Get up there!"

He broke into motion, raced for the hall, and tore up the stairs.

Later, when Katherine descended the stairs, completely composed, Marian lurked from the kitchen, ready to pounce. She restrained her attack and observed, searching for some flaw in that perfect poise. Katherine went into the parlor to join her daughter.

Sliding into a chair before the scorched roast on the table, Marian held her grumbling stomach. *What will it take to crack the widow*, she wondered. What must she do to convince T.B. away from whatever Mrs. Koryn was already convincing him of? Marian scratched her hair and breathed fire. Control was one thing she valued highly in her life.

She maintained control of her household, including the guests that resided therein, at least to the best of her ability. She cherished, even required, a position of control. As a girl she had manipulated her mother, and in school she had been able to manage her teachers, for they proved far too wary of disciplining the unbalanced child who, when distressed, would cross her eyes and collapse into fits on the floor.

In her own cunning ways, Marian ensured that she, and only she, dictated the course of her life, from the way her time was utilized, to the way her friends behaved, until she lost her friends. She labored to keep each aspect of her life in perfect order. Perfection was paramount, and perfection was the goal.

She kept everyone precisely where and as she wanted them, in straight lines. Except for George, except for Mrs. Koryn, and if she was not tactful enough, even T.B. might slip out of her perfect order.

Losing George nearly sent her over the brink. She deemed herself considerably well-adjusted, even if others believed differently. At the recollection of those days, when she quaked with anger for the loss of her domination, when she was repulsed by the chaos of disruption, the walls crumbled around her, and she stared at the vast ugly sea, ignorant of where it took him, she lost the ability to see straight, and fresh fury increased the temperature of her blood.

What vexed her most was Katherine Koryn; the charlatan, an intruder in her own house, disturbing the balance she had reclaimed at last. No! She had come too far and worked diligently to recover from the trauma of losing George. She prevented calamity before, and she would prevent it once more. T.B. was owed to her and she would keep him, and over him, her control would endure.

With a twitch of her eye, Marian stood up. Resolved, she prowled silently up the stairs.

⚅

As daylight slipped away the windows darkened and with few lamps lit, the hall appeared bleak. Tarl hovered in the doorway of his room, postured as seductively as he could, with one elbow over his head against the door frame and a demure smirk sprawled across his rubbery features.

Unmoved by the display, Marian slipped into the room and beckoned him after with one severe jerk of her head. By the moonlight through his window, along with the flickering glow of a candle on the chest of drawers, she examined his face and prepared her ears for the news.

"So, on with it, what's happened?"

Tarl seated himself in the chair by his window and crossed his lanky legs. In the faint light his complexion was pale and green. He drew in his breath, puffed his cheeks, and with eyes bulging let the air leak out slowly.

Marian's impatience mounted and she stabbed him in the stomach with her pointed shoe, expelling all of the air from him at once. "What did you hear?"

"Nothing." He tilted his head and went on in his dragging manner, "Well at first nothing. I heard waves, then straight away, I had to try and interpret their meaning, because they, well, I missed the beginning while I's downstairs seeing you pummel the roast, so all I got is, it's more like a summarization really, it's not word for word or anything, the basics of it, I think."

"What?" she screamed in a whisper.

Tarl was an insufferable dimwit naturally. It did not help his case that he also slurred when he spoke, reeked of liquor, and stuttered. Nonetheless, he was easy to push around.

He looked at her, as steadily as he could manage with his tics and tremors, and leisurely muttered, "So my basic, general, overall generalization is this: she's no doctor, she's maybe a patient, or should be! She's weeping, telling him a story about this guy's life, like things he did, where he lived, that he painted and such, and she's saying she's his lady, that she's been looking for him and found him, and how he painted her, and he don't sound real impressed with it right, he sounds kind of, well, quiet. There's no sound from him at all, until he's cross and saying he don't know what she's talking about, don't know her or anything, and can't say it sounded like she liked that a whole heap," he released the air he somehow retained after the clumsy anecdote.

Marian propped her chin on her fist and considered his account.

"What do you make of it?" Tarl asked, scratching his nose with fervor.

"It's just as I worried," Marian announced. "She's telling him she knew him, hitting certain nails on their heads, telling stories, telling him about his past—"

"I didn't hear no hammering—" he slurred.

"—and she's no specialist, and I'm sure she's gone and told him that too."

"It's true what she told him?" Tarl asked. "He didn't think so."

"No, and he won't think so. It isn't true one bit! You watch, Tarl. Just watch!" Marian slapped her knee and whirled around. "Wait here!"

❧ 24 ❧

To Marian's knowledge, T.B. never before took the liberty of locking the door to his room. Although with the simple turn of a lock, the door could be secured from the inside, Marian had always come and gone freely. She never expected it to be otherwise. Until that moment, she forgot about the only key to the room, having lost it somewhere in the front parlor among her collections of knickknacks, or in a drawer with other useless odds and ends. She failed to predict that he might take charge of the room.

When Marian took hold of the doorknob and it would not turn, her thwarted expectation nearly upended all good sense. Before she snapped, she tried the knob again. Tugging, twisting, and wrenching accomplished nothing.

He had indeed locked her out. A hot rush of anger ripped through her, however, instead of slamming and kicking against the door with wild abandon, as she was compelled to do at first, she twirled around and shot down the stairs like a stampeding bull.

Crashing into the midst of their tranquility, Marian appeared in the archway, a ruddy flash of light. The hall lamp at her back set ablaze the wild frays of hair standing in jagged wisps around her forehead. Over crimson flushed cheeks, green fire smoldered from eyes that fixed their heat on Katherine's face.

The widow, with composure well intact said, "Marian? You look dreadful! What's the matter?"

"What have you done to him now?" she spit.

"I don't understand," Katherine said.

"The door is *locked*! He's locked my door!" Marian stamped her foot as a child throwing a tantrum.

Angelle looked at her mother. Katherine gently patted her hand and addressed Marian with a quiet, firm tone, "Since when is privacy a crime? Calm down, if you please, ma'am."

"I'll not be told to calm down! I can't *get* to him! What if he is hurt? I can't get in, he's locked inside!" With each utterance, Marian breathed more briskly.

"So he wanted to be alone, so he didn't want anyone barging in on him. Let him suit himself for once."

"Of course, you don't care!" Marian stiffened and crossed her arms. She eyed Katherine from head to toe and back again. "Whatever lies you've told him have vexed him, and he shouldn't be left alone!"

They sat idly by, helpless to extinguish the tempestuous frenzy with which Marian commenced her search for the key. She attacked the parlor first. Katherine held Angelle close against her, their eyes wide with surprise. Marian ripped open the door of every cabinet and took to the shelves, shifting the knicks and knacks aside, muttering under her breath.

Glass and porcelain clanked and scraped. Ceramic bells rang and clapped. When the shelves provided no prize, she slammed door after door, and bent to the nearest bureau drawer. She tugged it open and rummaged through the papers and sashes stowed there. With a grunt she yanked open the next drawer, and forgoing rummaging, spilled its contents onto the small space of rug at her feet.

On hands and knees, wedged between the piano and tea-table, Marian raked through a collection of coins and tangled necklaces.

The efforts yielded nothing, and each remaining drawer was spilt in the same erratic manner and the floor was combed, and still the search proved fruitless.

Katherine and Angelle cringed when she swept passed them with a curse and rushed into the hall. Marian fell on the hall table and ripped out its drawer. She disemboweled the armoire and the roll-top desk beside it.

Proceeding into the kitchen, she took to the cupboards and drawers. Curses were flung into the air and the slamming of drawers, and the clattering of glass and metal revealed Marian's temper in the fullness of its power.

Katherine smoothed a dark curl from Angelle's forehead with one finger. "It's important to learn, darling, to curb the irrational compulsions that might accompany strong, negative emotions."

"It's rather disturbing," Angelle said, watching the hall as if she could see through walls. Her ears piqued to the riot of noise resounding from the kitchen.

"More than you can know, my love." Katherine sighed and glanced vacantly toward the stairs beyond the arch.

Holding the key to Trayten's room was enough to prevent Marian from getting at him. However, to shield him from what-ever persuasion Marian had planned would be to exert control over the situation, and Katherine would rather trust him to recog-nize the truth, than be as Marian, and seek to dominate him.

The memory of the tender moment, when Trayten entrusted the key to her, crossed Katherine's mind and she hesitated to break her promise. Next, she envisioned him unconscious behind the locked door and fear pricked her heart. Katherine had to let it go. With the wearied, lingering faith that the truth mattered enough to penetrate the cloudiest memory, the thickest deception, she stood up.

As Katherine entered, she could hear Marian rustling about inside the pantry. The kitchen was in bedlam, conveying the tumult that befell it. Cupboard doors stood open, and drawers hung from their tracks. The floor was littered with pots, pans, utensils, and dishes. The casualties of the hunt stretched before her path.

Katherine reached inside the collar of her blouse and pulled out a necklace. At the end of the chain dangled the key, which she gripped tightly in her fist for a moment. She unfastened the chain and slid the key from its tether.

Noting the continuance of Marian's occupation in the pantry, by the clanking of bottles that echoed from within, Katherine bent down among the mess to place the key on the kitchen floor.

Inside the pantry, Marian was busy tearing through a crate, canning jars and bottles littering the ground at her feet.

"May I make a suggestion?" Katherine asked.

Marian glared.

"Right, well," Katherine cleared her throat. "In my experience with searching for lost things, I've learned that the more hurried the rate, the more likely you are to pass right over it."

With hands clasped loosely behind her back she wearily tiptoed through the debris and toward the stillness of the dim red parlor.

❧

Without warning the doorknob jostled, a click sounded, and in the next moment Marian swung the door open wide. Trayten drew back from his painting and Marian sighed loudly. Relieved to see him alive, she smiled an awkward grin, the lines of her face straining. She closed the door behind her.

At last, his gaze drifted to the object clutched in her fist. A shadow covered his eyes. His left hand gripped a paintbrush and the other slid the marred canvas from his lap onto his bed. His eyes remained fixed on the key to his room.

"T.B.! Thank heavens you're all right! How'd you ever lock

it? Did that foolish girl Suzan mistakenly lock it? What if you had a seizure?" She clutched her beating heart.

"How'd I lock it? I turned the lock. And where did you get that key?"

"What a question! This is my house, is it not? I have keys."

He narrowed his eyes. "What's this about?"

"Exactly! Right, what *is* this about?" she parroted, swaggering toward him. She surveyed the canvases laid across his bed and abruptly snatched one.

"What, is she forcing you to do this as well? Is she pressuring you into another collapse? Do you wish to wake the anguish that we finally put to rest?"

He greeted her hysteria with a grave, low tone. "Is my ability to think and act for myself impaired?"

Marian forced a sardonic frown. She sighed extravagantly and fell to her knees before him.

"Oh my dear, dear T.B., how can I bring you such disappointing news? How can I hurt you? But if I must, to keep you from being deceived, and confused."

"What's wrong with you?" he asked, disgusted.

"I'm saying that I'm sorry I ever exposed you to this, that I allowed a person in who would feed you lies and manipulate you! I want you to always be protected and safe. I want to make sure that no one harms you, no one and nothing. I have sworn to protect you, and I must tell you the truth, having just discovered it myself, before it's too late."

"And what's *your* version of the truth?"

"Only the *most* true, and you must listen to me, T.B.! Surely you must understand that I have your best interest at heart. Time has proven that! What I have to tell you is awful, shameful, but it's the truth above all. I've cared for you too long to let you ever be deceived." Marian's eyes gleamed with tears and she waved her hands expressively.

He stared at her, revolted and wearied by her wild appearance, with beads of sweat shining along her forehead and upper lip. "The truth about what?"

"About the widow." Marian's voice dropped, and she crossed her arms. "I received a visit today, from an officer from Portsmouth. He was looking for Mrs. Koryn, and having discovered her in England recently, he followed her back here and came to warn me, to warn us all! She's wanted in England, and she came here to hide out, to escape! Of course, *that* makes sense.

"She heard about you, well an embellished rumor about you. Maybe it was the loony Saunders sisters who suggested it, but she got the idea that you're worth a fortune. You've got money somewhere, hidden, or put away and believing that you could, well... die soon, she thinks she could get a piece of your wealth!

"She planned on coming to you as a doctor, to get close to you and find out what she could about you. Meanwhile, she's been telling me that she knew who you were, that you had a lot of property, and that she knew you before your accident, and was trying to have you reinstated to your wealth, but her story was always changing, and she's told *you* she's just a specialist until she can't get you to talk. Then she goes and tells you she was your lover, so she can persuade you to leave with her, allowing her the liberty of scheming for your wealth!

"But, to add to the disgrace, the woman is already rich! It's true, because she inherited all that her husband had since he's dead and do you know why she's wanted in Portsmouth?" Drawing breath, Marian delivered her line with perfect conviction, "Because she killed her husband! Yeah, *she* did that! Wouldn't you believe it? She's a liar, a deceiver, and it's why they've had such trouble catching her, and that's why she's working on *you*, because she thinks you're someone worth money. If she can get you to believe that you knew her and loved her and marry her, she can do away with you and be even richer than she already is!" She gasped heartily for air.

Trayten was speechless at first in the wake of her rant. Finally, he said, "You're really something."

Marian closed her eyes and patted his shoulder with a nod. "Thank you." When she opened her eyes, she drew back at the ire covering his face.

"How did she kill her husband?" he asked.

"By stabbing him! Yes, she did! Twice, at *least*!"

"That's the problem with a rumor; unreliable information. She told *me* she poisoned him."

Marian was thrown as he expected. After an instant, she struck again, "How dastardly awful! It's amusing to her! She's a wicked woman, I tell you!"

"You may leave now," Trayten said directly.

"Well, I…" Her eye twitched. "I understand if you need some time alone to digest this awful news. It's all right, and don't worry, I will handle sending her away."

"Why? Isn't your *officer* going to arrest her?"

"Worry not over the details T.B.. I will take care of everything."

"Just get out," Trayten ordered.

She tripped clumsily backward, clutching her throat with both hands. Marian opened her mouth to object and his booming voice rattled the walls. "Get out!"

Winter 1901

The black shape of her figure slightly filled the space of an upstairs window where white light blinded. A powerful alliance of sun and snow cast Katherine as a silhouette. Perched like a raven in the windowsill she surveyed with red-rimmed eyes the barren touch of winter, its colorless sky, the sharp dingy coast of Portland, and the frigid sea.

From her high window in the rickety, rotting house, the lawn stretched, brown, crisp, and dead. Along its narrow sweep, few trees sprung from the hard, unyielding earth. Their branches were bare, revealing unsightly gnarls, twists, and cracks. Not far from the front porch, past the woodshed with a rusted tin roof, the narrow yard fell away, ending at a cliff. Deep below, the ocean waters crashed and pounded against the shining rocks.

Katherine pulled her gaze from the desolation and felt the sting under her eyelids when she blinked. Deep indigo irises appeared faded, set in bloodshot orbs. She focused on the red leather book in her cracked, weathered hands. Strands of oily hair hung in her face, shielding her ashen skin from the light through the window. From the pocket of her gray skirt, she withdrew a quill and a bottle of ink, and prepared to write in the book she had discovered in a drawer in the closet of the bedroom.

She decided it would be her confessional, her book of truth. She addressed each entry to Trayten, speaking to him with the romantic hope that somehow the act of writing to him would bridge the gulf between them, that in some way his heart would hear it.

⚜

Dear Trayten,

 I am in exile. The world of warmth has cast me out.

 I am imprisoned in winter, in anguish, mourning the love I almost possessed. And there is no one to blame but myself. I yielded to this, to Reuben, to the confinement of my obligation as his wife. I pay the price for my choices. Here, in this repugnant house, I am sentenced to endure.

 It was naïve of me to think that Reuben Koryn would simply stand aside and allow me to leave him, and humiliate his reputation, crush his ego. No. He did as any respectable husband in his position would do to bar a wayward wife against temptation, and he moved us to Portland.

 Spirited away in the early morning like convicts fleeing. No word was left to our families. In the blink of my tear-filled eyes, the atmosphere was altered. My soul passed from life into death.

He has business interests here. The area is occupied by fishermen and their toughened wives. In the harbour, the waters are teeming with fish. The company established by Mr. Koryn Senior pays the fishermen for their catches and exports them where they are sold at high prices. Less than ten percent of these profits are returned to the fishermen, who slave away for the portion and live in the row houses along the docks, provided by their landlord, Reuben. They are grateful for a lifestyle more civilized than their former sea gypsy ways and they in turn fatten the pockets of my tyrant husband.

This is my asylum.

This ancient, wind-beaten structure that ought to be condemned is the new Koryn estate. A hill ascends to a precipice, on which sits the house where I wither and fade. The cliff at the end of the yard is supported by jagged rocks that look down on a churning, cruel sea. They beckon me, the cliffs and the sea, promising swift release from this living death.

It is this damp place, the winter rolling over me and being without you that smothers the life from my soul. No warmth, no light, no love is here. In this decaying house, in a room of my own, I am shut away.

And yet I wonder if I am truly alone. Since arriving here, in fact before we came to Portland, I have been ill. There are other irregularities I have noted that stir my suspicion that I could be carrying your child. And still there is a part of me that warns against such an irrational hope.

My appetite has failed me. Nonetheless, the sole servant Reuben retained delivers meals on a regular schedule. They kept the door to my room locked from the outside. I began to suffocate within days, filled with rage like a caged bird.

Before my fire died, how I raged.

I destroyed the contents of my cell. I raked my fingernails at the door.

I thought my punishment would be the gradual onset of insanity by isolation. But he saw fit to shatter the last of my resistance. He visited my room at night, to claim his right as a husband. I cannot write another word of what he has done.

I wish I could erase it from my body, my memory.

I could not bear to be shut away and kept as a helpless victim. So, I ambushed the servant, poor girl, one day as she was leaving my meal. I wrestled her for the key to my room and won it. I locked my door from the inside to guard myself against Reuben's assaults.

And I let myself out when I please, to creep around this mournful house and to peer over the edge of the sea cliff. Beyond that, there is nowhere to go, nothing to see. I can imagine Portsea, a world away; alive, in colour, the place where you are. I can close my eyes and see your face, hear music and laughter, feel loved for an instant.

Reality is a shock in contrast.

Reuben, upon discovering my freedom, was swift to encourage, rather to demand my servitude alongside the rest of the fishwives. From the hour before the sun allegedly rises until the dark returns, I stand on the docks in the stench and the damp, gutting fish that are brought in baskets, arriving in a never-ending procession from the arms of returning fishermen.

There I stand, day by day, in a line of worn-down women. The air off of the sea bites my nose and ears, and numbs my fingers, which I cut often because I cannot feel them beneath my knife. My penance is emotional and physical disfigurement.

He will walk the docks, between our cleaning tables and the rows of ships in the harbour, flaunting his imperialism. He supervises us, and when he is bold enough, he does not hesitate to berate me especially, determined to shame me publicly.

Like a frigid shadow I dare not tremble but stand firm to face what I have merited. In my shell, in these rags, I hide my fire. My health is failing. I've had frequent pains and tremendous weariness.

Yet, I think of you, constantly aware of how I deserve to suffer this way.

I sacrificed you, our love and in the chilling shadow of our bright, warm summer, I will rot in eternal winter.

Forever frozen,
   Katherine

One by one, Katherine plucked fish from the basin, slit open their bellies with her knife, and tore out their innards as slimy juices spread over her skin. She watched the mechanical repetitions of her hands through glazed eyes. All appeared hazy and submerged beneath a murky damp. The air was gray with fog, the ocean white, and the docks, always wet, gleamed oily and black. Ships bobbed alongside the docks, with fishermen passing heavy baskets, untangling ropes and nets, dropping or pulling anchors. The sound of their voices, deep and commanding, filled the otherwise quiet atmosphere, accented by the weary chattering of the women at their tables.

She held another little corpse in her hands to slice open, disembowel, and toss onto the pile. Katherine's vision smeared away, until she was looking through her raw hands, her expression fixed, lips like stone. She pulled, cut, ripped, and chopped. She disassembled each fish as frenzy increased within her, boiling within her shell.

Memory assaulted her, tugging at her awareness and delaying her progress. Visions of Trayten haunted her. They might have transported her from her present hardship, yet a strident voice prevented them.

"You're thinking about *him*, aren't you?"

Pulled from the bittersweet aura of the past, Katherine cringed against the voice she loathed to hear. Reluctantly she faced Reuben, blinking the veil of memory from her vision. She bristled against his provoking glare.

"I can always tell when you've got that pathetic look in your eyes!"

Katherine remained silent, unflinching.

"Are you so stupid, Kathy? You think he could actually love you? Does a parasite love its host? No, he has another host and has forgotten you!"

The chattering around them ceased. The women eyed Reuben with timid curiosity. Katherine stared back, grinding her teeth.

"It is over. Say it's over!" He captured her by the shoulders. "Say it now, because he doesn't love you!"

She refused to react.

"You need to say it, I need to hear that it's over, it has ended. Say it!"

The more he shook her, the louder the chatter from the onlookers. Reuben appeared crazed, his usually slick hair broken apart and waving in his eyes, his shirt hanging loose, his breath reeking of alcohol. The less she responded, the more he unraveled.

"Shut it!" she finally said. "Everyone is watching you!"

He let go of her. Reuben raised the back of his hand and released it with a slap across her cheek.

Gasps echoed across the docks. Katherine braced herself with one hand against the table, holding her stinging cheek with the other. She stared back with searing eyes.

Reuben ran a hand through his hair, fumbled for a word, and whirled around to escape the glares that followed him.

"Mrs. Koryn, are you—" One woman crept near.

"Do not call me *that*! And get back to work."

The women shuffled back to their tasks, gossiping with heightened intrigue.

ॐ

Mournfully Reuben called, his voice echoing along the corridor. When the sound reached her in the kitchen, where she lately occupied herself cooking, she recoiled. Loathing to leave her only comfort, Katherine suspended the ladle over the stewpot, and waited for him to give up. Not only had she been cooking for several weeks, but she had also been eating with equal effort.

Although, with her healthy weight gain and increased energy, Katherine appeared to be at peace, the servant was ordered to remain as her shadow, checking for erratic behavior or perhaps escape. The maid studied her closely, while Katherine dismissed Reuben in her mind, and returned to stirring. Of course, he called again.

"Ma'am, Master calls you."

"Does he?" she asked, unconcerned.

He called a third time and the maid jumped, pointing to the hall. "There ma'am, hear him?"

Katherine's shoulders sagged and she set the ladle down in defeat. "All right." She surrendered, took a shawl from the hook, and slung it around her shoulders before abandoning the shelter of the kitchen.

When she entered, he was hunched on the edge of a stool with his elbows on his knees, his forehead in his hands, and his dull blond hair gripped between his thick fingers. On the tea-table a cigar smoldered in an ashtray. Pale light bombarded him from the two tall windows. The rest of the den was empty.

He sensed her entrance and raised his head. She recognized the tears in his eyes, and she narrowed hers. "What's gotten into you?"

"Katherine, come here." His voice was hoarse.

"Are you ill?"

"Not really, no." He rubbed his red eyes. "Come here. I have something to say to you."

She neared and he grasped her hand firmly, flashing pitiful eyes at her face.

"What."

"Kathy, I—" he gasped and squeezed her hand.

"What is it?"

"Why? *Why* have you done this to me? I only wanted to be your husband." He pulled her close. "No. Listen to me. Don't struggle. How could you come to hate me so much? That isn't what I wanted! I wanted to be a part of you. How could you turn to someone else? Kathy, where have I gone wrong? Have I been so unbearable to you? I never wanted to hurt you. I admit, later I allowed my temper to get the better of me, but you've hated me so thoroughly it's driven me to it! You must forgive me. I hurt when I hurt you, but it can change, can't it? If you'd come back to me, if you, if—"

"No." She tried to withdraw, but he constricted her.

"Do you think I wanted to resort to this? Bringing us here. I am not happy either. Yet if we begin again, if you let go of him, he who, who doesn't love you, I swear I never meant to sound spiteful, but it's only the truth, Kathy. He is a rogue, a junkie. How can he *love* you? How could he ever be good enough for you? He wanted to steal from you. Believe me, I know his lot. He cannot love you.

"I will be your husband through eternity. I will stand beside you, provide for you, as he could never have done. I'm not a monster. I don't want to punish you. Come back to me."

"Reuben, stop!"

"No!" He slid to his knees and wrapped his arms around her waist. He clung to her, sniffling and sobbing. "I love you, don't you know I do, Kathy? I love you so much! Why could you never love me?"

She could not break free from his hold, though she fought and cringed. She stiffened, waiting out his emotions. When he drew back to wipe his eyes, she pried free, and fled in a flash. He groped at the air in her wake, crying her name.

🌿 25 🌿

1909

The room was thick with dreadful, sullen air. Trayten languished in it, in passionate frustration, endeavoring to paint and failing. Marian dared not enter again, since last he ordered her out. Objects smashed against the other side of the door when she attempted to open it. He refused his meals. He sank into a pensive isolation.

The open window cooled his frosty confinement. The discomfort comforted him, enlivened him, sitting paralyzed in his chair. His hands clutched a paintbrush and the edge of a canvas. No amount of either focus or emotion could reproduce what he held in his mind. The inability to paint what he desired to capture infuriated him.

The dreams inevitably faded, leaving him trapped in the barren room alone. If only he could record their impression in oil, he believed they might save him, somehow. Trayten had been dreaming and shouting. The inhabitants of the house could hear his despair, even if they could not understand it.

Katherine felt it most acutely. She left him alone after the explosion between them, tearing out her heart and praying for a miracle. Marian was the last to set him off, and Katherine waited for his temper to ease, unsure who he would believe. He demanded his privacy, and Katherine respected his need of it for two days.

With her courage amassed, Katherine entered his room to face the heat of his glare. He detected the guilt showing through her mask and he burned away her strength with a superior facade.

"Come back to tell more stories?" he asked.

"I'm not finished yet."

"Marian says you'll kill me. Come to kill me, have you?"

"You know that she's out of her mind."

Trayten rubbed his stubbly jaw. "Maybe you *both* are."

"I want you to make your own decision, believe what *you* choose to believe. Nothing is more important to me than the truth. But before you close your mind, there is more I need to tell you."

"Careful what you say. Miss Boley, in her expertise, has pronounced me to be in critical condition, at risk of another relapse from this stimulation. I value my life so highly, you know. I wouldn't want to lose all that I have."

"Can't you stop with the sarcasm? Is nothing ever serious to you?"

"Serious? Serious is my situation! Serious is the fact that my legs are useless." He slammed his hand on the arm of his chair. "Isn't that serious enough? You want me to be serious when I speak as well?"

"So, you *are* angry with me."

His eyes darkened. His blood began to boil. "How sharp you are, *Doctor.* Shall I lay it out for you?"

"You might as well. I've my own truths to lay out." She folded her arms.

Trayten wheeled around to face her and said with a fierce tone, "I'll admit something to you, but bear in mind it doesn't make any difference after all! I actually trusted you. You were the only warmth here. I wanted to be able to tell you what I saw in my dreams, although it wasn't much. Still, I've been fighting against the blackness in my mind to discover the truth, my past, who *you* are, but now…I'm not sure I *want* to know you."

Katherine shuddered.

"You betrayed my trust. All that warmth was stripped away because you lied to me, for whatever you were hoping to gain for yourself. You're not who you told me you were, and I can't believe anything more you say.

"I'm tired of wondering about you, of shifting between uncertainty of you and fondness of you. I'm tired and I want to be left alone! I don't want you here pretending warmth to try and persuade me to *your* truth, and I don't want Marian hovering, treating me like some idiot to coddle. I'm done being manipulated by you both. You don't belong here. I don't want you here."

Katherine bit her lip. "So, full of spite, *are* you? Full of self-pity?"

"Didn't I tell you to leave?"

"I told *you,* I'm not through!" Katherine snapped. "Go on Trayten, hate the world! Wallow in self-reproach, languish away in your hermitage. You never much cared for the world anyway! But you might as well go on hating with good reason … and better aim." She wiped the hair from her eyes. "Do you want to know *why* you're like this?"

"Sure. Why not."

"Blame me!" she demanded. "As you are today; without feeling, without memory, scarred and not knowing who did this to you, well, I am the reason. I did this to you!"

Astonished, he stared silently. The intensity of her eyes stole the breath from his body, leaving him speechless. Her raw, unguarded vulnerability moved him, yet he dared not let her know it.

"I'm not afraid to admit my failings anymore. There's no one to impress and none left to judge, aside from yourself. And you *should* judge me. I was selfish, and my selfishness tore us apart.

Poverty terrified me, and I was a hypocrite as I scorned the ease to which I clung.

"I never deserved your patience, your efforts. Your love. And as I denied us, you fought for us! You shed your blood when I wasn't worth a drop of it! The trap you walked into, I set. I stoked his anger. I provoked the beast and he turned on us!

"You told me to be free. I didn't have the courage to leave when I should have, before the consequences of my mistakes fell back on us. I was a coward, terrified of the life you lived, of having no money for food! All I knew was abundance, never struggle. Well, I caused a struggle more fierce than poverty. And I lost you!" Katherine put her hands on his, feeling them stiffen.

"Trayten, you came to me and wouldn't let go. And I did nothing to spare you, when I knew his anger, when I felt his wrath and should have foreseen he would only act out in violence. I made you like this.

"If you're livid, which has been apparent since I found you, and which you *have* been for these eight years of isolation, I'm telling you: linger no more in that stupor! The woman you loved *failed* you. If you want to yell, go on. Curse me! *Really* let me have it, because I'm the one responsible. It was me."

For the next excruciating moment, he kept his gaze on the floor and remained still. Then, he tore his hands away from her.

"So, this has been what, your penance? Your desperate chance for redemption?" his voice broke. "You've sinned, transgressed against loyalty, truth, and love. And what else? You're a murderer? You think you can ease your conscience by taking care of me?"

"It matters little what more I tell you if you are determined to be angry with me. I can only hope you will believe the truth. I'm here because I love you. I came to find you because I needed to tell you that, and it's all I can do. Tell you. I can't *make* you remember. I don't know how.

"But your life is your *own,* remember that, not Marian's. If you'd rather remain here, wasting away, smothered by her obsession, than come home to the people who love you, well it's your decision. You *like* your misery, and I'm sorry for you. You'll die this way, wallowing in your pain and festering in your anger!"

"I won't be yours to pity!" he bit. "I don't want to be your punishment!"

"Then stay here! Let Marian be *yours*!"

"Selfish as you say you are, it's just as well. I'm to trust a woman I can't remember who tells me she wasn't trustworthy at all? Leave me alone! I'm exhausted. I'm tired of being pitied."

"So you'd rather pity yourself? Be alone with your disturbances?" Katherine cried. "You've got a narrow window of time then I'm gone, and your fate is sealed here!"

"Go! I've told you before, so has Marian. If you're so inclined, stay no longer!"

Katherine stared at him with her heart aflame, her feet like lead, and her pride shriveled beneath them. "I can't believe you."

"And I, after all, can't be expected to believe *you*."

"You're right. You are right." She opened the door.

Before she removed herself, broken and reluctant to give in, she revealed cheeks streaked with tears. "I'm so sorry, I *am*. You've no idea. That you ever felt any pain. If I could have taken it for myself I would, in an instant. I'd gladly trade places with you. To *not* remember is a freedom greater than mine."

۞

A creak of the door announced her entrance, the small shadow of a girl, slight in the morning light, her boot-heels clicking on the floor, her little hands closing the door behind her. Trayten stilled, his heart breaking its beat at the unexpected vision before him. A peculiar notion struck him as he looked into Angelle's brown eyes. They fixed on him a bold, open gaze.

She climbed into the chair against the wall. Her feet dangled in the air above the floor, and she slouched against the seat-back casually. Dressed entirely in black, she appeared to be in mourning. Politely she folded her hands. Those eyes, like mirrors, flashed firm and steadily watched him.

His pulse thundered through his body. More breathtaking than her stare was her silence. She said nothing to him, waiting for him to respond to her presence, the way Katherine stared silently at him once. Angelle remained focused. She frowned. Her dark hair rest in ringlet curls around her solemn, porcelain face.

Wind outside the window animated the tawny grass and it danced erratically toward the sky. Trayten's eyes were red rimmed, and in the wheelchair, he slouched, his hair sticking to his sweat beaded brow. His shirt was loose and rumpled. Under his breath he asked, "Who are *you*?"

۞

When the child ordered her away from T.B.'s door and ventured into the room herself, Marian Boley decided she had enough of the nonsense. She hurried down the stairs. In the front hall, Katherine jumped back to avoid being trampled. Marian's twisted grimace drained the color from her cheeks.

"Whatever is it now?" Katherine asked.

Marian's hair sprang up all over her head. "You need to explain a few things to me!" She grabbed Katherine's sleeve, swung her around, and tugged her into the nearest room.

The sitting parlor was warm and dim. The drapes were drawn, and a small fire burned on the grate. Although two couches framed the floor, neither would lower themselves to sit.

Marian huffed. "I had my suspicions from the beginning, and I know when people are dishonest. Now you owe me an explanation, the truth of it all. You're not any kind of physician!"

"Of course, I'm not," Katherine answered plainly.

"So, what is it? I have an idea of what you're doing, or *trying* to do here, but I'd like to hear it from you."

"I won't deny you the truth. Trayten, your boarder, he's no stranger to me. We were in love and were separated. Now, the eighth winter since I lost him, I *found* him and I'm going to bring him back to me," Katherine said soberly. With the color gone from her cheeks she was ashen, her eyes were dull and bloodshot, and her usually composed appearance lay in shambles.

As Marian studied her, she stammered, "You...you." She shifted her weight. Her control failing, she stuttered, on the brink of delirium in the heat of her frustration. "I can't *believe* this. Do you have any idea how serious his condition is? That man upstairs, he's unstable because you're stirring up his thoughts, telling him these stories! I *heard* the shouting! Mrs. Koryn, you definitely are no doctor. If you were, you would care about the trauma you are causing him!"

"You needn't raise your voice at me, Miss Boley—"

"Oh, needn't I?"

"No. I don't see what's upsetting to *you*," Katherine challenged.

"Of course not. No, of course you don't, because you and I don't see eye-to-eye! We don't understand each other. You haven't any grip on reality, where I on the other hand am clinging to it for life!"

"Is that so."

"Yes! Leave it be!" Marian demanded. "I say leave T.B. here and stop confusing him! I'm sick of it, sick to death of it! It will not stand. I want you to leave! Go get that frightful child and leave! I will not have him relapse again!"

"I don't think it's appropriate to insult my daughter! And as for leaving, no, I will not. I won't turn away from him, not after everything I've been through. Years will have been wasted if I leave now."

"He doesn't remember you! How can I believe that you actually knew him before?"

"Of course I knew him." Katherine scoffed. "What would I gain by lying?"

"You lied to *me* from the start!"

"You made assumptions that I did not amend," Katherine corrected. "I allowed them because I needed to get close to him."

"All that you've ever said was shrouded with falsehood. How can anyone believe a word you say?"

"I'm not asking *you* to believe me. I don't really care what you think. I know the truth!" Katherine proclaimed.

"Which is?"

"That he's dear to my heart, that he knew me and loved me once too, and that Angelle is our child. Whether or not you want to believe it, or even accept it, he *has* a family, people who love and want him. He's not a lost stranger and the darkness you want to keep him in will kill him!"

"The past is over and gone, Mrs. Koryn! He does not remember you, or any of what you claim! If you meant so much to him before, why doesn't he remember you now?" Marian sneered. "And if you don't mean anything to him now, why should he still matter to you? He *has* nothing for you! He's useless and helpless!"

"I'm not like you, you said it yourself. You can't understand what I feel for him, or what it is to want someone, not for what you can *get* from them, but for the sake of loving them, for what you can *give* them! It's you who wants something from him."

❧

Angelle took another deep breath. Trayten stared through the window, endeavoring to ignore her stirring presence, as well as the faint echo of raised voices below them.

"Are you not speaking with us?" she asked.

Trayten studied her, bearing the peculiar notion that cut him. "Us? You and who?"

"Me and my mother."

"Who is your mother?"

"Honestly." Angelle groaned. "Are you going to pretend to be stupid?"

"So, I'll guess your name is Angelle. You look like her."

"I look like you."

It struck him like a blow to the head and he flinched. "I hate to ask what you have to do with me."

"Do not hate. Ask what you will," she coaxed.

He sighed, scratching behind his ear.

"Go on," she prompted. "Think about it. Deep down, the answer is there."

"I know nothing. Haven't you heard?"

"How sad. Nothing at *all*? You're feeling sorry for yourself, behaving like a child."

"And I presume you'd like to claim that you are mine," Trayten said at last.

"Not 'like to,' but will claim."

He clutched his chair.

"You feel attacked, don't you? It is understandable. But it's time to come home."

"Home? This is the only home I know," he said.

"That will change."

"Do you never smile? What sort of child are you?" he broke in, panting and sweating.

"Is smiling appropriate?" Angelle asked. "You never smile, right, Father?"

"I'm not your father. I don't remember you." He looked around, searching for a way out of his chair or the room.

"Oh no, of course you don't remember me. You were gone before I was born."

"How!"

"If *you* don't know how babies are born, I'm not going to tell you." Angelle drew in her chin and shook her head with disgust.

"How was I *gone*."

"We don't know." She slid off her seat and took a tin from the large pocket of her smock. "Maybe if you have one, you could stop shaking and sweating so much."

Suspiciously he snatched the tin away as though she might

bite him. Angelle returned to her chair and seated herself exactly as before. He lit a cigarette, inhaled, and ran a hand through his hair. It calmed him, momentarily.

In her meticulous way, she studied him. Her stare made him shift around and tap his fingers. He shrugged at her and she remained staid and set. Trayten glanced around the room, but always returned to find her gaze pinned on him.

☙❧

"What I want from him, Mrs. Koryn, is peace and rest for his own sake!" Marian insisted. "I want to help him. It's you who I can't understand, you who can't help him. Leave us at peace! You aren't doing him any good! His life is here. I'm providing for him. I *have* been! He needs me."

"You are deranged. Delusional! He doesn't need you at all!" Katherine said. "The reality is he belongs where he is *loved*! Can you grasp that? This is what I'm doing; bringing him back home, where he has a purpose, because I need him, his daughter needs him! He must go where he can be alive. Because here, he is dead!"

"Maybe he isn't who you think he is and even if he is, maybe he doesn't *want* to remember! He's comfortable here, he needs stability! You can't storm back into his life throwing a child at him, telling him it's his, and that he should leave with you! You can't! It's too much! You'll kill him!"

"You never knew him, but I did. I do! He has hope. He can recover! Even if he never does, I'll take care of him."

"I've been doing it for years! I have!" Marian shouted, pounding her chest with a fist. "The shock of that kind of change could be detrimental."

"He could be happy. Happiness is something he hasn't known as long as you've taken care of him! And it isn't up to you! You can't control him! He doesn't belong to you, he isn't property! He's a human being!"

"I know he is!"

"Then let go of him. You can't save him!"

"You let go! You're only confusing him!" Marian fired.

"But you are the one who has suppressed his progress all these years! Like the painting, let's talk about that! The one you lied about."

"What do you accuse me of?" Marian squawked.

"Even *you* lied! You said you knew nothing about it, but Russell Danby told me Tratyen saw it and had a seizure! It affected him, but you locked him away and you shut out his chances at discovering the past! You wanted to deny he could recover so that he would remain here for you to keep!"

"No, I—"

"You are killing him slowly! You are! He doesn't *care* about you. He hates your cooking! Tell me, have you ever made him smile? Have you?" Katherine inhaled. "Well, I have."

છુ૪ઝ

Angelle regarded the door and turned back to face him. "They're *shouting* about you."

"Why do you look at me that way?" Sweat gleamed at his temples. He lit another cigarette. "She sent you here to do this to me. You're both making me crazy! Is that what you're after?"

"Don't be foolish. I can't figure you out. What scares you? That you don't remember? Trusting us who appear to be strangers?"

"Child, I am not scared."

"Let me persuade you." She pulled from her pocket a journal, red and leather-bound. It was worn and thick with rumpled pages. Angelle opened it, revealing the fancy script that covered the pages. "Let me tell you about my mother."

"What is that?"

"Her journal. She filled it with letters to you. There. It's your name." She pointed and he squinted. "Trayten." Angelle placed it open in her lap, flipping through the pages daintily.

"We have searched a long weary time. Yes, we have. Momma told me the stories, the memories. She wrote them down. Things that you said to her and places you went. They are all here, if only you would accept them."

She flipped several pages and pursed her lips. "You liked the name Angelle. She told you it meant messenger and you said you liked it, so that's what she named me. Can't you remember?"

"I can't say."

"Oh, you can, you just don't! Tell me if you recall this." She bowed her head and placed her finger on the page to follow the words. " *'Wherever you go, and whoever you will see, I am the whisper at the back of your mind. I am keeping the greatest part of your heart. I have taken up your soul and entwined it with mine, ensuring you cannot forget me, lest you forget yourself. Even if you leave me, my warmth will still linger like heat from the sun. These things I promise. I will be with you, and I will see you every day when you cannot see me watching. I will always find you.'*

"You told her that. She never forgot it and it's true. You stayed with her. People called her mad because she was trying to find you. You have to believe it. And you can't deny me! I'm the image of you." She laid the diary in his lap, her curls bouncing at her shoulders, and a pout on her mouth when she plopped back into her chair.

"Listen," he said weakly. "I don't know what to think of what I can't recall."

"They say you have dreams."

"Common myth. My dreams are so hurried, they burn right out of my memory in a flash. What I'm trying to say is; how can I be expected to accept this? If I can't spark a recollection, what sort of life would that be for you? For your mother?"

"You would spark. You would fall in love with her again."

He breathed a laugh. "*There* it is, finally, the childishness in you!"

"That isn't fair!" Angelle pouted.

"*Whatever* is?"

"You are so pathetic!"

"Am I?" He chuckled at her temper.

"You are! You remain snide and ignorant! You must like it here!"

"It isn't simple—"

"It's not hard! You *are* my father! You think she's lying to you, but Momma would never lie to you. She tells the truth!" She stood on her chair and wiggled her finger. "And even if she was lying, which she's *not*, what would it be for? That's stupid! You have nothing to offer us. She came here knowing only that you were a nameless recluse!"

Trayten smirked, as she threw her arms about.

"Don't you laugh at me!" she warned. "I'm not here to amuse you. Momma rejected all comfort to find *you*." His smirk faded away. Angelle preached on from the platform of her chair. "Her husband was a rich man. Reuben Koryn."

"Reuben?"

"Yes! When he died, his properties went to her. His money became hers. Did she buy a big house? No. Did she buy more land? No. She sold the lands to the people who worked them. And when she's in Portsea, do you know where we stay sometimes?" Angelle's eyes were large and expressive. Trayten covered his mouth, his eyebrows knitted. "She bought a rickety flat in Sun Street."

He gave no reply. She slouched in the chair. "That flat has creaking floors stained with paint, a leaky window, and dark walls. The man who lived there vanished, so the paintings were left on his walls."

"You are very persistent, aren't you?"

"I have to be." Angelle nodded.

"Like your mother. And you both get angry, so quickly. You like to snap."

"One never *likes* to snap." She looked at him. "But you are good at encouraging it."

"I apologize."

"No, don't apologize. Agree! I would not *have* to snap."

He chuckled. "I enjoy your company."

"Good. But you'll be able to appreciate my company more when you come home," she said.

"You don't quit."

"Didn't you say I'm persistent?"

"Right, forgot." He tapped his temple. "Must be the memory loss."

Angelle glared. "That isn't funny."

"No, I don't imagine you'd think so." Trayten smiled.

"You are mocking me. Stop playing. I'm serious."

Trayten wheeled in a circular motion away from her.

❧

"I have been most tolerant." A cruel expression crossed Marian's face. "I have tolerated you changing routines, taking him outside! I endured you spitefully going against my rules, my words. He's been worse these past months than the whole time I've had him! You are *more* than finished here!"

"I'm not finished until he leaves *with* me!" Katherine said.

"You'll have to go through me!"

"That's no barrier!" Katherine stepped closer.

"It's my house, my life, my man!"

"You might be desperate to keep him, but he doesn't belong to you! I think it's revenge for you! You couldn't force George to stay, so you planned to keep Trayten, who couldn't run if he *wanted* to! It's sick!"

"You don't know anything about George! And you don't know me!"

"I know you're unreasonable, and that's enough!" Katherine said. "I would have asked you to consider what it's like to be me, to try and understand, but I don't think you can!"

"I should hate to be like you! You expect to get what you want because of your privilege and power! Well, I see you for what you are. You're a liar and you're selfish!" Marian backed Katherine against the wall. "It's awfully convenient that your rich husband is dead! It wouldn't surprise me if you killed him yourself!"

"I tried, really, I did."

"I knew it!" Marian gasped.

"I didn't kill him. But you, you're killing Trayten!"

"I'd never harm him!"

"You already have. You've confined him, suppressed him, and fatally bored him!"

"You need to leave!" Marian closed her eyes.

"I paid for my week." Katherine sat on one of the couches. "It's been my prayer since the day I lost him; to find him alive. I don't care that he can't remember now. I'll spend the rest of our lives hoping for him to recover and even if he doesn't, *I'll* be the one to prepare his meals and look after him.

"I believe God has given me a chance to make it right. I owe a great debt and I will pay it gladly, thankfully. No one else can pay it for me. No one else can care for him as I can. No one can love him as deeply as I do. One more week, and I'll get him to come with me. One week, and I'll be finished here."

"You aren't asking me, are you?"

"I can't afford to," Katherine said quietly.

"Well, I suppose now we know what we think of each other!" Marian folded her arms.

"Now we know."

❦

Angelle stomped her feet as she marched around to face him. She bent over his wheelchair and put her face close to his. Trayten tilted his head, wondering, and drew back. She followed him with a stare. When he would try to wheel away from her, Angelle would follow him and slam her hands on the arms of his chair, forcing him to see her. After fruitless efforts to shake her off he said, "Stop it. What are you doing?"

"Does it bother you?"

"Angelle, stop it! Go sit down!"

"You can't order me around," she huffed.

"What are you doing?"

"Why?" she asked.

"Why? Because it irritates me," he said.

"Does it bother you?"

"It certainly is aggravating." He pressed the heel of his hand to his temple.

"I thought you enjoyed my company."

Trayten stared back. "I forgot that, too."

"Have I taught you nothing?" Taking a blanket from the arm of the chair, she tucked it around her small frame. She pulled her feet up. "I'll sit. But I'll stay here. I will stay until you are honest with yourself, and with us."

"You want me that much?"

"We do," Angelle proclaimed.

"Why."

"I'm not sure, since you have proved yourself to be vulgar and messy, rude and stubborn. You don't have any nurturing qualities, or even humane qualities. However," she sighed deeply, "we have noted these things and believe that your greatness in the past is enough to want you with us in the future. We have invested our efforts in you, and we believe in miracles, above all things."

His expression softened. Tired of staring at him as the sun's rays filled the window, Angelle curled up, resting her head on the arm of the chair. Trayten scarcely moved after her haunting eyes closed. Many hopeless, powerless sighs were released. Many frustrated wonderings collided within.

Dinner proved an awkward event that evening. At the table four were seated. From her plate, sunken and small in her chair, Angelle glared directly at Tarl. Her curls were flattened, and her cheek was red where she had slept on it. She did not move to chew her food. Instead she kept her face directed to him with a studious stare, her head tilted slightly back, shoulders turned in.

The wobbly headed boarder, his eyes blinking drowsily and mouth constantly agape, juggled his spoon. He could not lift the utensil without losing the food on it. By the time it reached his mouth, it was empty again, and the shaky process was repeated. He fumbled to catch his cup and missed his mouth with his biscuit. He coughed with morsels of food on his tongue. Angelle sneered with disapproval.

Between Katherine and Marian, tension sizzled. Gruffly, Miss Boley would ask for something and Mrs. Koryn, after passing it, would make a point to slam a bowl or a glass down. The meal was a serenade of thumping plates and utensils. Katherine was aggravated by the atmosphere. She dropped her knife, tapped Angelle's arm, and scolded, "Stop gawking at him. Eat."

Angelle groaned and continued to stare with disgust anyway. Katherine returned to hacking at her steak. Marian ripped a bite from her biscuit and chewed loudly with her eyes narrowed.

❧ 26 ❧

1901

Night was the time when Katherine haunted the confines of her self-secured room. The battering of the wind, shifting against the old house kept her from rest. She lay on the narrow bed, body curled in around the small swell of her stomach.

Suddenly, she sensed Trayten. Faintly she detected his voice, a submerged echo. She opened her eyes to the bare little room.

Disappointment. Immediately tears formed and she curled in tighter, clutching her pillow, digging her fingers into the fabric. She closed her eyes again, squeezing out the tears. She inhaled but held her breath. Katherine felt a warmth crawl along her spine, a notion, and in desperate dizziness she sat up.

The floor was brisk against her bare feet and she slipped them into a pair of boots. The eerie bluish white of the snow through her window illuminated her face when she drew near. A sharp aura enveloped the glass, but she placed her palms firmly against it and glared through the dense mist.

Movement caught her eye; a tall, dark form, gliding between

the crooked trees. Katherine broke into motion. Her intuition drove her, and she threw on a coat. She unlocked and tore open the door, and raced through the skeleton of the shivering house to break into the night below, desperate and on fire.

Outside she tramped heavy and reckless through the snow, exhaling stacks of white mist into a thick, smothering fog. Katherine swam the air with her arms, the cold climbing under her skin. Snow fell into her boots as she sloshed through it.

She ran to the trees, believing desperately in what she saw. "Trayten!" she called and arrived at the row of trees. Spinning around, she searched the mist, heart thumping loud inside her chest.

She did not find him there. In her stillness, the beating of her heart filled the silence. The defeat crushed her. She cast her gaze to the snowy ground and noticed, merely yards from where she stood on trembling legs, a folded piece of canvas in the snow. Her spirits ignited once more. Katherine tucked her wild hair behind her ears and took hold of it.

It did not vanish into air, as the rest of her dreams. She unfolded it and beheld his handwriting in paint:

Katherine, My Love,
   Look for me. I am coming for you.
   Trayten Basel

The impact of the message knocked Katherine to her knees. The shell that had sustained her melted and left her a puddle in the snow, weeping wildly with a bliss that struck deeper than pain. The hopes and the beliefs rushed back in waves, awakening the part of her that had been dying. Her heart warmed, for the first time in an eternity. Even there in the wintry night air, she was protected by his presence, his message clutched eagerly between her hands.

1909

"What more can be done?" Katherine asked.

She and Russell Danby faced her portrait in the corridor of the museum. Katherine twisted her hands and rubbed her neck, catching small dark strands of hair that fell from her chignon. Russell glanced from her to the painting and back again, taking in the likeness.

"How desperate are you?" he asked.

"That is fearful talk." Katherine furrowed her brow. "What do you mean?"

Before he could respond, two figures skipped toward them. Mary called, "Of course, you are back, of course!"

Katherine weakly smiled and shook their willing hands. Louisa rubbed her arms, having come in from outside. Her nose glowed as red as a cherry.

"Doctor, nice to see you out of the clinic for once." Mary nodded. "Don't I say it, Louisa? The man's got to be awfully lonely keeping to himself."

"I'm quite all right, Mary." Russell flashed a sweet grin. "And you are both well, I trust?"

Louisa laughed. "With our thick Saunders blood, Doctor, we are *always* well!"

"Are *you* well, dear?" Mary asked Katherine, touching her arm.

"Yes, how is everything going with the cripple?" Louisa asked, creeping close to Katherine with heightened interest.

"She has told him everything," Russell answered after watching Katherine grapple for words.

"Everything?" Louisa shrugged.

"The truth," Katherine admitted. "His name is Trayten Basel and he was a painter. This painter." She turned to study the portrait and their eyes filled with wonder. "This is a portrait of me, and he painted it because…because he loved me. I came to find him, I wanted him to remember me, but he doesn't."

"Well, there's more hope for him now than ever before!" Louisa cried. "Oh dear, here you are!"

"What'll you do?" Mary asked.

"He won't accept the truth. I'm not sure what more I can do." Katherine shook her head and bit back the tears.

"Russell," Mary whirled around. "Haven't you still got notes on those studies? The mental ones you were talking about?"

"I asked you how desperate you are," Russell said to Katherine.

"You did." She turned back toward him.

"Well, how desperate?"

"I have less than a week before I must leave Marian's. Less than a week, to try and take him with me, but he's lost trust in me, by my outburst. I've already ruined everything."

"Desperate then," he confirmed.

"Cautious," she corrected.

"I can work with that. There's a medicine that well, let me go back." Russell paused to compose his words, then continued to their undivided attention, "Studies were conducted by physicians and medical students in Vienna a few years back. A friend of mine who practices there keeps in contact with me. These were experiments for mental maladies. Their efforts involved manipulating and testing substances to open chasms in the mind. From the reports and a combination of my own research and study, I discovered a combination of laudanum and herbs that, when consumed as a steeped brew, could induce the mind into a dream-like state, while keeping a patient coherent and awake. Like dreaming while awake. Asleep, yet alert. It proved in some cases to relax patients, who could then speak about traumas. It's possible it might open pathways previously locked. Perhaps open the memory to things buried deep."

Mary gave Katherine an impressed nod. Louisa clung to her sister's side apprehensively.

Russell drew in a breath. "I could apply this to Trayten and see where it would lead us. Perhaps, if some doorways open, we might help him through to find the answers. We may be able to do more than hope that his memory will recover."

"So you mean we have to drug him?" Katherine touched her heart.

"It's like a sedative. It should not harm him."

"Should not?" she gasped. "What if it does the opposite; erases the pieces he has remembered?"

"I can't guarantee anything. We can only discover it for ourselves."

"But *drug* him?"

"Listen to the doctor, Miss Katherine," Mary suggested. "He is a gentle man. He would go out of his way to prevent anyone harm."

"Best to do all you can, yes?" Louisa encouraged.

"He might also benefit from a little more reminding," Mary said. "Who he once was. Who he could be again. Tell me, Katherine, do you know anything about art?"

"What do you mean?"

"I've heard that artists leave traces of their selves in the work of their hands." Mary took the painting from the wall. "If it be so, take his work to him."

"Do you think it could help?" she asked. Reassuring nods surrounded her.

"You must not be nervous, so he won't fear a thing," Louisa said. "You must make him comfortable. Doctor, make that concoction and I'll brew a pear cider potent enough to cover any drug."

"Go to him," Mary said, handing Katherine the oil painting.

"Trust us," Russell told her. "I wouldn't harm him. Go with Louisa and I'll come by to get you. We'll do this together."

Outside the door to his room Katherine glanced worriedly at Russell. She held a pitcher close against her chest and he carried a bag on one shoulder, cradling the portrait.

"It's good that Marian's gone," he noted. "Otherwise, we'd have to sneak me through the back."

"When she returns, she'll see your carriage."

"Pray for her delay. Let me go in first. After you've said a good long prayer, you come in too."

She nodded. Russell smiled, touching her shoulder gently.

ぶꙮꙮ

Russell's first impression of Trayten was that he appeared rough and disorderly. Whiskers darkened his face, and his eyes were severe. His clothes were in need of laundering.

Slackened in his chair, tightly gripping its arms, Trayten dully perceived Russell. The drapes were drawn, leaving a shred of light between them to illuminate the room. Russell moved toward the lantern at the bedside table. Trayten animated to stop him. "Leave it out."

Nodding, Russell set the bag down and waited in the darkness. Trayten's hair was unruly and dark bags stretched beneath his eyes.

"Do you remember me, Trayten?"

"Doctor, how are you?"

With an easy smile, Russell shrugged, pulling up a stool and sitting before him officially. "Well and good, truly. And you? What, are you waiting here to die?"

Trayten stared blankly at the far wall, black beyond the small stream of light. He snorted and wheeled around to face the shrouded window. "Sure. It doesn't matter though, does it?"

"It matters a lot."

"Does it? I doubt that. Why not leave me to the dark." Trayten focused on the darkest corner of the room. "What good am I?"

"Nothing is more important than restoring you to the light."

"Are you trying to be spiritual? I thought you were a man of science."

"They are one in the same to me." Russell smiled.

There was a glint of appreciation shining in his eyes when Trayten looked at Russell. He asked, "Where did you disappear to, anyway?"

"Don't you remember?"

"Are you serious?" Trayten leveled him with a hard glare.

"After your relapse six years ago, Marian decided that my right to treat you had expired. I haven't been allowed near you since then."

"I believe it. And have you met this…this," Trayten flapped his hand into the air several times, "I don't even know what to call her."

"Katherine Madison?"

"Sure."

"I've met her, yes."

"And what is your professional opinion?" Trayten scratched his temple.

"Well, she is—"

"I know what Marian told me."

"What's that?" Russell asked.

Trayten did not answer him. Russell waited in the silence awhile, wondering. The door opened and Katherine entered their pathetic pool of light bearing her pitcher. She was immediately crushed by Trayten's glare and hesitated under its weight.

With a deep breath she poured the cider into a cup on the table. Russell noticed her unsteady hands and took the cup from her with a reassuring nod. He passed it to Trayten, smiling. "It's frightfully cold outside."

"Lucky we are inside. What's all this? A tea party?" Trayten took the cup and snidely squinted at Katherine. "Where's that precocious little person of yours?"

"Asleep, restoring her energy." She smoothed her skirt, sitting farther away from them on the outer perimeter of the light.

"Good," Trayten said. "She'll be ready to terrorize some other hapless invalid tomorrow."

"Oh, but you're the only one she's interested in," Katherine softly chimed.

Tratyen turned his attention to the cup in his hand.

Russell talked of obscure and impersonal things. His voice became a low surrounding drone, the words soon incomprehensible to Trayten who drank his cider and leaned back in his chair. Even as Russell's voice filled the air, for Katherine it was silent. Even in their midst, she sat alone beyond their dim halo.

She was acutely aware of every sip of cider that he took into his mouth. The air was concentrated, stagnating her breath and blurring her vision. Trayten became a hazy mirage in her tormented view, inexact and reminiscent.

In the dimness of the room and the distraction of her apprehension, Katherine could envision him as he once was. She held her breath, fearful that he would vanish away. There were golden flecks shimmering from the depths of his eyes. Health painted his features.

She tried to remember the last time he kissed her and the sensation it had stirred; the lightning striking her palms, the fire scouring her blood. With her eyes tightly closed, she dared follow the daydream. He was there to lift her up, holding her with both the assurance of his strength and the power of his devotion. His image, sitting withered in the wheelchair, returned to her mind and Katherine jolted.

She blinked as though she had been sleeping, the dimness blinding her, while both Trayten and Russell noticed her jump. Russell raised his eyebrows and glanced with overemphasis at Trayten. He slouched low in his wheelchair, his cup full again and his eyes so wet that he appeared to be weeping.

Katherine waded through a waking dream. A frightening, powerful dream. In the dim, with a heart strangled by fear, with a loss of confidence, anxiety found her easy prey. She wiped the sweat from her temple and swept a strand of renegade hair from her eyes. It fell back down again. She was increasingly self-conscious while Trayten's gaze locked with hers, refocusing with inquiry.

Russell directed his attention back to Trayten and stuttered on, "That...that is true, it must be colder on the shore. Inland might be warmer."

"It must always be colder somewhere, I suppose," Trayten uttered. "There is a color other than white sky somewhere, bleak winter white is so barren, I'd prefer it to be night here if it's warmer for lack of cold white. But it's black always, in a way. Black like the sea, like the night, underneath. It's not blue anymore...just black."

"Under the sea?" Russell asked.

"Under the surface, out in it. Like being in the eye of a storm, like the waves disconnect down there. They go all ways. They pull, they—" Trayten labored to illustrate some shape with his hands. His gaze drifted to the window.

Her stomach twisted into a fast knot and she sank back a little farther into the darkness.

"Were you in the sea?" Russell asked.

"Ha." Trayten laughed morbidly. "Are you a good man?"

"What? Me?" Russell asked, surprised at the question. He shrugged. "I suppose I *try* to be—"

"How very good of you. I can't say the same."

"Why not?"

"Why are you a good man? I...I did something awful. Wouldn't you believe? Awful deeds left men before me in the dark, in death. But my death isn't death, it's life. Good men don't have to know what that's like, men like you...men like you...like you—"

"Men like me?" Russell sat stiffly. "What about men like you?"

"Men like me, Doctor, aren't men like you." Trayten was beginning to tick, twitch, and loll. "Ever feel like you're going to be cut to pieces? Cut so deep you think, surely something has to be severed, but it isn't."

"Trayten, do you believe you were bad?"

"I don't believe anything anymore. But I—no." He stopped and squinted, concentrating on the darkness. "Murder consigns a man to living death. Don't you think so?"

"I don't know anything about it."

"Oh, well, that's because you're a good man. Right. Well, this is living death. Emptiness, loneliness as white as that snow, all the color gone, never any blue in the sky. A perfect mirror, the same isolated view, same absence. No one in the water."

Russell looked at Katherine, who sat listening intently, her face solemn, eyes focusing on Trayten while he gazed off, his head drooping.

"Trayten," Russell called.

"Yes."

"That *is* your name," he affirmed.

"So some say. Russell. That's your name?" Trayten asked.

"It is."

"You know where it came from, probably. Some uncle's name, a grandfather, a father's middle name. Names mean something. Mine means something." He ground his fingers against his forehead.

Katherine wanted to remind him, but she held her tongue. Trayten sipped from his cup and Russell took it to refill.

Trayten rambled on, "I'm a god. Well, it's a god. Ha! God of pain, god of the lost, the left. How many miles is it to Alderney from England, is it far? How far? How many miles? All this blood, how can it all be mine, no, it wasn't, then it was. Cuts. Sand clots blood, sand gets inside of you. God of the shore, sand swimming in his veins, salt sea sealed in there. God of the sea…"

They were silent, allowing him space to run free in the vehicle given him. Trayten poured cider past his lips, missing them. It ran down his shirt and he dropped the cup. His eyes scanned from the door to Katherine and Russell. Their faces were glazed and distorted.

He heaved with his head spinning and used his hands to support his speech. "Can't feel my lips, like my legs. Can touch them but can't feel the touch. Were you ever touched, Russell? Tell me, you're a young man, you have your mobility. If I were touched, I couldn't feel it now. She kissed my cheek once, my cheek, this one," he tapped it, eyes foggy, "and I don't even know why. Her hair holds the rain. Why kiss a man like me? Empty man. Half a man. I'm homeless, did you know? This is not home." He laughed brokenly. "If it were, God help me, how did I get *here* with that Marian?"

"Did you have a home before here?" Russell asked. He took the cup and filled it again, but Katherine grabbed his wrist. She shook her head, eyes full of warning. Russell nodded.

"Of course I have a home," Trayten barked. He took a deep breath, shuddered, and began to cry. Russell waited, preventing Katherine as she instinctively reached for him.

"I lived alone. Alone. I live the longest nights, alone," he muttered through tears.

"Were you always alone?"

"I was always without, alone and there is a bleeding." He pinned his fist to his heart. They stared as Russell held Katherine's wrist. The discordant mix of hope and anxiety within her resulted in a subdued numbness.

Trayten narrowed his eyes. "I was a watcher. Once, when I could watch her. Like an angel, but here I'm a devil, doomed."

Katherine could neither breathe nor move. Russell let loose of her wrist and waited. Footsteps broke the silence, and Katherine caught Russell's alarmed expression before whispering, "Marian!"

Russell leapt toward the door and locked it. "Does she have a key?"

"Yes, she got it recently. I hope she's lost it by now!"

The dreaded knock sounded, and they all jumped. The doorknob jiggled, followed by Marian's shrill voice, "Mrs. Koryn? Doctor? You're in there I know it! Open this door immediately!"

"Go on to bed, dear," Russell said through the crack. "We are working here."

"What are you doing?" she demanded.

"Go to bed."

"Don't order *me* in my house! And don't lock me out of my rooms!" She grumbled. "Where's that blasted key?"

"We're all right in here," Katherine consoled. "Don't worry."

"I'll have the authorities here if you don't unlock my door!"

"The deuce you will! We're having a tea party!" Trayten sneered.

There followed a shocked silence. Russell spun away from the door back to Trayten. Shaking off the resonance of Marian's interruption, he said, "You speak as though someone has broken your heart."

Katherine detected Marian's breathing on the other side of the door. Silence resettled. Trayten lifted his head, took another drink and said with dreadful assurance, "I have no heart."

"How can you have no heart?" Katherine asked.

"How do people lose things? They are stolen, ripped out, even misplaced. But I wasn't a forgetful man."

"You still have it. You must, and isn't anything repairable?" Katherine asked.

Marian pounded at the door. "I'm going for the authorities!"

They ignored her.

"Do you know what *she* told me?" Trayten fixed his stare on Katherine.

"Who?" Russell asked.

"Marian told me about you, Katherine." Trayten pointed lazily. "That I have something…something you want. That's why you're here, to say you knew me, to say I have a child, isn't it, is she right?"

"What could I want from you?"

"I don't even know!" He laughed. "She's crazy!"

"I *told* you," Katherine said.

"What happened to your husband?"

She was hesitant to answer, "He died."

"Yes, I heard. How did he die? Did he die like I died, or did he get sick and stop breathing? But that happened too."

"What happened?" she asked.

"I stopped breathing. There's no air in the water. Once you swallow enough it clouds your brain, your lungs, and makes you disappear. But that is forceful, not like sleeping and stopping breathing. Was he sick? Did he get sick and die?"

"He was not sick. The man never got sick."

Trayten studied the shadows on her cheeks, the fallen hair around her face. "So, how did he die?"

"He was killed."

"How?"

"I don't know exactly."

"Didn't someone tell you?"

"Well, I saw it. I saw him," she admitted with a chill.

"And you don't know?"

"No," she affirmed.

"Of course you do! Was he wounded? Was he smothered? What killed him?"

"I don't know which killed him."

"Which what?"

"Which of the wounds. There were many of them."

"And this doesn't affect you?"

"Why would it." She held her chin high.

"Someone killed your husband, and you saw him. Didn't it hurt?"

"I wasn't the one killed."

"Didn't it hurt to see him," Trayten pressed.

"It hurt more to *not* see someone else." She turned her face to the floor.

He scratched his face with rubbery fingers. Leaning forward as though he would get up, he looked at his legs, and laughed with a shrug, "Oh, right. Can't walk." He looked at Katherine and asked, "Didn't you love him?"

"I never loved him, Trayten."

"But he was your husband."

"I couldn't love him."

"That bad of a man, yea? We have something in common. But I'm badder—worser— or more bad…I'm the worst."

"What have you done?"

"But, I said it right; bad men like me get hurt, get killed, get lost."

"What have you done, Trayten?" she asked again.

He lowered his chin onto his chest. In the lingering quiet, Katherine moved close to Russell's side. They were exhausted in the stifling air of the room, the silence heightening their sensitivities to his movements and sounds. The cider was entirely consumed, except for what had spilled on Trayten's shirt.

"What's happened?" Marian asked. "Is he all right? What are you doing in there? Doctor, I warned you—"

Trayten raised his eyes, red and blinking. "A drug runner, running drugs for the smugglers. Night travel, deceiving the guards. To cities, to the other sellers. Taking threats and delivering them back and forth, to … he's dead now, he died. He died."

Russell felt Katherine's hand slap against his forearm. He looked at her and her brow tightened with an angry sorrow.

"Is it?" he asked.

"I think. I think it is—" Katherine brokenly replied.

"Then they got it. They got it and my only employment, gone. I had nothing else. I had rotten potatoes for half a penny. Dirty. The floor dirty, my hands. Felt the ground through my shoes. A dog starving in the street. No. The dogs did better than I."

"You're remembering," Katherine said. "Trayten."

He would not respond to his name. He drifted off into other places and departed from them into the air, into a dream. Words fell from his lips like water draining out. They listened, collecting every drop he offered. The fragments and revelations seeped freely from his loosened mind.

"A vessel, drifting in the sea, lost or roaming, wandering on the waves, under misted skies, onboard, top deck, exposed to the air. A storm brewing in fog, only wind, only turbulence; no rain, no thunder, no rain like her hair. It was night and on the shallow deck, tumbling on the sea, I would freeze, paralyzed and frozen, all warmth gone.

"I would die, she told me, I would freeze. White fog turning to gray and looking out over the hazing waters I knew fear, a dread. Motion of the waves, throwing us about but I couldn't leave the deck. I was freezing, frozen, already. I spoke to someone. She came to me and opened her arms to me, her hair to shield the coming storm, circulating our breath close between us, and she held onto me, tightly. Sharing the heat of our bodies; though I was already frozen, my legs frozen.

"She told me I'd die, held on, preparing me, comforting, covering me from the fog, keeping me warm, alive. So I breathed again." His dark eyes filled with terror. Katherine's nails dug into her throat, her heart stilled.

"There was no storm. Only the waves and the fog. I felt her cheek against my face, my love. Waves tossing, tumbling us about. We would hold enough heat to survive it, I couldn't move … couldn't get up. White clouding air closed down, comfort holding me, but my eyes wouldn't close.

"Awaiting death, seized by the sea, strange, entangled in her comfort, while dying, while forgetting her. In her arms, I was leaving, ready to go. And then I was alone. She had gone. Only the fog covered me, and I couldn't get up, willing myself to move, but couldn't get up, frozen, I had frozen. The more I grasped to move, to hold onto her, the more I was forgetting, I was losing her. The cold crept over me. Cold crept over and left me dead. And I forgot her."

"What does it mean?" Katherine whispered to Russell. "He

was pulled out of the sea and brought here in winter. He remembers it, is that what that was?"

"You did love," Russell said to Trayten, who practically lay in his chair.

"Love...love," Trayten repeated with empty sound.

"What do you think of it, Trayten?" Russell asked.

"I don't. I try *not* to. Love, shouldn't it be true? Shouldn't it last? Shouldn't I remember it, if *ever* it was? How could it have been? Love is entrapment. Crippling dependency. All things crippled for me. By love, there's the truth of mortality, aware of all the small things, pattern of breath, every word held sacred. Alone, stricken with constant aching. Chains of indulgence, weakness, a killer, a gift—"

"From God," Katherine's voice cracked. "Love is the world's greatest disease."

He turned his eyes on her and jarred, completely stunned.

"What, Trayten?" she pleaded.

Russell glanced from one to the other.

Katherine asked again, "What is it?"

Trayten avoided her gaze.

"You *see* me. Trayten Basel, you saw me, just now!" Katherine rushed to kneel at his feet. "Tell me, what is it you see?"

"Stop it! I can't see it!" He covered his head with his hands.

"Of course you can, please!"

"No! I don't!"

"You do!" Katherine took Russell's bag, talking as she worked the painting from it. "Remember Portsea, the night travel you did for Jack Conway, that was his name, Jack Conway. You remembered that. You can remember me! You painted, you painted me, Trayten look!" She brought the portrait to face him, and his gaze moved across the beam of light through the drapes to behold it.

The blood drained from his face until he appeared blue. Sweat glistened on his skin. His eyes flickered, horrified.

"Look, it's your work! You sold it in Portsea and it's here, your art!"

"No—" He breathed faster, shaking his head, blinking. There were four of her, his vision splitting, blurring, dancing. He touched his head and felt nothing, although cold and heat raced violently through his chest. Delusions swam through his consciousness, threatening to fade into blackness.

"But she's," he choked, unable to complete the sentence.

"What is she?" Katherine handed the portrait to Russell.

"Everybody stop!" Trayten put up his hands.

"Come back to me, Trayten." She touched his face hesitantly with both hands and tried to catch his gaze, but it remained locked on the painting. "You have to remember me, please!"

"We can help you!" Russell offered. "You're getting there again, Trayten. You have uncovered so much! Only now you have to believe it, trust it. Leave this place and go with her."

"She's frozen. She's frozen!" Trayten jolted and his body spilled onto the floor. The chair rolled backward when he fell, and Katherine and Russell rushed to get ahold of him. He convulsed, heaving, gasping, and swimming as though he were drowning. He seized and quaked. Marian beat on the door.

With his thrashing they struggled to get near enough. Russell took several punches and elbow jabs, trying to lift him. Katherine called to Trayten, frantic as he palpitated. He managed to hurl himself near the table and he knocked the stools over with flying fists. Russell juggled to catch his wrists. Katherine reached around his chest, but his arm thrust back and knocked her down. Russell lunged and hoisted him halfway up, his body fighting senselessly.

Marian pounded and squawked behind the door. Katherine slithered to the wheelchair and brought it closer, and Russell tried to lift him. Trayten clutched his head, howling as though in agony and folded, throwing Russell off balance. Clumsily they crashed to the floor. Trayten landed first with a loud, cracking thump.

Katherine gasped. Trayten lay stiff and still, his head against the hardwood floor. She screamed his name and threw herself on him.

"Don't touch him, Katherine, don't!" Russell ordered and unlocked the door.

When it opened, Marian rushed in, her shriek filling the room. "You've killed him! I knew you would!" She pulled Katherine by the arm and spit into her face. "Get out of my house! Get out of here!"

Katherine stuttered but was cut off by Marian's fiery hand, slapping across her cheek. "Get out! You ever come back here, I'll have you arrested!"

"Trayten, do you hear me? Wake up!" Russell crouched over the stilled body, checking hastily for signs of life.

R oused from a warm bed at a dreadful hour, Angelle was bundled up and carried away. Katherine had strapped the suitcases together with a belt and dragged them behind her through the snow, carving a trail away from the narrow house. In the bitter cling of night's wintry breeze she fled, away from the room where the dread of his death lingered. She was convinced that this time, she had completely failed him.

Mary was quick to let Katherine in, when she knocked on the Saunders sisters' door. She did not question Katherine, only brought her to a spare room where she could tuck Angelle in for the remainder of the night. After closing the door, Katherine collapsed on the bed. Tears covered her cheeks, catching in her loose flowing hair. She laid a hand against Angelle's cheek as the child drifted back to sleep.

In the thick silence, the sound of Trayten's distorted ramblings filled her head. The distress of her heart became heavier with each recollection. She inhaled deeply, painfully, fighting the compulsion to sob openly.

1901

Curious, Katherine shuffled to the door in response to a knock from the other side. She opened it to the fair glow of early morning. A lifting, leaping quiver rocked her from within to see Trayten standing before her. Warm tears fell as freely as the elation rushing through her.

The vision who visited her dreams towered over her, stunning and substantial. His black hair and dark features boldly contrasted the bright white of his dress-shirt. Against the dull, hazy chill, his eyes burned with glimmers of gold and warm shades of russet. They feasted on her tenderly, sweeping Katherine into a helpless swoon. When he smiled, the radiance buckled her knees and she threw herself into his arms, trusting he would catch her, lift her from the ground, and crush her in a tight embrace.

He did not vanish. He was no dream. Katherine pressed her cheek against his neck, savoring his warmth, breathing him in. As she shivered with relief, he held her safe in the cradle of his arms. His lips searched her neck and face, covering both with soft, melting kisses. Under his touch she was gasping, her eyes spilling tears, ecstasy bursting through her body. It rushed along her spine when he implored, "Come with me, Katherine, now and forever."

"I will! You're here! I can't believe you are *here*!" She squeezed him, kissing his cheeks.

"Of course I'm here!" Trayten took her face between his hands and stared into her eyes. "I found you. Didn't I say I would? I had to line up our departure, to find you alone so we can leave quickly. Our boat is leaving on the hour and I'm taking you with me." He held her, his hands firm against her back.

"I'm so sorry! I brought this on—"

"Hush!" He kissed her lips. "I love you! It's all that matters. I love you and we are leaving." He kept his eyes locked on hers, his hand in her hair. "Let's get anything you need and be quick."

"I don't have much. Follow me and don't leave my sight!"

She took his hand. Their footsteps clapped, climbing the stairs and racing down the corridor.

Quickly and roughly, Katherine stuffed raggedy clothes into a suitcase, circling the room with her heart racing. He leaned against the door frame. She shoved the red journal into the bag. Sliding her tattered coat on, her hair hung in her face and Trayten smiled firmly at her.

Katherine paused in the act of tying her hair back and asked, "What?"

He beamed. "I'm in awe, to take you in at last."

Her eyes glistened in rapture. Artfully, Trayten moved fallen strands of hair from her eyes, tucked them behind her ear, and tilted her chin to him. "I love you." His smile was full of charm.

She remained in the spell of his gaze. His allure was magnetic, powerful like the tide. Beyond the excitement to be with him at last, a penetrating dread whispered at the fringes of her mind.

All time and distance between them dissolved. She followed him out of the house. In desperation she had dreamed of him finding her. Fearful of being returned to a waking hell, she pinched herself, thankful for the sharp bite of her fingernails against her skin, affirming her wakefulness.

Trayten carried her suitcase, leading Katherine from the porch into the snow-covered driveway. A horse stood tethered to the nearest crooked tree. Following behind, her eyes were fixed on his motions, studying the familiar lines of his back, his shoulders, and the length of his arms. Against an empty sky, hints of blue shined in the black of his hair, as inky as the roaring sea beyond the near cliff. His beauty and strength led her forward, breaking her heart with the love that consumed it.

Powdery snow that lay in sheets on the road whipped and clouded the air when the carriage came rushing toward the house. Reuben perched haughtily on the seat, his green coat distinguishable against the snow.

When he recognized them, two forms standing in the path, his nostrils flared, his face tightened, and his hand slid over the hilt of the gun on his hip. He slowed his horses, the carriage sliding in the snow. As he drove near, staring hotly, he straightened up.

Under Trayten's arm Katherine cringed, feeling the rise and fall of his chest as he breathed evenly. They faced her gravest mistake. Reuben's eyes settled on Trayten. They stared at one another, a threatening current traveling between them.

Reuben threw down his reins and sucked in his cheeks, his pale eyes narrowed to sharp daggers.

"So this is it?" he asked with an eerie calm.

"This is it." Katherine swallowed her fear. The sea rushed beyond the cliff and the air flowed frigid between them.

"Basel." Reuben sighed as though he would laugh and kept his gaze steadily on Trayten. "Here you are."

"You are very astute," Trayten said.

"What are you doing?" Reuben demanded through gritted teeth.

"Didn't you expect it? I'm leaving, Reuben," Katherine answered curtly.

"No, you are not."

"It's true, she's leaving you," Trayten confirmed. "She's already left."

"You never left me *before*, Kathy. You can't go. You'll have nothing, and your junkie is incapable of supporting your superior tastes."

Trayten covered her hand on his heart and reiterated, "I'm taking Katherine Madison with me."

Reuben huffed, puffs of white breath trailing from his mouth and his arm tightened, his hand gripping the gun. With a frightful yell, he withdrew the weapon. "There's no such person as Katherine Madison. Her name is Katherine Koryn and she's my wife!"

At first sight of the gun, Katherine screeched. Reuben stood, aimed, and pulled the trigger. Sparks and smoke filled the air behind the ringing blast. Katherine was shoved aside and Trayten flung backward into the snow. Horrified, she sprang for him, but Reuben yanked her from the ground in one savage sweep.

His fat arms squeezed her ribs, his sweat dampened body oppressed her, and he pulled her away from Trayten. The more she bellowed, the faster Reuben dragged her. She fought as he carried her away, her fists pounding at him, legs swinging above the ground.

Into the air her piercing, frantic cries reverberated. He slapped his hand over her mouth. She kicked him in the shin, and he collapsed to his knees for an instant. Reuben fumbled with her swinging arms until he snapped both wrists in one hand and staggered up to drag her onward.

Her heels dug into the snow. Her body pulsated with hysterical alarm and she continued to call for Trayten. Reuben brought her to the woodshed with sure, determined strides.

Tearing at his hold on her wrists, she struggled. He pinned her against the wall of the shed and with his free hand slapped her fiercely across the face. The hit slammed and silenced her, blinding her for an instant.

Reuben crushed her neck with both hands, leaving her hands free to scratch at his vise-like fingers with futile desperation. Blood trailed from her nose to her lips.

"I did love you. I would have taken care of you. I would have never harmed you." He squeezed her throat as icy tears covered her eyes.

She managed to shake her head. With her voice low and cruel she gasped, "And I hated you!"

"Hate me then. Die hating me!" He wrung her neck with fearful, determined lights in his eyes. Katherine gasped, her lungs begging for air. A twisted grin marred his face as the color changed in hers, the deep red under her skin transforming to purple. Her eyes rolled back, her grip on consciousness slipping.

Reuben released her throat and as she sank, he caught her by the hair with one hand and raised the bolt on the woodshed door with the other. With her senses draining, Katherine was dragged into the dark space. Coughing and gasping, she weakly croaked, "You shot him, you shot him!"

"At least he died quickly!" Reuben released her hair and shoved her into a pile of firewood. As she clamored to catch herself, Reuben retreated and slammed the door behind him.

Katherine hurled herself against the other side, the rigid door an impassable barrier. He barred it from the outside. She slammed her fists into it and cried, the terror descending in sharp waves. Every gasping breath she inhaled pierced her lungs. Every broken cry bounced and pounded off the close, secure walls of the shed.

"Reuben! Leave him! Leave him alone!"

She went hoarse, her throat cracking and aching. She beat at the door, each slam echoing. Katherine kicked and rammed at the door until her wrists were bruised and her toes stung. When her throat produced little sound, she shuddered pathetically, sliding to the ground, chest convulsing.

Muffled, far-off hollering caught her ear. With frozen tears on her cheeks, Katherine swallowed and pressed her face against the door, straining to peer through the crack of the hinged side. An ominous silence descended. With shaky breath and heart pounding loud, Katherine concentrated to hear anything.

She covered her mouth to catch and hold any warmth from her breath. Voices attracted her attention to the door, and she wrestled to distinguish the sounds.

A gunshot blast ripped through the air beyond the shed, thick in the distance. Her heart exploded with helpless peril. Several more blasts followed. Trayten's name, distorted and painful, expelled breathlessly from her body. The sound crashed back against her throbbing head. In exhaustion and torment, she persisted beating her fists against the door, to the dying rhythm of her battered heart.

A whimpering moan escaped from her dry lips and Katherine's ears acclimated to the clinking of metal against the door. Slightly raising her head from the numb pillow of her arm, she fell back, dizzy and weak. Two swift thumps, another clank, and the door sprang open, showering her body with fierce twilight. She reeled, blinded. Frost crystals clung to the strands of her hair. To the three men standing there, she appeared blue, her lips dark as if bruised, and her eyes unable to focus on them.

"How long has she been here? Pick her up, quick," one of the men directed, and two others swarmed. They picked her up. Her limbs were weary, and they carried her by the elbows.

"You're all right, Mrs. Koryn."

"Won't be once she knows," another commented under his breath. They helped her into the dying sunlight, throwing blankets around her. The sky was on fire, burning red and gold.

"Knows," her voice cracked and sputtered. A temporary dementia fogged her memory, and she tried to comprehend her situation.

The trio supported her and steered her through the snow from the woodshed toward the house, attempting to block her vision from a cluster of people gathering at the cliff. She blinked to clear the fog clouding her mind.

"What?" she asked with a sore throat.

"Mrs. Koryn, we gotta get you warm first, it isn't good—" the man at her left trailed off.

"Let go!" She jerked her elbows free from them as feeling returned to her body with a rush of adrenaline. She ambled forward with great effort, trudging through the snow that she had been dragged over by Reuben, fighting her way toward the commotion at the precipice. Depleted and with stiff joints she stumbled against her stinging toes. Her recollection of the last events before she blacked out crept through her awareness, bleak and sinister. It settled on her senses with dreadful realization.

They followed to catch her as gently as possible, and one

officer suggested, "Madame, listen to Officer Sears, you could be frost-bitten, and you need a doctor."

"I'm fine!"

As they restrained her, she glanced from one to the next, searching their glum, pitying eyes. She inhaled deeply and asked through the pain at her core, "Where's Trayten?"

"Who?"

"Trayten! Where is he?" She squirmed to see around them. Deep red clumps of snow lay where Trayten had fallen. Yet Trayten was not there.

"Madame!" Officer Sears approached. "Do you mean to ask about your husband? It is bad, it's—"

"Trayten! Trayten, where is *he*?"

They were puzzled, frustrating her like the empty spot in the snow. She escaped, hiking the cliff with clumsy speed, dragging her frost-bound skirt, gasping for air, pale and shaking. They called after and resumed their chase, however before they could reclaim her, she shoved her way through the onlookers and stopped before the body at her feet.

She understood. The sky tried to warn her. The snow was red, crimson ice. His eyes were open wide, petrified and disbelieving. Reuben was scarcely recognizable, his face sealed with a sheet of blood, his stomach blown open, the carnage crystallized in frost. His hands were raised with cuts zigzagging his skin, skin that appeared blue and purple. His body lay back awkwardly in the bloody snow, his legs folded underneath him, as though he had knelt and fallen back.

Katherine's knees buckled at the sight of him. The fishermen and their wives watched her closely.

"Mrs. Koryn," Officer Sears called.

She pinned her gaze on Reuben's corpse and sobbed, "What did you do to him? Where *is* he?"

The officer and his men held her back while Katherine spit and roared like a wild animal. "Where is he? What did you do to him? Trayten! Let go. You don't understand!"

"She's delirious!" one of the officers gasped, trying to help Officer Sears contain her arms.

"Calm down, Mrs. Koryn! Who is Trayten? Who are you talking about?"

"He was here!" She gasped, "*He* shot him in the snow! Trayten! Trayten Basel, and he's gone now!"

"There was nobody there, Mrs. Koryn," Officer Sears said. "Do you understand that your husband is dead? We didn't want you to see him like this!"

"What has he done to Trayten?"

"Who is Trayten? Did *he* do this?"

"Reuben shot him. I saw him fall! Where is he?"

Officer Sears fumbled to lift her as the pain sank into her muscles and her heart. He drew her tightly against him, carrying her above the slushy snow.

1909

"What do *you* want? I told you never to come back here." Marian drew the door open just enough to show her sullen face. Her eyes glared meanly, and her freckles were dark against the white of her cheeks.

Russell immediately stuck his boot in the doorway and offered graciously, "Miss Boley, you know that I must."

"Don't tell me what I know." She slammed the door against his foot.

"Miss Boley, I have to get in to see him." He pushed back. "When I left, he was in critical condition and I must check on him."

"He is fine. You may go."

"No, I cannot go. I need to call on my patient. I have other obligations, other patients to attend today, so don't waste my time. Be a polite host and move aside. I must verify that he's stable."

"He is stable, Doctor."

"You are not qualified to make that judgment. I must come in."

"No!"

"If you do not allow me to attend him, you are violating the right of a doctor to aid the critically ill—"

"He's not critical."

"—an offense that makes you liable to serve time in jail for neglecting a critically ill patient— especially if anything else happens to him. I have my rights and he has rights as well! To prevent such a thing will surely be reported and will not only affect your personal reputation, but the reputation of your establishment. Now, Marian Boley, if you would remove your door from my metatarsals!"

Marian reluctantly backed away and allowed him to squeeze through the doorway passed her. Once inside, Russell peered around the narrow corridor and up the steep stairway, pausing for a moment to sigh before he climbed the stairs.

Preparing for the worst, Russell inhaled deeply and touched the doorknob. When he opened the door, he was immediately taken aback. Anxiously he exhaled, "Oh, my word."

☙❧

1901

Eliza answered the door, allowing Officer Flarrity and his partner into the flat with a meek smile. She knew why they had come. Wringing her hands and glancing toward the den, she gently whined, "I understand your purpose and I understand it's your job. However, I don't think you should try to *talk* to her about it."

"Do you know something?" Officer Flarrity asked. He

gestured to his silent partner, who scrambled to ready his pen and notepad.

"I know only as much as the rest of you," she said.

"We'd like to talk to her ourselves."

"We got the paper today and she's likely cross about the headline," Eliza said.

"Likely?"

"It's quite harsh. She's said nothing about it. But, how would *you* feel? Someone suggests you killed someone, your own husband worst of all, or even that a lover did?" Eliza lowered her voice. "And that she's with child has gotten out, and they're making a mockery of her."

"Eliza, I understand, but maybe we can clear up some of the accusations and rumors," Officer Flarrity suggested.

"I don't like it. I'll be straight with you. But it's *her* choice to talk with you or not."

Officer Flarrity nodded. His quiet comrade mimicked him.

"Where is she?"

"In the den, sir," Eliza said and directed them with the wave of her hand. Quietly they followed her to the archway that opened into the room.

"Katherine, Officer Flarrity and Officer Parson are here to speak to you. Gentlemen." She curtsied to the men and remained in the archway.

Two large, uniformed figures invaded the room, intrusive vibrations accompanying their hasty approach. In response to their disruption, Katherine raised her head. She was curled into the corner of the couch. Her body was hidden beneath layers of black; the nightgown a mourner's shroud, the bountiful robe wrapped around her slight form, the cloud of despair shadowing all. Tangles of hair were tucked rashly behind her ears. She leaned a pale cheek on one hand, the wrist below it black from the bruising she had amassed. They sat rigidly in the chairs across from her, haunted by the glance of her white face and the eerie look of her red-rimmed eyes.

"How are you, Mrs. Koryn?" Officer Flarrity asked. The dreary gaze of her eyes did not change. "I saw your mother today. Have you not gone home?"

"I have no home."

"I'm sorry. Your family, they must be horribly worried."

Katherine glared.

Officer Flarrity inhaled deeply and said, "People want to know—"

"I don't care!"

"They wonder why you weren't at your husband's funeral. It's dishonorable, suspicious, that you would not appear."

"I don't care what any of you believe to be honorable or not."

"Why didn't you attend? Your husband—"

"You think I killed him," she broke in. "Well, I didn't do it."

"Who did?"

"You don't really care. You only want more fodder for the papers. You hear what you want, but I'll tell you this; I despised him, but I *didn't* kill him. When I saw him last, he was shutting the door to the woodshed with me inside. When they pulled me out, he had been dead for several hours. I couldn't have done it!

"Reuben shot a man...a man that fell in the snow before I was dragged to the woodshed. None believe me, because when they got me out, he was gone! They tell me there was no sign of another person who was involved anywhere on Portland! How is it possible that no one else saw Trayten Basel? No one will acknowledge that Trayten Basel lived, that he died, or survived. No one saw him, only me!

"Whether I tell the truth or not, they'll consider me insane. They say I was delirious, that I saw nothing at all. Tell them I lost my mind. I'm disturbed. Lock me away like you've done to Hilda Koryn."

"*I* didn't do that, Madam."

"I'm as mad as Hilda according to you people! But I'll still tell you that a man was there, that Reuben shot him, and he fell down beside me. I will tell you Reuben meant to kill me and that I know, I *know* Trayten Basel is alive, somewhere.

"If you've come here hoping to discover more than that, you must go away disappointed. I have nothing new to reveal, I have no desire to go through it again. I've related the events I recall and told you about Trayten, and I've been accused of inventing him."

"I am only sorry we can't help you," Officer Flarrity said, discouraged.

"I never asked you to. I can't be helped, anyway." She glanced at Eliza. "You leave my sister alone. No more questioning her, no more knocking at her door." Katherine folded her hands in her lap. "I'm sure you must be on your way. Good day, gentlemen."

Eliza showed them out. Katherine lowered her head into her hands, entangled her hair with her fingers, and squeezed her eyes shut against the anguish in her soul.

❦ 28 ❦

1909

Passengers scuttled about the breakwater in the briny air. Some of them had just arrived and others waited to board the ferry that now waited in Braye Harbour. The sallow sky was thick with clouds that smothered the distant horizon.

Angelle gazed at her mother's face, holding tightly to her hand. Bitter air stabbed her cheeks as the breeze battered them. Katherine's eyes were vacant.

"Why are we leaving?" Angelle asked.

Swallowing, she pleaded, "Do not ask me questions like that."

"What sort *shall* I ask? I don't understand."

"Some things we can't hope to understand." Katherine covered her lips with her glove. A whistle blew and she quivered. Minute by minute her heart shrank, smaller and smaller.

"But you always explain to me the things I cannot understand!" Angelle pouted.

"I can't this time, love. I don't even understand."

"Tell me why, Momma!" Angelle abruptly stamped her foot and crossed her arms.

"Angelle!"

"You can't do this. What's happened?" Angelle's eyes burned and her voice was strained with desperation. "You'd *leave* him? You would leave my father? Didn't you leave me alone to find him? All of that for *nothing*? Now we go home *without* him? What did you come here for? To leave him again?"

"It's complicated, Angelle." Katherine knelt down, a sharp pain cutting her in two.

"No! It's not!"

"Angelle."

"How—" She wept unrepressed, as Katherine held her hands and pleaded with her eyes. "How can we leave? He needs us and we need him. Don't leave him all alone!"

"Please, darling. There's nothing I can do…there's nothing—"

"There is!"

"We have to leave. We need to board." Katherine attempted to lure Angelle toward the ship.

Angelle pulled against her toward the inland, shouting, "Come back! Come with me, or I'll go without you! I will go back to him even if you won't!"

"Please, Angelle—" Katherine held firm as the child tugged at her frantically. She directed her glassy eyes to the looming ship and the weight crushed against her heart.

The resistance against her arm yielded suddenly. Angelle stood still, her eyes fixed on the inland horizon and the cluster of people appearing there. Wind swept the loose hair from Katherine's swollen face as she turned to look back. In an instant, devastation dared transform into hope.

Russell pushed Trayten forward in his wheelchair. A surly Marian, her angry eyed Suzan, and a wobbling Tarl followed after them.

Katherine was locked on Trayten's eyes, unsure whether she

could believe them. They were intent and they were affectionate. She fell into their depths and lost the ability to move.

"I told you," Marian's cross voice broke the hanging moment between them. "She's leaving! She doesn't care!"

"Quiet! What did I tell you?" Russell snapped as he wheeled Trayten to Katherine.

Trayten did not seem to notice his entourage. He concentrated on Katherine only, gripping the arms of the chair, his hands smudged with blue and red paint.

With a voice strangled by the wintry air she asked, "Trayten, what are you doing here?"

"You aren't leaving me again."

"If you want me to be your physician, I'm sorry. I can't. I'm not."

"I know that."

"Do you?"

"Trayten," he announced. "Trayten Basel. That's my name. Katherine, I know who I am."

Disbelief stunned her and tears fell from her eyes. "Do you remember *me*?"

"Yes," he breathed gently. "I remember you. You *were* there, Katherine. You were buried so deep that you were like a spirit to me. But you were there all along."

"And your memory is back, all at once?" she asked.

"No." His gaze was enlightened, determined. "I have to confess to you, that you became familiar to me as I fell in love with you, my peculiar *specialist*. And when you confessed who you were to me, when you told me of my life, then you came back to me...in foggy pieces, my memories started coming back to me."

"And you said *nothing*? You let me believe that you recalled nothing."

"You were playing a charade, weren't you? Well, I needed to know. I needed to be sure and to know how you truly felt. I still had to make sense of it all."

"I was afraid to tell you who I was from the beginning. I was a coward."

"Yes. You were a coward," Trayten affirmed. "But I forgive you." His tender smile quickened her heart.

"And what of all you said last night? Was that a part you played?" she asked, biting her lip.

"No. I remembered that. After they pulled me from the sea. That was my last memory before I forgot everything. I remembered that last night and with it, the horrific truth of what happened that day. My darkest memory, my darkest deed."

"You know what happened to you?" Katherine choked as she stepped closer to him.

"Take the child away." Trayten nodded to Angelle. "She shouldn't hear such things."

Angelle stepped forward. "In time I would inevitably know. Let me hear it from you and I'll never have to wonder."

Trayten smiled at Angelle with an openness in his expression that revealed a filial affection now understood. Then he looked at Katherine with all of the clarity and recognition of years past. "I thought you died ... that he killed you. I heard you screaming for me, and I couldn't get up. I've dreamed it, a recurring nightmare."

Katherine wept.

"I envisioned you, there with me, on the boat. They took me out of the sea. God of the sea. Katherine, I didn't drown, but I couldn't move. I couldn't feel a thing. I didn't know what was happening to me. I thought I was freezing, and that you were dead. They pulled me onto a boat. I heard them speculating that I wouldn't survive, and I didn't want to. He had dragged you away and you were screaming for me, and I couldn't get up. I resigned myself to death until I *saw* you and felt you holding onto me on the deck. You were so real, but you *weren't* there.

"Living, after I survived was nothing short of a curse. You vanished, and everything I knew before also faded. I've had this vague impression haunting my dreams; the rage, the devastation because he hurt you and I didn't stop him. The loss of you, my failure to save you … that pain would come back, and I forced it down until it was completely obscure.

"So many memories have flashed through my mind lately, flooding back to me. I couldn't place them until you articulated them, I couldn't recognize you, but now, I remember *more* than the pain." He gasped and tilted his head. "I remember you." He whispered the last word and it settled into her soul.

"Do you *really*?" she gasped, desperate to believe it.

Trayten wheeled closer. "You recited a poem in a tavern, and I fell in love with you on the spot. It hit me like lightning. I was stricken and I didn't even know your name! I watched you, and I discovered who you were and loved you more. I tried to paint you, to recreate your presence, to keep you with me always. I used my hands on the canvas." He held them up to illustrate. "I bled my soul into portraits of you. The painting *here*, my master-piece, it brought back the pain, the dark sea, your screams. I remember how I couldn't sell them, your portraits, not until you had left me."

Katherine sank to her knees in the snow and beheld him in rapture. She drank in every word, as though she had been wandering the desert without water for as long as she had lost him.

"I loved you so much I couldn't think of you with him," Trayten remembered. "And Jack, my friend, he was killed. I worked for him, driving at night, saving up to buy you a ring. I did buy one. It was pathetic, but I bought you a ring with what I had…and you became the wife of another."

She covered her mouth, weeping. Silence pervaded and even Marian was still.

"Reuben Koryn," Trayten said disdainfully. "I wanted you to marry *me*, didn't I, Katherine? But you married him. He hurt you! I couldn't bear it. I got up too late. It was too late."

"When he shot you…when you fell down, I thought he killed you! I couldn't get out of the shed. I couldn't get back to you."

"And I thought I'd never see you again in this waking world," Trayten said with a grim expression.

"Did you kill him?"

"Don't!" Marian squawked. "He'll only lose it again! You'll disturb him! That's your fancy isn't it, to terrorize him?"

"Enough out of you!" Russell fired back at her.

Marian reconsidered her advance and Suzan glared, holding onto her arm.

Katherine focused on Trayten's face and cried, "For eight years I've wondered what happened to you, my darling."

Trayten inhaled and gazed at her remorsefully. Then, he pulled her close to speak in her ear as quietly as possible, "His shot didn't kill me. It felt like it, at first. I'd never been shot before. I blacked out."

※

1901

Reuben charged through the snow dragging a shovel behind him. His face fell flat as he viewed the indent in the snow beside the carriage, and he spat. Blood spattered the ground, yet Trayten's body was gone. There was a groan and a shuffle.

Disoriented and covering his bleeding shoulder with one hand, Trayten had just pulled himself to his feet beside the carriage.

"What did you do!" he demanded of Reuben. "Where is she?"

Reuben raised the shovel high and drew it back, exerting, "Join her!" before he swung it out. On impulse Trayten dropped and was missed; the blade clanking against the side of the carriage. The horse stumbled and jerked forward between the two men, dragging the empty vehicle off toward the road.

Reuben charged Trayten, who stumbled to stand, the skin torn at his shoulder, bleeding trails around him.

"What did you do?" Trayten staggered to gain his footing.

"She's gone!" Reuben raised the shovel again.

Trayten sprinted forward and jammed his good shoulder into Reuben's middle, knocking him down. In the glaring snow that scattered and flew, Trayten fought him, threatening, "I'll kill you!" With red-stained hands he reached for Reuben's neck, and Reuben smashed his face with open palms, fighting beneath him. They tore at each other with vicious, graceless fervor.

They were a flurry of limbs and fists on the ground, smashing each other into the snow, rolling, kicking, and pounding at faces. Trayten yelled, wild and enraged. He shoved Reuben backward and scrambled for the shovel.

Trayten took the splintering handle in his slick hands and got to his feet. "Come on!"

Reuben crawled on hands and feet before pushing himself upright. Then he bolted in the opposite direction toward the cliff. The cloud darkened sky and sea stretching vast beneath it bore witness to the struggle. He careened up the hill, frantic wheezing echoing from his throat.

Behind him Trayten hiked, feverish and determined, rage in his eyes, his teeth clenched. His expression ferocious. He could hear the panicked gasps of his prey, his limbs flinging forward, desperate to escape. At the top of the incline and startled by the immense drop-off before him, Reuben tripped and fell on his face, which had been cut and bruised by the fury of Trayten's fists.

A fast blow struck him in the back when the shovel crashed down. Reuben bent backward, howling. Trayten kicked him in the side.

Reuben heaved, trying to get up. Through his labored breathing he managed to cough, "She never wanted you—"

"That's a lie!" Trayten swung the shovel to crack it across Reuben's face! Blood sprayed from his mouth and he crashed against the snowy ground headfirst. The rage in Trayten burned and boiled and Reuben groveled, spitting blood, his nose cracked, crawling on his hands and knees.

Trayten was shocked at his own lack of remorse and,

forfeiting the shovel, he jerked Reuben by his collar to face him. He punched him, cracked him between the jaw and neck. With a muffled snarl, Reuben wretched and then with a burst of adrenaline, he was on foot.

There ensued a race for the blade lying hot and bloody in the snow. Reuben limped, his back cut and body doubled, Trayten slid for it, and they collided. Elbows and feet struck and stabbed at one another. Trayten jabbed Reuben once more in his bloodied face and he flung back, his coat flying open, and something shiny plopped into the snow. Recovering, Reuben rushed at Trayten and kicked him in the chin as he attempted to get off of his knees.

Reuben stepped on his neck, held him down, and wielded the shovel like an axe.

The horrified wails escaped into empty air, flinging across the face of the sea. Birds fled the trees, startled. Trayten attempted to drag his body away as he gasped, but he was held and prevented, feeling the blade, brutal and constant. The rigid edge of a shovel, with every blow, rendering him less and less likely to escape the next.

Reuben groaned through his own wounds, growled in his own rage, and swinging fast he hit and hacked at Trayten's legs, disabling his movement in the immense shock of pain, breaking bones, tearing flesh. He could have swiftly ended it, but instead he prolonged the suffering. The blood spattered back at him from the swinging blade, into the snow, onto his mangled face. He grit his teeth, howling past the blood in his mouth.

Trayten gasped, hyperventilating in the shock, shrieking and grinding his jaw, his legs torn and cut. His chest heaved, his face twisted, and he reeled. He saw metal in the snow and wailing in agony, he took hold of the gun.

Screaming, bloodied and butchered, Trayten turned the gun, squeezed it, and fired on Reuben. He did not stop. He shot again and again at close range, the smoke bursting hot and high, until the clip was spent. Reuben gyrated and burst open in the blaze.

He stared with petrified eyes through the rising smoke. The

blood-soaked shovel blade sliced into the snow at his feet. Reuben tilted his head, the green of his jacket black across his front. His mouth opened as if he would speak and instead of words, a river of blood flowed down his chin as he fell on Trayten.

In his last effort, dying and aware, Reuben used his weight to ram Trayten, holding his throat, driving to shove him over the cliff. Reuben's abdomen was blown open. His face revealed the vestige of a man, slipping out of life. He used all force that remained to propel Trayten, whose hands alone could not prevent Reuben from inching him toward the cliff's edge.

Unable to use his legs, Trayten fought with his arms, the ground beneath him giving way as Reuben released his neck. He clung to the edge, endeavoring to grip the slick, icy rocks that stabbed the brink. With another shove, his lower body slid over the edge.

He was powerless and frantic at the last moment, the cold cliff firm against his chest, his legs hanging over the edge. Reuben spit blood, his stomach erupting as he kicked Trayten's hands, stomping with his heels, lagging before he dropped back. Reuben's last kick wrested Trayten's desperate hands from the solid rock cliff. He fell the drastic distance into the churning sea below.

❂

1909

Katherine recalled his legs, the deep purple scars, and she flinched. It left her speechless in anger, sorrow, and guilt. For everything she did to contribute to those last violent moments, she bowed her head in shame. Her eyes were swollen from crying. The tears had fallen as Trayten described his fatal struggle with Reuben.

A silence fell that none could break, and none dared, until

Trayten said, "I can look at you and see the past, Katherine. Please don't cry. I wish I could've remembered. If my mind hadn't shut down, if I had tried harder that night on the boat, wouldn't I have found you? Didn't I always find you?"

Katherine threw her arms around his neck. He held her fast.

"I am so sorry, Trayten!"

He replied, lips close and warm against her cheek, "Katherine. Don't leave me again. I can't carry you anywhere, not as I *once* could, but I'll never leave you. And I won't lose you again!"

"I'll never leave you," she vowed, drawing back to admire his eyes. Again, the whistle blew, and Katherine wiped the tears from her face with her glove.

"We'll go together." She held her hand to their daughter. Trayten compared their faces in loving contemplation.

For the first time since arriving at Alderney, Trayten's eyes were full, a reflection of his soul. He pulled Angelle into his arms, kissed her hair and announced, "My Angelle."

With relief and acceptance, Angelle clung tightly to him and for the first time was introduced to the love of her father. They were images of each other, father and daughter. Katherine wept with gladness.

Russell's smile deepened and he winked at Marian. Scowling, she dragged Tarl by the hand in retreat. Suzan trailed dutifully behind them.

"I painted," Trayten exclaimed. "I was able to, like I'd never forgotten! I picked up the brush and was carried away."

Angelle held his hand, rubbing and spreading the paint on his fingers. "We've missed you too long. All my life."

"Am I any good to you like this? I'm not what I *was*. I can't be—"

Katherine put her finger to his lips and replaced it with a kiss, driving away his self-doubt.

Giggling, Angelle covered her face.

Memory flooded back to Trayten, awakened by Katherine's

kiss. She felt him shiver the way he used to. The reaction had remained. The response she always cherished had survived.

Giddy, Katherine smiled against their kiss. She set her sparkling eyes on him. "I love you!"

Removing her glove to feel the rough of his cheek with her fingertips, she stared at the ring on her left hand. Sighing, she slipped it from her finger and flung it into the air.

"I've waited a long time to absolve myself from that error and begin anew, free from its shadows and sorrows."

Trayten smiled brightly. "No more shadows, no more sorrow. We have the spring to look forward to."

With laughter in her voice she shouted, "Trayten Basel, I love you!" Her declaration climbed the air. "I *love* you! And I'll love you more, more than you ever thought possible."

He kissed her forehead and his eyes burned gold, remembering her with loving elation.

THE END

Don't miss out on your next favorite book!

Join the Satin Romance mailing list
www.satinromance.com/mail.html

THANK YOU FOR READING

Did you enjoy this book?

We invite you to leave a review at the website of your choice, such as Goodreads, Amazon, Barnes & Noble, etc.

DID YOU KNOW THAT LEAVING A REVIEW...

- Helps other readers find books they may enjoy.
- Gives you a chance to let your voice be heard.
- Gives authors recognition for their hard work.
- Doesn't have to be long. A sentence or two about why you liked the book will do.

ABOUT THE AUTHOR

Jillian Kae Reimann writes romantic historical fiction. She knew that she was a writer at the age of seven and has been writing stories ever since. Her mother instilled in her a love for history and reading. Her father passed on the inspiration that music can bring. When not writing her novels, Jillian is likely to be found pouring over history books and Victorian novels with a highlighter in hand.

An air-force brat, Jillian grew up in Montana, but had the opportunity to live in Panama for three magical years. After a short sojourn in central Texas, then Ohio, she returned to her home state and graduated college with a BA in Social Sciences with concentrations in Education and Psychology.

She lives in Montana on the windswept prairie at the foot of the Rocky Mountains with her husband, four kids, and a spoiled Black and Tan Coonhound named Beags. Her husband is a gifted musician and Jillian has been known to join him on stage to sing every once in a while.

Jillian is a visual artist, particular to oil painting and graphite portraiture. She enjoys Oolong tea, Pink Floyd, and hiking the Montana wilderness with Beags.

www.jilliankae.com
www.jilliankae.com/blogjilliankaereimann

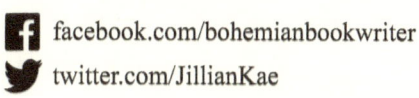 facebook.com/bohemianbookwriter
twitter.com/JillianKae